# Fate and Flame

## FAE RISING

MIRANDA LYN

Copyright

Fae Rising

**© 2020, Miranda Lyn**

Cover Designer – Tairelei – www.facebook.com/Tairelei/

Editor – https://secondpassediting.wixsite.com/website

**CONTENT WARNING**
Violence, Language, Explicit Sexual Situations, Death

Also by Miranda Lyn

# FAE RISING

Blood and Promise

Chaos and Destiny

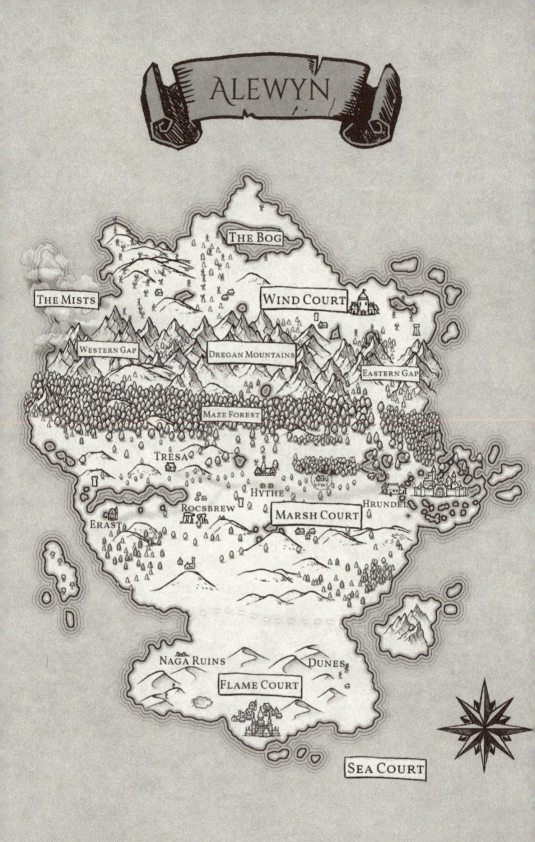

# ALEWYN

THE BOG

THE MISTS

WIND COURT

WESTERN GAP

DREGAN MOUNTAINS

EASTERN GAP

MAZE FOREST

TRESA

HYTHE

ROCSBREW

HRUNDEL

ERAST

MARSH COURT

NAGA RUINS

DUNES

FLAME COURT

SEA COURT

# Dedication

*To my eight-year-old self that had a far-fetched dream of doing something impossible:*

*We still haven't won the lottery, girl. We didn't marry a billionaire, but we work really hard every day.*

*And that's enough.*

# NEED A RECAP OF BOOK 2?

We started with old King Tolero. He and his buddy Inok discovered the snake (let's go with eel), Morwena, was responsible for so much of his own personal pain and was trying to poison the minds of his kingdom. But he was a smarty pants and captured her, causing his mother-in-law to stop being an asshole and finally get on Team Tolero.

Ara was locked away, she found out her parents weren't her real parents, she got a cool cat-suit from Nadra's mom and then set off to get lost in a forest, chained to Fen, released from Fen, played a game with a dragon and finally accepted her mate. I'm just going to say it . . . She was an asshole. But she's fine now, so it's fine.

Tem . . . Poor Tem. He joined the rebellion and had to balance all the jobs. He thought he might finally win Gaea over only to realize he no longer loved her the way he'd hoped, so she bounced because she didn't want to watch him fall in love with someone else or die first (I mean, can you blame her?) and then he found out his mate had been in front of him the whole time. He saved her and her mom to his own detriment as he ends the books in chains. GASP! Oleo tried to tell ya, buddy. #justiceforoleo

# Ara

"I hope you killed her."

"You don't mean that," I told Fenlas as we stood together, hand in hand, staring down the backside of The Mists. Thick gray clouds swirled beyond the invisible barrier, beckoning us forward. "Nealla bound me to keep me safe. She made sure our mating bond couldn't be severed. She's fucking twisted, but she's good. In her own way."

"Say that part again." He stared into the depths of my eyes as he brushed a strand of my auburn hair from my face. "Say it a hundred times." The deep timbre of his voice felt like home.

I wrapped my arms around him. "Our mating bond wasn't severed."

"It wouldn't matter if it was." He pressed a tender kiss to one cheek and then the other. "It wouldn't change the way I feel." His velvet lips brushed my neck, leaving a trace of that icy fire that sat within his soul. Our soul. "I would still choose you. I would follow you to the depths of hell, if only to live eternity in torment, just to be with you."

I dug my fingers into his thick black hair, tilted my head back, and tried to restrain the pressure of my endless magic as I let him memorize every damn inch of me. I didn't deserve him—his utter devotion, his fearless nature, or his very deliberate hands. I parted my lips as he pulled my face to his. Sliding my knuckles down the rough stubble along his jaw, I brushed my thumb over his lips, and smiled.

He closed his eyes and took a deep, ragged breath. I felt the seductive possession within him, right down our bond. He meant to claim me. Purely instinctual, the feral beast had yet to mark his mate, so his hard body pressed against me. Still, he took his time and moved as gracefully as a feline hunting its prey.

Again, he kissed my cheeks, my nose, the tips of my long ears, and finally, he held the sides of my face and pulled my lips to his. It wasn't our first kiss, but it absolutely was. It was the kiss that sealed the gap between my past and his future. I would forever be his, and the deep rumble within his chest as his tongue stroked mine was brutal and greedy.

One careful hand, now tangled in my hair, held me while the other roamed freely, right down my rigid spine. He squeezed my ass and I moaned. If he was a beast, then so was I. All fae were when it came to two things: sex and food.

"Mine." Fen's voice was husky against my fevered lips as he continued to meld us into one.

"Yours." The word left my lips like a promise.

He pulled away, resting his forehead against my own.

The abrupt absence of his muscled body left an ache within me.

"Your eyes . . ." He stared, fixated as he spoke. "They're silver."

"We're going to have to work on your pickup lines, Prince."

He shook his head. "No. They've changed. They aren't gray anymore." He took another step away, studying me. "What happened?"

"Nealla happened. She unbound my power and my secret. Everything's different now."

He turned his back and hung his head. Not from sorrow, but rage. His broad shoulders rose and fell with each measured breath as he tried carefully to calm himself, to contain that protective nature. "The world can hunt you now," he whispered.

I stepped behind him and brought my arms around his waist, laying my head on his back. "They could try."

"We need to get home as fast as possible. You aren't safe anywhere." He balled his fists and released them several times.

"Look at me, Fen." I could feel his hesitation, but eventually, he turned. I saw a shadow of the angry prince from our first meeting. Fen's desire to protect me always manifested in rage I hadn't understood before, but now I did. "I've trained my entire life. Every single thing my parents, all four of them, did for me was for this moment."

A bated breath lingered between us as he fought with his self-control. "Together, then?" He forced a smile, though I wasn't sure if it was for my sake or his own.

"Together." I kissed him and there was nothing gentle about it. After several minutes, he pulled away, and once again, we turned to face The Mists.

"Do you think you can clear some of it again?"

A nervous laugh escaped. "Yes, but you might want to stand back."

"I'm not afraid of you, Ara." He grabbed my hand and squeezed.

"I'm afraid of me," I whispered.

"Trust yourself. Think about what you want to do and infuse your magic into that desire. Do you know what your core magic is? Is it fire?"

I shrugged. "She didn't tell me. I can't feel it the way you can. It's different. There's so much." I pressed a palm into my temple as I tried to concentrate. The pressure continued to build, and soon, I'd burst no matter what. There was no need to reach for it, to let it build, to search within me. It was ready. Waiting.

"Just release a tiny bit. See what happens. Focus."

I tried. Gods help me, I tried. But that tiny bit ripped a gaping hole into the barrier I was using to hold it back. I clamped my eyes shut as magic poured from me like water through a broken dam. My veins, my mind, my very skin came to life as the purity of the first king's gift of power exploded from within. I fell to my knees as pain washed over me and lingered, reminding me that magic is dangerous.

"Are you still alive?"

"Fucking barely," Kai answered.

I peeked one eye open as Fen helped me to my feet and placed his hand on the small of my back, bracing me for what I had done. A boulder dropped into the pit of my stomach as I took in The Mists. Or the lack of them. They were completely obliterated.

If not for Fen, I would have stumbled backward.

My feelings were mirrored on the faces of our familiar companions.

In place of the famed Mists, there was just a massive expanse of absolutely nothing but uninhabited flatlands. The compacted dirt didn't budge in the still air. No birds flew overhead. Not even a cloud in the naked sky.

"Thank the gods." Wren rattled me from shock as she plowed into me. "I was so worried."

"Tell me you did that on purpose." Greeve's dark eyes watched me like a trained hawk as I pulled from Wren's arms and stepped away.

I opened my mouth to confess, but Fen took my hand and tugged me away. "She did. Let's go home."

"No hello? Nice to see you? Sorry you've been sitting in The Mists for hours?" Kai asked, stomping behind us.

I let go of Fen so Kai could shove him around. *Males.*

Wren nudged me with her arm and wiggled her eyebrows. "How'd it go?"

I jerked to a stop. "You knew Fen was my mate and didn't tell me." The betrayal stung. I'd thought we had established a bond while we traveled, but her loyalty was to her prince. I couldn't blame her, but it didn't change the way it felt.

She paused, hiding her face behind her chocolate hair as she looked away. "I didn't think it was my place." Her shoulders relaxed with an exhaled breath as she turned back to me. "I warned him you weren't going to take it well."

"That's the understatement of the century," I mumbled.

"That bad, huh?" She bit her lip as her eyes fell to the barren ground.

"Yes. So, next time you learn some life-altering shit about me, a heads up would be nice."

She smirked. "You know what this means, right? You're basically the princess of the Flame Court now. Your words are just as powerful as his."

The world went silent.

All those times he'd called me princess . . . I thought he was only mocking me for calling him prince. I jerked my head to Fen, who had Kai pinned to the ground. Fear trickled from him. For whatever reason, I hadn't even considered that. But he had. Of course. He thought I'd tuck tail and run, leaving him behind again.

Rather than using words, I sent him a mental picture of his arms wrapped around me. I wasn't sure if it would work until a beaming smile spread across his beautiful face as he shoved off of Kai. He was stuck with me.

We spent the entire day walking through the desolate lands heading toward Lichen. The air was lighter. Our hearts were lighter. Greeve and Fen used their magic to pick on Kai for over an hour until he threatened to chop their balls off in their sleep if they didn't stop. Then Greeve got bored and wind cleaved away, promising to hunt for dinner.

By nightfall, our limbs hung heavy, and our feet ached, but we happily arrived at a nice warm fire with searing hot coals and a spit impaling some unfortunate mountain beast. I ate more than I had eaten in days, weeks even. I think we all did. Belly full, I leaned comfortably against Fen's chest as we sat huddled around the fire.

He bent down and whispered, "I never thought I'd wish to be home so badly. I'll never take a locked door for granted again."

I chuckled, and he sent a wave of his fire magic. In turn, I sent the memory of being pressed against him, moaning during our *magic lesson*. He growled in my ear and everyone looked at us.

"How is it that there are four of us and two of you and somehow I still feel like a third wheel?" Kai asked.

"Their mating bond emerged." Wren laughed. "These two need some privacy, like yesterday."

"No." The pitch of my voice was higher than I'd intended. "We're fine." I hoped she could read the 'shut the fuck up' look on my face.

She cocked her head and raised an eyebrow to me. She wasn't even kind of sorry. Kai and Greeve couldn't look at us after that comment while Lichen was wholly unaware of the world around him, as always. I was still pissed at him, so I didn't care if he was uncomfortable. I knew he swiped Nealla's book from my bag. I didn't have proof, but I just knew it.

"A walk?" Fen offered, standing.

I took his hand, and, as we shuffled away, most of the group whooped and whistled behind us.

"Literal children." I shook my head, but the minute I did, the pounding began again. I tried to hide it from him, but he knew. He would always know.

"We're going to have to do something about that, or you're going to start demolishing the world."

"I'm open to suggestions." I pinched the bridge of my nose trying to alleviate the pain.

He hung his arm around my shoulder. "Well, the good news is, this is the perfect place to work on it. There's no one here and we know you can't hurt me."

"I have other ways of hurting you, Prince. Don't get *too* excited." Fire lit his eyes and that familiar heat caressed my body. "Or do. That's fine."

In a blink, he was inches from me, reaching to curl a strand of my hair around his finger as his other hand brushed a fallen snowflake from my cheek. A sad smile curved his lips as he sighed against my skin. "I am such a fool. I should have come for you sooner. All I can think about is the time wasted. Time we didn't have together. I've known my whole life you were missing. But now that I've found you, held you, it's so much more than I thought it would be. You're more than a missing piece slotted into place. And I am more because of you. Because of who I want to be with you. It's like I finally make sense. I knew the world needed saving, but now it's your world, our world together, and somehow, that makes it so much more important."

I pressed my lips to his. He pushed his hands into my hair and held me as I poured everything I was feeling into that kiss. We were the lucky ones. No matter what happened, we would have each other. There was comfort in that security, even though I had spent so much time fighting against it.

He pulled away, searching the snow-filled sky as he forced out his next words. "About what Wren said earlier. It's still your choice, Ara. It will always be your choice."

"Save it, Prince. You've already won. I'm not leaving. Let that be enough for now." I pulled him forward, continuing our walk.

The fresh blanket of untouched snow crunched below our boots as we trudged through. Starlight lit our breaths and the fresh air was so crisp, a whisper would have carried for miles. I'd barely noticed the cold because Fen used his magic to keep us all warm, but as he swept it away, a chill ran up my neck. We were still in the Wind Court.

A soft breeze tickled my neck and I gasped.

"Are you cold, princess?"

"No. Suddenly I'm immune to frigid temperatures." I lifted my shoulders to cover my neck and blew puffs of hot air into my hands.

"Use your magic. Release the pressure."

I shook my head and shivered. "It's too dangerous."

He laughed. "Just try, scaredy-cat."

I shoved him away and spread my feet, bending slightly at the knees as he continued to tease me.

"It's not a swordfight. It's mental."

"I've only managed to destroy shit. I think a bit of fear is warranted." I closed my eyes, scrunched my face, and let the magic go, rushing because I was so cold.

The world shook below my feet.

"This is fine. We can work on this. This is fine." Fen pulled me into the comfort of his arms.

So basically, it wasn't fine. I peeked my eyes open. The snow was gone. All of it, for as far as I could see. "How do you do it? How do you control what form you magic takes? How do you keep it from all bursting out at once?"

"It's like a thought with intention behind it. I know what I want to happen. I visualize that, and then just let a tiny bit of the magic surround the intention. Then it happens."

"Mine is so different. It's raw. Uncontrollable. Before there was a shallow basin to pull from, now it's this overwhelming ocean that I'm barely holding back with mental fabric."

He rubbed his hands down my back to warm me. "Use something heavier, Ara. Think of a metal wall with a tiny window. Move all your magic so it's behind the wall. And just like your mental shield, you can add layers to hold it back, so it doesn't suffocate you."

I let the world fade away as I imagined an iron wall, heavy and unyielding. I only allowed a tiny needlepoint hole, but it was working.

The mounting pressure began to subside, and I used my bond with Fen to anchor that wall down.

"Now make a flame."

I opened my eyes to protest, but he looked at me so intently, letting a small flame dance above his palm. I held up my hand, mirroring his, and let the magic come through the small pinprick. The moment I lit up like a torch, I slammed the cover back down and Fen burst into laughter.

"Not funny."

"It's going to take some time and practice. We'll figure it out. I promise."

I lifted my hand to my hair to make sure it was still there. He chuckled, and I sent a direct wave of anger.

"Sorry." He jumped back just in case I went for a weapon. The lopsided grin was still plastered on his face though. "Let's get some sleep and we can try again tomorrow. It's going to be a long journey home."

"About that . . ." I linked my arm through his. "I have a plan and you're going to hate it."

"Yeah, that sounds like something you'd say."

"Mkay. Well, I'll wait until tomorrow to tell you. Maybe by then, I'll have myself convinced it's a good idea."

"Greeeaaaat," he said.

We made it back to the group but the only one who would look at us was Kai. "Damn, Fen, you've always been fast, but—" He jumped up, hooting and patting the flames under his bottom.

"You were saying?" Fen asked, winking at me.

Kai looked to Greeve. "I've been replaced."

The draconian shrugged. "She's prettier to look at."

"Finally, someone notices." I threw my hands into the air and Fen cleared his throat. "Don't be jealous, Princey Poo. He said it first."

He blew a wisp of magic around me in protest.

Lichen clapped once and stood. "Time to get some sleep. I'll take the first watch. Ara, could I speak to you for a moment?"

I knew this was coming eventually so I nodded and walked toward him. Fen tugged on our bond, and I could feel his hesitation as I stepped away from him. This ragey male fae shit was going to have to be dealt with.

"What is it?" I crossed my arms over my chest.

"I wanted to apologize." He took several steps away from the group. As if they couldn't hear us.

"For what?" I wasn't letting him off easy. He was going to have to spell it out.

"I shouldn't have opened your book. It wasn't my business and I hope you'll forgive me." His words were clipped and I was sure an apology was difficult for the old fae.

"That's the thing, though. It wasn't even my book. It was a doorway to a bunch of creatures our ancestors locked away. Someone could have died, Lichen. Even if it just fell out, as you claim, why didn't you just ask me first?"

His face was devoid of all emotion. I almost found it hard to take his apology sincerely, but I guessed he wasn't used to delivering them.

"I should have. To be honest, I don't travel well. I thought something new to read might distract me from the long nights on the hard ground. I'm a scholar first. Can you forgive me?"

I looked away, studying the snow-capped mountains in the distance. I could barely see them through the darkness of night, but

11

they were there, like a memory. "I forgive you, Lichen. Just don't touch my shit again."

I spent the night wrapped in Fen's warm arms. He didn't wake as I tossed and turned. The pressure of magic had finally subsided, but I lay there wondering what it must feel like for them. They were finally headed home, but what was the south to me? My home was ashes on the wind. Everything that mattered to me, gone. I only had them now. In their minds, I was headed home also. But it didn't feel like it. It just felt like another step on this long, arduous journey. There was still no end in sight for me, and I wondered if my life would ever be my own.

"Morning," Fen whispered in my ear just as I began to fall asleep.

I rolled over to face him and let him hold me for several minutes. I would take this journey with him a thousand times if it meant I'd always land here, in the comfort of his arms. I matched my breathing to his, listening to his heartbeat until the others started to stir. I didn't want to talk about the circles my mind had traveled over the night, but the thrumming apprehension was hard to hide from your soul.

"It's going to be okay." He hugged me tighter, pushing his confidence toward me.

I nodded and pulled away.

"So, what's this genius idea you have?" he asked loudly so everyone else could hear.

I smirked, remembering my plan. I stood and tucked my blanket into my bag and wrapped my cloak around my shoulders. "How do you guys feel about skipping the long ass walk home and finding something quicker? Maybe getting back today?"

"Even I couldn't get everyone home that quickly." Greeve stretched, his tattoos peeking out from below the cuffs of his shirt.

Kai sucked a sharp breath between his teeth. "If you're talking about Aibell, hard pass."

"No, it isn't Aibell. Let's just say I know a guy that owes me a favor."

"Is he single?" Wren asked, rubbing her eyes.

"You can ask him yourself," I told her, holding back my grin.

We packed up camp fairly quickly and started our journey south. The first—and hopefully only—obstacle was the giant pile of sleeping dragons blocking the Western Gap.

A scattered and scaled rainbow of colors lay before us on the frozen ground of the Wind Court. From a distance, something in my heart told me danger was near, but as we approached, I couldn't force myself to look away. The deepest purples and the brightest greens. The faintest reds and the richest blues of beasts. They were so very large, smaller only than the mountains surrounding them, yet they curled so far into themselves to slumber, it was a miracle they could untangle themselves to take to the skies.

"How much do we trust that dragon's promise to let us through?" Lichen squeaked.

"One hundred percent." I hid my trepidation, though Fen eyed me cautiously.

We edged around the scattered heaps of sleeping dragons, with Greeve keeping his eye above as we moved. My heart thundered in my chest as I sought the one I needed. Thick plumes of smoke and the rancid scent of sulfur permeated the air, but we pushed forward as one until we stood before the yellow sleeping behemoth. A layer of dried dirt nestled below the dragon's warm belly. Snow would never settle where a dragon hoard lived.

I hadn't warned the others and when they saw me stop, I heard Kai lean into Wren and whisper, "Want me to find out if he's single for you, baby bird?"

Wren stuck her nose in the air. "Pretty sure he nearly ate you for lunch and his brother shredded your shoulder, so keep laughing while you can, prick."

Greeve snorted but Fen was still as a statue.

I sent a wisp of confidence to him before I clapped several times to wake the dragon in front of me. Lichen jumped, then stepped behind Greeve as the beast moved like a snake until his head laid on the ground in front of me. He opened both of his slit eyes and inhaled slowly.

Fen stepped forward, trying to block me from view.

*Hello, little liar,* he hissed into my mind.

*Hello, Pathog the Unyielding.*

As I thought his true name, a great shiver of discomfort crawled down his body, his pearlescent-coated scales shimmering in the morning sunlight.

*What rank are you in your hoard?*

He sat silent for a moment as his eyes narrowed on me. Fen grabbed my arm and hauled me backward when the rumbling within his chest began.

"Don't piss off the dragon, Ara," Greeve warned as he drew his curved sword.

"You are an evil little liar," the dragon said out loud.

"You will answer," I demanded.

"I think you already know." He huffed a thick cloud of smoke into my face until I coughed.

14

"Answer," I demanded.

"I am the Sengen. The leader," he snorted.

"My friends and I require a flight to the Flame Court."

"You would demand the Sengen to give rides like a common horse?" He stood, his great muscles tightening as he coiled and soared into the sky, bellowing while leaving us all in a heavy cloud of dust.

*I would and you will. There is no negotiation here. I've not shared your name, nor the power over you it gives to me, but don't think I won't.*

"If I agree, you will release me." He moved across the sky until his great wings blocked the sun, taking the tiny bit of warmth with him.

"I don't feel like negotiating. Now be a good dragon and let us up."

"You have got to be kidding me. I'd rather walk." Lichen inched backward until he stepped into Greeve's solid form, then yelped and moved away.

Wren's eyes were wider than a wagon wheel, but she didn't step away.

"You're perfectly safe, Lichen. He can't and won't hurt you," I assured him.

"I need specific details. How are you commanding him?" he asked. "And what about the other dragons? Are they under this new authority also?"

"That's between him and me. Best let your balls drop, Lich. We're riding a dragon today."

"I want to laugh, but I'm afraid I'll piss myself," Kai whispered.

Greeve chuckled and I smirked at him. At least I knew he and Fen would come with me. They were fearless. I think Wren would too. She looked scared, but not as much as Lichen. When we left the dragons last time and the others didn't make a move toward us, I knew I had ensnared the Sengen. They were all bound to him, and thus to me, because I knew his name. The name of a dragon was a powerful piece of information.

He landed, lifted his long neck to the sky, and roared a stream of fire until the ground shook and the heat beat down on us.

I tapped my foot impatiently. "When you're done with the dramatics, dragon. It's time to go."

He snorted a murky cloud of smoke and lowered his stretched wing until it was flat on the ground.

*One more thing, if one of my friends even gets the feeling you're going to attempt something dangerous, life-threatening, or scary, I'll order you to kill the others and then yourself.*

The rugged sound of dragon laughter filled the air as he hissed and his body shook. "I think I quite like you, little liar."

"Seriously can't believe you just made best friends with a dragon," Wren said as the six of us moved up his wing and sat on his massive back.

"Well, you know what they say." Kai chuckled nervously. "What doesn't kill you will just give you a lot of unhealthy coping mechanisms. Or a sparkling personality."

"How are we supposed to hold on?" Lichen cried out.

*Are you sure you don't want me to drop that one? His scent is fishy. His mind is void of loyalty to you, unlike the others.*

*Stay out of their minds. Lichen is just a whiny old fae. He's fine.*

16

*The mind of your mate is quite scandalous and even now the draconian contemplates ways to kill me.*

*Out of their minds, Path.*

*The blond one is funny. I quite like him.* He tremored with laughter.

"Can you guys put your mental shields up? Damn. He's reading you all like books right now."

"Calm," Fen whispered into my ear. "Not all mental shields can hold out a dragon. You're just an exception to every rule."

"You're a scary bitch." Wren linked her arm with mine. "Let's get out of here."

"Whenever you're ready, dragon." I laid my head on her shoulder. In that moment, I knew home was where my people were. They were mine and I was theirs.

# CHAPTER 2

# Temir

*I* could have killed him. Maybe not, but I wanted to reach out, use my dark magic and force the disgusting life from Autus' body. Unfortunately, he was more powerful than I was. It would have been the match to my pyre. So, I stood in that giant throne room, surrounded by a hundred rigid guards, as King Autus walked the marble steps to his dais, sat calmly upon his unjust throne and gestured to Eadas to deliver his twisted tale.

"We received word that Temir was seen among the rebels during the Volos attack." Eadas paced between me and the king, painting his theatrical picture of my betrayal. How could he have known that? "We believe he was working with the rebels long before that, my gracious king. Today, he has successfully helped two of the rebellion leaders escape our dungeons. Days ago, we believe he kidnapped your concubine and we also have reason to believe he killed Thane and Oravan."

"What reason do you have?" Autus answered, snapping his head toward me, though he addressed Eadas only.

"Although you received what you needed from Oravan, Temir could not have known that. He could have been trying to thwart your plans. And he was never a fan of Thane. We all know that. He may have even killed Gaea. At this point, there's no reason to count him out of anything."

I clenched my jaw as fury burrowed within me so deep my bones rattled. "I didn't touch her."

"Of all the accusations, and there are many, this is the only one you protest, *lesser*?" The king spat the last word like it was a weapon meant to slice my throat.

I pursed my lips shut and said nothing, infuriating him further. I didn't care. They could kill me. Should kill me. Put me out of my own lifelong misery handcrafted by a callous king, his loathsome court, and vile council. I held my head high and stared right back into the king's dark, cold eyes, knowing it was the only weapon I had against him. He thrived off fear and cowardice and I would feed that monster no longer.

"Beat him," the king ordered as his lips curled into a wrathful smile. He slumped back in the comfort of his throne as the soldiers moved in.

I stood tall while fist after fist flew through the air, making perfect contact. They were relentless, yanking me by the stubs of my horns. Eventually broken, I fell to the floor. They took turns kicking me, breaking bones I refused to heal, as blood poured from my body until I became lethargic. I closed my eyes and imagined the curly red hair of my abandoned mate. I reached for her through the bond for an ounce of comfort in a desperate moment, but there was nothing to satiate me. Only eternal silence.

That stillness carried me away as I lost consciousness and woke to find my hands and feet wrapped in chains, lying in the cold, damp dungeons I had just helped two fae escape from. I coughed and a surge of pain tore through my abdomen. Still, I would not heal myself. I would rather die in the dungeons than be used as a weapon for the king.

Eadas' damning words haunted me. They knew I was in Volos. All of the king's soldiers were killed that day. Which meant one thing. There was either a traitor amongst the northern rebels or amongst the southern prince and his crew that fought with us. I likely wouldn't live to learn the truth, but I did worry for Rook and the rebels. My mistakes were not theirs and somehow I hoped they lived to watch the king die. That was the only hope I had left in the world.

I laid my head back on the cold stone floor and listened to the constant dripping of stale water from the seeping walls. In the dark room, it was nearly impossible to see anything beyond the solid metal bars of my decrepit prison.

I knew only one truth: I was alone. I coughed again and watched as blood spattered the floor. I had six days, maybe seven, until the wounds would fester into something life-threatening. Perhaps the king would have me killed before then. I doubted it. I was the key to his immortality. If he learned of the barrier ring on my finger, he would have it removed, and I would forever be a mindless puppet. He'd always refrained from using his enchantment, believing he could force his kingdom, the world, into blind submission. I had only to lay in wait until he called me.

I woke again to the angry shrill of the rusted hinges as my prison bars swung open. A copper-bearded guard spat on me and dropped a metal tray to the floor. The small bit of colorless food splattered everywhere. The guard took the brass cup he carried and kneeled, drinking every last drop of water before slamming it across my face, sending me right back to the comfort of mind-numbing oblivion.

"Wake, lesser," a familiar voice grated out some time later.

I peeled my eyes open to see Eadas standing just outside the bars of my dank cell.

He pulled out a knife and dragged it across each rail as he watched me. The crooked smile never left his monstrous face. He nodded to the guard who opened the door and strode in like he was the king himself. "Stand him up."

"I don't want to fucking touch him," the guard retorted, twisting his face in disgust.

Eadas slammed his fist into the guard's face, and I smirked as the guard moved to lift me from the ground.

I offered no help, letting the rusted chain's additional weight drag along the damp floor.

"Tell me how you resist the king's enchantment." Eadas' smile faded into pure hatred.

I didn't answer. Didn't even look at him. He planted a knee into my gut, and the sharp end of a broken rib pierced a lung. The shock of the breath forced from me caused me to cough and Eadas to laugh. He had no idea what he had just done. Taking additional time off my already shortened life.

"Answer." He lifted my bruised chin with the tip of his blade.

I stared back into his beady little eyes and dared him to kill me. My silence ignited a fury within him, and he slammed the knife into my shoulder.

I winced at the searing pain. That single motion had given him just what his twisted mind had begged me for. A semblance of control. He was mistaken though. He would never control me. I was ready to die. There was not a single thing in this world worth living for.

He yanked the knife out.

Warm blood dripped down my broken arm. I pulled only slightly at the chains around my wrists, forcing myself to stay conscious.

"Answer, Temir, or I swear when I find Gaea—and I will—I'll break her bone by fucking bone until she screams, begging me to kill her."

"I already killed her."

"You lie," he screamed, slamming the knife into my other arm.

I didn't feel the blade go in, but he grabbed the handle and jerked it downward, slicing me from shoulder to elbow. Tendons, muscles, nerves, everything damaged.

"Heal yourself."

Even if I wanted to use my magic, I wasn't sure I had the strength to heal that wound. I let my head drop and sway as the blackness began to creep in from the sides of my vision.

"Heal yourself," he snarled again.

"Suck my . . . limp . . . cock," I rasped.

Somewhere in the distance, I heard him roar as once again I faded into oblivion.

I was not sure how long I had lain on that frozen floor until I woke again. My head was damp with perspiration, which meant a fever had set in. I eyed another tray sitting in the corner with half a loaf of moldy bread and something I couldn't make out. I would have to scoot myself across the floor to get to the food, and even if I wanted to, I was in too much pain to move.

I closed my eyes as a jolt fired through me. She was near. Somewhere within the castle, the king's lover—my mate—had returned. She sent me nothing down the bond, but still, I reached out to feel for her. Foolish high fae female. The king would use her just as thoroughly as he had used everyone else. Something deep within begged my battered body to go to her. To find her. But just as she had turned her back on me, I did the same to her. There was no way for me to save her now anyway. I realized that the dark hole I had found her in was the same one I was currently digging within myself. There was no deliverance for either of us.

Again, the obsidian took me.

The shivering of my own body pushed me to life once more. I struggled to breathe, feeling the deep pressure on my chest. I began to cough, and once it started, it took forever to stop, until I was nearly choking and failing to drag a breath in at all. I barely had the strength to lift my head.

Murmurs from the guards at the bottom of the steps filled the scattered silence. They came and went on no particular schedule. Sometimes they would stay for an hour or two while other times they would only peek in and leave again. At one point, they brought down another prisoner. He lasted one day until he died, and it was two more before they dragged his stiff body through the dungeon.

*Lucky bastard.*

I'd be close behind him if they would just leave me alone, but Eadas was too conniving to let me rot in the dungeons before he got what he needed out of me. An admission of anything he could serve the king on a silver platter to solidify his position before the king moved to war with the south. The keys rattled against the lock, and I prepared myself for another battle. One I probably wouldn't win again.

He brought two guards this time. They hauled me to my feet, each holding under my armpit. "Time for games is over, Temir." Eadas stood in front of me as one of the guards held my face up to stare at him. "Do you really think you can save them? Any of them? The king will find the rebels whether you disclose their hideout or a weaker lesser does. It's only a matter of time before he starts lining up the staff for questioning."

The faces of Iva and Roe flashed through my mind, but I kept my face neutral.

"Tell me where the rebel compound is, and I'll bring you a full meal." He cracked a fist across my face and paced as he let his anger fester. "He will kill you, Temir. Do you think you're safe? You think because you haven't healed yourself, he will feel sorry for you? He hates you. Hates that he tried to see past what you really are. You're nothing, and he will never release your soul to the Ether if you don't cooperate."

As if an eternity of living in limbo would be worse than my lifetime of living in hell. His fears were not my own.

He reached inside his long, gray robes and pulled out a pointed rod, no thicker than the shaft of a feather. He grabbed my hand and lifted my arm, causing the stab wound in my shoulder to burn in pain.

I held my breath but did not cry out.

He took the pointed end of the small rod and shoved it into my index finger below the nail. I called enough magic forward to numb myself from the pain he so ardently sought. There was only one small mercy—he hadn't grabbed the hand with the barrier ring. My stomach rolled as I watched the bone in my hand splinter as the device was shoved up my entire finger and out the other side of my hand. He yanked the torture device out, anticipating a scream from me that he did not get.

24

He destroyed my entire hand, finger by finger, living solely for the pleasure of knowing I'd likely never be able to use that hand again. He knew at this point I couldn't heal myself entirely. I'd keep myself alive, but I'd never be able to gain the strength to heal those types of wounds unless he granted me the provisions to do so. And he never would.

Instantly, I was distracted by a feeling of desperate need, frantic searching seeping down my abandoned mating bond. I wanted to vomit. Not only would I suffer in the dungeons until someone finally killed me or the infection became severe enough, I would live out these days feeling the satisfaction the king would give my mate until I passed.

"I'll be back soon with more toys. Perhaps I'll bring the one your large, winged friend loved," Eadas said, bringing my thoughts back to my cell.

His guards dropped me to the floor, and my head slammed against the stone. I watched their blurred feet fade away. They left the barred doors open, knowing I wouldn't be able to escape if I wanted. Mental torture.

Eventually, another guard came down, dropped a tray of food onto the floor, set down a glass of water, and shut the gates behind him.

I listened as his steps filled the stairway and he closed the door above.

I was completely and utterly alone, and for the second time in my life, I felt a tear slide down my cheek. Was I well and truly ready to die?

"Temir?" a familiar feminine voice muttered from somewhere within the emptiness of my cell.

# CHAPTER 3

# Ara

"I hope I never see you again, little liar."

"I'll miss you too, buddy." I smirked at the enormous dragon as he extended his wings, coiled his legs, and vaulted into the scorching desert sky, leaving a sheet of red sand raining down on us.

"Now, see? That would have been way more appreciated if everyone could have seen it." Kai pouted as we started the last leg of the journey on foot.

Fen grabbed his shoulders from behind. "Ara's right, Kai. Dragons are beasts of great honor. He didn't want to be seen by the others. It was the right thing for us to do."

"I still don't understand how you were able to convince him to give us a ride." Lichen adjusted the pack on his shoulder, his stance was more stooped than it was when we first met. The journey had taken a toll on the old fae.

We were all sore. We had ridden that dragon most of the day, and as the sun trekked through the sky and toward the horizon in the Flame Court, we still had a bit of a walk ahead of us.

"I just asked nicely," I lied, leaning into Fen as we trudged through the deep desert sands.

I would never share the secret of the dragons. They would become enslaved to a world of fae that murdered each other for sport and spread hate like a disease. Dragons were incredibly beautiful creatures, and while they could change the tide of war, it was not their war to fight. It wouldn't be right for me, or anyone else, to try to use them as weapons.

"I think he likes you." Fen nudged me, a playful look on his face.

"Who?" I held my hand up to block the warm glow of the sun.

"The yellow dragon."

Sweat dripped down my back as I shook my head. "I think we just understand each other."

"How so?" Greeve asked, removing several layers of clothing until the tattoos on his arms were on display like artwork.

"Neither of us are fond of the idea of pulling dragons into the war for starters."

"Are we at war, then?" Fen asked.

I shrugged. "You tell me, Prince."

I needed to tread carefully. I hadn't shared my fate with anyone. I couldn't find the words to tell Fen I was charged with killing his father. He'd already lost his mother, and I was intimately familiar with that pain. I was also in denial. But fate was not a question of if, only when. It would happen, whether I wanted it to or not, unless I died first, because that's how it worked. I knew I needed to tell him. It was a constant rotating truth within my ever-wandering mind.

"There it is," Wren yelled, jumping up and down as we crested a hill.

I looked down to see a great city of twinkling lights with droves of people wandering the crowded streets as the sun sank below the horizon, leaving a chill in the air. Before I knew what was happening, everyone was running. Even Lichen, though he trailed behind.

Fen held my hand, looking back at me with a boyish grin, as we reached the road that would take us inside the lively city. "Welcome to Halemi."

Greeve turned and looked far into the distance. He must have been feeling the call of the draconians. The city was probably a place of a thousand nestled memories for the others, but for us, it wasn't quite home. Maybe that was why I felt so close to Greeve. Not because he looked at me like a sibling, but because we'd always understood each other. In our darkest moments, when no one else seemed to notice the world around us, he and I always did.

One step at a time, we walked into Fen's city. At first, a few scattered fae gasped, calling his name, and then more and more until we were met in the center of the city by a crowd of lesser and high fae intertwined like they didn't mind standing next to each other. They called his name and the names of the others, cheering and celebrating as they welcomed their prince home.

Kai ate it up. Bowing, waving, handing out hugs and a few winks as he walked beside Greeve, who stood taller than I had seen him in days, with a fierce, emotionless face. He was playing the crowd as well, just not in the same way Kai was. A tall female with her hair wrapped in fabric ran from the crowd, gathered Wren into a hug, and held her for several moments.

"That's Sabra." Fen pointed.

The sisters were nearly identical, apart from their wardrobe. Wren's traveling clothes were a far cry from Sabra's beautifully printed cloth.

As they laughed and hugged, we shared smiles until we were approached by an older high fae with a stern face and watchful eyes. His gruff voice was hidden behind his beard. "The king will see you immediately." He spoke directly to Fen, not bothering to look at the rest of us.

"Let us get settled in first, Inok," Fen answered.

"There's no time for that. Something has happened." His dire tone pushed Fen into motion.

I felt the panic and worry for his father as we ran through the rest of the busy city, up the worn road to the castle, through the gates, and into the large front doors. I expected the messenger, Inok, to have stayed behind or have struggled to keep up, but he was right on our toes as we moved.

"Meet us in the kitchens when you're done." Kai disappeared into the castle in the opposite direction. He was right at home.

Fen hadn't let go of my hand. He slammed open a door at the far end of the hallway, where we found an old high fae sitting in a stuffed chair staring out of a window. A perfectly made bed sat along a far wall. It took me a moment to realize I was standing in the bedroom of the king of the Flame Court. I knew Fen was the prince—I'd used that word as a weapon against him forever—but only now did it feel real.

The old king stood, leaning on a staff, as his kind eyes surveyed us both. His eyes rested on our coupled hands. "My boy." Water pooled in his old eyes. "You've found her." In two steps, he was across the room and pulling Fenlas into a welcoming hug.

Fen dropped my hand and held his father for several moments. I felt a tiny crack in my heart knowing the world would have me kill this male. This kind, old fae who had eyes for only his son. I thought of what a reunion with my own father would feel like right now, after all I had been through. I had to fight back my tears, mixed with happiness and sorrow, as I watched their reunion and longed for my own parents.

"Father." Fen cleared his throat and stepped away. "I'd like to formally introduce you to Ara, my mate."

He looked at me and beamed.

I started a perfect curtsey. "It's nice—"

He grabbed me and pulled me into a firm hug. I stood there awkwardly as he whispered, "We've met before, but my have you grown into a beauty."

"Thank you, Your Majesty."

"Please, will you call me Tolero? Or Father? Whichever you prefer. I wish to be more than a king to you, child."

"Yes, Your Majesty . . . Uhm, Tolero. Sir."

He chuckled, and Fen reached for my hand again. "We need long baths and big meals, Father. But Knocky—" A grunt from the back of the room interrupted him. "Inok," he corrected himself, "said something happened. What is it?"

"You might want to sit down, son."

"Father," Fen drawled.

"I've got the sea queen locked in the dungeons," he blurted out.

"Morwena?" I gasped.

"She is the only sea queen, my dear." Tolero pulled his staff in front of him so he could lean on it.

30

"Warded?" I asked.

He looked at me, stunned, and then shook his head.

"You'll find she's more than a pretty face, Father." Fen winked at me, sharing a smile with his father.

"Greeve is the only one trained with wards. Apart from him, we haven't had anyone skilled with them since the boys were young, so we've got her locked up the old-fashioned way. Chains and deaf guards."

"What's the rotation?" Fen went directly into military mode.

"We are doing ten-hour shifts between the upper and lower guards.

"How did you even manage it?" Fen asked.

"That's a long story for after your dinner, I suppose. For now, just know that she is down there, and we are working on a plan to figure out what to do with her." He tilted his head toward the door. "Head to your rooms. I'll let Loti know we'll have dinner in the hall tonight a bit late."

"Let's just meet in the kitchens, Father. There's no need to make a fuss."

"You're sure?" He looked to me alone, as if it were my decision.

I shrugged, giving a half-smile.

"I'll see you there in half an hour?" Tolero asked.

"Make that a full hour." Fen spun on his heel and dragged me out the door.

"Fen." I laughed as he hauled me through the castle. "Slow down."

"Sorry." He gave me those bedroom eyes as he slowed. "I finally get to have you alone, and I intend on using every minute as productively as possible."

"So, no bath?" I whined.

"I will bathe you." He grinned, sending a wave of heat through me.

We rounded a corner and he stopped short, staring at the uniformed soldier standing outside the only door in that hallway.

He held his hand up to cut the fae off. "No. Not now, Brax."

"But Sire, she says it's urgent."

"Who?" he asked, squinting.

"She won't say. She requests only to speak to you."

Fen growled, groaned, moaned, and then turned to me. "Duty will always call when I am here in the castle. Will you forgive me?" he asked, kissing my fingertips.

I tugged him forward and kissed his cheek. "I promise I'll be waiting for you when you come back."

"Five minutes." He lifted my chin and kissed me soundly. "Ten max."

He and the soldier disappeared down the long hallway as I let myself into his room. I walked around long enough to realize he had not only a room but an entire wing of the castle. A castle that had the sea queen hiding somewhere below. I glanced at the door and looked away. Not now, but soon, I'd find a way to confront her.

Intricately woven pillows of every jeweled color lined the floor with matching artwork and tapestries covering the walls. A slight breeze brought my attention to the silk curtains billowing in the room from the open columned balcony. I stepped outside and sighed as I watched the stars twinkle over the ocean. If there were heavens, this was one of them.

We'd made it. Through everything, all the chaos, all the fighting, we were here. So close to being lost in only each other, I leaned against the railing and watched the stillness of the ocean beyond the sands, longing for something. I couldn't quite decipher what was missing, but as I closed my eyes and listened to my heartbeat in the night, I realized what it was. *Home.* I hadn't had that feeling for so long, and perhaps I was envious of my companions and their newfound comfort while I still sought my place. Or maybe I was reluctant to let myself feel at home, knowing I'd come with the biggest secret of all. I felt the call of my power even now and hated it.

I would never look that old fae in the face and think ill of him. He was kind. You could see it in his ancient eyes. In the wrinkles around his smile. Fate may have brought me to the Flame Court, but somehow, I'd find a way to fight back. To still have a choice in my promised future.

I stepped back inside and searched for the bathing room. The main room was massive with the bed directly across from the balcony, but beyond that, there were several closed doors. I opened two dressing rooms before I found the one I wanted. He didn't mess around when it came to baths. I reached down and turned on the water to the giant tub, recessed into the floor, and it began to fill from the bottom up. I couldn't help my squeal.

Finding a drawer full of oils and lathering creams, I plucked the lavender and citrus bottles and poured a heaping amount into the rapidly filling bath. I undressed quickly and let myself sink all the way down into the near-boiling water. I sighed and sent Fen a mental picture of my feet in the tub. He jerked on the bond, and I giggled as I waited for him. His five minutes were up. I washed myself and my hair several times until all the grit and dirt from traveling for so long rinsed clean from my body.

Still no sign of Fen. We were supposed to meet the king in the kitchens soon, and that was where Kai said to meet him also, so I reluctantly pulled myself out of the water, wrapped a cloth around myself, and padded back into Fen's bedroom. The breeze from the window was just warm enough that I could have curled up naked on his bed and fallen asleep for days.

A knock on the door pulled me from that little daydream.

"Who is it?" I asked reluctantly.

"It's Frair, my lady," a female voice called out. "I've been sent to assist you."

"Assist me with what?" I opened the door but kept my body hidden behind it.

A high fae female with long, slender legs and ashen hair stood before me with a stack of fabrics and a smile. "Dressing, my lady," she smirked. "The prince sends his apologies. He will meet you in the kitchens."

*You can kiss my ass if you think I'm using a servant.* My inner thought was doused in sarcasm. I didn't think he'd hear me. It was mostly internal frustration. I was so used to having him right beside me I just sent thoughts like I had been sending the mental images.

*She's employed, not a servant. And trust me, no one is more irritated than I am,* he answered.

I jerked at his clear voice in my mind. *Holy fuck, Fen. You just answered me. In my brain.*

*Well, this is a welcomed new development. Shall I tell you what I wish I were doing right now?*

*Save it, Prince.*

34

I felt his joy and it tugged on my heart. Something about having him with me all the time was so comforting. I'd never be alone. "Come on in," I told Frair as she waited patiently for my mental conversation to be over.

I'd never seen a high fae working as a servant by choice. I hugged my towel close as she sauntered in and tossed her armful of fabrics onto the enormous platform bed.

"Prince Fenlas has requested the seamstress to see to your wardrobe in the morning. For now, I've brought several items for you to try." She watched me expectantly.

"I can dress myself, thanks. And a simple riding shirt and trousers will do just fine. I'm not fancy."

"But you will be the queen one day," she gasped. "You must dress appropriately."

"Listen, lady. I don't care what title everyone thinks I'll be taking. For now, just keep it simple."

She put her hands on her hips and stared me down. A picture of my mother flashed before me. "The prince likes blue, so shall we start with that?"

As if I hadn't said anything at all.

"You and I are going to fight by the end of this day and that's not a great thing for you," I threatened.

"I appreciate the fire, I do. But I grew up in the southern kingdom. I can hold my own. Shall we fight now or later, my lady?"

I couldn't help my laugh. Of course, he would send me the servant ready to throw down. "Trust me, you don't want to go there. Show me what you brought."

Her face reddened, but she bit her tongue and held the blue option out. There wasn't much to it. Still, I put it on. The top was beaded

35

fabric that ended below the bust, exposing my entire midriff. The bottom was a lightweight square fabric that Frair tied around my waist. I knew instantly I was going to have to be careful how I moved, or the slit that went from the floor to the waist was going to show the world my ass.

"I might as well just wear the towel down," I grumbled and shifted in the chair she had ordered me to sit in.

"I'm sure the prince wouldn't mind." She smiled, brushing through my hair.

"I really can tend to myself. I don't need help. I'm already going to be late."

She yanked on another knot, jerking my head back. "It's a lady's prerogative to arrive when she wishes. You're a far cry from the dirtball the prince walked into the castle with. Let me finish. I bet they won't even recognize you. Did you know your hair is actually beautiful?"

"I'll take that backhanded compliment." I crossed my arms and huffed, throwing my back into the chair.

She nodded and continued ripping through my hair until all the knots were gone, and honestly, as she began to massage my head, I forgot she was pissing me off.

She braided my hair down my back and stepped away. "Well, it's the best we can do for now. Tomorrow, we should try a few powders and a bit of rouge."

"Hard pass." I headed for the door. "Oh, shoes?"

She shook her head and smiled. I walked out and realized I had no idea which way I was going. I had to wait for her to lead the way, and for some reason, that annoyed me more than anything else. I didn't like relying on others. She'd only have to show me one time though. I was still my father's daughter.

I strolled into the kitchens to find everyone but Fen. *Where are you?*

*Almost there,* he answered.

The kitchens of the southern castle were not as elaborate as I'd thought they might be. Warm wood features, an alcove carved into the walls kept the room warm and cozy. Void of any windows the space, though dusted in flour, reminded me of an oversized version of the kitchen I'd grown up in.

"Holy. Shit. You're a full-fledged female?" Kai asked, wiggling his eyebrows as he leaned over an island in the middle of the kitchen and took a bite out of a crisp apple.

"I'll still kick your ass, Kai." I glared at him.

"You could try."

That was the southern motto. I couldn't count how many times I'd heard it. As if none of them were scared of a thing. I bowed graciously to the king standing across the room and sat on a tall stool beside Greeve at the table in the middle of the kitchen probably meant for rolling dough.

"Loti," the king said to a plump little female with tight brown curls and an apron tied around her. "This is Ara, Fenlas's mate and my future daughter-in-law."

Kai snorted, and I shot him a glare. Loti swung a towel at him, and he ducked to miss it. "Where are your manners, Kaitalen?" she fumed. "It's nice to finally meet you, dear." She curtsied and Kai snorted again.

"Turning into a piglet Kai-*talen*?" I looked back to Loti. "Please, you don't need to do that." I shook my head, trying to hide the revulsion.

"Nonsense. Have you eaten? You look half-starved."

She looked from me to Kai, and he shrugged. "She can out hunt me, trust me. If she's starving, it's her own fault."

"Can you really?" the king asked, moving to sit beside me.

"Kai talks so much he scares away the animals," I answered.

This was quite possibly the most casual and informal family dinner I had ever seen outside of my own home, but it was such a welcomed surprise. I had imagined the king in a thousand different ways. I wished I could hate him. It would make my fate simpler. But he was kind and lovable, and that made everything more difficult.

Loti sat a heaping plate of roasted boar, fried agraroots, and various fruits before me, and I didn't hesitate to dig in. Greeve smiled and added more to my plate. Once full, I sat back and finally took the time to notice that he and Kai cleaned up pretty well. They certainly smelled better. Greeve wore all black and his clean hair was tied behind him with new leather.

"Shopping tomorrow?" Wren asked as she stood and moved across the table to stand next to Kai.

"She's already got plans." Fen strode into the room and slipped a hand around my bare stomach "You're stunning," he whispered, kissing my neck.

Wren slammed her hand on a counter. "Damnit Fen, you don't get to keep her locked up in your room anymore. You have to share."

"Anymore?" Tolero asked, pinning his son with a stare.

"Don't ask," the others said in unison.

I looked at Fen, but he hadn't taken his eyes from me. *Where were you?*

"We have a new guest. She claims she comes from the Wind Court and she offered a large amount of information on King Autus. I had to debrief her. I'm sorry I'm late."

"Is she hot?" Kai asked, not missing a beat.

"What is wrong with you?" Loti smacked him in the back of the head.

"Ow," he mock whined until Loti's cheeks pinkened.

"He truly is just as whiny as I thought." I shared a smirk with Greeve.

"What's the plan with the new girl?" Greeve asked as Fen stepped away to make his own plate.

The Flame Court continued to surprise me. If Coro could order someone to blink for him, he would have. Fen took care of himself. They all did.

"Not sure yet. I thought maybe Wren and Sabra might take her to the others?" He looked to Wren.

"Sure. Tomorrow, if that's okay. I'm going home and sleeping until midday."

"That's fine. She has magic. Just so you know."

"What's her gift?" I shifted the delicious food around my plate, too full to take another bite.

"She calls it spiriting. It seems similar to Greeve's ability."

"Feline eyes?" I asked.

He nodded.

*I've seen her with him.*

*Me too.*

"We'll have to be careful. She could be a spy." Greeve leaned his arms on the counter, the delicate breeze he commanded stilling.

"She knows about the rebels but claims she isn't one. Let's worry about it tomorrow."

The king simply ate his dinner and listened to the conversation like it was music to his ears. Smiling as he watched his son take full charge.

*My father and Inok are going to want a full report of everything after dinner. I can make them wait.*

I shook my head slightly. *There's no need to rush, Fen. We have our whole lives to love each other. Handle whatever you need. I'm not going anywhere.*

"Is there cake?" Greeve asked, completely unaware of our mental conversation.

"Of course. Just for you, my dear." Loti crossed the kitchen, lifted a massive white cake from another counter, and set it in front of him. Tolero cleared his throat and Loti shrugged. "He's always been my favorite." She reached up to pinch Greeve's cheeks.

He beamed. I'd never seen that smile from him before.

"I'll just be over here wallowing in self-pity if anyone needs me." Kai stuck his lip out and lowered his chin, pinning Loti with a full pout. I guessed he'd stolen many hearts with that look.

"If you weren't such a pain in my behind, Kaitalen, I'd bake for you too."

"Oh, Loti. We all know I'm secretly your favorite and you have lemon tarts stashed away somewhere for me."

She giggled. "Here, you big baby." She opened a cupboard, pulled out another tray, and the whole room erupted. Even I couldn't help myself. Kai, with his handsome boyish features, was hard not to love,

40

especially when he grabbed her around the waist and pulled her in for a hug while she swatted at him until he let her go.

"Welcome home, my dear," Tolero said, leaning toward me.

CHAPTER

4

# Temir

"Nadra?" My voice crept through my throat like a knife. "What are you doing here?"

The dripping water in the otherwise silent prison was maddening. There was no answer. Would be no answer, because, in my own delirium, pain, and sorrow, I'd only imagined she came for me when no one else would.

But then the silence was broken with a gentle whisper. "You saved my mother."

I coughed, and the familiar pain of my wounds, of this wretched life, of her voice, ripped through me.

Her voice trembled. "Are you okay?"

The spots grew bigger in my vision and I had to force myself back to clarity. "I've been better."

"What can I do to help you?"

"Go away." I never wished I could turn away from someone so bad—from my own shame or my ire, I wasn't sure, but she couldn't be trusted. It didn't mean the bond wasn't there somewhere, buried within me, but when I closed my eyes and saw her lying beneath the king, it was all I could do to keep myself from heaving.

"I can't." Her voice faded away as a rustling in the corner of my cell replaced it.

I didn't even bother asking why I couldn't see her. I closed my eyes and went back to sleep. She couldn't use that against me.

The heavy cell door slammed shut, waking me. A hunched sentry dropped a tray to the floor and walked out. I thought she'd leave with them when they brought food, but she didn't.

"Do you need a drink?"

Tears stung my eyes as I laid disgraced on the dank floor and tried to ignore her. Maybe that's what Autus wanted. To show me that even my mate wouldn't really want me. I was just a joke to all of them.

"Please let me help you." Her voice was full of so much sorrow, it blended with my own, drowning us both until we could have swam away in it.

"If you're down here to prove some point or to report to him, save yourself the trouble. He's already won, Nadra. I've given up." I tried to drag the heavy air into my lungs after such a long-winded sentence, but fluid compressed them. To say those words out loud crushed the small bit of strength I had left, and my eyes fell shut again.

"Why would you think I was down here for the king when you saw what he did to me?"

I didn't bother answering. I willed myself back to sleep until I felt water splashing my face.

"Maybe you gave up, Temir, but I didn't. You need to drink."

It was room temperature and tasted stale, but the moment it touched my lips, I desperately wanted more. It was gone far too soon. "Why?" I wheezed.

Her sharp tone became soft again. "You wrote me a letter full of kindness and compassion. You saved my mother, despite the danger to yourself." She paused, sighing in the dark. "The pull to you is still here. It won't go away until I deny the bond. Despite everything, I can't find it in me to turn my back on you. Anyone who gives everything to save someone else is good. Is worth saving. Maybe even worth loving. And I need to know if that's who you really are."

"No one knows who I really am. Not even me."

"Then show me, Temir. Fight back. You didn't stop protecting me when you saw me at my worst. So don't ask me to. I am changed because of you and that has to mean something. You are mine and I am yours, and there has to be a reason for it."

Something deep within me moved. It might not have leaped as she would hope, but it shifted. The desire to take in a full breath without pain resonated within me. If nothing else, if not the will to live, then at least that. I tried to pull on my magic, but I had no strength. The damage was already done.

"You need to eat. I've got a bag of food I stole from the kitchens."

"You have a wh . . . Why can't I see you?" I groaned.

"My mother made a gown for a friend of mine. When we came north, we brought it with us. Iva helped me steal it from my rooms. As long as no one touches me, I can remain unseen. I'm going to hold out some bread. Can you lift your head to eat something?"

Too weak to answer, I simply lay there. She held the bread to my mouth, and I attempted to eat. It was doughy and not dry, which made it easier. I closed my eyes and took a careful breath as I willed that small bit of sustenance to give me enough strength to test the mating bond for any semblance of deception. I wanted to believe her. In fact, I think I was desperate to.

"Tell me something about yourself." I tried to be gentle. She was still fragile. The female I'd left behind at the Keep was still broken in so many ways, but so was I. We'd have to tread lightly. If it didn't work, then fine, but at least we tried.

"My mother owned a seamstress shop. But I guess you knew that. I have worked for her for many years. I've done everything she's ever asked of me aside from really trying to settle down. I was shallow, Temir. Awful, even. I think about the way my mind worked before the king twisted it into something horrid and I'm ashamed of it. I was petty and daft, but I was happy." She moved, the fabric of her dress shuffling against the dirty floor. Her voice was distant and sad. "I went from happy to not being able to string two thoughts together. It was like he dug talons into my mind and just spun until it was scrambled. I wanted to die. To end the madness. And then there was this light in the darkness." A careful breath caught in her throat. "You. And now that I feel myself coming out of the other side of that torture, things that seemed important before are nothing to me, but things I would have never considered seem like the most important things in the world. Maybe I'm still twisted, or maybe I always was."

Her words were so raw and there wasn't an ounce of a lie in them. She had really come for me. When no one else had. Without any form of training, and at great risk to her own life, she had come.

I whispered. "Maybe you're just processing what happened to you. That's okay."

"He broke me," she muttered.

"He broke me too, Nadra."

"He wanted me to love him. To worship him. And I wanted to. But you were here, and it seemed wrong, even when it felt right. It was like being split in two."

The familiar pull of my own magic brought a trace of comfort as I began to slowly let it heal my inner wounds. Starting first with the punctured lung and then the excess fluid. I had only enough magic to enable myself to breathe without rasping. It was bliss.

"Would you tell me a happy memory?" I asked, my voice hushed as I listened for the door of the dungeon to open.

"If that's what you need." She adjusted herself again, coming closer so she could speak quieter. "There's this old couple who lives in Hrundel. They are notorious for their bitter nature and I'd never seen Chire's wife smile. Ever. One day, the king commissioned my mother to make him a band of fabric that he could wear on his wrist that would make him a better lover. My mother did of course. She left the fabric on the counter, and when Old Chire came to pick up his monthly tailoring, I accidentally sent it with him." Her tone was lighter, as if I could hear the smile.

"What happened?"

"Hours later, I overheard my mother speaking to one of her friends about the fabric, and I instantly realized my mistake. I headed to Chire's home, and just as I was about to knock on the door, I heard his wife screaming in the throes of passion. I gasped and ran home as fast as I could. I spent hours sewing a duplicate, though mine didn't have magic, of course. And then my mother asked me to have it delivered to the castle without checking it. The next day I saw Old Chire's wife with the fabric tied around her wrist and smiling from ear to ear. I've never been able to look her in the eye since."

The first smile I'd had in a long time struck me. I tried to turn toward her further, but the pain was still immense as I stifled my groan.

"Can you tell me about your parents?" Her voice was cautious and tender.

"I never knew them. I don't know how I came to be in Autus' court. But there was an old fae who raised me." I took a deep, shuddering breath. "This might not be a story a high fae is used to hearing."

"A long time ago, before I was born, my mother knew your friend, Rook. She maybe even loved him. I'd like to think that there really is no difference, so if it's all the same to you, I'd be happy to listen to your story, Temir."

"Okay, well Oleonis was his name."

"Was?"

"He died in my arms."

I heard her quiet inhale of a sharp breath. "Go on."

"He was the best fae I'd ever known. He promised to take care of me when I was young after the king collected me from the stables. Oleo, that was what we called him, used to give me and my friend Gaea lessons at the same time. I was quite a bit older than she was, and she would always get so jealous if he gave me the attention she coveted. I think you've met her, right?"

"I've seen her with you, and she is the one who brought us here."

"Yes, well, she was quite a spitfire when she was young." I paused. The energy it was taking to hold the conversation caused my heart to thunder in my chest. I needed to calm it. Or maybe it was the memories.

"We can finish tomorrow if you need to rest?"

"I'm okay. But before I continue, I need to warn you. Others will come and they will do horrible things to me, and I need you to promise you'll look away. I don't know when they will come, I'm not sure what they will do, but just promise me you won't watch."

"I promise, Temir."

"Thank you, Nadra. Thank you for coming, for staying. For pushing me."

"You're welcome," she whispered.

I pulled at the chains to turn in her direction. Huge mistake, as a wound in my arm ripped open and blood seeped out again. I had to distract myself from the pain. "Are you cold?"

"This dress is massive," she said as the fabric rustled below her. "It's plenty warm enough if I tuck it around me."

I gritted my teeth, willing my voice to sound calm. "I'm sorry I can't do more for you."

"Don't apologize to me for your circumstances when I'm the one who put you here. I'm fine, you're going to be fine, and we are going to find a way out of this."

"Should I continue my story, then?"

She yawned. "Yes, please."

It was odd. She was only a voice in the darkness—I couldn't see her features at all—but as we settled into whatever madness this could be classified as, I felt her without touching her. I knew her without seeing her. She was giving me far more than I'd ever imagined possible as the will to live began to burrow deep within me once more.

"One day, the three of us spirited to the Marsh Court because Oleo wanted to find some mushrooms for the garden. At that time, Gaea's magic wasn't strong enough to carry two people at once. So, she started with me, as Oleo instructed. She dropped me off in the middle

48

of a forest and then went back for him. Only they never showed up. I spent three days wandering that forest until a high fae who worked for Coro found me. He took me to his home, sent a messenger, and eventually, Gaea showed up to procure me. Turns out, she wanted the day alone with Oleo but then claimed she couldn't remember where she had dropped me off."

Nadra giggled. "Do you think they believed her?"

"Not at all. Oleo made her write paragraphs for a week. I think she hated me even more after that. Then we started having our lessons separately. We never really talked to each other again until we were older."

"Did you love her?" she whispered.

Of course she had noticed it. I think everyone had. "I thought I did. But now I don't know. None of it matters anyway. She's gone. I'll probably never see her again. We were doomed from the start, and I held that against her more than I should have." The blanket of exhaustion covered me as the pool of blood grew larger.

"I'm sorry."

"I think I'll sleep now."

"I think I will too. Good night."

I closed my eyes, completely drained, and fell asleep. I woke to her deep, slow breaths. I healed as much as I could, including repairing my crippled hand, and fell back asleep. I repeated that several times until I thought I could probably sit up if I wanted. Instead, I let myself sleep again. We spent days like that. Exchanging stories. I'd heal myself as I could, little by little. It was amazing how much you could get to know someone if the only thing you had to do was talk to them for days on end.

"Wake up, lesser," a guard called out one morning. If it really was morning. We had no idea. He opened the bars and dragged me to my feet.

I closed my eyes and hoped like hell Nadra really would turn away as she hid in the darkest corner.

"Sleep well?" he asked, just before hitting me in the groin. I doubled over and he kneed me right in the nose. He was lucky my hands and feet were still bound.

I heard a small noise from Nadra and coughed to cover it.

"The boss will be down soon. I hope you're ready to answer his questions today." He threw me to the floor and slammed the door as he went.

I waited and listened carefully. He didn't leave as the others had.

"He's still here. Stay quiet." I breathed, hoping only she could hear me.

She didn't answer. What she was about to witness would be a lot more difficult to bear than what the guard had done. I hoped she had an iron stomach. If she revealed herself, I was going to have to bring out my dark magic and hope like hell I could get us out of the castle.

I had healed most of my inner wounds, but I left the bruising and flesh wounds. Eadas would have no idea I'd been healing myself, and that's how it needed to remain for as long as possible. If I was going to get us out of here, he needed to believe I was weak. Unwilling to help myself.

"You dead yet?" he asked as he approached the bars with Autus' new winged twins at his side. He glanced over to the uneaten food and scoffed. "You forget you are a lesser, Temir. You're not too good for the food the king provides you. I can see how you'd be confused after all these years of privilege, but today, I think we'll remind you of your rightful place." He opened the bars and stalked in with that wicked grin of his.

Our fear intertwined as they lifted me to my feet. My fear was for her. I reached for the bond and held it, and she did the same. They could do whatever they wanted to me as long as she was safe. Undetected.

A guard handed Eadas a contraption, and I watched as he slipped his hand inside the glove and flexed the long knife-like fingers at the end of it while his nefarious laugh echoed through the shadowed dungeons.

I gripped the bond tighter.

The guards held me up, pinning my arms as Eadas made his first strike, slashing me with the claws of his glove across my chest. My skin ripped, and the blood seeped through what was left of my filthy shirt.

"Where are the rebels hiding?" Eadas asked.

I kept my head down and let my body hang limp. Perhaps if they thought I was weaker, they would leave sooner.

"Answer!" he roared.

He took another swing in the opposite direction, and the pain was so severe I wasn't sure I could stitch myself back together. I tried to use magic to numb my nerves so that I wouldn't feel whatever came next, but it was so damn hard to concentrate. I gave up and kept my focus on the beautiful female radiating fear and anger as she hid.

"Turn him," Eadas ordered.

The guards turned, and he slashed into my back repeatedly until sweat poured down my head and I couldn't help but cry out in sheer pain. He was shredding me.

"Tell me where they are, Temir," he demanded. He wouldn't have worked this hard if there was a rebel betraying us. He would have already known. Which meant, for now, all the rebels except for me were safe. And I still wasn't convinced the king would let me die. He would work tirelessly until he learned about Oravan's ring, and then he would destroy it and I'd be a slave to him for the rest of my life.

He ran his clawed fingers down my legs, pressing so hard you could hear the skin tear.

I yelled in pain. Nadra sent me comfort and strength, and that was all I could hold onto until the pain and blood loss became too much to bear, and I passed out.

I woke later to an empty cell and the heartbreaking sound of sniffles from the corner. "Are you okay?"

"You're asking me?" she answered. "They nearly killed you."

"I'm fine," I lied, refusing to move an inch.

"Please use your magic, Temir. Please eat something," she wept.

"Don't cry." I could hardly bear the sound of her broken voice. She was strong though. She'd remained silent through it all. "Just tell me another story. Distract yourself."

"If you promise to eat something. Can you move?"

"Give me just a moment. I've been working on it."

I let the magic coalesce through my body, clotting the bleeding wounds and strengthening myself. It was rough and exhausting, but I was able to sit up when I was done, though I was still soaked in my own blood. The root of all evil, magic was again my savior.

"Here," she said, "hold out your hands." The heavy chains dragged along the moldy floor as I did. A block of hard cheese and another half loaf of bread landed in them. "The food is getting low. I can try to sneak out and get some more the next time they come."

"Nadra, if you can sneak out, you should go someplace safe." I carefully took a bite of the bread.

"I've told you I won't leave you and I meant it. I can sneak away to get food, but I'm not leaving this castle without you."

I wasn't sure I deserved that kind of dedication, but I was grateful. The gods had given me a mate that wouldn't run, even though everyone else in my life had. She was exactly what I needed, and every minute with her, I felt our bond grow. "Tell me more about you."

"I'll make you a deal. I'll tell you more if you agree to stop asking me to leave. I'm trying here, Temir. I really am. But please don't push me away."

I listened to that drop of water for a long time as I considered what she had said. She was telling me what she needed and giving me what I needed. It wouldn't have been fair for me to deny her. So I didn't.

"Deal."

"I wasn't lying when I told you I was a shallow person. I went to tea with ladies that weren't my friends. I got my hair done to impress people I didn't care about. I worked in my mother's shop to make her happy. I lived my life for everyone else, always."

"That makes you a giving person." I finished the last of the bread and leaned my head against the wall feeling better than I had in a long time.

"No, I was still selfish. I think I had one friend in the entire world that wasn't afraid to tell me how ridiculous I was, and I don't even know where she is anymore."

"When we leave this place, we will find her, if that's your wish."

"I don't know what my wish is. The only thing that matters to me right now is you, Temir. I just want something normal."

Those words made the world brighter. "Do you mean it?"

"I'm not going to be a good mate for you. I'm sorry about that. But my heart is here with you. At first, I thought I couldn't accept the bond. But now, I can't deny it."

"I promise you, I will get us out of this."

"We can do it together."

I wanted to reach for her. I wanted to hold her in my arms and tell her I knew exactly how she felt. I wanted so many things I couldn't have. We were far from happiness, but we had each other, and something about that felt right. We fell asleep that night inches apart.

Our hearts began to heal our shared soul.

She snuck out the next morning when the guard brought us another poor excuse for food. The moment he'd opened the doors, she slipped behind him, as we'd planned. She sent wave after blissful wave of confidence as she traveled through the castle, so I knew she was all right. I felt the delight she sent when she succeeded in securing food from the kitchens and then calmness as she stood outside of the door, waiting for someone else to come back down. We'd agreed she shouldn't open it, even if she thought no one was looking, just to be safe.

The door above opened and heavy feet marched down the stairs. I held my breath as the soldiers approached. "You've been summoned."

They opened the cage door and dragged me out of the musty dungeons. Pure fear radiated down the bond, and I hoped Nadra hadn't followed them down and gotten stuck down there. If I was about to die, at least she could still get out of the castle.

The light from above burned my eyes. I'd grown accustomed to pure darkness. I expected to be taken to the throne room. Humiliated in front of the entire court. Instead, I was dropped onto the stone floor of the empty council room, practically naked with shredded clothing and covered in dried blood from head to toe.

"I am with you," Nadra whispered. "Until the end, Temir. I am here."

My heart wrenched. We both knew what was about to happen.

"Go now. Do not let them catch you. Find your friend."

"Until the end." Her voice was hard as steel. My mate.

# Ara

*F*en crawled into the bed just before sunrise. He was asleep before I could reach for him. I slipped out, threw his shirt over my head, and pulled out the riding pants from my bag. I'd probably never get away with wearing them again once Friar discovered I had them, so I enjoyed every last second of it.

I snuck out as quietly as I could and began my memorization of the castle. I could get to the kitchens, Tolero's room, and the entrance. From there, I had no idea. I passed a sleepy worker here and there, but none who paid too much attention to me as I went. Empty rooms with doors propped open and sheets covering the furnishings told me one thing: Tolero liked his privacy and didn't have a lot of guests.

The halls were designed with delicate, feminine touches of the same jeweled color palette that was in Fen's room. His mother, Efi, must have spent a large amount of time turning this enormous castle into a cozy home. I found stairs that led down below the castle and a hoard of guards keeping them secure. I didn't bother going any farther. I knew who they guarded.

"You're up early." Greeve appeared beside me in a gust of wind that nearly knocked me over.

"You're fucking sneaky when you want to be." I punched his arm. "Next time cough or something first."

"You're such a pleasure in the morning, Ara."

"Wait, why are *you* up so early?"

A vacant smile crossed his face as he slid a hand into his pocket. "Something about being in the south makes me want to go home. I get restless here in the castle."

I lifted a shoulder. "So, go home."

He pinned me with a hard look. "It's not that easy." I looped my arm through his, and we meandered through the halls, side by side. "Fen needs me here. Especially now that we have a murderous guest in the dungeons."

"Right. Morwena. Aren't you curious? What's her story? How did they even trap her?"

"Only one way to find out." He winked at me. His grin a contradiction to the honed weapons he always wore.

Greeve and I had settled into a different kind of friendship. Something along the lines of siblings, I imagined.

He knew he had me with that wink.

I stopped and pressed my back against an embroidered tapestry, crossing my arms. "Who are you right now? You can't be serious. She'll enchant you in a heartbeat."

"Yeah. You're right. Plus, Fen would kill me if I put you in danger."

"Okay, first of all, Fen's not my keeper. And second, Fen's not my fucking keeper."

"Mhm," he said with a conspiratorial gaze.

"Are you trying to convince me to do something we both know I shouldn't? What do *you* want to know? Why not just ask Fen or the king?"

"I don't want to know anything." He turned on his heel and continued walking. "But you do."

"How do you know me so damned well, Greeve?"

"Because the moment you sense danger, you need to run headfirst to be right in the middle of it, and I'd prefer be there to protect you rather than finding out about it later."

I shook my head, matching him stride for stride. "I didn't ask to go see her and I don't need protecting."

"I didn't say you did."

"But if I wanted to, could you get me down there?"

The corner of his mouth lifted. Greeve was dangerously beautiful, and if Fen didn't own my soul, I might have melted for that smirk. "If you wanted to, which you don't, then yes, I think I could manage it. If you kept it between the two of us."

I pressed my nails into my palms and turned away from him. As if I was protecting myself from the truth. "It's just that I want to know what she knows about me. Tolero has his reasons for locking her up, but she's been hunting me since before my parents died, and now she's here. Right here. I can't let that go."

"We could wait for Fen. You could go together."

"Something tells me he isn't going to be a fan. If anyone in this castle was going to get me down there, it would be you."

"Are you asking?" He casually rested his hand on the hilt of the knife at his waist, as if he already needed to protect me from something I couldn't handle.

I looked into his eyes with solid conviction. "Yeah, I am."

He reached to grab my arm.

"Wait. We need a plan though. You can't stay down there. If she tries to enchant me, it won't work, but if she aims for you, it will."

Razor-sharp cunning morphed into something steady and dangerous upon his features. "I can't leave you alone down there. It's not an option."

"Just give me a knife, I'll be fine." I scoffed.

"Not. An. Option," he said in his stern draconian voice.

"What if you drop me off and circle the room so she doesn't know you're there, and then if anything happens, you can grab me and we can go before she has a chance to enchant you?"

"Done."

It was only easy because he knew, if not for this, I'd find another way. He probably watched the hall all night waiting for me to show up. *Know-it-all.* He grabbed my hand, and within a split second, we were racing through the castle on steady wind he commanded, and then I was standing alone in a torch-lit dungeon staring into the cell of my greatest enemy. Morwena.

For a moment, I went back to the child who feared her. My heart raced. But then the faces of my fallen parents flashed through my mind and I raised my chin, straightened my shoulders, took a deep breath, and stepped forward.

Bound by her hands and feet, with a tie wrapped around her mouth, she was wide awake, glaring at me from the front of her barred cage with her piercing blue eyes. Her white-blonde hair a mess of tangles, pooling around her.

I paced in front of her, trying to collect my thoughts.

"Do you know who I am?" She blinked but said nothing. "If I take that gag from your mouth, are you going to play nice?"

She shook her head.

At least she was honest. I reached up between the bars, hooked my finger around the fabric, and jerked it down.

"You might be promised, but you aren't bright, girl." Her voice was raspy but strong.

"Did you order my parents killed?"

Her lethal eyes held mine as a wicked smile spread across her beautiful face. "Why would I answer your questions, girl?"

"Why wouldn't you? I'm just a lowly peasant and you're a magnanimous queen."

She snorted.

Clearly, I was going to have to bait her. I reached through the bars once more, quick as a snake, and yanked the massive jewel from her neck.

Her eyes lit up, but as soon as her evada pearl was removed, she began to gasp and then choke. "Okay," she rasped, fear flashing before she hid it away.

I clasped the long chain of the necklace and peaked an eyebrow until it was understood which of us was currently in control. I was destined to kill her, but she didn't know that. No one did. And I certainly wouldn't be doing it in the Flame Court, putting the blame on Tolero. I placed the chain over her head, and she dragged in breaths as she stepped out of my reach and gasped, her shoulders heaving.

"Such vulnerability." I tutted. "Did you order my parents killed?" I held my voice calm, calculated.

"Yes," she ground out.

"And me?"

"Yes."

"Why?" I asked, tilting my head to the side.

Silence.

"Why?" I barked. Facing my own fate was far worse than facing a mortal queen with an attitude problem. I could kill her. Right now. And there was satisfaction in that. Treacherous satisfaction.

"Your father signed his own death warrant when he refused to turn the Hunt over to me. Your mother was caught in the crossfire and you were just a happy accident when I realized who you were. You landed right in my lap."

"My mother was not caught in the crossfire. I was there. I watched her die."

"Oh, how sad," she said, a wide grin still slathered across her face.

"I will kill you. Maybe not today, but one day."

"You are a child. You have no idea what it means to kill. I've killed hundreds. Thousands. I'm not scared of you or your prince. You're all so worried about me when you should be looking farther north."

"I think we both know you are scared, Morwena. If you weren't, you wouldn't have hunted me. You wouldn't have killed my parents. You wouldn't have done a fucking thing other than sit on your pretty throne and stare at your beloved king you seem so infatuated with."Her eyes lit with fury, and I smiled as sweetly as I could. "Problem?"

"Only one."

I took my time inspecting the dank dungeons. I watched the light flicker on the walls and noted the selkies in the other cages now awake and watching me closely. I found comfort knowing Greeve was with me, though he hadn't made a sound. "I'd say certainly more than one. But what do I know? I'm sure Tolero has his reasons for locking you down here, probably because you're a—"

She laughed. A heinous, spiteful laugh. "He hasn't told you?"

"I've not asked. I don't care."

"You should care. If you're to save this world before one of us kills you, you should know the moves that are made. It was brilliant really. I nearly had him."

I waved my hand through the air. "In case you haven't noticed, nearly doesn't mean shit."

She huffed. "Autus knows about you. He knows there's a power greater than anyone else tied to the southern prince. How long until he figures out how to steal you away? Better yet, how long until he kills your prince and traps you when you try to seek revenge? Clearly, you have a penchant for danger."

"You can't possibly think you're a danger to me. You're hardly a danger to yourself anymore. When I kill you—and I will—I hope you'll go straight to the deepest pit of hell."

"I'll be sure to tell your father hello."

"You fucking bitch." I grabbed the bars, standing on the precipice of utter rage, as I considered dropping that iron wall.

"Time to go." Greeve snatched my arm

I gave him a pointed look, and he returned it. He let go long enough to put her gag back in place. Her muffled laugh echoed through the dungeon as I was swept away. I was still fuming in the hall.

"Feel better?" he asked.

"No, the fuck I do not," I answered, jamming my hands to my sides and staring at the ceiling.

"Did you learn anything?"

"No."

"Want to punch her?"

"Kind of."

His deep laughter calmed my racing heart. "I thought overall you were pretty nice to her. On Ara terms, that is."

"At least we know for sure Autus knows about me. Fen was already worried about it." I reached out to him, but there was only silence through the bond.

"Hungry?" Greeve asked, wrapping an arm around my shoulder.

"Always," I answered.

We made our way to the quiet kitchen, and I sat in the same seat I did last night while Greeve perused the larder and then the cupboards. He worked on his concoction as I sat watching him. He held a bowl under one arm, whisked in the other, and chopped vegetables like he was born doing it. Soon, the room was filled with the smell of whatever he was making, and my stomach growled just as Kai walked in with Loti hot on his tail.

"What in the gods' names are you doing in my kitchens, Greeve?" She peeked into his steaming pan and her shoulders sank. "Ah. Just like I taught you."

Greeve beamed when Loti praised him, and I guessed he'd spent a lot of time with her in the kitchens.

"She still likes me better." Kai took the seat beside me.

*Where are you?* Fen asked down the bond.

*Kitchen.*

*Who's cooking?*

*Greeve.*

*Be right there.*

I laughed, and Kai looked at me like I was crazy. I shrugged and looked down at the plate that Loti sat in front of me. I breathed in the sweet smell of fluffy honeyed bread, picked at a pile of red and blue berries, and let my eyes feast on the poached robin eggs over seasoned potatoes. I moaned as I tasted each thing and eventually everyone was looking at me.

"What?" I asked with a mouthful of food. "No one told me Greeve could cook."

"Glad I don't share a wall with Fen." Kai's boyish grin made me snort.

"You and me both, brother," Fen said, entering the room. "For so many reasons." He kissed my cheek and took a seat while Loti prepared him a dish.

"What's on the schedule for the day?" Greeve asked.

"I've got to check on the males in the lists, and then . . ." He paused as his fire magic wrapped around me. "I've got other things in mind."

"Pervert." Kai coughed into his hand.

"Entirely," Fen answered as he laid a hand on my thigh.

"Can we go see your cetani?" I figured I owed Greeve for smuggling me down to see the bitch queen.

64

He withdrew slightly. "If that's what you really want to do."

*I thought we might spend the day doing something else, Princess.*

*Scientific things?*

*I was thinking maybe a more hands-on approach this time.*

I looked at him and bit my lower lip. *Were you now?*

*Tonight, then?* he asked, raising an eyebrow.

I nodded.

"Does anyone else feel like we're missing something here?" Kai asked, shoveling food into his gaping mouth as his eyes shifted between us.

"They are Ameriala," Loti said as she smiled at Fen.

"Annoying. Riiight." Kai managed through a mouth full of food.

"No. Ameriala. It means their mating bond is stronger than most. They can speak without words."

"So that's what it's called." Fen's eyes lit with delight as his pride seeped into my own. As if it were a competition we had both won without doing a single thing.

"Yes, dear. It is very rare. It comes from old, old magic. I'm not sure there's a mated couple alive anymore that are Ameriala."

"Were my mother and father?" Fen asked.

She shook her head and turned away. Fen rarely spoke of his mother, and here in the castle, it must still feel like a fresh wound.

*Loti lost her mate a long time ago. I'm sure it's difficult for her.*

I leaned my head on his shoulder. I was sure asking about his mother was still hard for him also.

"How long does it take to get to the draconian village?" I asked, changing the subject.

"About half a day on a fae horse. Maybe a little longer. We could take the standard horses, but it would double the trip through the desert."

"So, if we leave now and stay for a few hours, we can still be back by tonight?"

"Well, we could take Gaea. Try to feel her out. She could use her magic to bring us back sooner or we could stay a bit longer."

"I'd like to feel her out," Kai said, because of course he did.

"Have you even met her?" I asked, rolling my eyes.

"Nope. I've got a good imagination though."

"You're disgusting."

"I know." He smiled, showing all his teeth.

Fen cleared his throat. "Greeve, if you could check in with Wren while I meet with Brax and the soldiers, we can all meet at the stables in an hour."

"I'll pass this time." Kai stretched his arms languidly above his head. "I've got a long day of napping ahead of me. Plus, I still have to find Greeve's blind date."

Greeve's head snapped to the side, his hair whipping through the air. "My what?"

"Oh no. We had a deal and you lost. You aren't getting out of it this time. I'm just trying to decide between which of the Luger cousins." He tapped his chin.

Greeve launched a hand towel into his face as Fen pulled me from the kitchens.

"Can I come with you to see the soldiers?" I asked.

"Friar is already waiting to have you measured for new clothes."

"Fen." I planted my feet, jerking him to a stop. "Can we skip the dress-up doll part? Can't I just wear this?"

"You could wear a burlap sack for all I care, but my father insisted."

I scrunched my nose and scowled. "He's lucky he's a bajillion years old."

"Give or take a few." He pulled me close, his piercing eyes melting me as he took a deep breath and leaned his forehead against mine.

My soul moved under his stare. As if it were a tangible thing, wrapping itself around him. He stroked his fingers down my arms, and I let myself settle into him, laying my head on his solid chest as his breath danced along the tip of my ear while I listened to the steady pattern of his heartbeat. He was strength and power. Fire and ice. But he was also just Fen. He was home.

He kissed me on the head and stepped away. "Come find me when you're done. Also, be nice to Friar. She means well."

I walked back to Fen's room to find the handmaid with a folded stack of gossamer clothing.

"I am not wearing that," I protested. "We're riding to see the draconians today."

"Plenty of southern females ride in skirts, my lady." Her words were kind, but her face was not.

"Not this one. You can take your measurements and torture me tomorrow."

"But you'll be meeting Umari. Surely, you'd like to wear something more traditional?"

"Tomorrow," I said firmly.

She huffed but didn't argue. I sat down in the chair and let her brush out my hair. Which was really just her jamming the bristles into my scalp and hoping it knocked me out.

*You forgot to tell Friar to be nice too.*

*Is she still alive?*

*Barely.*

She finished scalping me and took my measurements with only a few death threats exchanged, then stormed out of the room. I followed. We were either going to end up really good friends or killing each other on the lawn. There was no in-between.

"Hello, gorgeous," Fen said as I stepped beside him. "These are the lists, which is where we will be doing our training every day. I thought we could rotate training with Kai, Brax, and Greeve. Brax is the captain of our soldiers and answers only to Inok, Kai, my father, and myself." He gestured to the male in uniform beside him.

"I wanna fight him." I pointed to the giant trying hard to line up the weapons along the fence without knocking them all down with his clumsy fingers.

"Greywolf?" Brax asked. "He's a fun opponent. He's from the Wind Court." He motioned for the giant to join us, and we waited as he pounded across the arena. "Greywolf, this is Prince Fenlas and his mate, Ara."

I rolled my eyes. Of course, that's all I would be known as in this kingdom. Probably for the rest of my life.

"Hello, Prince sir," the giant said. "Ara, sir."

"No, Greywolf. We talked about this. She is a female fae. You call her 'my lady'."

"Ara's fine," I interrupted. Fen cleared his throat, but I ignored him.

"Ara wants to train with you someday."

"Nope. Can't fight my lady." He took three careful steps backward.

"Where are you from?" I asked, tilting my head as I tried to place the slight lilting accent.

"The Winterlands, my lady."

"Never heard of them."

He lifted his giant shoulders. "They are hidden."

I doubted that was true. I was well-versed in every territory in the Wind Court. I had to memorize most with my mother, but it was possible something slipped through the cracks.

"I tell you what, big guy. You let me train with you, and I'll see about finding you a proper pair of shoes."

Everyone looked to his feet but me as I met his stare.

"Okay." He grinned so wide I should have offered him a toothbrush.

His uniform was evidently made especially for him, but I doubted anyone in this kingdom could make his shoes. I happened to know a sly, old female in the Marsh Court, though.

"Should we go meet the others?" Fen asked.

"After you, Prince sir." I winked and swept my hand before me, bowing.

He gave me a roguish smile and turned to his soldier. "Keep working on those rotations, Brax. I'll be down in the morning."

"Aye, sir." Brax trudged away shouting orders to other fae, and Greywolf followed him with a high knee, exaggerated march.

"Only you would pick the giant to spar with." Fen lifted my fingers to his soft lips.

"I like a good challenge," I answered.

We approached the stables where Wren, Greeve, and another female that must have been Gaea waited. Her unique cat eyes were strikingly familiar to me. I had seen her with Autus numerous times. I tried to keep an open mind, remembering the rebel from the village we had helped, but Morwena's threat of the northern king weighed heavily on me.

"Ara, this is Gaea. She's come for refuge."

*Play nice.*

*Why do you keep telling me that? I don't walk around biting heads off, Prince.*

"Aren't you coming with us?" I asked Wren.

"No, I need to help my sister. She's been running everything on her own and I promised I'd help out today. I'll try to come for dinner." She leaned in to hug me. "Be nice," she whispered into my ear.

Fen snorted, and I elbowed him.

"Are we all riding, then?" Gaea asked.

"Do you ride much?" I asked in a really nice and not bitchy at all way.

"When I can. I use magic to travel most of the time." Her dark brown hair fell like curtains over her pale face as she answered. Talking openly about magic for any fae was likely uncomfortable, but having been collected by the Wind Court king and essentially escaping him probably made it worse. If she was to be believed. But we would hold her secret close. She didn't know that though.

"How does it work?" I prodded for more information. I was my mother's child, after all.

"I can only travel to places I've been. I call it spiriting. Do you want me to show you?"

"So you can turn me over to Autus? Hard pass."

Her gaze dropped to the ground.

*That's why.*

*What? Like you weren't thinking it?*

He didn't answer. He would have never let me go with her, and we both knew that. His protective nature runs deep. I looked to Greeve for backup, but his dark eyes were locked on Gaea. Interesting. I wasn't even sure he was breathing.

"I wouldn't," she said finally, as the huge black horses were brought from the stable. "I know it's hard to trust me, but I've finally escaped him. I've left my entire life behind to try to find something better. To breathe."

Fen stepped between us, taking the reins of the fae horses. "Thanks, Rah." He motioned to Greeve. "Let's get going."

We mounted.

I stayed next to Fen while Gaea and Greeve rode next to each other. He was deadly silent and still as we moved. Not to say that wasn't normal for him, but this was a whole new level of lethal. I couldn't decide if he wanted to kill her or undress her.

"Are you nervous to meet my grandmother?" Fen asked.

I plucked a piece of lint from my shirt—Fen's shirt. "Should I be?"

"Umari is a different character. Actually, no. She's just like you and should come with a warning. Why did I agree to this?"

I flashed him a sultry look. "Because I asked."

"Right."

I sped my horse up and Fen followed until we traveled in a line with Fen and Greeve on the outside. The fae horses kept at a steady pace as we moved.

"What did you expect?" I asked Gaea.

"I'm sorry?"

"I mean coming here. What did you expect to happen? That we would welcome you with open arms?" I caught Fen's rigid back at my blunt question, but he remained silent. Listening.

"Not at all. I expected your reservations more than I expected the kindness that Prince Fenlas showed me last night."

My head snapped to him. *How fucking kind were you?*

*As kind as we are to all the refugees, Princess. Calm your rage.*

"Tell me something about Autus. Something that he would hate for others to know."

"He's an insecure asshole who hates nearly everyone but himself?"

"Something more than the obvious."

She leaned down and patted the great neck of the beast below her as her mind worked. "He has no intention of marrying Morwena. He's been killing her forces in the north so they know he's still in charge. He's using his betrothal to secure her army so he can move south and take out Coro. Then he plans to keep Coro's soldiers and move south again."

"That's what I would do," I accidentally said out loud. "I met a fae conspiring with Autus to work against Morwena in the Marsh Court."

She shuffled the reins in her hands. "Even if he and Morwena join forces, which they don't need to be married to do, they still might not have enough to take out Coro."

"Agreed, if we can rely on the Sea Court's fighting numbers, but really I don't think anyone has a clue what she's hoarding down there," Greeve said, finally breaking his silence.

"Autus is calculated though. I think he plans for something worse," Gaea said.

"So, which is it? He's taking the kingdoms one by one or something worse?" I asked.

She shook her head. "I'm not sure. He's got it in his head that he is the rightful king of Alewyn. His ancient family ties are deeply rooted. I think the northern rebels are trying to figure out exactly what his plan is, but so far, they haven't. He had his magic welders sitting in on the council meetings, but he mostly spent that time going on and on about how much everyone around him hates him. Which was true, I guess."

"You sat in on his council meetings?" I kept the surprise minimal.

"Yes, but nothing war-related. It started after the Red Beach massacre. I can tell you his council is quite a bit smaller than it used to be. And a rebellion spy is sitting in on those meetings also. His name is Temir. I believe you all met him outside of Volos."

"We did," Fen answered. "The stag."

"You should check with the rebels to see if they have any news. He's reporting to them as often as he can."

Fen looked at Greeve and he nodded.

*We'll check in with our rebel contact tomorrow.*

*Do you trust her?*

*She hasn't given me a reason not to.*

*Famous last words.*

# CHAPTER 6

# Temir

*K*ing Autus always took his time. I laid on my side and kept my eyes shut, wishing Nadra didn't have to see me like this. It was so much easier in the dark dungeon. My voice had been strong, even though I'd been physically weak. I had healed all of the internal wounds and some of the flesh wounds, but the smell alone was putrid. She would never love me after seeing me like this. I wasn't sure I could love myself.

I didn't want to die anymore, but I didn't want the king to know that either. I searched for a balance, but it wouldn't take much to see that I wasn't covered in festering wounds down my chest and back. Especially here, in the light.

A deep breath shuddered through me and I listened to the thundering silence suffocating the room. It seemed strange to miss that water drop from the dungeon. I searched for peace that wouldn't come. The only one I had left in the entire world was about to watch my death, and there was nothing I could do to save her from it. She wouldn't save herself. The bond between us thrummed with our coalescing emotions and I held tight to that. When I died. I wouldn't go alone. She would never know what that meant to me.

The door swung open and two female high fae entered, their arms full of supplies, followed by four soldiers who stood rigid at the door. The females set their things down on the table. The brunette tentatively crossed the floor to me and unlocked the chain around my feet. She left my hands bound. Two soldiers came and lifted me. Finally, able to spread my feet, I stood on my own for the first time.

The blood rushed through my legs and I wobbled, using atrophied muscles. A guard held a hand on my shoulder until I could steady myself. I refused to look in anyone's eyes as the blonde removed the shredded clothing, just ripping it from my body. I closed my eyes as I stood bare in the room before six strangers and my mate. I felt the fear from her end, but I did not want her to feel the complete humiliation from my own, so I tried to picture only her face as they continued. I hadn't actually seen her in so long.

I considered the dark magic within me. This might have been our only window of escape, but I'd never be able to kill all six of them, especially bound. Still, I imagined myself doing it over and over again until ice-cold water poured over my head, forcing a gasp from me. Two of the guards chuckled, but again, I couldn't look at them. The blonde-haired female soaped and scrubbed my naked body, pressing so hard I thought the coarse bristles would shred my skin. I was lathered and rinsed multiple times, until every crevice had been cleaned. I let myself become completely numb, submissive even, to the complete degradation of my circumstance.

The king wanted this. To humiliate me in a way that would show me just how little I mattered compared to the rest of the world. The group gathered their things and left me silently standing clean and bare. My erratic emotions strangled me. I could hardly breathe. Hardly move as I thought about Nadra watching my debasement.

"You are strong and perfectly made," she whispered, standing directly before me.

I couldn't hold back the tear that rolled down my face as I stared forward and held my breath. Another followed and then another as I was forced to suck in small, short breaths to stop myself. He had won before he even entered the room, and as much as I already hated him, somehow, I'd found a way to hate him even more. I gulped. "Hide below the table, Nadra. The king will see through your mother's magic."

There was only a moment's pause before the door slammed open and the king walked in alone. He beamed, so proud of himself as he saw my tears and raw emotion. Terror slammed into me from the bond. The king's eyes dropped to examine my naked body, and somehow, I felt even more exposed than I already was. Still, he gave no indication he knew Nadra was there. Small victories.

"No one in the castle can do a single fucking thing right." He marched up to me, lifted my hands and yanked Oravan's ring from my finger. He examined it closely as the panic Nadra had sent became my own.

"So, this is where Oravan disappeared to. He wasn't murdered as Eadas had suspected, but he's hiding with the rebels. Some of whom don't have your iron will. You got that from Oleonis, I believe. That's why he is no longer with us, but you suspected that, didn't you?" He paused, grinning like a child, as he waited for the bated reaction he didn't get. "I had him killed. He was keeping secrets, and maybe I'll never know what they were, but you will not escape this life so easily. It's amazing how loud a lesser will sing when you remove a wing. Pity he didn't know many of their secrets. But you do, don't you?" He circled me, continuing his examinations.

I tried to keep my head high but felt it slowly sinking as I realized the king would not be killing me; instead, his confession of Oleonis' murder accompanied his promise. I would become his immortality forever.

"Tell me, Temir, where are the rebels?"

I pinched my lips and looked at the floor. He would eventually get his answers anyway, but I would not give them to him willingly.

He circled around and struck me hard across the face. Still, I did not answer. There was nothing worse he could do to me than what he had already done.

"Where are the fucking rebels?"

He stormed around the room and I flinched when he threw a chair. I had no idea how close he had gotten to Nadra. He was distracted though. He hated that he would have to use his magic on me. Autus wanted to believe that fear alone would work.

"I need the seamstress. Do not make me force it from your lips like I should have forced her. I try." He seethed. "I try to be generous. I try to be a good king, and this is how you choose to repay me." He ground his teeth together as his face slowly turned from red to purple with rage. "I saved you from that barn. I saved you from a life you deserved." His spittle caught the light before landing on my face. He took a deep breath and pulled his melody forward. "Tell me where the rebels are."

The will was suddenly pulled out from under me as I answered. I fought him, but in the end, there was no choice. There was a flurry of concern down the bond as Nadra brought me straight back to the room. The king's enchantment had put me into a distant state of confusion. I knew what I was saying but could not help but release the words. I could think about them but could not control them. My body was merely a puppet, his voice, the strings.

"Briar's Keep."

"Finally." He threw his hands into the air and sat before me, thrumming his fingers along the arm of the chair, and shook his head. "It didn't have to come to this, but now that we are here, you will kneel."

I felt my body jerk as I slammed into the ground with my bound hands in my naked lap. I hung my head. I would single-handily be the downfall of the entire rebellion.

"How do I enter the building?"

I explained in detail the rebellion compound. I felt my stomach coil as the words flowed from me. He made me tell him who to look for. He made me tell him the numbers of rebels, the reach of the rebellion. Every single thing I knew about it until I was eventually giving him Roe and Iva's names and the few others still in the castle.

I hated myself. I hated how weak I was. That I could not fight him. That I had chosen to come back for Nadra's mother when I should have left her. But then I remembered her crying on the floor of the castle and I knew, given the chance, I would have done it again.

"Where is Gaea?" His melodious voice grated on my ears.

"I don't know."

"Fuck." He rose and slammed his hand into the council's table. "What did she tell you of her plans?"

"Nothing."

For the first time, I stopped thinking about myself long enough to realize why Gaea hadn't told me where she was going or even when. She knew Oleonis had seen me cuffed. She knew I wouldn't leave the rebellion. She knew anything she told me would be a betrayal to herself eventually. She protected herself from me, far better than I had protected myself from her. It was the same reason she kept her room so bare. Her fear of attachment had saved her.

"Tell me who blew up the tunnels, Temir." His voice brought me back to the room.

"I did."

"How?"

"When the acidic compound of a flixeler leaf mixes with the compressed oil of—"

"I don't need the fucking molecular breakdown. I mean how did you manage it?"

"I had explosive chemicals placed at every entrance and had them all activated at once. I personally snuck around your guards to ignite one myself."

"Did you, now?" he asked, grinning. "And is this compound something you can duplicate?"

"Yes."

"You will begin as soon as we are done here. Just one final question, Temir. Where the fuck is my consort?"

CHAPTER

7

# Ara

"Jt's beautiful," Gaea said as we finally approached the draconian village.

"It's home," Greeve responded carefully.

Coming upon a desert oasis after miles and miles of the harsh, sweltering desert was like cheating the world. As if it had planned for the harsh climate to go on forever, but somehow the water found a way to defy everything. Trees surrounded the water to protect it from everyone. Scattered huts made from clay the color of the red sands of the Flame Court filled the terrain like patterned chaos. None equal distance from the next, none the exact same as another. The village was nestled below the largest dune I'd ever seen, as if it also protected the draconians.

"Are you ready to meet Umari?" Greeve asked.

"I guess."

"So you're not, then," he smirked.

*Let's just hope she's nicer to you than she is my father.*

I rolled my eyes. *How bad could she be? Honestly.*

We were greeted by several mounted sentries with long dark hair and beautiful tanned skin peeking out behind their intricate tattoos. The draconians were just another breed of beautiful fae.

Gaea and I exchanged a glance, and I knew our minds were in exactly the same place.

Fen cleared his throat.

*You're still prettier, Prince. Don't you worry.*

His grin was contagious. The riders dismounted their beasts and struck their chest with a fist, dipping their heads to Fenlas. He did the same, and they got back on their horses and guided us through the village to the largest thatched-roof hut with thrums of chatter within.

All the talking stopped as everyone paused to look at us when we entered. The walls were formed of red mud and simple chairs filled the room facing a raised platform. Instant cheers welcomed us as the dracs greeted Fen and Greeve, exchanging the same reception as the guards while we slowly worked our way to the front of the room.

"Welcome home, little prince." An older female stood at the front of the room with colorful fabrics wrapped around her and an intricately carved bo in her hands. Her eyes moved kindly from Greeve to Fen, and the moment they landed on me, the hint of a smile melted from her cold, hard face. I realized instantly who she was. Umari. Fen's grandmother.

"I see you couldn't take the time to dress," she said by way of greeting, not even looking at Gaea.

I looked down at my riding leathers and Fen's oversized shirt I had refused to change.

I said nothing as Fen stepped forward. "Grandmother, this is Ara, my mate."

Again with the mate thing.

"Is that all?" she said, still watching me closely.

Gaea shifted toward me, and for some reason, I appreciated the strength in numbers.

"Were you expecting anything else?" I snapped, matching her tone.

The draconians moved backward as Umari stepped down and crossed the room to me.

I stood still as she leaned in closer and closer, watching me for a reaction. I was not impressed.

"Your mouth will get you into trouble, mate of my grandson."

"Will it? I hadn't considered that before."

As quick as a snake she snapped her bo, intending to strike me in the stomach.

I was faster and caught it, holding it still, matching her strength.

"Grandmother," Fen barked, stepping between us as her eyes showed a glint of surprise at my reaction.

"She is a warrior?" she asked, still watching me.

"She is more than that."

"As are you, Fenlas," she answered.

Umari yanked her bo from my hands, spun on her heel, and went back to her seat. She waved, and the dracs sprang back into action as if that had never happened.

*That went well,* Fen told me.

*Yeah, she's a real peach, Fen.*

*To be fair, I warned you.*

"Welcome home," I told Greeve as his gaping mouth slammed shut.

"If you die in your sleep, it will be at her hands," he whispered.

"I've got worse things to worry about," I answered. "Can we go see the Cetani yet?"

"Wait here."

Gaea and I exchanged looks, and I decided I could at least try to be nice to her until we made it home. We waited together until Greeve and Fen made it back through the crowd and ushered us out the door.

"The draconians wish to show you a traditional dance followed by a parade of Cetani." Greeve placed his hand on the small of Gaea's back as we walked out of the building.

She stepped away from him and closer to me.

I tried to ignore the dejected expression on Greeve's usually indifferent face.

"We will sit on Umari's stage for the presentation in the arena," Fen said, pointing.

We waited a long time while the dracs lined the sides, eager to see the show as well. Eventually, a steady drum began to beat and the crowd of draconian fae chanted and hollered as painted male and female fae, naked as the day they were born, danced their way into the enormous arena before us. As one, we stood to watch. Some carried giant weapons, some small. The beating of the drum struck something inside of me as the warriors began their elegant dance, swinging their unique weapons and crying out as warriors.

I was completely hypnotized by the movement and the precision of each drac as they moved through the air and tumbled along the ground in perfect unison.

An ear-piercing scream sounded, and my head snapped to the back of the dancers as a female was thrown into the air swinging a massive double-ended sword like her entire life counted on that one moment. And it did. If she missed even a single second of perfect timing with that weapon, she would kill herself.

The draconians pounded their chest and chanted as her dance continued.

She was utterly stunning, with a lean, petite body and hair plaited back and tied with leathers, beads, and ribbons. She bent her body in half as two males swung their blades over her while she continued to dance with her own. The bedtime stories had not done the draconians justice.

"That is what my grandson deserves," Umari said from behind me as I stood stunned.

I glanced up at Fen, who, like me, hadn't taken his eyes from the female dancer.

*Enjoying yourself, Prince?*

He blinked and the world crashed back to him as he realized he was staring. He hadn't even heard what his grandmother had said, and as I looked back to her, she grinned in absolute satisfaction. So much for a deep and powerful mating bond. One naked female and he forgot I was standing next to him.

*I want that,* he said down the bond.

"I'm sorry, what?" I fumed.

"The sword, I want—Wait did you?" His vision snapped to the show and back to me. "Did you think I was looking at the female?"

"Don't pretend like you weren't." I scowled.

He grabbed me by my shoulders, leaned down until his face was so close to mine I could feel his breath, and said firmly, "There's a male drac in the back row with a silver-dipped sword, and the hilt has a jewel that is the same silver tone as your eyes when your magic flows. I want the sword, not the female, Ara."

"Oh." I paused, trying to hide my shame. "So you can just go around demanding others weapons now?" I was ridiculous. I knew I'd overreacted and played right into his grandmother's hands, who snickered in the corner as if she had won. Because she had. Damn it.

Fen pulled me into a hug, and I let him hide my face as the draconians in the arena finished. They had danced for him anyway. Not for me. I was just the stupid mate to Prince Fancy Pants.

*Here come the cetani.*

I didn't want to be excited, but I was. I faced the arena once more as the creatures that I had only ever dreamed about marched by. Their massive feline bodies were awe-inspiring, and their feathered wings and sharp eyes were every bit intimidating. The largest cetani led the others through the parade as they circled before us until there were so many moving in circles, I couldn't keep them straight, aside from the one in the center.

"That's Asha, my mother's cetani." Fen pointed to the large one. "And that's Cal behind her. He's grown since last I saw him."

Asha leaned her head back and roared, jolting me as the rumbling sound filled the air. As one, the cetani stopped. Frozen in place. The draconians filled the arena, mixing with the beasts, mounting them.

"You should go," I told Fen.

"I won't leave you here."

"I'm a big girl. You should go see Cal."

He needed no more persuasion as he hopped off the stage and weaved his way through to his cetani. Cal nuzzled him and then dipped low so Fen could mount him.

"Won't you join them?" Umari asked Greeve.

He glanced at me and back to her, then shook his head. I knew he didn't have a Cetani because of his magic, but he could still fly through the skies with them.

"You should," I protested.

"Next time." His eyes flickered with resignation.

"Prideful males," Umari grumbled and walked off the stage, leaving the three of us standing.

Asha moved first, stepping out of the crowd of beasts, lifting off, and one by one, the others followed until an entire aerial fleet filled the skies. Dracs from above and below screamed and whooped in celebration as we watched the riders fly, scoop and soar. I lost sight of Fen, but I could feel his stress melt away as he rode Cal.

Sometime later, the Cetani began their descent until, as one, they landed in a perfect line and let their riders off. I finally caught sight of Fen, and the smile didn't leave his face the entire walk back to us.

"Is there anything you wanted to do before we head back?" I asked Greeve. "You're the one who was homesick after all."

"You were homesick?" Gaea asked, probably before she realized she'd just shown her own interest.

"I'm ready to go back now. It's nice being home, but that's home too." A warm breeze circled him. His dark hair shifted around him as if he were underwater. The wind was his true home. His comfort and constant companion.

"Let me say goodbye to Umari and I'll be ready," Fen cut in.

"Send her all my love." I rolled my eyes, causing Gaea to turn away and chuckle.

As I watched Fen step away, I was overcome with desire for him. He'd come here just to cater to me, even though the other females eyed him carefully. I pushed the jealousy aside as his own yearning filled me, coalescing with mine. This was what it meant to have a mate. To be one.

Gaea cleared her throat, jerking me back to reality as Fen got lost in the crowd. "It's easiest for me to take you back one at a time. Do you care who goes first?"

Greeve stepped forward. "I'll go first. I am used to traveling on the wind."

"You are?"

"Yes," he said, holding his hand out.

In a moment they were gone. I stood waiting until Fen came back. "She said to tell you she'll miss you." He winked and I grumbled.

"I bet she did."

Gaea was suddenly back and standing right beside us.

"Who is next?"

"Ladies first." Fen leaned in and kissed my forehead.

"You take me to the northern king, and I'll gut you before you have time to vanish." She nodded, grabbed my hand, and then I was falling through nothing until I landed in a heap on the floor at the entrance of the castle. "I'm going to pretend that was an accident."

She laughed. "I'm sorry. It does take some getting used to." She helped me off the floor and I hated her for it. She looked up, locked eyes with Greeve standing next to Kai, and was gone again in an instant.

I faced him and put my hands on my hips. "You like her."

He shrugged and walked away. I gave Kai a look and he shook his head. "No. I already found the best blind date for him."

"Somehow I doubt that. Change it. Make him take Gaea out."

"But, Mother," he huffed.

I stalked forward and shoved him. "If it makes you feel any better, I think he will have his work cut out for him just getting her to agree to it."

"Fine, but if they hook up, I'm blaming you."

I mocked a gasp and placed my hand on my chest. "How terrible. I don't think I'd ever recover."

Fen and Gaea appeared. Kai flashed a half-smirk at me. The smartass in me loved the smartass in him. We might have been cut from the same cloth, but as he flicked his messy blond hair from those baby blue eyes, I knew there was so much more depth to Kai than he let on. His humor was his shield.

"You're sure you don't want to stay for dinner?" Fen asked Gaea as he stepped away.

"No, I'm headed out to the refugee place tonight."

"I'd prefer you to stay in the castle," he answered. "It will be safer here."

"I told you, I've had my fair share of castle life. I'd rather find my own place, if you don't mind. I want to be here and be helpful to you, but I also want it to be my choice."

"I'll make sure you always have a choice here," I said, moving to stand next to my prince. "No one understands more than me why that's so important."

"Thanks, Ara." A smile lit her eyes as she spirited away.

"So, you like her, then?" Fen wrapped his arm around my shoulders.

"I don't *not* like her. Does that count?"

"You guys coming to dinner?" Kai asked.

"I think we will take dinner in our room tonight." He tugged on my hand, pulling me down the long hallway. My laughter covered Kai's groan.

"Wren's coming to dinner," I protested.

"You can see her tomorrow. You can spend the whole day with her while I work. Tonight, you are mine."

"I'll make a deal with you." He stopped short, never able to resist a good deal. "You make it to dinner without touching me, and you can do whatever you want to me for the rest of the night."

His face flashed with intensity as he took a step toward me, locking his arms behind his back as he dipped his chin, fighting the smile. "Whatever I want?"

I sent him a mental picture of my naked body and his jaw dropped. *Whatever you want, Prince.*

He moved so close I could feel his breath like a whisper on my lips. Desire ignited our bond from both ends, clouding my mind. I moved to kiss him but he grinned and stepped away. "Deal, but we're going to dinner right now."

"It's a little early." I laughed. "And I rode a horse for half the day."

"Let me bathe you." He used his magic to brush a strand of hair from my face. "I'll keep my hands to myself until after dinner. You have a deal, but you will beg me long before then."

A spark of delighted anticipation ignited within me. "So confident, my prince."

Sending a wave of heat as we walked back to his room, he opened the door for me, and I strolled in, kicked off my riding boots, and sauntered to the bathing room. The soft breeze from the open balcony made my skin tingle as I passed, and Fen used that wind to lift my hair and send a shiver down my back.

He followed, shutting the door behind him and lighting the darkness with small floating flames scattered everywhere until a soft orange glow encased the room. His heated eyes held me as I faced him, untucked my shirt, and pulled it over my head. He stepped in, a growl leaving him.

I inched backwards.

*No touching, Prince.*

I moved my hands carefully down my body and unfastened the button at the top of my pants. Locking eyes with him, I gently pulled them down. All of the passion, emotion, and even a bit of his rage came to the surface. He looked at me as he had when I sat across that tavern from him, teasing him. His dark caress of magic moved down my sensitive body, massaging me as my heart pounded. I leaned over and turned the water on.

His magic left me as he stilled and made a truly guttural sound.

I stepped into the recessed bath and sat, waiting for the water to fill as the steam rose and danced with the magical flames. His winded fingers spread my legs apart, and I watched his jaw clench as he studied my naked body. His battle for self-control played across his beautiful face, and a very primal part of me nearly lost my own.

The brush of cool air across my thighs made me tremble. Two could play at this game. I released just enough magic to make his clothing completely disintegrate. I could control it in small increments. Progress. I intended to torture him, but quickly realized I had made a massive mistake. His muscled body glowed and he watched me squirm as my eyes dipped below his waistline to the enormous object of all my erotic fantasies.

The scorching water climbed in the bath, becoming a catalyst to my own budding arousal. Fen kept his fiery gaze on me as he reached down and grabbed whatever oil he wanted and dumped it into the bath. He moved for a cloth and lathered it slowly as those emerald eyes held my soul, then he jerked his arm forward, holding the cloth out to me.

*Wash,* he demanded.

I grabbed the cloth from his steady hands and dragged it first down my arms. Standing, I let the water fall from my body as I eased the cloth over one breast and then the other. Biting my bottom lip, I moaned as his heated magic traveled with my own hands across my nipples and down to my stomach. His magic was like fire on my sensitive skin as I went. I lifted one leg onto the edge of the bath and deliberately dragged the soapy cloth up until my thighs shuddered under his heat. I switched to the other leg and did the same as he continued to watch me until I sat carefully back down into the water and rinsed my cleansed, aching body.

I moved my hands up my thighs until I brushed over the tiny bud that ached for me to release the pressure the prince had built. I remembered the last time I had laid in a bath and stroked myself thinking of him. I tilted my head and moved my fingers back and forth as he growled. My breath began to hitch as the need for him grew and grew.

*Join me, Prince.*

I lifted my head to see he had taken his own length into his hands as he watched me. His warmth rushed through me as he began to stroke me with his magical fingers. It was not enough. I needed him, all of him, deep within me. Still, I couldn't push his power away as he sent wave after blissful wave of desire through the bond, still holding himself in place.

"Please," I begged.

*A deal is a deal, Princess.*

His last word cut short as I realized he could barely contain himself. I stood from the bath, stepped out, and strolled toward him. "You cannot touch me, but I can touch you, prince." I trailed a finger down his solid chest.

He stopped moving, stopped breathing, as I took his erection into my hand. I leaned up to kiss his neck, leaving a trail of kisses down his tanned body as I stroked him.

*Maybe you should be the one to beg.* I dropped to my knees and looked up to him.

His body shook as I licked him from shaft to tip. "Fuck." His smoky voice sent a thrum of satisfaction through me as I took him into my mouth and hummed as I moved. He reached out to grab me.

*Hands to yourself.*

"Ara," he warned, hands frozen in the air.

I didn't care. It could have just been a bath. He was the one who took it this far. I listened to his ragged breathing as I moved.

He shifted his magical fingers between my legs, and again the pressure began to build until I pulled away from him.

"Release me," he begged.

"Release you how?" I asked, echoing words he had once asked me.

"The deal. Release me."

I stood and dragged the tip of my finger slowly up his chiseled torso again, going to his neck and finally his lips until he closed them around my finger. "I release you from our bargain."

He lunged forward, grabbed my naked ass, lifted me up, and carried me to the bed.

I laughed as he tossed me down. I laid before him, spread wide open, wet, and waiting.

Again, he watched me. Studied me. The prowl in his steps as he moved every bit as seductive as his pointed stare.

"Will you still let me do what I want?" There was a hint of danger in that request, but then there always was with him. My breath hitched and I nodded slowly as again his gaze raked down my body. He crossed the room, disappeared into his closet, and came back with leather straps. He snapped them in his hands, and the reverberation of the crack jolted my lower abdomen. "We won't be making it to dinner." A devilish grin crossed his face.

"What did you have in mind?"

"I'm going to teach you a lesson," he answered. "I want you to see what it feels like to be forced not to touch. Raise your hands."

A jolt of excitement moved through me, and I couldn't tell if it was his or mine as I shifted forward on the bed.

He tied my hands to the posts, and then my feet. "Too tight?"

"Do your worst, Prince."

I felt more than heard the intense growl from him as he crawled onto the bed above me. He dragged an extra set of the leather straps up one leg, across my belly, and back down the other side. I gasped, and his greedy eyes gleamed. He dragged the leather over my breast and the ties were the only thing keeping me in place as I squirmed.

He tossed them to the floor with an evil chuckle and started with soft kisses against my cheeks, my tender lips, and down my neck, as his massive hands held my waist. He moved painfully slow down to my breast, using his tongue and his teeth as salacious weapons against me.

My body pulled against the ties. His heated fingers branded me his forever as he moved them up and down my taut body. He was hard. So beautifully hard. His tip pressed against my core, and I called out in sheer, brazen pleasure. The sexual tension had been growing between us for so long, I didn't think there was a thing he could do to satiate me.

He moved lower, massaging my thighs with his thumbs, as his mouth closed over my core, causing my body to buck in response. He was ravenous as he tasted me. The inability to move was torture. Euphoric, spellbinding torture. I panted and made small noises as he tortured me with his tongue until I was screaming and shuddering and begging him to stop so I could catch my breath.

He pulled away and slipped a finger inside while I writhed in glorious, growing satisfaction. I cried out as he moved two fingers in and out in perfect rhythm until I couldn't take it anymore.

"Fen . . . please."

*Say the words, pet.*

"I need you. All of you. Now."

He rose above me, staring down through thick, dark lashes, and rubbed himself against my opening until I tried to thrust my hips forward, begging him to fill me.

*You deserve soft and slow, but I'm afraid this is going to be nothing like that.*

My thoughts were not coherent enough to respond as he slipped the tip in and roared. He thrusted forward and I bucked, wracked with pleasure and pain as he buried himself to the hilt. I balked at his size, stretching to take all of him. My mate was a fevered animal as he leaned over and bit just above my collarbone, marking me. Claiming me. And then it was only passionate bliss.

I pulled at the ties, wanting to bury my hands in his hair, wanting to wrap my legs around his waist, but again, I was unable to get free. I was his in all ways as he used my body however he desired.

He slammed into me repeatedly, his eyes never leaving mine until his breathing was ragged, his body glistening and mine strained. He reached down to massage me, and my legs trembled. We climbed until, as one, we plummeted into oblivion, both throbbing and breathless.

He leaned his forehead down to mine and smiled. "I didn't know you made such sweet sounds."

"Neither did I."

He carefully untied my hands and feet and then laid down beside me, pulling me into his arms. He kissed my neck and then my shoulders, and again, I felt him growing hard against me. I scooted back, pressing into him, and he growled possessively into my ear. We stayed up, lost in each other for hours and hours that night. Fervent kisses turned into tender moments as Fen and I discovered a whole new world together.

CHAPTER

8

# Temir

*H*e wanted me to tell him where Nadra was. My body lurched to follow orders, but I bit back the words. I held them so tightly, I couldn't breathe, but even as his magic fought me, I felt it weaken. I closed my eyes, clamped my lips as I pictured her wild red hair and the dusting of freckles across her perfect nose.

"Answer me, Temir." Sweat built across his brow.

I tried to convince my mind that his consort was not my mate. That he had asked me where someone else was because she could never be his. He held up Oravan's barrier ring he had pulled from my finger. "You can fight it, but I've taken your only weapon against me. Where is Nadra?"

I refused to open my mouth, accepting death over telling him that she hid within the room. I visibly shook as I locked the information so far down within me, he could never pry it out. I studied the pattern in the etched stone walls, the variations of gray so very drab. I ran my eyes over the grooves in the table that held a thousand secrets. I longed for the sun. For a bit of warmth within the coldest place in Alewyn.

"Answer!" he screamed, throwing the ring so hard I believed it might have embedded into the stone wall as spit flew from his mouth.

I flinched but did not answer.

"Could it be? Did you find yourself a mate, Temir? It would explain your strong will against me." He laughed, the dangerous sound growing and echoing through the cold room. He stepped so close I could feel his breath on my face. "You have no idea what you've just given me. My spies tell me I'll need to break a mating bond in the near future. Now I have the perfect candidate."

I felt Nadra's hatred and then panic as the king crossed the room to stand next to the door. Nadra must have been on the back side of the massive table behind an alcove, and I was grateful.

"You may only move your hands, Temir." His magic struck me with a renewed force as he opened the door, gestured, and walked back in with the two females from before.

"Undress," he commanded. They did as they were told. I tried to look away, but I was unable to move. "Seduce him," the king grinned.

They crossed the room and reached for me. Nadra's fury burrowed into me as they moved their hands all over my naked body.

"Look at them, Temir," he ordered.

My eyes were forced to watch as they moved their hands over me and then each other. I kept my face dull as they touched their breasts and kissed each other. I felt sorry for them. The king hadn't enchanted them, only ordered. But their disgust was written across their faces all the same. Autus had no idea though. He was blind to anything but adoration.

"Tell me where Nadra is," he said, again using his magic.

It was less difficult than the first time to ignore him. My basic instincts told me to protect her, and I would until my dying breath. I watched the females move their bodies against me as I waited for the king to realize his plan would not work.

Instead, he crossed the floor, reached for one of them, and touched her, still forcing me to watch his perversion. He'd fuck her right there on the table and not think twice about it.

I swallowed the rising bile in my throat as the other female reached between my legs.

A growl came from the corner, and I masked it with my own as she tried and failed to induce a physical reaction from me. I would grow hard for one female only.

"Sever your mating bond," Autus said, though he was distracted by the female practically climbing him, much happier to be touching a king.

I didn't move, still saying nothing.

"Damn you, fucking lesser," the king roared, realizing he could not command away a mating bond. He grabbed both naked females and moved to the door. "Don't move until I return. I'm not done with you yet." He stormed out, causing a raucous on the other side of the door.

Several moments passed until Nadra spoke, her voice unwavering. "I'm going to slide this ring over your finger. There's a chance I might touch you. Are you ready?"

"Wait. Listen through the door. Make sure the hall is empty first."

"There's at least one, maybe two," she whispered several moments later.

"This is probably the only chance we are ever going to have to escape. There's a route really close to this room, but I'm going to have to use a type of magic I'm not proud of."

"Do whatever you have to do, Temir. You are safe with me."

I felt the cold bite of the ring against my skin and my rigid body dropped, no longer enchanted to stand still. I wasn't sure it would work, given a physical order rather than a mental one. I didn't take the time to consider the science behind it, instead I did a sweep of the room. Nadra remained hidden behind her mother's magic as I placed an ear to the door. "If there are two guards, stay inside until I come for you."

I yanked the door open, and a single guard stood stunned, staring at my naked body. I slammed my death magic into him, grabbed him by the collar, and dragged his fallen body into the room. Relieving him of his clothes, I rushed into his guard uniform, haphazardly buttoning but refusing to stop to explain to Nadra what she had just witnessed.

She was the only person in my life to have ever seen it happen.

The clothing was snug, but nothing would draw attention to me quicker than running bare through the halls. "If we can get out of this hall without being seen, we have a real chance. We have to get out of here and get to the compound as fast as we can if we want a chance of saving anyone."

"I'm ready when you are."

I longed to see her face. To take this single moment and hold her. But she was safest unseen. I took a few solid, deep breaths to steady myself before I opened the door.

The hall was fortunately empty.

"Keep your pace slow," I warned her, turning the corner sharply, then walking a straight line toward the tree nursery that would lead us to the only open tunnel. Rounding another corner, I stopped and casually redirected to go the other way as I realized several guards stood outside the doors we would need to use. Once I was alone, I whispered, "We're going to have to go out the front doors."

Nadra sucked in a sharp breath. "It's too dangerous. Why not the kitchens?"

It was a brilliant idea. The staff in the kitchens who recognized me would likely say nothing to alert the others, and, dressed as a guard, it wouldn't be uncommon that I would leave the castle that way. We would still have to get through the gates though.

I watched the faces of the court as I passed them, but none were observant or cared enough to even register my presence. I hoped Nadra was able to navigate the crowds of people okay, but so far, she hadn't complained. We made it to the kitchens safely, and I caught a glimpse of Iva.

She looked up, startled to see me, and dropped a small pile of dishes.

"Silly me," she said, keeping her head down.

I bent to pick up a bowl and she whispered, "What are you doing here?"

"There's no time. Get Roe and get out. The king has your names. He's going to storm the compound. Go somewhere else. Go to the Weaver or the southern kingdom, Iva. Just go. Now."

She didn't hesitate. She dropped the dishes on the closest counter and rushed out of the room.

I prayed to the gods she made it safely.

Getting out of the kitchen doors was easier than taking the tunnels, since I was in uniform. Most of the servants kept their heads down and a wide berth.

We crossed the bailey and my eyes flickered to the pile of ash that was once the stables. The rebels had made quite a distraction in our attempt to save Nadra's mother. I still wished I had a horse, but I was glad they didn't have any either. It would be a foot race to the compound, and we had the head start. If we made it through the gates.

I looked up at the guards working the gate tower, hoping I'd get lucky and see another rebel working, but I recognized no one. I kept my head down and shuffled at a steady pace. Not many people were coming and going, but I slipped into a small group of guards just as I passed through the gate and no one said a word.

I wasn't sure how far behind Nadra was, but I guessed she had to be a lot more careful through the people. If someone touched her, her bright red hair would give her away in an instant. I cut off to the side just down the road and waited until a hand slipped into mine and the most beautiful female in the world appeared before me.

I wrapped her in my arms and swung her around as she laughed until she cried. "I'm not worthy of you, Nadra. But I promise I'll spend my entire life trying to be."

She continued to cry in my arms, and I held her for several moments.

I pulled away, brushing her gentle tears with my thumbs. "I'm so sorry, love, but we have to go right now, or we are never going to make it in time."

She wiped her fresh tears, stepping away. "But we need horses."

"I'm sure the ones I left tied up are long gone."

Her eyebrows knotted for a moment as she tried to find a solution. "Do you think the one I left is?"

"I'm not sure how many days have passed, but I would assume it's gone too."

"It would be worth checking though. If it's still there, we could get back in plenty of time."

"Yes, but if not, we might have lost our lead on foot."

"It's not far from here. I remember walking up this main road to the castle."

An anchor settled in my gut with the choice we had to make. "Lead the way. Quickly."

I followed her as she moved in the direction we were originally headed, but then she turned at a trickling creek and started going the wrong way. I couldn't agree that this was the best choice, but she was right. If we had a horse, we would get there so much faster. She trudged on until she lifted her skirts to run. I followed as soon as I'd seen why. Not only did she have a horse tied up so he could drink from the stream, but it was a fae horse, a behemoth black beast with booming clomps as he begged to be released.

"You're brilliant." I pulled Nadra into my arms and buried my face into her curls. "Thank you."

"I removed his bit so he could eat and drink while I was away."

"You have no idea how many lives you may have just saved. Let's go." I grabbed her small waist and lifted her up onto the horse.

She shifted forward and I swung up behind her. I held her tightly, kicking the horse's flank and springing him into a thunderous run back the way we had come until we were on a direct path, running for the rebel compound through the eternally frozen forest of dead trees with twisted dark limbs tangling through the thick evergreens. With fresh snow upon the ground, they could track us easily. But the damage had already been done and now the king would know exactly where to send his army, traceable footsteps or not.

I tried to ignore Nadra's body moving against me as we rode, but I was only a male and I had been locked in with a mate that I couldn't even see for a long time.

"I want to look at you," I said into her pointed ear.

She laughed and leaned further back against my chest until I could look down at her beautiful face. "Better?"

"Much."

"Now that we are out of the castle, I should tell you what I know of the king and his plans."

"Not yet, Nadra. I want to be in a safe place when we talk. If it changes the trajectory of this world, I don't want to be overheard by a single sprite."

She looked around the frozen trees and nodded. It was sadly the truth. Though sprites were still lesser fae, they would trade that knowledge for coin, and I wanted to be extra careful. They hadn't ratted out the rebels yet, but I had a feeling Rook was paying the little beasts a hearty sum.

"What will we do, Temir? After we warn the rebels. Will we go somewhere else? Will we stay and fight?"

"What do you want to do?"

"I want to find my friend. The one I was telling you about. Then I don't care what we do. As long as we are together."

"I think it's time for us to go south. Join the rebels in the Marsh Court and see what use they would have for us. Maybe she would agree to come. I need my serum to work its way through the rebellion now more than ever. We have to sort out the good from the bad."

She took a long, measured breath and closed her eyes. "I wish it could be easier for us."

"I would take difficult with you over life without you. I'm afraid, it will always be hard for us. What will you say to your mother about me?"

She shifted and looked up to me. "What do you mean?"

"You may have forgotten, but she won't. I'm still a lesser fae and you are still a high fae."

"Believe me, she won't care. I told you she and Rook have history. She only wants me to marry and be happy."

"I'd marry you right now, Nadra. Right in the middle of this damn forest. After what we've just gone through together, even if you weren't my mate, I'd still marry you."

I kicked my heels into the beast, and we jolted onward as her body nestled into my own. Drawing on my warmth as we stormed through the night.

# Ara

*I* peeled my aching body out of bed before sunrise. I had done nothing the past several days but train and sneak away with Fen as often as we could. He had become nearly inundated with work and I found the lists helped pass the time.

I promised Wren we could shop, though Friar had filled my closet with more clothes than I could ever wear. I dressed, choosing something Fen would like, and stepped out onto the balcony, watching the ocean waves. The slight wind warmed my face as I leaned against the barrier and breathed in the comfortable peace that had become my life.

I'd nearly forgotten about my dreaded fate until I saw the king crossing the sand below me, headed toward the water. He must have felt me watching him because he turned and smiled. Though I could barely make him out in the early morning light, he gestured for me to join him, and I nodded while holding up a finger. I quietly padded out of the room, leaving Fen to rest. I dashed through the castle until I stepped outside and my bare feet dug into the sand. Still, I hustled along. I didn't want the king to have to wait for me.

"Hello, dear," he said as I walked up.

"Are you okay?"

"Oh, yes. I'm fine. I thought you might like to join me."

He began walking again and I followed. "Where are we going?"

"Efi's Isle."

Fen told me his father spent a large amount of time on the island that held his mother's funeral pyre. I only had Fen for such a small amount of time and already I couldn't imagine not having that brooding fae in my life. I couldn't even begin to imagine how the king felt every day living with only half of his soul. Living without the only female he would ever truly love.

We stepped into a shallow wooden boat, and though I tried to row, he insisted. I waited and watched as we glided across the still waters of the bay until the small isle grew close and the boat scraped against the sandy bottom of the shore. I jumped out alongside the king, dragging the boat onto the beach. I walked behind him up the grassy hilltop until he sat and gestured for me to do the same. We watched in comfortable silence as the sky began to glow and transform with the immaculate, fiery sunrise over the ocean.

"Fenlas has never been here." He smiled unhappily.

"Really? Why not?" I looked over my shoulder at the lavish castle in the distance with golden domes and aged white walls, turned red with years of exposure to the deep red sands. I could see his balcony far away from the others.

"I thought maybe you could tell me." He paused and reached for my hand. "I know you've also lost your parents."

The comment struck me out of nowhere and I couldn't hide the sadness on my face. "I can't speak for Fenlas, King Tolero. If I could, I would visit my parents every day." I looked away as the lump in my throat threatened to choke me, the mourning hitting me as fresh as the horrid day I'd lost them. Something about sitting with an ancient king left me feeling devastatingly vulnerable.

"Your father was a good male. Both of them were, Ara," he said softly.

"I guess I never really knew either of them." My voice cracked as a tear slipped out and the weight on my chest hindered my breathing. Grieving sucked. Flashes of my parent's faces, things I'd tucked away, too painful to remember, began to surface and I tried to swallow the lump and hide my aching heart.

"I'm sure that's not true. Perhaps you never knew Arturas, but Thassen raised you."

"Arturas? Was that my real father's name?"

"Yes." He smiled as a memory came to him. "And your real mother's name was Coraj."

I studied the horizon, letting their names sink in as I wondered if it would ever feel normal to know I had four parents. "Were they similar? All of my parents?" I asked, wiping another tear.

He chuckled. "There was no one like Thassen. Not in this world or any other, I'd wager. He was the greatest warrior I'd ever met, but the moment Greeve placed you into his arms, he melted into a thousand pieces. I remember one time when Thassen came to visit, Inok challenged him to a friendly duel. Your father beat him, of course, so the next day he challenged him to a foot race in the mud.

Your father won again. On and on they went, swimming, throwing knives, hunting—anything Inok could think of, your father was always better. One night," he said as his eyes lit up, "I caught them taking turns pushing boulders through the sand."

"Did Inok ever win?"

"No," he laughed. "And to this day I think it bothers him."

"Why didn't he just tell me, King Tolero? Why couldn't they find a way? Why did we stay in the Marsh Court? Why not here?"

"Your father was a member of the Hunt before I even met him. He came here once, and we became instant friends. But as soon as we learned of your fate, and Arturas and Coraj made plans to take their own lives to protect you, I called upon him. We agreed the Marsh Court would be the safest place for you. He forced me to enchant him. He knew you'd be strong of will and they would struggle to keep the secret at bay. He believed he was protecting you. Who was I to deny the request of a father?"

"I still wish I had known." I picked at the grass. "If they could have told me somehow, maybe we could have saved them."

"Your father died protecting you, Ara. Let him have that sacrifice with no regrets."

The king was so sincere. For a moment, I questioned everything I knew of the world. I'd made my own assumptions of him, hated him from afar, but there was not a single thing to hate about this old fae. "Do you think they know? That I made it here to Fen?"

"I have to believe all the ones that have gone before us are still here, watching over us." He moved his fingers over the grass, as if drawing power from our world into his palm. His old eyes found mine and held them. "This is the land of the fae, after all. Anything is possible."

Those words settled deep into my soul. As if he'd known something he wasn't telling me. As if he challenged me to defy my fate, though he hadn't spoken a word of it.

He cleared his throat and looked back to the bay. "Some days, thinking she is still with me is the only way I make it through."

He became distant again, and I let him have his moment of mourning while I sorted through my own. We watched the waves dance in the distance and listened to the hungry bird's caw as they soared above the cerulean ocean. There was peace here. Perhaps that's why he came.

"Ready to go back?" he asked eventually.

"I can give you a moment alone, if you'd like."

He nodded and I stood, dusted the fresh dirt from my pants, and walked back to the hill, letting my eyes settle on the pile of dried flowers he'd apparently brought for her. The words of my prophecy rattled around in my head. Never, ever would I kill that fae. Not even at the cost of my own life.

After only moments he joined me and we went back to the castle together. As we approached, several guards and Inok ran to us. "I need a moment, my king," he said frantically.

"You may say what you need to in front of Ara. She will be queen one day."

"It's about the other queen. The one we had in the dungeons."

"What do you mean *had*," he barked, stepping closer.

"She's gone. The selkies too."

He was instantly moving and I followed.

"I'll go wake Fen." I ran past them and up the stairs, slamming the door open as he jolted upright in the bed. "Your father needs you. The queen is missing."

He was out of bed, dressed, and to the door in an instant. I moved to follow him, and he turned, tossed me a knife, and kept going. I was more lethal than most of the males in this castle. Leave it to my mate to arm me and set me free.

We ran through the castle, down the stairs and to the main study where the others had gathered. Fen started giving orders, settling into his role as a leader, while I waited. Listened. After several minutes, we spread out, searching the castle for any sign of them. Several times I passed Kai and Lichen as they hunted together. Greeve cleaved through the castle on his own. After hours and hours, we ended the search, finding absolutely nothing.

"I don't understand," Fen said, as we all sat eating in the dining hall later that day. "We have a guard schedule. The guards below are not changed at the same time as the guards above. There should have always been at least four on duty."

Greeve and I exchanged a glance. There had been no guards below when he and I had gone down to the dungeons. It was possible they were still above and the guards below were switching shifts, but I couldn't believe we had just gotten that lucky.

"There's nothing we can do about it now. We will just need to keep our eyes open and be sure that everyone reports anything fishy," Tolero said.

"Pun intended," Kai followed, but his smile didn't reach his eyes.

King Tolero clapped him on the back while Fen stepped forward, taking his commanding tone once more. "I want all guard duties doubled up. Each point, twice as many sentries. They will take shorter shifts to balance the time, and Kai, I'll need you to help Brax in training. Ara and I will be visiting Sabra and Wren today. It's time to start training the refugees."

"They didn't come here to fight, Fen," Lichen said, his voice neutral, though the consternation on his face said far more.

"No, but they came here to live, and with that comes an obligation to help protect the court. I won't force anyone, but I think we all know Morwena's move against us will not be her last. King Autus isn't far behind her either. They are making war plans. I can promise you that. Ask Gaea."

"You ask us to trust a northerner?" Lichen bit out.

"He doesn't have to ask your permission for shit," I answered.

*Easy,* Fen said down the bond.

The disappointed look on the king's face caused mine to flush.

"Gaea can be trusted," I said more calmly. "She trains with me and Wren every day. I haven't seen a single red flag, and believe me, I've been watching. Don't you think so too?" I asked Greeve, searching his face for a hint of solidarity.

He nodded once and the discussion was dropped.

"It's time," Tolero said. "With or without the trust of the *former* northerners." He dipped his chin to me and I smiled. "We have to start preparing this kingdom for the inevitable. That includes the *former* northerners. Just as we do not use the terms lesser and high fae in this kingdom, we will stop referring to the newcomers as northerners. They are all southerners now. Accept it."

He looked firmly at Lichen, who shrunk an infinitesimal amount in his chair.

*Looks like you made a friend.* Fen grabbed my leg under the table, and I sent him a mental image, sticking my tongue out at him. *You're training with me today, just for that.*

*Don't threaten me with a good time, Prince.*

112

Later, we stood facing each other in the lists. Each time I had come, the crowd swelled. Fen had teased me that beating up the males had become a southern spectator's sport.

I didn't care. I hoped it made all the females feel stronger.

"Begin," Brax called from the side.

Fen conjured his infamous fire magic, and, as always, I sent magic forward, smothering it. The crowd loved a good show. We had agreed ahead of time to make it fun, lighter, in lieu of the bad news. But something was happening. I could feel it each time I used the magic. Like a pinprick of pain. I kept it to myself. Since Nealla, I'd only ever used the magic in small amounts. A hint of pain was nothing to fear.

Fen shook his head and swirled his fingers as a dust storm brewed between us. I dodged to the side, leaped forward, and smacked him on his bottom with the flat part of my wooden sword. The onlookers cheered as he spun around, and I punched him right in the gut. He didn't even flinch. It always hurt me more than him to slam my fist into that solid wall.

The ground below me rumbled, and I looked to the giant first, thinking he was doing it, but he stood still, watching. I jerked my head to Fen, who laughed as I nearly lost my footing. He used that opportunity to swing his sword. I barely blocked it, giving him the time and space he needed to lean in and kiss me quickly. The crowd cheered again as he beamed. I used my magic cautiously against him. The last thing I wanted to do was actually hurt him. He insisted that I wouldn't, but I was not convinced.

We fought, teasing each other back and forth for quite some time, until Kai and Greeve ran in and pinned him to the ground while I pretended to jab him repeatedly with my sword. We stood, bowed to the crowd, and walked out. We could have gone on for hours, but Fen and I had to meet Wren soon.

"Ready for your hot date tonight?" Kai asked Greeve as we waited for the lists to empty so we could leave undercover.

"You convinced her?" I asked.

"Convinced who?" Greeve said warily.

"I basically had to pay her, but she said she would go for a drink."

"Who?" Greeve asked again.

"Just some fae I found wandering the city," Kai said, showing every single one of his teeth.

Greeve actually groaned out loud. "I'm not feeling so hot." He wrapped his hands around his abdomen.

Kai shoved him. "Oh no you don't. You're going. A deal's a deal, Greeve."

"Fine, one drink. But I'm not bathing or anything." He shoved Kai back.

"Good. You'll match her stench."

I punched Kai square in the gut.

"Fine. Fine," he rasped. "It's Gaea."

Greeve's eyes doubled in size as he jerked his spine straight and shook his head, no.

"You don't get a choice. You have to go."

His face turned red and he punched the wall before storming out.

"For some reason, I thought that would have gone smoother," I said from a few paces away.

"Similar to someone else in this circle, he doesn't like being forced to do something."

"It will be good for him," Fen said. "Ready?"

I wrapped my cloak across my shoulders and pulled the hood up. "Why are we hiding again?"

"We have no idea if Morwena is still in the city. I'd rather notice her before she notices us."

Fen's concerns were valid, but we made it through the city and to the compound without a single hint of the sea queen.

"Shall we go in?" Wren asked, leaning her shoulder against her sister's as they welcomed us.

"Lead the way." Fen dipped his chin and Sabra smiled warmly at him.

I wasn't even a teeny bit irritated. Fen cleared his throat and I realized they'd all moved toward the entrance while I stood watching Sabra like she'd grown a second head.

Ragey fae shit, I guess.

We entered the compound, finding so many fae. Many more than I ever realized had fled to the Flame Court. There were fae of all species here, cohabitating in peace. I marveled at the high fae female working side by side with the pixies, just as they did in the castle. It hadn't been normal for them before, but they had all adjusted and found a new way of life. I'd never been so inspired. I watched a centaur give a high fae child a ride, both giggling, and my heart nearly exploded.

"This is the way it's supposed to be. This is the way the world should look," I said to no one in particular.

"This is the way of the southern kingdom, Ara," Fen answered.

"I've barely left the castle though. I've only seen the fae that come to watch us train. This is . . . This means something."

"Isn't it beautiful?" Wren asked, bumping me with her shoulder.

Her heart was so damn good. Wren, the mother hen, loved so fully, the rest of us would truly never compare. She reached out and took my hand. I squeezed and she knew exactly what I was trying to say but couldn't find the words to. I was so beyond proud of my friend.

"You've given them all hope," Fen said. "Let's see if they are willing to fight for it."

"Shall I call a gathering?" Sabra asked.

"Please do," he answered.

The refugees poured out of the metal buildings scattered through the compound as we moved to a small, raised platform. Fen stepped forward and, like a wave through the ocean, every single one of them took a knee and bowed their heads.

I'd never seen this level of reverence before.

"Please, stand and hear me," Fen called over the mass of people. "Our borders are open to those that need safety, food, and shelter. We continue to provide as much as we can in the Flame Court. I stand in awe of you. That you've put your own prejudices aside and have learned what we have known for thousands of years. Peace among us is the only way forward."

He paused, waiting for the cheering to stop.

"I come to you today, humbly asking for anyone willing to please join us at the castle tomorrow. We are looking for soldiers, fighters, wielders. Anyone who has a score to settle with the north, join us. This life you're creating is worth protecting, but we cannot do it alone. We need help, and I'm here today to ask you to come forward. We are on the precipice of war."

The crowd went still as Fenlas' grave words settled over them.

"We have information that has led us to this point. We know the other kingdoms are making calculated moves, and we cannot be

116

caught unprepared. I hope to see as many of you as possible in the morning. Please speak with Wren or Sabra if you have questions or need anything at all. We are still here for you, and it is our hope that you will also be here for us. Enjoy your evening."

Fen turned to me, hugged me tightly in front of the crowd, and pulled me off the stage. He had done everything but beg.

*I've never been prouder of you than I am right now.*

*Do you think they will come?* he asked.

*They'd be fools not to.*

We said goodbye to the identical sisters, but just before we were about to leave, a makara child ran up to us. Her face was furry and her wide eyes were adorable. She barely came up to my waist but still tugged on my skirt.

I knelt to her as she kept one hand behind her back.

"Are you a princess?" she asked.

"She is," Fen answered for me.

"A princess should always have a crown." She brought her hidden hand forward, and I leaned even farther as she placed a delicate flower crown upon my head.

"Did you make this?" I asked, touching the petals.

"My mother helped a little."

"It's absolutely perfect. Thank you so much."

"You're welcome." She dug her toe in the dirt before looking up to Fenlas. "I don't have anything for you."

I laughed, and he knelt beside me. "I've got something for you instead." He leaned and grabbed a handful of sand, placed it in his open palm, and moved his fingers until a tiny cyclone formed. "Reach inside," he said to the wide-eyed child.

She lifted her hand and eyed us both before she reached in and pulled out a coin Fen had hidden in his palm. "This is for me?" she whispered.

"Just for you. Please tell your mother we thank you both for the crown."

She bolted away and we stood watching until she disappeared.

*I'm going to let you do very dirty things to me tonight, Prince. Just for that.*

*Where's Gaea's magic when you need it?* he asked, wiggling his eyebrows at me.

We crossed the city, cloaked again, and made it back to the castle just in time to see a freshly bathed, shaven, and cologne-covered Greeve stomping out. "Looks like he had a change of heart," I said.

"I don't think he did at all," Fen answered, dragging me up to our room.

I was restless that night. Each time I fell asleep, I dreamt of the sea queen and her evil laugh. Of her murdering my parents. Of a bloody battlefield where I watched each of my friends die. Eventually, I gave up and slipped out of the room. After aimlessly wandering for the better part of an hour, I found myself standing on the beach, watching the reflection of the moon in the still water and listening to wave after wave crash in the distance.

I saw something foreign in the bay and continued to watch it until I realized a sea fae was coming ashore. I hadn't grabbed a single weapon, but still, I was not afraid. For a split second, I thought of calling for Fenlas, but he'd needed his rest, and a single fae was no match for my power.

A female walked carefully toward me, letting the ocean's water drip from her as her eyes glowed green in the moonlight. She hid behind long, dark hair and a villainous smile. "Hello, Promised One."

Instantly my hand flew to my empty neck. My mother's necklace had protected me from detection and now it was gone. I hadn't even noticed. "I wouldn't come any closer," I warned.

"Your beloved king has been poisoned while you were away today. Make a move to alert your mate and he will not be given the antidote. We have spies watching the prince's room."

"Who?" I demanded

"That is not important. You will come with me now, silently, or the southern king will be left to die."

My heart raced. I could alert Fen, but if what she said was true, Tolero would die. I couldn't rob Fen of the only father he had left. I still had my power, I'd kill an entire ocean of fae for him.

"Now I'm not saying I'm the world's most intelligent person here, fishy. But"—I gestured between us—"land fae, sea fae? Catch what I'm saying, or do I need to *scale* it out for you?"

"It's your choice. You or the king, Promised One."

I kicked a hip to the side and rolled my eyes, dramatically. "I will drown in the sea, you twat. Then I'm dead and you kill the king anyway."

She cackled. "I'd love to witness such a thing, but the queen has ordered your capture. You will remain alive. I have a gift for you. You will wear it to breathe under the water, just as I breathe now." She held out her hand.

I pictured Fen. He'd been absolutely livid when I raced into the dragon's pit. This was not the same though. I would save the king and be back by morning.

"How do I know you aren't lying?" I asked.

"You don't." She placed an earring into my hand. "Put it on."

"Bold of you to assume my ears are pierced."

"I've no time for your mouth. Put it on."

I jammed the earring into my ear and gasped, drowning in the fresh air. I tried to yank the earring out, but it did not budge. Again, the sea fae laughed as she walked toward the water. I needed water so badly I ran ahead of her and jumped in, sucking it into my body like it was the air above.

She removed her evada pearl and her feet turned into a fin. Mermaid. In a flash, she circled me while I still struggled to adjust. She slammed a pair of familiar handcuffs onto my arms and I believed I nearly died as my magic and my bond with Fen instantly vanished. I panicked as she grabbed my wrist, dragging me deeper and farther out into the foreign ocean.

As we moved, my body became acclimated, followed by my eyesight. I looked down at the cuffs that had nearly ended me and realized the last person I'd seen holding them had committed the ultimate crime. I should have guessed when the sea fae found us in the forest, though I wore my mother's necklace. I should have guessed the moment the banshee appeared. I should have guessed with every stupid question he'd asked me.

Fucking Lichen had betrayed us all.

# Temir

*I* held Nadra close to me the entire ride to Briar's Keep without a single rest. I leaped from the horse when we arrived, helped her down, and we ran, hand in hand, down the stairs and into the compound.

"Rook!" I yelled, turning to Nadra. "Go to the room and pack everything. I'll meet you there as soon as I can. Stop only to warn your mother."

She darted away, passing Rook as his wild eyes sought immediate danger.

"Temir, I didn't think we'd see you again." He leaned his hand against the wall, willing his breathing to calm.

"No time. The king knows everything. He knows where we are and it won't be long until his soldiers get here. I've come on horseback, but I assume their horses were freed in the fire. They will be marching on foot."

His eyes bulged as he stumbled back a step. "They saved a good portion of their horses. They'll probably be here sooner than you think." He turned to run down the hallway, barking orders as he went and beating on all the doors. "Emergency meeting, go to the hall!"

I rushed to the large meeting room and waited for it to fill with fae.

Rhogan entered, saw me waiting at the front of the room, and rushed to me. "Glad you made it out. We've been trying to organize a rescue party. What's going on?"

"The king knows where we are. He has several names."

His mouth fell open. "He enchanted you?"

A pit of guilt tumbled in my stomach. He wasn't accusing me, but I felt the shame anyway. "He took my barrier ring. I couldn't fight against him entirely. I tried."

"It's not your fault, Temir. It's something we all knew would happen eventually." He patted me firmly on the back and stood beside me, at the head of the room, until Rook ushered the last few fae in and nodded to me to begin.

"We don't have a lot of time. The king's soldiers are coming for us and they could be here at any moment. We might have a few hours, we might have a few minutes. We need to decide quickly what we are going to do."

Sidelong glances from a silent audience met us. Some seemed to shrivel in place while others frowned and looked to the ceiling for easy answers.

"If we stay," Rhogan said, "we can fight, but not from down here. We have to get above the ground."

"If we fight them from down here, there's only one entrance," Rook countered. "If they are bottlenecked into the compound, we can take them out at the door a few at a time."

"Or we could run," a lutin called out. "We could flee south and combine forces with the Marsh Court rebels."

"Either way, we need to decide quickly," I urged.

I recognized a male that stood. He and I had fought our way out of the tunnels below the castle together. "I say we stay and fight inside the compound."

"It doesn't make sense to stay here when they could just send more soldiers. It's not safe anymore. We have to flee," a kobold said from the back of the room.

"Consider this." Rhogan took a step forward. "If we all pack our things and go above ground, we can send the females and children ahead first. The males can stay behind and fight the first wave of soldiers. We would still be able to catch up to the others and there wouldn't be a possibility of being trapped down here."

That was his biggest fear. After being trapped in the dungeons, which I completely understood, he couldn't stand being underground if he thought there was even a possibility he would not be able to escape. He was a winged fae. He needed to fly.

Another spoke up, slamming his hand on the table in the center of the room. "We can't leave the females and children. If the soldiers catch them . . ."

"They won't. We know which way they will come," Rhogan said. "I can watch the skies and make sure the soldiers don't reach them."

"We'll need you on the battlefield, Rhogan." Rook placed a careful hand on his shoulder. "Let us all split now. Run to your rooms, pack your essential things, only what you can carry, and I will discuss this with Rhogan and Temir. We will decide what the best plan is and go from there."

Within minutes the room was empty.

"We don't have long to make a decision," I warned them.

"I know we don't. I just can't be down here. I can't fight down here," Rhogan said. He looked up to the tip of his raven wings, and I noticed for the first time they were nearly touching the low ceiling. He probably couldn't even stand straight in the rebel headquarters.

"Then it's settled," Rook answered. "We send you to guard the others while Temir and I will run the battle in the clearing outside of the Keep."

"I think we'd be better off fleeing. As long as we have a head start, it doesn't make sense to sit here and wait for a fight, potentially losing lives we could have otherwise saved."

"I know it's your nature to try to save everyone Temir, but I don't think we can just take off running," Rook answered. "We will be slower on foot than they are on horses."

"Do we have no horses of our own? I thought we were stealing them from the king."

"We have a few, but not nearly enough."

I nodded. "I don't see how we have a choice, then. We'll have to fight them on the field. Do we have weapons?"

"Plenty." Rook smiled at Rhogan. "Gather your things and let's get going."

"I'm not sure my mate will agree to go with the others."

"Neither will her mother," Rook answered, rushing out of the room.

I followed suit, scanning every nook and cranny I could on the way to Nadra. The rebels were moving quickly. I found Nadra and her mother hugging and crying, and I gave them only a moment until I interrupted. "I'm so sorry, but we have to get prepared. The soldiers will be here sooner than we thought."

"Mother, this is Temir, my mate. Pack your things. We need to leave."

Her mother stood as tall and beautiful as she did with the same copper hair, but her eyes were blue and she didn't have a single freckle. Her face was serious all the same.

"We've met," she said with a gentle nod in my direction. "I have nothing to gather. I should find Rook and see what I can do."

"The plan is to grab everything we can and send the females and children ahead while we stay behind and fight the soldiers."

"That's great for the rest of them, but my daughter and I will stay and fight."

"Are you trained?" I had seen no indication that Nadra could fight at all.

"I am. I'll protect my daughter."

"With your life?" The growl that escaped me startled Nadra.

"Always." She smiled and fled down the hallway.

"We don't have a lot of time, and we need nearly everything in here. Can you pack this up while I get weapons? Lock the door behind me."

"Temir, wait. I need to tell you what the king has planned."

"Now isn't a great time."

"It's important. Someone else needs to know. Just in case." She looked down at the floor.

"You are not going to die today, love. I promise."

"Still, just listen. Because it's never going to be a good time and someone else needs to know."

I pushed the door shut and waited as she began.

"The king believed that I would be his prisoner forever. He twisted my mind until I was so lost, it didn't matter what he said to me. He believed I didn't understand. He thought his enchantment would keep his secrets. It starts with the mate of the southern prince. The last time I saw him, I was with my friend Ara, and I don't think Prince Fenlas was mated."

I let my mind connect the dots as she spoke. I thought of the last time I'd seen the prince and his company. Nadra's fiery friend had threatened to have me mounted. I'm sure it was her. "I met them near the mists. They are together."

She sucked in a gasp. "Oh my gods, Temir. Are you sure? Could she be his mate? She is the friend I want to find. Her name is Ara. She has dark red hair, like wine. Same height as me? Grey eyes?"

"It was certainly her. It's possible they are mated, but what about them?"

"King Autus believes the southern prince's mate is Alewyn's Promise. Morwena told him."

The anticipation fled. "That's a fable. A child's bedtime story, Nadra."

"I thought so too, but it's not. And the king is on a hunt to break their mating bond and bind her to him instead. Don't you remember what he said to you in that room? He needs practice breaking a mating bond. If he kills the prince and splits her soul, he will never be able to bind her. He has to find another way."

"But even if he figures out how to break a mating bond, how can he bind her? In the stories, the promised one had unparalleled magic." I scratched the back of my head, attempting to work out the puzzle.

"He's hunting artifacts, Tem. He sent for the Gryla in the bog to read an ancient text to him. She told him he had to gather things in order to bind the promised one to him."

"And you're sure it's her? She was an amazing fighter, but I didn't see her use magic."

"Maybe it's not her, but I'm sure that's his plan, and I know for sure the southern prince's mate is the key."

"Gaea and I assumed he was scheming something. Do you know the recipe? Everything he's hunting?"

"I wrote it down so I wouldn't forget." She reached into her gown and pulled out a worn piece of paper.

"He requires a fabric woven from lies. My mother's reason for being useful to him, I'm sure. Also, a sword forged in death, blood of the king and queen, ashes from the first oak of Alewyn, a lost artifact in the southern sand dunes, and something called an adda flower."

I jerked at her last words. I opened the door, listened to make sure the king's guards had not yet come, then closed the door and locked it. "I have the final item," I whispered. "Gaea and I hunted it down, had a replica made, and turned that over to the king." I waited for her reaction. She gave none. "I would guess in less than an hour, the king's soldiers are going to be here. We have to make a decision right now. Either we stay and fight, or we flee."

"We can't stay down here, Temir. We're completely trapped. We must get out of the compound. We have to protect the artifact." She paused, biting her lip. "There's something else. The king believes if he can bind the promised one to him, he can use her power to take over the entire world, enslaving every fae who ever moved against him. He genuinely believes he is the rightful king of the realm. But he stumbled upon the binding spell by accident. He was searching for something else."

Legs weak, I moved to sit on the tidied bed in the small room. "What else could he possibly need?"

Nadra pushed her hands through her hair. "There are dangerous creatures trapped somewhere within this world. Behind a hidden door. He intends to find it and release them upon Alewyn. That's why he needed Gaea. He wanted to send her to find the door. He has been hunting for it but can't find it. He was trying to find a seer, but last I knew, he still hadn't found one."

My mind faded back to Oleonis. His visions, and the king being so incredibly suspicious—that had to have been the truth behind his death. The king had found out Oleonis was a seer, and when he refused him, he'd had him killed. Of course, he would have never admitted that to me, even in chains, he didn't think he owed me that. I scanned the visions in my mind, the female on fire, another lost underwater, a group wandering in a dense fog. Nothing fit.

A tingle of doubt embedded itself within me. There were too many things to do and only two of us. We needed help. We needed to find somewhere safe and craft a plan. "We have to tell the others," I said, still pacing.

"We have to wait. I think we have to warn the southern prince. But first, we need to find the ancient tree and steal the ashes before he can get to them. If we have two things he needs, the flower and the ashes, we can go south, warn the prince, and hopefully, he can secure the artifact in the dunes."

I stopped and took her hands into my own. She stepped between my legs and I hugged her, laying my head against her stomach. Taking a single moment I probably didn't have to caution her. "You're sure you're up for this? It isn't going to be easy."

"As long as we are together, that's all that matters, Temir."

"We need the truth serum and only people we can trust as we get through this."

"Where is the adda?" she asked.

I pulled away, reached under the bed, and lifted out my hidden bag. "It's here." I removed the glass box from the overstuffed bag and set it on the chest of drawers.

She crossed the room in a trance and reached out, gliding her fingertips across the top. She turned the artifact back and forth several times until finally I took it away and placed it back into the bag.

"It has that effect on people. It draws you in so powerfully you can't help but reach for it."

Her face slackened as she moved forward, her cheeks flushing. "If that's only one of the missing items, I'd hate to see what the others feel like."

"Well, we know he's been hounding your mother for the fabric, and now he can't have that either. He does have the sword from Oravan though."

"It won't do him any good if he never gets the other pieces. But I think the only thing that will stop him from hunting is his own death."

Nadra paused, her racing mind likely realizing the finality of her own words. This would never end until we found a way to kill King Autus. He would continue to hunt us and the pieces until he could steal the power and conquer the world. It was the only thing he had ever wanted. Complete control of every single fae.

I opened my arms and she stepped into them. "We'll do this together. And we are not alone. Let's get going."

We started frantically shoving all my things into the bags I had brought, trying not to break anything. I double-checked the room and turned the lock to open the door just as the screaming began.

The soldiers had come, and we were trapped underground.

# Ara

Fucking fish. The mermaid—with her siren's high-pitched laugh—dragged me through the bay and out into the deep cold waters of the ocean. I hadn't grown a tail or a fin, thank the gods, but I could breathe. Under normal circumstances even my fae sight wouldn't be able to see this far below the surface, but the earring she had clipped into my ear had transformed me. I wondered if my mysterious magic would have allowed me to save myself, but with the handcuffs Lichen had kept from the dragons, I would never know.

I would kill him. I was foolish for believing the king was poisoned. Was it possible? Yes, but I should have been sure. I should have reached for Fen. The void, the great chasm of space that was once my mating bond with him, was incapacitating. Only that tiny flicker of a flame remained within me. A reminder of where my prince once was.

I heard stories of Morwena's grand castle under the sea. Some said it was made of coral, some said it was made of millions of pearls, but no one mentioned the bones. No one mentioned the aura of trepidation pulsating through the water as we got closer. On top of a shelf of coral, there were millions of tiny bones framed to the shape of a sea beast's tentacles holding up the castle pillars. Towers equally placed on each side donned massive pearls the sun would never touch. If Morwena was going for elegant death, she had accomplished it perfectly.

I kicked my feet behind me as the mermaid dragged me between the doors, through the castle, around the sea fae, and shoved me toward Morwena. She sat in her true form: a leviathan. Terrifyingly enough, she reminded me of a slightly smaller version of Pathog, the dragon, with her upper body in her high fae form and her lower body a massive sea serpent with shimmering blue scales the size of my hands.

Unable to sit on her throne, she sat coiled around it possessively as she laughed. "My, how the tables have turned."

Her eyes twitched sideways, and I followed her line of sight to Lichen, standing in the crowd like the slimy little fish he was. I lunged for him, seeing nothing but red. It took six armed guards to pull me back. "How could you?" I screamed.

"How indeed." He stepped forward and locked his arms behind his back. "I've been working for Morwena for years, stupid girl. And while none of the southerners were smart enough to figure it out, not even when I slipped poison to their queen, you were so skeptical. Right from the start." He walked back and forth along the sandy seafloor like it was the most natural thing in the world. "This all began during the Iron Wars, you see."

"Oh great. A life story," I said behind clenched teeth. I looked around him, up to Morwena. "Just kill me now and save me the headache."

"You won't be dying, girl. I intend on controlling that power of yours, but until I learn how, you'll stay locked up. I plan to keep you from Autus' hands."

"I'm not really interested in your sloppy seconds anyway."

Lichen turned to face the queen and grunted.

She waved her hand through the air. "Yes, yes. Carry on."

"The only court Autus didn't seem interested in was the sea. I tried to make Tolero see that, but he was so blind and disconnected. Then, when his mate showed up, he pushed me even further to the side."

"I mean, obviously. Did you think you were prettier or something?"

A few chuckles from the crowd had him turning red as he continued. "When Queen Morwena approached me with an offer I couldn't refuse—"

"Let me guess, she said she'd fix that receding hairline? No, wait, she promised to make you her little sea baby. No, a bigger penis?"

"If you do not stop interrupting me, I'll have you gagged."

"Too late, I'm already gagging. Also, I don't care. You hid in the Flame Court for years and years, poisoned the queen, got stuck with the prince, tried to have me captured in the forest and again with the banshee, which is why it didn't attack me, and then finally you got your jollies off, completing the final betrayal, poisoning the king. Good story. We done now?"

He stood with his jaw open. He'd probably practiced his little monologue in front of the mirror, and I'd just ruined it for him.

"Not sorry." I shrugged and smiled in his direction.

He faced Morwena again, fuming.

"Shame we cannot keep her here. I believe she would be quite entertaining." Morwena dipped her head, and several guards swam forward, grabbed my arms, and dragged me through the castle until the final traces of light faded away and the sea became a black chasm of danger.

A single light illuminated the end of a long hallway, and I was thrown into a pitch-black room. I held my hands up, hoping to find a way to break free of the cuffs, but I couldn't see a thing. My fae senses were on high alert as my neck crawled—the tingling sensation that meant something ominous lurked in the darkness, watching me. I was blind though. Staying close to the door was the safest thing I could do. I didn't want to get lost in the depths of the ocean if I had been thrown into a magical endless dungeon.

Time was completely irrelevant here.

Eventually, the door opened, and a tiny glowing female slipped inside. My eyes, adjusting to the light, went instantly to the exit, and she quickly pulled it shut. She, too, wore chains around her wrists, though she carried a tray. The glow from her small frame wasn't enough to give detail to my prison.

"Hello," she said in a high-pitched voice. "I've brought you some dinner if you're hungry."

"I'm not," I snapped.

"I promise it's nothing bad. And I've brought a second helping of the kelp if you'd like."

"As if I would trust anyone from the sea."

"Oh," she said, her glow dampening. "I'm sorry. I meant to be helpful. I'll just leave it here then, in case you'd like it later."

She looked into the depths behind me, shuddered, and slipped back out, taking the light with her. I slammed my hands on the door, but it didn't have a handle and didn't budge. I bent to the area where the tray was left, sniffed the food, and nearly vomited. Maybe nothing bad for a sea being. Definitely bad for me. Living below water with the earring the mermaid had forced upon me was so similar to being on land. The water pulled at the ends of my hair, but everything felt normal. There were still smells. There was no need to force myself to stay on the floor of the castle. It was not at all what I'd expected, and had I been here under any other circumstances, I imagined I could even enjoy it: this different world within my own.

Sitting on the soft sands of the seafloor, I examined the bleakness around me. If I were alone in this room, or whatever this prison was, I had to believe the water would be still, but it moved, and not fluidly. It jerked sometimes and tossed me around others. I was unquestionably not alone. I leaned my head back and closed my eyes, picturing Fen. I sat there for hours upon silent hours. By now he'd know I was missing, and I could only imagine the fury. Especially if his father really was poisoned. He'd watched his mother die, and now his father could die from the same coward's weapon. Not at my own hands though, so my fate had changed, it seemed. Which wasn't supposed to be possible.

Again, the door opened, and the lighted sea faerie slipped in as quickly as she had the last time. "Good morning." Her trill voice matched her smile.

"It's morning already?"

"It is. I've brought you something different to try. Apparently, your kind like your fish cooked."

"Cooked, not soggy."

"I've wrapped it in seaweed to try to help."

"Why are you being kind to me?" I asked, reaching for her tray this time.

"You are not the only prisoner here. I am also." She held up her chains and rattled them, though there was no sound.

"You're a prisoner *and* you're a servant?"

"All of the lesser fae in the sea are either soldiers or servants. Isn't it that way up there also?"

I hesitated, but what harm could answering a question bring? "In some places, I suppose."

"I have to go now," she said, abruptly straightening. "I'll bring you something nice for lunch." Again, she slipped out of the room.

She was a servant, but she was obviously able to come and go through the castle. That was enough to become an ally as far as I was concerned. I waited and waited for her to return, and, reaching a new level of boredom, I tasted the fish. It was awful. But she had tried. She had given me some kind of crunchy seasoned vegetable that wasn't bad.

Hours later, could have been forty-two days for all I knew, she returned bringing another tray of food.

"Can you stay longer?" I asked.

"Only a bit. I've got rounds to make. I work for the kitchens and deliver the private meals around the castle."

"Do they always feed their prisoners so well?"

She shook her head slowly, the water pulling her in waves "Not all of them. You are special though. You're not here to die."

"That's only because the queen is an idiot," I mumbled.

She beamed so brightly the radius of her soft golden light doubled. "You shouldn't talk like that, though it is nice to hear from someone else's mouth."

"Do you have friends?" I asked casually as I shoved whatever was on the tray into my mouth and swallowed whole so I wouldn't have to taste it.

"Oh yes. There are lots of servants within the castle to talk to when we are allowed."

"Good gods, what is this?" I held up the slimy mass that was on the tray.

"Oh, that is very good. It's a mollusk. The red ones are my favorite."

"Mmm," I said with wide eyes the size of a Grendel's ass as I looked down to the oozing creature in my hand.

"Try it." She smiled, nodding her head like she was excited to prove me wrong.

"You first." I held it out to her.

"Oh, I couldn't take your lunch from you."

"I don't mind."

She grabbed the sea slug from my hand, ripped it into two, and shoved half into her mouth. She closed her eyes and shook her bottom until she swallowed.

"Your turn." She handed me the other half, leaning in, waiting for me to eat it as she bit her bottom lip in an attempt to hide her excitement.

I closed my eyes and shoved it into my mouth, instantly gagging as I swallowed. The thick, salty slime trailed slowly down my throat.

"I told you." She clapped, as if the look on my face was contentment and not absolute torture.

"What is your name?" I cleared my throat and wondered what would happen if I vomited at the bottom of the ocean.

"Leora."

"I'm Ara."

"I know. All the servants are talking about you and how you aren't afraid of the queen."

"She is far less intimidating in her land form. That's for sure."

"She's a monster no matter what she looks like." Her light dimmed as her eyes fell to the sea floor.

"You shouldn't talk like that," I said, repeating her earlier words. She giggled and then floated closer to the door. "Are you leaving already?"

"I know it must be terribly boring for you. I'll be back at dinner time." She gathered her tray slowly. She wanted to stay, and that was a small win.

I wanted so badly to ask her to help me, but I needed to build a rapport with her first. The room felt a thousand times bigger when she was not there to light it. Leora's small smile and sweet personality were not what I had expected from a sea fae. But slowly, I began to realize they were just like the rest of us. Living in a flawed world and only trying to survive the reality of their circumstances.

I spent the next several days laughing at her absurd jokes about food, I ate whatever she brought, and it became a game between us. She made it her personal mission to find something from their kitchens that I liked, and I made it mine to brighten her glow each time she left the room.

I still felt the lurking disturbance in the waters, and eventually, I remembered a bit of important information. Something Aibell, who had been irritatingly absent, had said to me.

"Leora, do you think you could get a message to the shore for me?" Her eyes grew wide and her light nearly faded as she sunk to the ground. "Eventually the queen is going to call for me, Leora. I cannot give her what she is going to demand. She wants my power. The only way I'll be safe is if you help me."

"If I'm caught, she will kill me and my family," her small voice whispered.

"But if we make it out, I will free you from her. I'll make sure she cannot hurt you. You can move to the castle if you want. Be a guest and not a servant."

"I couldn't eat your food," she retorted.

I laughed. "We could figure it out together."

The glow within her grew as an idea came to her. "I think I can do it. I know someone that could sneak me out."

"My message is specific, Leora. You'll have to remember every word."

She nodded. "I promise."

"My mate is the prince of the Flame Court. If you can go to the castle and ask for Fenlas, he will come. I promise. He will be scary, but if you say these words to him, he will believe you. Tell him, 'Ara is trapped in Morwena's castle. Lichen betrayed everyone and I am wearing the cuffs. Bring the keys.' Tell him I said to call him Prince Fancy Pants." She scrunched her face at me. "Just trust me. He'll know I said it. Oh, one more thing. I need you to get a message to Greeve also. He'll be somewhere close to Fen. He's a bit dark, covered in tattoos, and will likely be the first to make a threat."

She whimpered. "What is it?"

Afraid to say the words out loud, I leaned in and whispered into her ear. She gasped, looked out into the water, and nodded before slipping out the door. I could only hope she could swim far and fast without getting caught. She was cuffed, but I hoped that helped Fen to see she was on our side. I knew Leora would not betray me, but that didn't mean she wouldn't die trying to help.

# Temir

"The soldiers are here," Nadra whispered, sending a tidal wave of her own worry crashing into my own. We stood inside our room in the rebel compound and listened to the battle outside begin.

"This was foolish. We should have just started running."

"It wouldn't have mattered, Tem. They were all on horses, we would have been outnumbered."

"Rook says there are about three hundred rebels in the compound right now. I won't be able to save them all."

"No one expects you to." She took my hand and pulled me closer to her. "It's not your job to save the world."

She was desperate and terrified and, had I any less will power, I might have resigned to stay locked in this room with her. But they needed every edge. Every male. "I will hardly be able to save any of them."

"What about the magic? The one you used against that guard at the castle. Will that help?"

"That type of magic is incredibly draining. I won't be able to use it more than a couple of times and then I won't be able to heal anyone." A battle cry came from down the hallway and I jerked for the handle.

"Temir," Nadra whispered, reaching for my arm once more.

"I have to go. I have to do what I can. The minute I leave the room, lock the door, move the chest in front of it, and then the bed. Do you hear me? You have to protect yourself and the flower until I can get us out of here."

She nodded solemnly.

I wanted to kiss her so badly, but I didn't want our first kiss to be rushed. I wanted to take my time with her. Stepping into the hall, I heard the lock click behind me as I sprinted towards the fighting.

The way the compound was set up, the entrance would lead the guards into the main landing area. Based on the sounds coming from that direction, that's where the battle was being fought. From that entrance, several halls stemmed off to form sleeping quarters, the dining hall, and the large meeting room.

As I entered the main landing, I tried to make sense of the chaos, but it was useless. Rook was trying to hand out weapons to any rebel willing to fight while Rhogan and a few others were battling the northern soldiers as they came barreling down the stairs.

"Rook. Weapon!" I screamed.

He tossed me a sword, heavier than I would have liked, and I jumped into the madness. The stark white walls and floor were already splattered in blood. A rebel to my right was just about to be killed when I stepped in, blocking the fatal blow from the soldier.

He turned to me, panicked, and then scurried away.

"Someone needs to guard the halls. Don't let them leave this room!" I yelled.

"Alto, Griv, Weben, and Hage, take the left four, Rhogan and Vertu, take the right," Rook ordered.

His confidence and direct nature were a far cry from the rebel leader I had seen in the past, but in this moment, it was the only thing that might save us all. The outside males moved into their positions while Rook, three others, and I continued to battle the soldiers who came down the stairs, into the compound. The bottleneck theory was working, but we were not without our losses.

Now covered in blood, we had to start moving the fallen bodies so we wouldn't trip over them while fighting. At first, the soldiers filled the stairwell and were pushing each other to get into the room, essentially shoving the first guy onto the sword of the rebel standing there, and we were able to fight them off easily. Then they got smarter and sent only two or three at a time.

A battle cry echoed from behind me and I jerked to see Rhogan fighting two soldiers at once while still trying to protect his hallway. I ran for him and relieved him of one soldier while he continued to fight another particularly large foe, leaving his wings spread as far as he could to block the hall.

"One got past me. You'll have to go catch him," he said breathlessly as he brought his broadsword above his head and swung it down onto the large fae he battled.

I sprinted down the hall, listening until I heard screaming. Standing at the end of the hallway were most of the rebel females and

Nadra's mother holding a sword out in front of her as the king's soldier lurked closer. Her eyes met mine, and I pressed my fingers to my lips. She continued her battle stance, stepping forward to help protect the females and few children within the compound.

The soldier lunged forward. Megere blocked the blow perfectly and then parried, nearly taking out the soldier before I even got to them. He tried to catch his breath and took a step back right into the tip of my sword. He jerked upright, and a few of the females turned away as I thrust my blade farther and yanked up.

"Rhogan is at the front of the hallway blocking it so others cannot get in. Are you okay back here?"

"Perfectly fine," she said fiercely.

I ran back down the hall and called out so Rhogan could let me through while again he fought another soldier. Arrows were everywhere. Apparently, the soldiers had changed tactics, and it looked like it was working. I tried to take a tally, but the yelling, running, and chaos of the main room was too fluid to track.

"Rotate hall guards," Rook called out.

It was smart. They weren't struggling as much as the rebels in front, so a reprieve of any kind was likely the best idea.

I ran to the hall that led to Nadra. "I'll take this one, Griv."

The rebel, bouncing on the tips of his toes, was antsy to join the fray, and I was most content to guard the hall that housed my mate. He ran onto the blood-soaked floors while I stood waiting. A soldier slipped past the others and ran for me. Clothed in tattered gear, proof of his earlier fighting, he completely ignored the trickle of blood seeping down his face. He was strong and fought me halfway down the hall until I was able to gain momentum and push him back.

The sword I used was heavy at the tip, something I wasn't used to, and it threw off my balance multiple times as we fought. Eventually, he moved in so close he stabbed me with a knife he held in his other hand. A fury poured over me as I realized if he got past me, there was one person he would be headed toward. I could not let that happen. I lunged and screamed and nearly lost myself in a feral rage as I killed him and then yanked the knife from my side, running back to the entrance of the hall.

I used magic to heal the small wound, panting while another soldier came for me. I cut him down and kept moving forward until I heard a rebel call for me.

"Rhogan needs help. They've pushed him into the meeting room."

"Take my hall!" I yelled, leaping over the dead bodies while my heart still raced with anger.

I slammed open the door to the meeting room to see Rhogan fighting four soldiers. Three were on top of him and one had a knife about to penetrate his wing.

*Why do they always go for the damn wings?*

Rhogan screamed in rage, his veins bulging as he struggled.

I bolted across the room, tackling the soldier on top of him as I kept my sword in my left hand and pounded my fist into his face with my right. I heard the scuffle behind me and took the hilt of my sword and slammed it down into the soldier below me.

Three soldiers circled Rhogan like prey.

I ran into the middle beside him, and we stood back-to-back, weapons out, ready to fight whoever moved forward.

"Thanks for coming," he said from behind me.

"Apparently, saving your ass is becoming a habit," I answered.

The soldiers moved as one, and Rhogan dealt one lethal blow while I blocked the swing of another. The third got me in the arm, so Rhogan began fighting him as I continued with the one in front of me. Within minutes, the king's soldiers lay on the ground, blood pouring from them.

Even if we didn't have to leave, I wasn't sure I would have been able to stay here again. I would never think of Briar's Keep and not remember this day. The bloodiest day the rebels had ever seen.

We left the room and exchanged a glance as we realized the rest of the compound had gone utterly silent. Rushing back to the steps, we found so many more fallen fae than were there before. Something had happened. I looked but couldn't find Rook among the fallen.

Rhogan pressed his hand to his ear and then pointed down the hallway Megere and the females were in.

We moved silently forward, listening, weapons ready. The hall curved to the left, but the moment we turned that corner, we would be visible. We stopped and waited with backs pressed against the wall until I heard Eadas's deep, dark cackle and instantly moved to rush forward.

Rhogan grabbed me and slammed me back against the wall. "Don't," he whispered into my ear. He peeked around the corner, and his face dropped. He moved back against the wall and took a deep breath. "Eadas has Rook by knifepoint. Megere is on her knees with two soldiers holding her down."

"Just the three soldiers then? We can take them."

"Not before Eadas slices Rook's throat, Temir. You have to make a decision. We can storm that hallway and potentially save Megere, but Rook will die. Or we can wait and see what he wants from her."

"I know what he fucking wants from her. We have to save her."

146

He nodded.

"Move," Eadas screamed.

We paused, and Rhogan opened a door just in time for us to slip in as the five of them passed us, moving toward the front steps. I hadn't felt anything from Nadra, and I had to believe that meant she was still okay, still barricaded into the room. I had to try to save her mother. We slipped out of the room together and stayed all the way back until they entered the landing before the exit.

"We have to go now, Rhogan. They can't take her."

We rushed forward, no longer worrying about staying quiet, rounding the corner just before they made it to the door. Eadas' eyes flashed with amusement as he caught sight of us. "Oh, Temir. I was hoping I would see your body among the dead. It seems you are forever resilient." Eadas stood behind Rook with a knife to his throat.

"Let them go, Eadas," I seethed. "You know the king wants me more than he wants either of them."

"That may be, but he's requested something your mate's mother just isn't willing to give up."

I met eyes with Megere. I could tell her iron will was faltering. "You can't do it, Megere. Don't give him what he wants."

"You can and you will. Don't think I won't hunt down your daughter. She's got to be hiding around here somewhere." Eadas pressed the knife further into Rook's throat.

"No, please." She shook with fear.

Rhogan and I moved together, going for the soldiers.

"Stop," Megere cried as she watched the blood pour from Rook. "No one move. I'll do it. I'll do it."

"You can't," I roared.

She pulled out a tiny spool of thread. Calling forth her magic, she wove a small square of fabric as she looked to Rook and said, "I never loved you." She held it out for Eadas and he nodded to a soldier to take the fabric she had woven from lies.

Rook's eyes never left her.

"Now, was that so hard?" Eadas asked, dragging his knife across Rook's neck and tossing his body to the side while Megere screamed and ran to him.

One of Autus' soldiers held her back, but she punched him in the face. Rhogan and I both leaped forward to pull her away, but it was too late. The male sank his sword right into her chest. Rhogan roared again, killing both males as I moved to Megere. Eadas had slipped out, and if I chased him, Megere would die. She might die anyway, I realized, as I grabbed her hand and pulled on my magic.

The sword the soldier had used was wide and short, impaling her entire torso. Large tears fell down her face as she tried to move to Rook's fallen body on the floor.

"You have to hold still. Do you hear me?"

She didn't. Blood poured from her nose, ears, and mouth.

I slammed my magic into her so fast she jolted. I moved first to her punctured lung and then realized the sword had pierced her heart. I fought like hell to save my mate's mother. I gave as much as I possibly could to her, grasping the cusp of life within her and holding it firmly as I worked. Until a white-hot, searing pain came from Nadra. I lost my breath, my vision, my entire grip on reality as I realized something terrible had just happened to her while I had been trying and failing to save her mother.

"Temir," Rhogan yelled, grabbing me.

148

I couldn't respond. Couldn't move as every muscle in my body locked up and I too, had blood trailing from my nose and ears. He called for me in the distance, but I couldn't respond. One moment I was in the rebel compound and the next I was a million miles away, drifting through the rolling pain within my body.

# Ara

*L*eora never returned. At first, I was glad she probably found a way to get out of the castle and deliver my message to Fen, but as time passed by so slowly, I worried that didn't happen at all. I knew she was content to stay in the sea, and she hadn't complained about her job once. Maybe she didn't mind being enslaved.

I tried at least a million times to get the cuffs off my hands, even cried out to Aibell. Once utter boredom took over in the unending sea of black hell, I began speaking to the beast that lurked somewhere beyond. I had decided he was a male, lurky, ocean beast. A female wouldn't have been quiet for this long. She probably would have eaten me days ago.

He never answered, but as time went on, I became more and more confident that I was right about something else being in here with me. He knew most of my life story, what I really thought about Leora's food, and all the ways I planned to kill the sea queen the second I figured out how to free myself.

The water would still when I talked and jerk me around when I was done. The presence became like a distant pet I couldn't touch or see. But I couldn't even see my hands, so I didn't hold that against him.

"I had a pet once," I told him. "A tiny tree sprite I kept in a jar by my bed. I had him for a whole two hours before my father forced me to apologize and let him go. Now, I know what you're thinking. That's not a real pet. But one day his mother came after me with a pair of kitchen shears and I locked her away for three days until she apologized. But then I let her go too. She wasn't nearly as pleasant as her son, but also, my father was right. Being a prisoner sucks."

I moved my hands through the sand and continued the longest endless day of my life. Without the sun, it was so hard to tell how much time had gone by. It was probably a year. Or maybe even two. I was starving. That's all I knew. So hungry, I think I would have eaten another sea slug.

Finally, as if my thoughts were heard, the door opened. I whipped around, expecting to see Leora, but instead, it was the dark-haired mermaid who had captured me, her silhouette lit only by the faint light in the hall behind her.

"Enjoying yourself?" she asked.

"Oh yeah. It's a real party in here. You should come back later."

"The queen has called for you to be brought before the court."

"Oh, shoot. My schedule's full today. Maybe another time."

She didn't appreciate my humor as she reached forward, grabbed the cuffs, and pulled me from the room. A rush of bubbles circled me and swept away as my eyes adjusted to the light. The mermaid didn't seem to notice. Apparently, solitude was not great for my mind.

Past the crowds of sea fae, down the darkened halls of embedded seashells and sculpted bones, I was once again dragged to the center of the throne room and shoved before the queen. The creepy eyes of a thousand gathered fae watched me. Some in chains and some not. I noticed more servants than I had the time before as I searched faces looking for Leora, for her comforting glow, but I couldn't find her.

"Something catch your attention?" Morwena asked, bringing my gaze forward.

"Just wondering how you eat fish when you literally are one."

"No matter. I've brought you here today because I've come to a rather disappointing conclusion."

"It wasn't just a rash?"

"You are insufferable, girl," she snapped.

"We all need goals, Morweenie." I shrugged, letting the weight of the chains pull me down.

Her lips pulled back to bare her teeth as her body coiled like a muscle. "King Autus will never stop hunting you. He's after the Wild Hunt and some damn door. I hoped that would keep him distracted, but alas, it has not."

"Guess you should have kept your mouth shut about me. Then he wouldn't have known."

The room shifted at my boldness, and it brought me a small bit of joy.

"Oh yes, but you know how royalty can be. Always trying to show off the upper hand."

"Or fin," I quipped.

She dropped her gaze and glared.

I matched her bitch face with my own, refusing to blink. I was pretty sure I was winning the staring contest until the entire castle began to shake and rumble. She jerked, tilting her head at an odd angle. The corners of my mouth lifted as a gentle, familiar hand glided across the small of my back. Leora was a fucking hero.

"What was that?" Morwena snapped at her guards.

Her face became frantic as reality crashed down on her. A great lament, a cry unlike anything I had ever heard called from deep within the castle and Morwena circled her gilded sea throne, coiling her leviathan body so tight, I thought she might crush it.

A small click at my wrist, and the cuffs fell to the sandy floor. Power surged through me as strongly as all the emotions Fen had sent down the bond while I was away. I was overcome with fear, worry, anger, and determination.

*Hello you,* he said, his hand still planted firmly on my back.

My shoulders dropped in relief. *Why can't she see you? She can see through Wren's magic.*

"Guards," Morwena called. "Protect me."

*Not in this form. She is practically blind in her true form.*

*Does everyone know that?*

*I've been researching.* There was a haunting stillness to his words.

*She is mine, Prince, but Lichen over there? He's all yours.*

Again, the castle boomed, the walls rattling as the light that hung from the high ceiling swayed.

Morwena shrieked. She hadn't noticed I'd lost my cuffs yet. "Kill the girl and seal the doors. Someone has freed the hydra and she's coming for me."

"That would be me," I said, raising my freed hand.

"You?" Her head snapped sideways. I wondered if she could see the missing cuffs at all.

"And a few of my friends."

"You'll die now, promised one. You will die and I'll feed you to that beast myself."

"Unfortunately for you, we're best friends now. Although, I *am* surprised it's a female."

The guards rushed for me, but Fen let loose his air magic and sent them flying. Morwena unwrapped herself from her throne and moved like lightning through the water toward me. Fen shot sideways, in Lichen's direction, and I had no idea where Wren—who had kept Fen hidden from everyone else—was. Morwena was upon me, wrapping me in her coils as all hell broke loose.

I wasn't afraid as I dug my hands into her scaled body. Just before I plunged into my cresting magic, the doors slammed open behind us, and all three heads of the hydra called Morwena's name. She tensed, squeezing me so hard the edges of my vision blurred. As much as I wanted to watch them fight, for a couple of rounds at least, I wasn't patient. I let the entire wall holding my magic vanish and completely obliterated Morwena before she could make another move.

I had a lot to learn about magic.

I had no idea that using that powerful of a force, that swiftly, would knock me out. My body fell to the ocean floor, and the last thing I saw was the hydra coming for me at full speed.

Standing on land and facing a hydra, it would tower over me, its size equal only to the Kraken. One of her razor-sharp teeth was the length of my body. The sea castle was, by far, the largest of all the castles I'd been to. It had to be, to accommodate the beasts below the surface, but still, the hydra had to be the biggest of them all.

*Ara!* Fen called. *Ara, wake up.*

His voice was calm and steady, but I felt his fear trembling through me. I tried to draw myself from the blackness, but I was stuck, the force of my own magic holding me down. There, but not there at all. I wasn't knocked out. I was pinned below the magic I was meant to control. Panic rose like a boiling pot as tremors took over.

"Rise, friend. Tell me who to kill," a hissing voice said so close to my ear the vibrations trembled down my spine.

I had actually made friends with the hydra after all.

I needed to rein in the magic suffocating me, but I was dripping with despair, the force foreign and overwhelming. I closed my eyes and tried to right the spinning world. Nothing. I opened the iron wall and tried to force the magic back behind it. Numbness trickled up my fingers and through my arms, and if I didn't get the magic under control quickly, I would become completely lost to it. I reached out to the bond and held tight. Fen tugged and I held onto the essence of him while I pushed and pushed until I felt my body convulsing.

Slowly, so fucking slowly, the magic began to move as I willed it. If I hadn't feared it before, I would from now on. The weight of a thousand worlds pressed down on my chest and numbness still moved, creeping up my body while I continued to force the magic until, at last, I was able to open my eyes. Three terrifying faces looked down on me as I lay in the fetal position on the ocean floor. My power had destroyed half the castle.

*Fen?*

*Thank the gods. I'm here, Ara. I'm here. The hydra hasn't let anyone move. She waits for you.*

155

"Hello, friend. You are well now?" the three melodic voices of the beast asked in unison.

My heart pounded, and it took every ounce of self-restraint to keep the fear from my face. "I am well, I think. If you could just move off me a tiny bit so I can breathe, that would be helpful."

She jerked, realizing she was crushing me, and slithered back, but only inches.

"My mate," I coughed. "Please let him come."

She leaned so uncomfortably close. "There are several menacing males with weapons that look like they want to try to kill me. Which one do you request?"

"The most handsome one."

"You may come forward," she said to someone in the crowd.

She shifted only slightly as she let him in. I closed my eyes and coughed again, but when I opened them, Greeve stood above me. I couldn't help my smile. "The hydra thinks you're the best-looking male in the room," I laughed and wheezed.

He didn't think I was funny at all. The fierce look on his face was only brutal.

"Glad you got my message to take out her wards. Help me up?"

He reached out a hand, and I used it as leverage, pulling my stiff body to stand. Anger radiated from him. He was pissed at me, and I had a feeling that only meant Fen was even angrier.

"All right, let us out," I told the hydra. She gave me a questionable look, and I patted her. I had no idea how to comfort a sea creature. "I have to deal with these people now, so you have to let us out." She opened her coiled body and Greeve helped me walk over to the other brooding males and one pissed off female. "Hey guys," I said tentatively.

156

"What in the fuck—"

I held up a hand to stop Wren from the ass chewing. "Not now. Later."

I reached for Fen's hand, and he let me take it, but he would not meet my eyes.

"Only you would make friends with a hydra, Ara," Kai said.

Looking around the frozen crowd, I was surprised to see Lichen still standing. "You didn't kill him?" I asked Fen.

"The world exploded before I could get there," he bit out.

"Care to take your anger out on him? He's the one who trapped me, after all."

Fen's eyes finally met mine, and he drew his sword. Each of my crew had earrings similar to mine. Leora was still nowhere to be seen, but I had a feeling she had something to do with that.

"Who do you wish us to kill?" the hydra asked, watching me carefully.

"Keep your panties on," I answered.

Her faces contorted into what I believed was supposed to be smiles, but Wren still moved behind me.

"Lichen," Fen called. "Where is the antidote?"

My head whipped around so fast I thought I'd injure myself. "It's true, then? Your father has been poisoned?"

He dipped his chin as he watched Fen. Lichen hadn't moved.

I wanted so bad to shred that fae into tiny fucking pieces and feed him to the hydra bit by bit. But this was not my kill. This was Fen's. For the years and years of betrayal. For his mother and maybe even his father.

"Where the fuck is the antidote?" Fen yelled.

He crossed the floor to stand in front of Lichen and the hydra followed behind him, leaning down so that when Lichen looked at my mate, he was also forced to look at her. The rest of us moved closer, showing absolute solidarity as Fen made his demands. Lichen trembled with fear. Not from watching Fen, but from the looming beast above, poised and ready to kill.

"Shall we force him?" the hydra asked, staring down at Lichen.

"It . . . it won't matter," he stuttered. "There is no antidote. There is no saving the king."

"Liar," Fen snarled, swinging his blade until it pressed into Lichen's throat.

*Say the words and I'll ask the hydra to step in.*

His nostrils flared as he flexed his hands into fists. *I don't need your pet.*

His words were fierce and hurtful, though I knew he didn't mean them to be. He was on the cusp of losing his father. Desperate to save him. Lichen remained silent and, though fear was written across his face, a smile pulled at his lips, and that was all it took to push Fen over the edge. Lichen lost his head in a single move and the hydra instantly devoured his body.

"We need to get back," Fen said, void of all emotion.

"The sea fae have just lost their queen. Someone has to stay and pick up the pieces," Wren answered.

I looked at Greeve, but he shook his head. I turned to Kai and drew back. I'd never heard of a land dwelling fae gaining a tail with a charm, but there he was, every inch the sea god with his flowing blond curls and a tail as blue as the night sky, gold flecks shimmering within. "What the fuck, Kai? You even dressed the part."

He looked down and back to me, shrugging as he examined the sea glass ring on his finger. "I've always loved the sea."

"Will you stay?"

His eyes flashed to stone-faced Fen who dipped his chin. Kai mimicked the gesture in my direction and that was that. "I will for a bit to get things settled, but it won't be long term."

I could see the struggle on his features. His clenched jaw and worry as he watched my mate. He didn't want to leave Fen. I turned to the rest of the sea fae watching us. Some with hatred, some in awe.

"I need a servant named Leora. Has anyone seen her?"

"She's at the castle still. She's working with Loti in the kitchens," Kai answered.

I turned to the hydra. "I will send someone back here to help find peace and decide what to do. In the meantime, you're in charge. Anyone so much as whispers about killing someone else or joining the northern king, eat them."

She smiled and nodded. Greeve grabbed my arm and whisked me away before I could say another word. The moment I was on land, he was gone again. I easily pulled the earring from my ear and waited for them all until we stood in a group, dripping wet and panting. Fen crushed me into his arms, and I mumbled an apology into his chest. I turned to the others. "I know you're all really pissed at me right now, but you have to understand. There was a mermaid and she told me if I cooperated, the king would be saved."

"You should have told me, Ara. You could have alerted me down the bond." Fire coated his clipped words as his jaw clenched and released, breaths ragged.

"I thought I was helping. I could have killed them all with my magic. I only realized too late that Lichen had turned over the dragon's cuffs."

Greeve's lethal voice was hardly above a whisper as he forced his words out. "I've spent the last week watching my brother suffer because of the choice you made. Next time, we do it as a group or not at all, Ara. We're a team now. I can't protect you if you don't let me." A harsh wind whipped around his feet, the damp sand flying everywhere. "You should have sent a signal. Something."

"None of you knew there was a traitor here for years, so don't blame me because I didn't figure it out. I had a plan and it all went to shit. I think we're all familiar with that. Wait, it's only been a week?"

"Yes, and I don't think my father has much time left. We need to go to him. He's been asking for you."

# Temir

*T*he world came crashing back to me as I lay on the floor and began crawling toward Nadra. Something terrible had happened. Unable to save her mother, I refused to lose her also.

"Let me help you." Rhogan put his hands under my arms and lifted. "What the fuck just happened?"

"You saw it too?"

"The ground shook, Temir."

"Shit."

Limping down the hallway, Rhogan stayed beside me, carrying the majority of my weight. I tried to push the door open, but as I had asked her to do, she had moved the chest of drawers in front of it. Rhogan helped me shove on the door until we created a big enough gap for me to slide in.

Nadra lay still on the floor with shattered glass all around her.

I scooped her up and laid her on the bed. "Nadra," I whispered.

"What's happening?" Rhogan asked from the hall.

"She's breathing. I've got this handled. Go round up the others, we have to get the hell out of here. Make sure everyone has a weapon. Especially the females.

"Got it." He pounded down the hall. I could hear his wings brushing the walls as he moved.

"Nadra?" I gently shook her shoulders. "Please wake up."

She groaned and cracked her eyes open. "Am I dead?"

"No." I forced a smile. "You aren't dead. What happened?"

"I packed both bags like you asked me and I left the glass box on the top of the dresser and waited. I heard the screaming from everyone and then everything went quiet. I was so worried something had happened. I lifted the flower, intending to put it into the smaller pack so I could carry it out, but the moment I touched the glass I got that feeling."

"Like you needed to touch the flower?"

"Yes. And I didn't mean to Temir, I promise, but somehow the box opened and I'm so sorry."

I took a step back shaking my head. "What happened to the flower?"

"I think I broke it." Tears pooled her eyes as she placed her hand on her chest, flashing a new mark on her skin.

I reached for her, examining the back of her hand for a wound I needed to heal. "Nadra, the box was charmed to only open if I willed it. But it was linked to my soul. Our soul. You didn't break the flower." I showed her the raised skin in the shape of an adda on the back of her hand. "I think you absorbed it somehow. How do you feel?"

"I've a pounding headache, but I think I hit my head."

Traces of the flower must have been left behind. The residue on her hand was enough to regenerate my nearly depleted magic. Pressing my hand to her clammy forehead, I pulled away her discomfort, and she moved to lay back down.

"I'm afraid you can't go to sleep just yet, love."

She sat upright again, finally remembering the current situation. "Is everyone okay?" She clutched my arm, filling the bond with equal parts hope and fear.

I couldn't say the words. I knew she felt the hesitation and she shook her head. "She's fine. My mother is fine. I know it."

"I'm sorry, Nadra."

"No," she cried, jumping out of the bed. "No, Temir. You can save her. Come on, you have to help me find her." She squeezed out of the room, and I followed, feeling the devastation slam into me as she found her mother's fallen body. "You have to do something," she wailed. "She can't die here. Not like this." Her shoulders trembled as tears refilled her honey-colored eyes.

"I'm so sorry, Nadra. I tried to save her. I tried. I was too late."

She shook her head and fell over her mother. I stood guard over her until Rhogan joined me, where he knelt beside Nadra and took her hand. The room was the embodiment of death. Piles of bodies and puddles of deep red blood covered the floor. Eyes of the fallen watched me as their deaths replayed in my mind.

"Your mother was a beautiful soul taken far too soon. I spent a lot of time with her down in the dungeons. She was the only bright light in the worst part of my life, and I'm so sorry you've lost her."

She leaned her head onto Rhogan, and I tried to withhold my jealousy. I was no good at comfort. Never had been.

"Come now," Rhogan told her. "We have to leave, or she will have died for nothing."

Nadra stood, hugged that giant winged male, and walked back to me, taking my hand. She would never be able to properly mourn her mother, and I wished I could change that.

I went back to the rooms, grabbed the two bags and the furs from the bed, then we left the rebel compound. Rhogan and another filled the headquarters with an accelerant, and we stood together for only a moment of prayer to release the fallen souls to the Ether as the compound burst into flames. I painted a red "x" on the broken wagon so passing rebels would know not to bother.

There were only about forty survivors, and most of them were females. We traveled for two days together until we reached the Eastern Gap. Stopping only when we had to, we ate as little as we could, and pushed ourselves harder than most of them had ever been pushed.

"What will we do?" a rebel female with a kobold's long nose and tufted ears asked as we stopped.

I shared a look with Rhogan as Nadra squeezed my hand. "You will all travel with Rhogan to the Marsh Court. You'll seek the Weaver. She will help you. You may continue to travel south with the refugees to the Flame Court, or you can stay and help the Marsh Court prepare for battle. Autus is only headed in one direction."

"What will you do?" Rhogan asked me.

"Nadra and I have a mission we have to see through to the end. Take this." I handed him one full bag. "Inside is a truth serum. Get it to the Weaver and start questioning all the rebels. If you can, plant half the seeds. The flowers bloom quickly, and we need to cultivate them. Save the second half until I get there in case we have to move again. Blue is serum, red is the antidote. They will not be able to tell a lie if they take the blue. Weed out the traitors and I'll find you as soon as I can."

He took the bag, slung it over his shoulder, and led the rebels away, leaving me and Nadra standing hand in hand on the path. I took the deepest breath I'd taken in my life. I wanted to rest. I wanted to just spend time with Nadra, feel the loss that had been weighing on us both and live in that moment, but we couldn't. We had to push on.

"What's the plan?" she asked.

"The king has the fabric, he has the sword, he has the blood of the king. He needs the ashes, the artifact, and now you and your friend in order to complete the binding. I intend to foil those plans as thoroughly as possible."

"So, you think Ara is Alewyn's Promise?"

I shrugged. "We have to assume, so I guess."

She blew into her hands for warmth, trails of her breath dissipating in the cold air. "Do you really think I have the power of the adda?"

"Can't you feel it? I touch your hand and it's nearly vibrating within you."

"I hadn't noticed at all," she said.

"I wonder . . ."

"What?" she asked, stepping away from me.

I faced the wall of mountains beside us and pinched the bridge of my nose, trying to sort my thoughts. "Do you have magic now?"

Her shoulders lifted and she shook her head. "I don't know."

"Can you access it within you? Can you feel anything out of the ordinary?"

"Nothing at all."

"We need to explore this again when we have time to sit down. For now, we have to climb a mountain."

"I'm already so cold," she protested.

"Here," I said, taking off my fur coat and wrapping it around her shoulders.

I'd made sure she was warm before we left, giving her the furs from our bed, but she was right to worry. The farther we got up the mountain the colder it was going to get. I couldn't protect myself from the cold, but I could use my magic to take the pain.

"I'm not sure exactly where we have to go, but I have a general idea. Oleonis and I had a discussion about this tree once. He told me the gods planted one tree and the northern winds carried its seeds, filling the world with saplings. It's said the wind transformed the seeds into millions of different species, but they all root from the first oak, touched by the gods."

"Do you think it's true?" she asked.

"At this point, yes. I think it's all true."

We started our long and arduous trek up the mountain. Several times, the reality of losing her mother struck her and Nadra cried. I tried my best to comfort her as Rhogan had, but there was nothing I could do but be there for her.

By nightfall, we found a shallow cave after I had killed two rabbits with arrows as we walked. We probably could have devoured both, but we shared one, saved the other, and I kept the pelt and let it dry over our small fire. They were small, but the only thing Nadra had brought with her was the needle and thread from her mother's pockets. She intended to make gloves from the rabbits.

"How long do you think it will take us to find the tree?" Nadra yawned.

"If we can get to the top of this mountain, we will be able to see down the mountain range more clearly. The tree is atop one of these mountains. I'm hoping we can see it from here and then we'll have a better idea. I want nothing more than to get out of the Wind Court."

"Me too. I'm freezing," she said.

"Come sit by me in front of the fire."

She stood and moved to me, sitting in my lap as I wrapped her into my arms and then covered us both with furs.

"I don't think I ever thanked you," I whispered into her ear.

She shrugged a shoulder, pushing away the sensation of my voice on her skin. "For what?"

"I thought I'd die in the king's dungeons. I had given up the will to live, resolved to let myself rot down there. But you saved me. You gave me more than someone to talk to."

"Do you think you would have gone through with it?"

I pulled her closer. "I thought you had denied the mating bond. Maybe you hadn't said it out loud yet, but I thought, in your heart, you had already given up on me, and you were the only person I had left."

She turned on her knees to face me. Her unruly hair blowing in the breeze entering the small cave. Her eyes enraptured me as she leaned in so close, we shared a single breath. "I could never deny you, Temir. I was lost and confused and processing a thousand different emotions, but you saved me. I could have betrayed you, but you did it anyway. The fae in the castle, they talked about you. They said how good you were, how much you helped the stable boy, and how you were always so kind to the servants. The king hated it. He wanted that kind of devotion to himself. But that's how I knew you were good before I knew you at all."

"I don't think I'm good, Nadra. I think I'm just going day by day and trying to make the best of a terrible situation."

"We are sitting in a cave on the side of a mountain. I have on my coat and yours. You're still trying to comfort me, though you are colder than I am. You are good, Temir. Even if you deny it."

I wanted her so badly, though I knew her heart was hurting. I began to crave a single touch from her, needing her skin next to mine like I needed air to breathe. She leaned in closer and I felt the desire down our bond. I slid my hands behind her neck and pulled her to me, pressing her lips to mine. She opened her mouth and I slipped my tongue in, finally tasting the mate I had longed for.

She moaned as our lips massaged each other, pressing her body to mine and stirring a heat that was not there a moment ago. Slowly, she pulled away from me, her phantom lips still lingering on mine. "We should rest," she said in a husky voice.

We laid on the cold ground and covered ourselves with everything we had. We couldn't let the fire burn because we didn't want to draw predators, so instead, we spent the night clothed but wrapped in each other's arms. I fell asleep to the soft sound of her gentle snores as she laid across my chest.

The next morning, it was hard to leave our warm cocoon of blankets. The moment we did, the heat we had created was sucked away and we were both quickly shivering. Nadra tried to insist I take my coat back, but I refused. It was only going to get colder, and I still had my magic to heal the frostbite. I wasn't comfortable, but I wouldn't die.

We left the cave behind and followed the trail up the side of the mountain. There were still fae and beasts that climbed these peaks, so we had to be careful as we traveled. I had nothing that would save us from a fall. The slope grew steeper and the trail narrow, but by midday, we had pushed to the top.

"Can you see anything?" Nadra asked as we looked down the hazy, snowcapped range.

"The fog is too thick. I think we will have to wait to see if it clears."

With wind pelting our faces, we moved down from the summit to try to protect ourselves from the frigid temperature. The rays of the sun were warm, but still, we squinted in the snow and shivered as we waited. We sat huddled, wrapped together in the furs, trying to use our breaths to keep us warm. Nadra took the time to sew the rabbit pelts. There were two gloves, she took one and I took one, squeezing both hands inside.

I left our cocoon several times to check for danger and clearing fog. On the third walk up the mountain, I still couldn't see the tree I was looking for, but I did find a familiar face. One I wasn't exuberantly happy to see.

"Mountains are time. Rivers are deceit. Do you really think you can cross the mountain rage dressed like that? Mush for brains, all of you."

"Hello, old female," I said to Aibell as she stood with her long gray hair flapping in the relentless wind.

"Gather your mate, it's time to go."

I stood still and glared at her.

"The clock moves on the wind, boy. Identical faces are almost there. You must come now."

I spun and walked back to Nadra, grumbling as I went. "It's time to go. We've earned a ride, it seems."

"What do you mean?" she asked, gathering our scattered things.

"Ever heard of Aibell?" She nodded. But clearly didn't understand. "Let's just say the nursery rhymes were wrong. Still, we need to move quickly."

We hurried back to Aibell, who eyed Nadra carefully. "What have you done, child?"

I looked to my mate and back to Aibell. "Are we going or not?" I demanded.

Nadra pinched me, and Aibell smirked. "Good girl," she said. "Now take my hand."

We placed our shivering hands on hers and the world faded away, but just as quickly as it had vanished, it slammed right back into place. Again, we stood atop a mountain, only this time, we were under the shadow of the largest oak tree I had ever seen.

"You have a day at the very most to see this through. Don't get caught."

"Can't you help us?" Nadra asked.

"I can't touch the tree, child. It comes from the gods. Temir knows what to do. I've got somewhere else I need to be as well." She handed me a large jug and said, "It's an accelerant. You're going to need it. I'll see you again."

"Hope not," I complained as she vanished.

# Ara

*Y*ou think I don't know that you are grown?" Fen stared down at me. "Do you think that changes the way my heart feels? Does it change my soul? Our soul?"

I stood in our room with my arms crossed over my chest. "No, I didn't say it did. I'm just saying that I have to be allowed to make my own choices too."

"Look what happens when you do. Greeve told me he took you to see her. Why? Why was he the one to tell me?"

"Because I knew you'd act like this," I said, fuming. He was broken. I'd done that to him. But it wasn't intentional, and he acted as if I'd purposefully cultivated this horrid situation.

He threw his hands into the air as he paced before me. "Of course I would. Do you not see the danger you're constantly putting yourself into? I'm not just your mate, Ara. I'm your Guardian. But I can't do my job if you don't fucking let me in."

"I wasn't leaving you out. I thought I was saving your father."

He blanched at that. The gaping wound of his father's current health was still fresh.

I crossed our bedroom and wrapped my arms around him. No matter how furious I was, I needed him to be okay. "I'm sorry." And I meant it. "Obviously, I didn't expect the betrayal. I sat on that seafloor and replayed that night over and over in my mind. I'm not sure if I would have done it differently, Fen. I lost my parents. Both of them. I know the pain of that loss. I would save you from that over and over again if I could. But it doesn't mean I'm not sorry for all of it."

He held me close and laid his head on mine, taking a deep, shuddering breath. We stayed like that until our hearts beat as one and the tension slowly faded away.

"You killed the sea queen," he said finally. "What will you do about the sea now?"

"I don't know. I can't worry about them right now. Only you."

"I'm sorry for being so upset with you. I know the choice you had to make wasn't easy." He pulled me tighter, and I ran my fingers through his thick black hair. "I've just been lost without you. I've lived in a constant state of panic and rage until that little sea fae came to me. I nearly killed her. Even with Kai and Greeve holding me back, I still nearly killed her. I don't just want days, Ara. Not even weeks with you. I want an entire lifetime. And even then, I don't think it will be enough."

"I didn't ask to be Alewyn's Promise. I didn't want to have to kill Morwena. I want a normal life too. But you and I, Fen, we are destined for something greater, and even if I only get one more night with you, we need to make it the best night of our entire lives. We cannot take a single moment for granted. We cannot fight like this."

He pushed back from me, his eyes searching my own. Convincing himself that I was really there. In his arms. He swept a lock of hair behind my ear and leaned his forehead down to mine. "If I didn't care so much, I wouldn't fight at all." He kissed the top of my head, and I ran my hands up and down his muscled back.

"How is King Tolero?" I asked.

He pulled me in closer, locking his arms around me. His voice broke as he whispered, "I thought we had it figured out. They'd saved the Cetani with the same poison by using my father's blood. But it's not saving him. The healer thinks it has to be foreign to the host of the poison. Coro won't take a meeting. Autus isn't an option. I think I'm going to lose him too, Ara. I think he is going to die."

I forced a breath, pushing back the tears threatening to come. This wasn't my Fen. He was always strong. Always sure. Something in his vulnerability shook me to my core. "Shall we go see him?"

He nodded and we left, our footsteps as heavy as our hearts as we rounded up the others and stood outside the king's bedroom door. Asha, Efi's cetani, paced on the roof above us, as if she knew what was happening below. I tried to swallow the sharp lump in my throat as Fen trembled. My dark and fierce warrior was lost in his own sorrow.

"I can't do this. I can't walk into that room knowing it might be the last time I see him alive," Fen said, completely broken.

"Can you guys give us just a few minutes?" I asked the rest of the group standing with us.

They walked halfway down the hall. I gave them a fierce look, but they only backed up a few more paces. They would not leave their brother, and I couldn't blame them for it.

"When my parents died, I only had the chance to say goodbye to my mother, and she wouldn't let me. She was too busy shoving me toward you. If I could go back and do it again, I would stop her and tell her how much I loved her. How much she meant to me and how desperately I wished I could have changed so many things. Take the opportunity you're given and say goodbye to him, Fenlas." Tears filled my eyes, and I squeezed his hand as he forced a breath.

"Come with me?"

"Always."

He opened the door and we found Inok, sleeping, hunched over the king's bed, holding his hand. Tolero groaned and shifted. "He hasn't left my side," the king whispered.

Fen crossed the room and shook him by the shoulders. He jerked awake and jumped to his feet. "Take a break, Inok. Go see Loti in the kitchens. She's a mess."

He cleared his throat and looked to the king, who nodded softly. "I'll see you again, brother," he promised.

My heart wrenched at the weakness of his voice. I could barely swallow as I watched Inok leave the room. The king began to cough until he could scarcely drag a ragged breath into his wounded lungs.

Fen sat next to him on the bed, helping him sit up.

"Hurts," he rasped.

"We're going to find a way to beat this. We'll find the antidote, Father."

I could feel the guilt within his lie down the bond, and I could do nothing but stand and wait beside him, exuding calmness that I did not feel as I watched the kindest soul suffer.

*You have to tell him goodbye, Fen. You have to say the words or you will regret it.*

Time slowed as my chest tightened and my eyelids burned. *I know.*

"There's something I want to say to you," he began. His father reached for his shaking hand. "I'm sorry I never went to visit Mother. I'm sorry you've had to go alone for all these years, wearing the burden of the crown and the loss of your mate alone."

"You lost your mother, Fenlas." He coughed, covering his mouth with a handkerchief. "I'll never fault you for how you chose to deal with that."

"You've always taught me . . ." Fen cleared his throat, trying to hold back the tears. "You've always taught me to be better, to do better. I promise I'll always keep those lessons with me. I won't leave this world as damaged as I found it, Father. You've raised me better than that, and I want to thank you for it."

He burst into tears, and the king pulled him into his arms. I stood and watched the male who held himself a thousand feet tall transform into a child seeking comfort in his dying father's arms. Tears tracked down my face as I witnessed the devastation and wished more than anything that I could save them both.

The king began to cough until he was retching up blood. Tremors wracked his body, and Fenlas pulled away to hand him a fresh handkerchief.

"Ara," he wheezed, reaching for me. "Give us a moment, son."

Fen looked at me, still crying, and I audibly swallowed as I nodded to him. He silently stepped out as I moved to sit beside King Tolero on the bed.

"Come closer, my dear," he whispered.

I tried not to jostle the bed as I scooted in.

He took my hand and placed it into his lap. "When I go, you must take care of my boy."

I nodded, biting my lip and holding my breath so I wouldn't cry.

"I will join my Efi soon, and I don't want you to be sad about that. She's waiting for me. Make sure he knows."

Again, I nodded, sniffling and clenching my teeth to hold back the wail.

"Soon, the pain will be so severe, I will suffer greatly, just as she did. I'm already feeling the poison working through my body. You're the only one," he coughed. "You're the only one who can end the suffering. No one else is strong enough."

"I don't understand." I broke, tears racing down my cheeks.

"You do. You must put me out of my misery. Send me to be with my mate."

I shook my head and stood from the bed. I took several steps back, trying desperately to fill my lungs. I couldn't do what he was asking of me. I wouldn't. "He would never forgive me."

"Give me a moment alone with my son."

I moved to the door and cracked it open. Fen was somewhere lost in the arms of the others standing just outside the door.

*He's asking for you.*

We traded places. Me standing outside and Fen entering the king's room alone. I felt only sorrowful despair, and I had no idea if it was

Fen's or my own. I stood inches from that solid wooden door remembering a king who sat beside me on a hilltop and told me stories of my own father with a gleam in his eye.

Wren slid her hand into mine as I struggled for air. Greeve took my other hand and Kai stood behind me with his hands on my shoulders. Tears covering all of our faces we waited, knowing these were Fen's last moments with his father and there was nothing any of us could do to spare him.

The bond jerked the moment the king told Fen what he had requested. Denial, rage, and then understanding moved through me until the door cracked open and Fenlas, with red-ringed eyes, stepped out and nodded once to me. *Do it.*

"Are you sure?" My voice cracked. I sniffled and moved to the door.

He nodded, and they all pulled him back into their arms. I could do this. I could do it for Fen, who couldn't do it on his own. I would end the king's suffering. No one deserved to die in pain. I stepped back into the room, and though the king was sitting up, his eyes were closed, and I thought maybe he had already passed.

"Please." This king's soft voice flooded my ears.

I moved to sit beside him on the bed and pulled out the knife I'd strapped on after returning home. The cold metal bit into my skin and my hands shook.

"Don't let my boy spend his life ruling. Make sure he gets to live. Give him a child," he rasped. "And make sure someone looks after Inok."

I bowed my head, no longer trying to hold back my stinging tears. My sobs.

"Your parents would be so proud of you, my girl."

I nodded. "Are you sure?" I gulped, my throat so thick it was nearly closed.

"Do it now." He laid back on the bed, a smile upon his ancient face.

*Forgive me.*

I plunged the knife into King Tolero's heart and the Cetani's scream from the roof matched my own wail as I ended the king's suffering and ignited my own. I pulled my knife, dropped it onto the floor and walked out of that fated room. Fen tried to stop me, but I didn't halt. I passed Inok, who ran into the king's chambers, and I heard his body crumble to the floor.

My feet moved below me until I was outside of the castle, away from prying eyes. I fell to my knees and screamed for all the world to hear because life was never fair and even the good ones died. Because I wasn't strong enough to look into Fen's eyes and I wasn't sure I ever would be again. He had allowed me to kill his father, but there was no way he'd truly forgive me for that. It was the only thing I was good at. Destruction.

Something within me shifted as the word came to mind. Annihilation. Obliterate. My heart stopped. The world stopped. All this time I hadn't known what my magic was. What moved and pressed upon me, even now, even in this utter misery. My magic was simply destruction. I was built to ruin it all. And be ruined. My soul chipping away each time I chose to use that so-called gift.

"It is not fair, girl. Your life never will be." Aibell stood in front of me with her boney arms extended, the arms of her robes nearly touching the ground.

I wanted to hate her for not saving me from this, but how could I? This was fate. She didn't have a say in any of it either. She pulled me from the ground and held me while I sobbed. "I don't understand why."

"Not everything is to be understood, child." She gently pushed me away, and I stared into her giant eyes, wondering what she was trying to tell me. "There are still things in this foreign world I do not yet understand."

Foreign. I wouldn't push, wouldn't even ask tonight. But she'd just confirmed this was not her world. But why would she stay here?

I stood straighter and wiped the tears from my eyes. "I'm being selfish. This isn't about me. For one brief moment, I had a father again, and now he is gone by my own hands. But Fen . . ."

*I'm sorry.*

He didn't answer.

"He does not blame you, child. His parents are already together, but you must go to him. He is a king now. His first duty, as king, will be to plan his father's funeral. He will need you."

"Will you stay?" I asked as I turned to face the illuminated castle in the distance.

"Apparently so," she said. "But you must know something. About your power, Ara. A rock may be crushed as easily as the mountain. Like all things, magic comes with a cost. Fenlas is your Guardian to protect you from your own magic, not from others. Each time, there will be a tear in your soul if you use the magic as you did with Morwena. Fenlas will be the anchor that brings you back, but he will also suffer. There is a limit. You will destroy yourself if you aren't careful. That is the cost of that much magic."

"Just another thing I can't actually control." My chin quivered as I pushed down those feelings. They wouldn't change anything.

Walking back to the castle was like dragging boulders. I knew eventually we would get where we were going, but each step was its own journey. As we walked into the king's bedroom, I knew I'd have to face what I'd done. They were all there, silently paying their respects. Someone had pulled the quilted blanket up to his chin and my knife was no longer on the floor. I walked to Fen, who opened his arms to me. Loti and Inok stood hand in hand crying together. Kai held Wren as she shook with tears while Greeve and Fen stood stoic. I thought they'd hate me. I thought they wouldn't be able to look at me, but instead, they took turns embracing me.

When Greeve pulled me into his arms, he leaned in and whispered, "It was a gift." My knees buckled and he held me upright as I began to cry again. Fen pulled me away, and though his sorrow was greater than my own, though the tears were still fresh in his eyes, he still offered me comfort. He ran his hands up and down my arms as he studied my face, making sure I was okay.

We stayed with Tolero until Loti made everyone go to their rooms. She promised dinner would be delivered, and we all obeyed, knowing she needed to be in the kitchens, moving her hands and keeping herself busy.

"Where do we go from here?" I asked Fen as he stood on the balcony staring at Efi's Isle.

"Now, we make plans. Now, I have to rule a kingdom." His voice was numb. He was a million miles away.

I made him tea and placed it into his hands. Then I poured in half a glass of liquor and lifted it until he drank.

It wasn't long until the knocks on the door became frequent and we were soon joined by Kai, Greeve and Wren. They couldn't be apart. Not now. Not when they knew Fen was hurting so badly, though he didn't show it. He showed almost no emotion. He just stood, watching the ocean waves.

"The pyre will be ready tomorrow night?" he finally asked Greeve.

"You're sure you want it on the isle?"

"It's what he would have wanted."

The guys continued drinking on the balcony while Wren and I lay in the bed. "Do you think he'll be okay?" I asked, pulling at the threads of the blankets.

"I know he will be. If nothing else, running the kingdom will keep him distracted from his own mourning."

"That's what I'm worried about. If he doesn't deal with it . . ."

"Then make him deal with it."

"I can't make him do anything."

I watched his profile in the moonlight. Silent tears slipped down his face at random times. I noticed the way Kai and Greeve tried to get him to smile and failed. I felt the pain a thousand times stronger than any emotion Fen had ever sent me before. Eventually the entourage left, and though I tried, he didn't come to bed. He stayed on the balcony until the sun rose. He didn't eat. He barely looked at me until the sun began to fall and it was time.

We dressed in silence, walked the halls in silence, and passed the gathering fae filling the beach in silence, until Fenlas turned to the crowd of thousands of sorrowful faces, fell to his knees, bent to the ground, and wept with them all as Greeve began to sing over the crowd. The crowd moved as one to join the prince on the ground as the vibrato in the song cut through the stillness in the chilled air. They all reached forward, a hand on the fae in front of them until they were connected like a web of fae. I knelt beside my prince and tried to stay strong as his body shuddered, finally letting go and crying for his fallen father.

I couldn't help the guilt that crept up my body. I let Greeve's song pull every emotion from me as he sang so beautifully. The deep voice of a male in the crowd joined him and then the harmony of a female, and within several minutes, a sobbing kingdom was on their knees singing for a king that changed the world. A king that harbored fae the world would have killed. A king that raised a son on his own after his mate was taken from him. A king that cooked in the kitchens and prowled the streets like a soldier. A king that set the bar so high, no one would ever compare.

We stood and Fen helped me into the boat, leaving Wren, Kai and Greeve standing on the shore while Inok joined us as we rode the still waters to the Isle. I felt out of place. Like one of them should have been here instead of me. I was the fraud. They had all lost a male they had known their whole lives.

The boat slid onto the shore and we stepped out. Fen pulled it onto the beach as we stood on the shoreline. Inok climbed the hill. We watched him from behind as the faeries across the bay remained quiet and still. He lifted the torch to the sky and Fen waved his trembling hand, his power igniting the torch.

This was the first time Fen had stepped foot on this isle. It was the one thing his father had always wanted from him, and he had come without protest. He would never enjoy his time here, but now that his feet dug into the sand and he was rooted to this land, it would always mean something to him.

Inok dropped the torch and the pyre ignited.

"I never said the words," he whispered as the orange light from the distant fire danced in his eyes.

*Which words?*

182

"I never said goodbye to him."

"The words you did say were beautiful. Thank you is just as good as goodbye."

"I'll never be as good as he was." He clenched his jaw and his shoulders fell. "Did you know the Flame Court used to be filled with fire faeries? The icaris. Tiny flames with wings that burned so hot they were blue. They are legends here mostly." He paused, studying the empty sky. "As a boy, I learned they appeared on the day of my father's coronation, long ago. They vanished during the Iron Wars when the world went black. They've been gone for so long, I've never seen one. I don't think my mother ever saw one either. But my father would tell me stories of their revelry and how he'd learned they were hiding from the hopelessness in this world. They were an omen for him. For his reign as king. He'd seen a million things; he'd experienced it all. Each of his decisions came from years and years of wisdom. I'll never fill those shoes."

"You already are, and you will, because you are his son."

He covered his face with his hands briefly, then pulled them away as his voice shook. "Do you think they are together now? My parents?"

"Of course they are. All six of them are looking down on us now. They will guide us from the Ether."

"Thank you," he said, finally looking down at me.

"For what?"

"For being strong enough to ease his pain when I couldn't."

"Never again." I shook my head. "Please never ask me to do that again."

"I promise," he said as the voices from the shoreline began to pray, and we joined them.

*"Into lightness and darkness, into shadows and mist, may you rest for eternity. Over the mountains and beneath the sea, let your souls find peace. May nature keep your soul, the wind hold your memories, the river bless your spirit and the fire carry you away."*

Fen held me in his arms as we said our final goodbye to the king that lived two thousand years.

# CHAPTER 16

# Temir

*I*n theory, the next part of our job was simple. Burn down a tree and hide the ashes so the evil king and his henchmen couldn't use them to help destroy the world by taking control of an unparalleled power. In theory. But as Nadra and I now stood at the base of the biggest tree I'd ever seen, while the clock ticked in the background, there was no questioning the challenge we were about to face. Fifty fae could have circled the trunk.

I knew how to grow trees. It was what I had spent most of my life doing with Oleonis. But I also knew how to kill them. I would have to use the power I'd kept to myself for so long and trust that Nadra wouldn't be terrified of me when it was done.

"Stand back," I told her, setting the bag and the accelerant on the ground at her feet.

I walked up to the tree, put my hands at the base and called forth the magic that took life instead of giving it. As I pushed it through the depths of the tree, it began to die, but I also knew I'd be drained long before I could push my magic through the roots. Still, I worked and worked until it dawned on me.

"Nadra," I whispered, "the adda."

She sat beside me and rubbed her hands for warmth. "I'm so sorry, Temir."

"No, no. I'm not blaming you." I placed my hand upon her cheek before I realized what I was doing. She closed her eyes and leaned in like it was the most natural thing in the world. I rested my forehead against hers, our frozen noses touching.

"Temir?"

"Sorry." I pulled away, refocusing. "I'm pulled to you the way you were pulled to the adda. Every time I touched the flower it replenished my magic and now it's your power."

"Let's try, then."

I held out a hand and she took it into both of hers. "I'm going to call my magic forward on the count of three. I have no clue what's going to happen, so whatever you do, don't let go of my hand."

Tension and worry settled on her face more prominently than I could feel down the bond. She was trying to shelter her nerves from me.

"One … two … three." The tiny bit of magic I called forward became a rush of death. "It worked. Not only did it work, but my magic isn't drained."

"What does that even mean?" Her hands trembled.

"You refilled my magic with a simple touch. You just became a thousand more times valuable to the king. We can't tell anyone, Nadra. Are you hurt?"

"N-no," she stuttered. "I'm fine."

186

I watched her carefully, looking for signs of fatigue or pain. Only trepidation. "One more time should do it, then, if you're sure?" She nodded and closed her eyes. "One . . . two . . . three."

Again, the magic ripped from me and into the base of the tree until it was completely dried out and cracking in the breeze. We had to burn this tree down as quickly as we could. Fortunately, at least the wind was blowing south. The ashes wouldn't go directly to Autus, but a burning tree at the top of a mountain would be the biggest beacon we could ever make.

Nadra stood back as I doused the tree in as much of the solution Aibell gave me as I could. I wanted to climb the tree and pour it down the trunk, but there was no time, and I'd never be able to get back down without getting it all over me.

I knelt at the trunk once more and placed kindling along the bottom. Nadra blocked the wind with her hands and I struck the flint until one tiny ember sparked the dry bits. I took her hand. We jumped backward as fast and far as we could while the first tree in the world burst into blue flames.

I had no idea what that old hag gave me, but whatever it was worked like a fae charm because within minutes, the tree was completely engulfed. I never believed we would burn that tree to ash within twenty-four hours, considering how wide the trunk was, but as I watched the top crack and splinter, I now believed it was a possibility.

"I think I can feel the magic in the tree, Temir. It's like it calls to me."

I moved to sit behind Nadra and held her in my arms as we let the tree's pyre warm us. "I'm sure it shares a type of magic with you. Something in Autus' binding spell probably calls to the power of the adda. I guess now we just wait. What shall we do with our time?"

A wicked little smile crossed her face.

I matched it with my own. "As much as I'd love to show you what I'd rather be doing right now, I'm not sure this is the best place for that."

"I'd rather not freeze my ass off," she giggled. The sound was music. Literal music as a hint of happiness resonated between us like pealing bells. "Should we look and see if the king's soldiers are coming?"

Moving to the edge of the jagged mountain, we peered over the side to find nothing but a frozen landscape of fir trees and endless winter. "The wind is starting to pick up, so even if they are climbing this mountain, they will have to stop for the night."

A giant crack from the burning tree snapped through the air and a massive branch crashed into the rugged mountain top.

"Good thing we weren't naked," Nadra teased as she pushed away the floating embers filling the air.

We spent the night watching the tree fall apart bit by bit. By morning, there was a blanket of gray smoke and the ashes were thick, layering the ground like fresh snowfall. Still, we tried to sweep them away, counting our blessings that the wind continued to blow south, into the Marsh Court.

I'd been watching for the soldiers over the northern edge of the summit, and early in the morning, we finally spotted them climbing. They had some distance to go, but there was still about four foot of stump burning like molten lava within the hard, outer core of the blackened bark. Nadra and I were both covered in soot, and no matter how much we tried to keep them away, there were ashes everywhere.

"Seriously, Temir. Do you think it's a lost cause?"

"Do you want to give up?"

188

She rubbed her red eyes and shook her head, coughing. "I'm in this with you. If you want to stay and try to see it through, then we will. But we have no idea how deep into the mountain those roots go. I don't think we can fight all six of those males on our own and continue this fight. If the wind shifts at all, it will all be in vain anyway."

"You're right. I've been thinking the same. The only thing I know for sure is that the fire moved down just as much as it moved up. The roots are practically lava right now." I wiped soot from my face and my hands came away black.

"So, what can we do?"

"I could try chopping at the burnt bark with my sword until that molten part spills all over the ground. I believe it would become cool and then frozen. Not ash, but also not something they could reignite."

She tilted her head and eyed me warily. "Why do I sense hesitation?"

"Because it's going to ruin the only weapon we have, and we still have to travel down this mountain and through the Marsh Court."

"We can find another weapon, Temir." She bit her lip and looked toward the edge. "You have to do it."

I stood and pulled my sword from the sheath lying on the ground next to our pack. "It's going to come pouring out and I can't predict where it's going to go. Just stay back."

She nodded and I moved to the opposite side of the trunk. I hacked and hacked the sword against the burnt crust of bark until it slowly began to crack, and just as I expected, it poured out of the hollowed-out trunk, causing what was left of it to collapse.

"It's time to go," I told her. "There's nothing else we can possibly do here. We can only hope that tar dries and seals off the rest of the tree.

"And the ash all over the top of the mountain?"

"It's in the gods' hands now."

"But it's not really," a familiar voice said from behind us. I spun around to see the damn twin harpies Autus loved so dearly, their wings flapping loudly as they gathered ashes from the ground. "The one true king thanks you for doing all the hard work." In an instant, they soared off the edge of the mountain, their large, veined wings opened in the wind as they drifted away. The males climbing the mountain were only a distraction.

"Shit." I slammed my damaged sword into the ground. "All of that for nothing."

Nadra grabbed my hands and pulled me. "Come on. There's not time for this. We need to get out of here before they come back."

"It makes you even less safe. If he finds out about the adda, Nadra . . ." My voice softened. "He will hunt you, and there's nowhere in this world you can go."

"The safest place we can be is with the southern prince and his mate. If the king is hunting her, then he will have an army between them. We have to go south, Temir."

"We've got to stop on the way. I need Rhogan."

She nodded. "Then let's go get him."

The trip down the mountain was long, steep, and by the time we made it to the bottom, my muscles ached, but I had never been so happy to stand on flat ground. The air was warmer on the south side and we were able to travel just off the main road, avoiding the maze forest since I no longer had a weapon. Still, we traveled mostly at night, when it wasn't safe to sleep, and we rested only when we had to.

Within a week, we were standing just outside of Hythe, staring at a little barn I knew was covered in glass inside.

"What are we doing here?" Nadra asked.

"I'm checking on a friend before we find Rhogan." I opened the door to the barn and smiled, dragging Nadra behind me when I heard a young boy's giggle. We walked up the glass steps, and I cleared my throat.

"Temir," River shouted, running for me and flinging himself into my arms.

"Hey Rock," I said, ruffling his hair.

He hugged me tight for several minutes and then pulled away, looking at Nadra. "Where's Gaea?"

"Haven't you seen her?"

He shook his head. "Not for a while."

"I'm sure you'll see her soon. Can you take my friend Nadra down and show her the glass sculptures while I talk to Alavon?"

"Sure."

He dragged Nadra down the stairs, and I faced his new father.

"Good to see you," he said, watching River closely.

"He's fine, I promise." I smiled. Happy to see that little stable boy was so well cared for. "We need to talk."

"Have a seat." He gestured to the familiar glass chairs, adjusted his glasses, and sat across from me.

"I don't have a lot of time to spend here, unfortunately. I've come to beg you to go south. I know you're working with the rebellion and

I'm sure they keep you plenty busy here, but I can promise you Autus is about to come and it's not safe here anymore."

He looked around the room, studying his life's work and shaking his head. "I'm not sure I can leave, Temir. The beautiful things I've created are the only things we have. What would we do in the Flame Court? What use would we be there?"

"The same use that you are here, only there you could live freely. Sell your wares from a shop without fear."

His eyes met mine, and I could see he considered it.

"Tea?" his wife said from behind me. I had no idea how she always knew to bring tea.

"What do you think?" he asked her.

"I think we've no choice, my love. We have to keep our River safe. If Temir thinks it's the only way, then I suppose he's probably right."

"I'm headed to the rebel headquarters this afternoon. I'll have a talk with the Weaver and see what she thinks," he said, not committing one way or the other.

"We'll join you. I'm headed there myself." I stood.

"I'll stay here with River," his mate said while we walked down the stairs.

"Be extra cautious of guests," I warned her. "King Autus will be coming."

She rushed to River's side, and he hugged her, leaving Nadra behind. I knew she'd have questions for me later, but for now, we had to get to the rebels and see what was left of them.

Before long, we were riding in the back of the glass maker's covered cart, headed for the large village. Nadra studied the outdoors as the flap lifted in the wind. She missed home. I could feel the peace within her as she closed her eyes and let the calm of familiarity settle over her.

"We could stay. If this is what you want."

She shook her head. "Someday, I want to come back here. This is where I want to be more than any place in the world, but right now, we have to go south. You know that."

I nodded. "Thank you for being so understanding and logical."

"Just don't tell anyone. I have a reputation to uphold around here," she said, winking at me.

Something about the warmer weather had lightened her spirit, and I could hardly get enough of her these past few days. We'd come so close so many times, but rationally we knew it wouldn't be safe to stop for frivolous activities. We had to travel quickly, but the moment we were somewhere relatively safe, she was all mine. And she knew it.

"Just ahead," Alavon called out. We braced ourselves as the carriage pulled to a stop.

I stepped out and Nadra followed, taking my hand as she always did.

"It's that building there. You'll want to knock three times, pause a beat and knock twice more. I've got to take this piece over to Beften's place, but I'll be there shortly," he said, tapping on the glass gnome he had brought along.

We followed instructions and were met by several rebel guards at the door. They let us in, only because we knew the knock, but eyed us carefully as I asked for Rhogan and the Weaver.

"They're in the back," one guard said, stepping closer to me than I liked.

I pulled Nadra behind me, and he smiled carefully as he passed, leading us down the dimly lit hall into a room filled with lesser fae having intimate conversations amongst themselves as they dined and played cards at several tables.

"Thank fuck," I heard Rhogan say as we entered a large warehouse room. "I can take it from here, Grend," Rhogan said, clapping me on the back.

"I bet you can," the guard mumbled and went back to his post.

"Sorry about that," Rhogan said. "Everyone here's been on edge lately. The truth serum has revealed a few traitors and we are cleaning house."

"I suppose we have you to thank for that," the Weaver said, moving over to us. "It's been quite helpful."

"I'm glad to see it finally put to use."

"We haven't gotten any of the other flowers to grow yet, but I kept half the seeds, like you asked."

"Good. The flowers will likely need a bit more time."

"I think you need to take your serum to the new king. He's going to need all the help he can get," the Weaver said.

"New king?"

"King Tolero was killed. Fenlas is soon to be crowned king of the Flame Court. And since they are mostly funding the rebellion and taking in anyone who needs sanctuary, we need to get him some help."

Nadra and I shared a glance. "Great. Because that's just where we were headed. And you're coming with us?" I asked Rhogan.

He flashed his toothy smile at me, and Nadra giggled.

# Ara

This was it. This was the day Fen had to get out of bed and take on a kingdom. I knew his heart was still heavy, the loss of his father so very fresh, but today was more than that. Today, before he left this room, we had to have a very difficult talk, and as I lay wide awake in bed, his naked body curled up with mine, I stared at the ceiling, preparing for the thousand different reactions he might have.

"Fen." I nudged him.

"Five more minutes," he grumbled, pulling me into the warmth of his body.

And I would give him those minutes because this day was the single day that would change the rest of his life forever. This was the day the prince of the Flame Court became the king. I could feel all the emotions he was feeling, and our bond became a weight between us as I tried to help him. But there was nothing more I could do for him than what we all were doing. Offering him support as he stepped into his father's shoes, feeling inadequate and lost the entire time.

The small castle staff had already tried to talk him into taking his parent's rooms, and not only was that a no, it was a hell no. Officially, Wren, Kai and Greeve moved into the castle and were added to Fen's new council, but Kai and Leora had gone to the ocean to try to help the sand settle there. I would attend the public meetings but decided to keep my distance from the things they discussed in private. I knew if there was anything Fen wanted to talk to me about, he would. Eventually.

It had been just over a week since his father's funeral, and his work as interim king had already demanded so much of his time, we were barely seeing each other. If not for our bond, I would have been worried. He still came to bed every night, and somehow, we began to define a new normal.

"Has the sun risen yet?" he mumbled into my ear.

"I think you can see the light in the room." I laughed.

"Let's pretend like it didn't," he protested, squeezing me until I could hardly breathe.

"Happily." I pulled the blankets up over our heads as his heated hands began to roam my body.

Since I'd been home from the sea incident, he'd taken me in every room and every way that he could, as often as he could, and I'd let him, never getting enough of him. Never fully being able to let him go as he was called away time and time again.

Eventually, we got out of bed and I poured him tea as we stood together on the balcony. "I know this is the biggest day of your life," I started. "But there's something I want to talk to you about.

196

Something I should have told you as soon as I saw you after Nealla, but I just couldn't find the words."

"I'm listening," he said, blowing on the hot cup of tea.

His captivating eyes met mine and for a second, I hesitated to say anything at all. This could change everything or nothing.

"You've never asked me about the second half of my prophecy, even though that's what we went through The Mists to figure out."

"I assumed if there was something to tell me, you would when you were ready."

"I think I'm ready now."

He set his cup down and took my hand, lifting my fingers to his mouth and gently kissing each and every one while he stared into my soul.

*I love you. It won't change a thing. I promise.*

*You've never said those words to me.*

"I love you," he said out loud, leaning down to kiss each side of my neck, my ears and my head. "I've loved you since the moment you socked that asshole in the bar."

I laughed. Actually, genuinely laughed.

Fen held me so tight I could feel his heart beating. "I know you're worried. I can feel it through our bond, but I'm not going anywhere. I promise."

"Nealla told me," I began and then paused, taking in a deep breath. "It's just easier if I tell you the poem."

"Whatever you need." He rested his chin on my head as he held me.

"Four thrones, four crowns,

North, South, Sea and West.

One Fae, One Will,

Must kill them all and free the rest."

His hands dropped to his side. He shook his head and stepped away as the shock rattled our bond. "You knew?" he accused, squinting. "You knew you were fated to kill my father and you never told me?"

"I never would have done it, Fenlas. Under any other circumstances, I wouldn't have."

"That's not the point," he said as he looked away, gripping his dark hair. "And now you have to kill Coro and Autus too?"

"We do," I said. "You're still my Guardian."

He scoffed. "Some fucking Guardian I am, huh? I can't protect you from being kidnapped. I can't protect my father from being poisoned under my own nose. I can't even protect myself from the shit that keeps happening. It's just blow after fucking blow, and some days it's a miracle I'm still standing."

"Fen, none of those things were your fault. I should have told you. But how do you tell the only person in the world you love that you're fated to kill his beloved father? How does one even find words for that?"

"I guess you don't. You just keep it to yourself until the opportunity comes up and then you kill two birds with one fucking stone. Fate is happy and the king is dead."

He stormed out of the room, slamming the door behind him, and for the first time since we'd arrived, I wished I had never come to the Flame Court. Where everyone loved him, and I was just the mate. Just the baggage.

Within minutes I was standing in the training ring with Gaea, armed to the teeth with wooden knives and mad as hell.

"If you kill me, I'm going to fucking haunt you," she warned. Any other day I would have laughed, appreciated her fire, but not today. Today I just wanted to fuck something up.

"You're sure you want to do this?" Greeve said from the sidelines.

"For the thousandth time, yes," she snapped.

She wasn't armed. She wore shallow padding and her job was simple. Dodge the wooden knives before they hit her. I'd tried to be gentle, but I just didn't have it in me today. I flicked my wrist so fast the first one landed right in her chest before she could spirit away.

"Fuck." She rubbed her chest, grimacing.

"Say the word and we can stop." I raised an eyebrow to her.

"Not today, Princess."

Wrong choice of words. Again, I flicked the knife. This time she spirited but took the knife with her, and it still smacked her in the arm. The banter stopped as she nodded. She was ready again. This time I faked it, waited for her to reappear and nailed her in the thigh.

"Damnit Ara, give her a break," Greeve seethed.

"If you can't handle it, go find something else to do, you broody ass male," she growled at him.

I fucking liked her.

She nodded again, and I flicked the next knife, barely missing her shoulder. She paused to celebrate while I tumbled and cracked her in the back.

Greeve was nearly beside himself. Apparently, *he'd* signed up to be *her* stupid Guardian.

"Go find something else to do, Greeve," I ordered. Not that I had any right to order him around. I didn't have a right to order anyone around because I was just the darn mate. Still, he stalked off.

"What's his deal?" Gaea asked, panting.

"Don't ask me for advice right now. I'm just as miserable as he is."

"That bad huh?" she asked, wiping her neck with a cloth.

"It's just, Fen expects me to be perfect—to do every single thing exactly as he would, even though we are two totally different people, raised in two entirely different ways."

"So, you don't just sit around staring at each other? I thought mates were madly in love forever."

"Don't get me wrong, I love him. That doesn't mean I agree with him. I have my own mind."

"Trust me, I don't think anyone would argue with that," she said, tossing the towel down and nodding to begin again.

I threw the next knife and it missed, but the next three hit her hard, and she had to break again.

"I've been meaning to ask you. Morwena mentioned The Hunt several times, you said."

I nodded.

"Well your father was part of The Hunt, right?"

"Yeah."

"It just seems important, that's all. Like of all the things he could have been doing, he chose to stay a member of the Hunt, even though working under King Coro would have put you at greater risk."

"I mean, as far as I knew, that was his job before they adopted me."

"Right, but your father was a warrior. He could have done anything. He could have walked away. Why would he choose to stay with them but also refuse to lead them, like you said?"

I shrugged. "I'm not sure."

"I think it's important and we should look into it, that's all. If it mattered so much to your father, it should matter to us too. If he was as smart as everyone says."

"He was," I said coldly.

"Okay." She nodded again, ready for another knife.

I flicked the final knife in my hand. She spirited away and it thunked right into the fence post. "Swords?" I asked.

"You really are pissed at Fen." She walked to the wall of practice weapons and grabbed two. "You know I suck at this, so be gentle."

"I'm always gentle." I smiled.

"Liar." She laughed.

We practiced, and I taught her move after move, until we were both drenched in sweat and I had to get back and bathe before Fen's coronation.

"Did I miss the show?" Greywolf asked as I walked past him.

"Sorry. Maybe tomorrow. Hey, I wanted to ask you about something." I pivoted, walking back to him. "You said you were from the Winterlands?"

His eyes doubled in size and he slowly nodded.

"Is that a secret you're not supposed to tell?"

Again, he nodded.

"But we're friends, aren't we Grey?"

"Sure, yes, Sir. We are friends," he said with a crooked smile.

"So, if I needed to know about your home, you could tell me, your friend?"

He shrugged.

"Maybe not today, Grey. But we should talk about it soon. In case it's important."

"Okay," he said, relieved he didn't have to say anything more.

"I'll see you tonight? For the coronation?"

"I'll be on guard duty," he said, his face dropping a little.

"I'll make sure Loti saves you a plate."

He clapped and I walked away. I still had to find Fen. Even though I was mad at what he said, I still wanted to be there for him. Opening the bedroom door, I found him sitting on the edge of the bed with his head in his hands, hair a mess from tugging at it.

"Fen, I—"

"I'm sorry," he blurted out. "You deserve so much better, Ara."

I closed the door, crossed my arms, and waited.

"I told you it wouldn't change anything, and it doesn't. I'm not mad at you. I never was. I'm mad at everything else that's happening. I'm mad that I can't protect you from your fate. I'm mad because the only thing that stops fate is death and I can't protect you from that. I'm mad because my father died. I'm mad because I'm just not ready at all." He lowered his head again, letting the utter devastation consume him.

"Do you think your father was ready, Fen?"

"He never told me, and I never got to ask."

"You may always look to the past, but you must never stay there. It's okay that you didn't ask and aren't ready. It just means you understand how big of a role this will be. But you will never fail, Fen." I crossed the room and kneeled before him. "I don't know what's going to happen tomorrow, or the next day, or in ten years, but I know one thing with absolute certainty. You will run this kingdom and leave

202

a legacy, just like your father did. One day, our son will sit where you do now and wonder how he will ever be as great as his own father."

His eyes met mine. "You've thought about children?"

"I've lived our entire lives in my dreams."

"Will you tell me about them?"

I moved closer and sent him a vivid picture. *It's only what I imagine. What I hope for.*

*It's perfect,* he whispered.

"We will get there one day at a time. Today is only the beginning and tomorrow is just another day.

"I wish I had your confidence." He pulled me onto his lap.

"I'm drowning in all of this, just like you are. But I'm not going to sit here and dwell on it. I refuse to let the reality of our circumstances compromise our happiness."

"So, your aggravated training session with Gaea was just showing off all your happiness?" he smirked.

"Greeve is such a tattletale."

"I'll be sure to pass the message along."

"Must be a drac thing." I rolled my eyes.

He huffed.

"There's something else I wanted to talk to you about. Something that Gaea said."

"Can it wait? Just for one day?"

A firm knock at the door interrupted us.

"I guess it will have to."

"Come in," he called.

Frair walked in with several other staff. Some carrying fabrics and soaps, some food. Thank the gods. "It's time," she said, kneeling low to the ground.

I was allowed a quick bath and then Fen was shoved into the bathing room while I tried not to complain as she draped my body in a long-beaded fabric that covered my breasts, crossed over my navel with a ruby circle band, and then draped around my lower body, pinned low at my hips. She added a necklace. It was tight and dainty in the front, but a long band of perfectly spaced, matching rubies lined my spine.

She pulled my hair back and pinned it only on the sides, leaving a loose plait at the top. She lined my eyes with kohl, added colored powder to my cheeks and stained my lips a deep blood red. I stood before the mirror and hardly recognized myself.

"You are nearly the queen now," she said, standing behind me. "You must remind our people what that means."

I nodded, not able to tear my eyes away from the reflection. The door to the bathing room opened, and Fenlas walked out shirtless, with black trousers matching the dark ink on his chest. The hair on his jawline was trimmed and his jet-black hair was slicked back. The moment his eyes fell on me, the bond snapped tight.

"Out," he ordered the room full of servants.

"You mustn't touch her," Frair warned.

"Out," he barked, his feet already moving toward me.

They scurried out of the room, not bothering to grab their trays as he wrapped his firm hands around my exposed waist, reminding me that he was strong, fierce and lethal. Heat rolled from him so heavily, I thought he might start the room on fire. Those beautiful eyes of his roamed every inch of my tingling body.

"Save it, Prince. You've got a tight schedule."

"You are mine," he growled.

I could only nod as the beast within him spoke directly to my own. He dipped me backward and began kissing the space between my breasts until every inch of me was pleading for more. He moved his hand below the jeweled circle, and so damn slowly, went lower until his fingers were stroking that sensitive bud and I was helplessly panting. He moved two fingers into me while his thumb continued to circle. He played me like an instrument, and within minutes, I was shamelessly climaxing, my body quaking below his skilled hands.

He lifted me, still placing soft kisses along my burning skin as I stood upright again.

"When this is over tonight, I want you in that dress, waiting for me."

"Yes, my king," my husky voice complied.

Desire radiated down the bond and it took every ounce of self-control we both had to walk out of that room, his hand firmly on the bare skin of my lower back. We walked down the steps together as our friends stood in a group, dressed just as sharply, waiting.

We were escorted to the arena where they held The Rights. The entire kingdom had come, and as we looked over the endless cheering crowd, it seemed a lifetime ago that we had watched the same faces mourn their former king.

Inok stood in the middle of the field before us and lit a giant fire, the heat from those fated flames so strong, sweat formed on my bare back. Umari, Kai, Greeve and I walked forward, as we had been coached to do earlier in the week and waited as Inok placed three iron rods into the base of the roaring fire. I noticed Kai's shaking hand and chastised him under my breath.

"It will hurt worse if you're shaking, Kaitalen. Get it together."

"Yes, mother," he mumbled.

He'd come back from his mission under the sea for the coronation, but I hadn't had a chance to talk to him yet. Eventually, we would have to figure out what to do with them, but tonight was about the Flame Court and tradition. Not the Sea Court I'd left in shambles.

Fen moved to his knees in the center, letting the fire heat his bare back.

Inok stood, facing him. "This fire represents your new place amongst our people. May you burn bright, Fenlas."

Fen leaned all the way down, placing his nose to the ground. Umari stepped forward, bedecked in flowing, ornate fabrics and moved to stand in front of the future king. "May you never forget the hard lessons of those that came before you."

Fen rose from the waist but remained on the ground. Together, they placed a metal circlet, forged in fire and shaped into a hundred tiny flames, on his head.

Greeve walked forward, nearly gliding across the ground to his brother. He pulled the first red-hot rod out of the tumultuous flames, then turned to Fen and pressed the first part of the brand into his back. Only our bond reacted to the pain, Fenlas did not move. "May the reach of your rule spread across the world." Greeve set the iron down and returned to his spot beside me.

Kai took a deep breath and walked forward, claiming the second iron. He pressed it into Fen's skin, and though I flinched, he did not. "May the fire within remind you to always protect your people."

He walked back to me steadily and then it was my turn. I stepped forward. A single brand remained, glowing in the base of the fire. I wrapped my hand around the warm metal and lifted as I stilled myself.

Greeve and Kai had done the left and right sides of a flame, and I was to brand the top of them into his skin. I held my chin high and pressed the rod forward, though it nearly killed me. I burned him. I yanked the rod away after only a fraction of a second but he was permanently marked. I stepped backward and set the rod down. "May you always protect the weak, encourage the strong, and may your fire burn eternal."

I felt the tremble down the bond as my words struck home.

"Rise a king," the crowd said in unison.

And so, he did.

# Temir

"*I*s this it?" Nadra asked, looking around.

Slowly, the grassy roadside turned into sand, and after over a week of traveling with more than twenty people, including Rhogan, who snored louder than anyone should ever be able to, we made it to the Flame Court. Or at least the outskirts of the kingdom.

"It's time to see how they really treat us down here," Rhogan said.

"Murtad? Is that who we're looking for?" someone from our group asked.

"Yes. But based on our information, we have to get through the border lords first and then we're supposed to find the refugee leader for shelter. Not everyone who travels south is a member of the rebellion. We're supposed to wait to hear from Murtad," I answered.

The desert was strange. So hot and blank, no trees for miles, hardly any landmarks, only an occasional homestead. We dragged our tired legs through the red sand until we were approached by a high fae on a fae horse loaded down with jugs of water. She hopped down with a smile on her face.

I was instantly on guard. I think we all were.

"Welcome," she said cheerfully. "Where are you coming from?"

We exchanged glances, trying to decide suddenly who the leader was and who should talk, if anyone. Rhogan shoved me forward and Nadra snorted. Two against one, then.

"We come from the north." I had no plans for revealing how far north most of us came from.

"Obviously," she said. "My name is Sabra. I've brought you some water." She pulled the jugs loose and handed them off to the group. They drank eagerly, passing them around as I fought with myself to reveal anything at all.

"We were told we could seek refuge in this kingdom."

"Indeed, you can. I'm just out here checking on some of the border lords. I've got a friend with me, she can get you all to the city pretty quickly, I think. She's new to the south also. If you want to follow me, we will have to head back to my father's place."

We had no choice. We followed the cheerful high fae, exchanging glances of disbelief as we walked. I couldn't shake the feeling that we were walking into a trap. High fae were never nice to lessers without enchantment or serious motivation. It wasn't how things were done. I expected her to treat Nadra nicely, but not the rest of us.

Eventually we saw the farm in the distance, and it took forever to get there. So long that the sun began to set, and the unbearable heat transformed into a bitter cold. My body struggled with the adjustment and Nadra shivered beside me.

We followed Sabra onto her father's land, and though she invited the whole group of us in, we preferred to stand outside, shuddering but together. Where we could run if we needed to. To my utter shock, Gaea walked out of the house holding a tray of goat meat, cheeses and more water.

Nadra sucked in an audible breath and I squeezed her fingers, hoping to reassure her. Gaea hadn't noticed me yet, but Rhogan recognized her.

"Isn't that your friend?" he asked, waving like a giant troll.

"Yes," I hissed.

He turned and walked away, suddenly too busy to be a buffer between us as Gaea walked over.

"Temir?" Gaea asked, nearly dropping her tray. "Oh my gods, Temir!" She shoved the tray into Sabra's hand and pulled me into a hug.

I kept my hand in Nadra's, but the awkwardness was suffocating me.

"I see you've finally realized your mating bond." She smiled as she looked between me and Nadra.

"We have," Nadra answered, unfazed. Was the tension only my own?

"I'm so glad you're here, but how did you get away?"

"It's a long story," I answered. "Maybe another time."

Gaea knew me well enough to understand that I wasn't comfortable with any of this. Her, Nadra, the uncommonly nice high fae, none of it.

"I need to start spiriting the crowd to the city anyway. We've got a place there. There isn't much privacy, but it's safe." My eyes flicked to Sabra and back to her. "You'll get used to it, Temir. They don't even use the terms lesser and high fae in the Flame Court. There are no servants, and no one is demanded to do a single thing. It's a different world in the south."

She walked away from us and I instantly pulled Nadra into my arms.

"What was that for?" she asked.

"Because I think you were right to want to come here. And not because Gaea is here, but because I think they'll let me love you. I think the looks we've been getting about a lesser fae and a high fae together will stop."

"Let them look, Temir. And I'm not worried about Gaea, if that's what you think. I think we're going to need her."

"How so?"

"I'd bet my last coin she's already working with Ara and the prince. We must get to them as soon as possible. They have to know what we know."

"Right."

Gaea spirited each of us into a makeshift village within a city. We stood in the center of a compound of buildings labeled on the outside for clarity. Barracks and wash houses and a dining hall filled one side. It wasn't immaculate, but it was freedom.

I wanted nothing more than to finally have alone time with my mate. She'd slept in my arms for weeks, but that was as close as we were able to get while traveling with a group of people. I needed to get her safe and then get her naked. That was it for me. Basic mated male needs, and I wasn't even ashamed of it.

We were shown to the barracks where cots with blankets folded at the end of them lined both sides of the long room.

"Someday, I hope to have housing available for those who need it, until they can find work, but for now, this is the best we have," Sabra said.

"Temir and I both have marketable skills," Nadra said, pulling me forward.

"Do you?" she asked as the others began to claim their beds.

"I can sew. I helped my mother, who was a famous seamstress."

"Oh, that's wonderful," Sabra answered, writing a note on the paper she carried around. "And your mate?"

"Temir is a healer. He's magically gifted."

Her head snapped up, her eyes wide with shock. She took a moment to remove the desperation from her face. She knew a war was coming and what I could offer. It was strange though. Most wielders spent their lives trying to hide their magic. And Nadra had just outed me within hours of meeting this high fae.

"You won't be forced to use your magic here, Temir. Of course, we would welcome your gifts, especially in the training arenas, but you're free to use them as you wish. If you choose to work, you will be compensated by the kingdom. It's our goal to get everyone out on their own as quickly as we can."

"Thank you," Nadra smiled.

Several unoccupied cots nestled in a corner opposite the door. We moved through the refugees, stepping over some and around the others to settle in, unloading the bags from our tired shoulders.

"When are you going to tell her about the serum?" Nadra asked, sitting on the edge of her cot.

"I plan to talk to Murtad first, and then make my plans from there."

At least she'd kept one thing a secret. For now.

"Please make yourselves as comfortable as possible. I know you've all had a long journey to get here. Tomorrow morning, breakfast will be served in that first building we passed and then each person will be given a chore to help our community. If you're unable to work, we won't ask you to, but if you can, we'd love to have you. Welcome to the Flame Court." Sabra walked out.

Rhogan plopped down on my cot, nearly tipping it with his massive body. "She could probably kick my ass." He watched the door with a grin.

"What?" Nadra laughed.

"I'm just saying, they breed them for fighting down here. Anyone worth watching fight has always come from the south."

"You can daydream about getting your ass kicked from your own cot, Rhogan," I said.

"Oh, I took this one." He pointed to the cot right next to me.

"Oh. Great," I mumbled. Nadra smacked my arm. "What? He snores."

"It's called nighttime ambiance," he said, standing. "You'll grow to love it."

"How are you even going to fit on that cot?" I asked as he fluffed his pillow and sat, causing the wood to bow from his great size and massive wings.

"On my stomach, like I always do."

The next day, the three of us went to breakfast together, and Rhogan was pleased to see another high fae who looked similar to Sabra dishing out the food.

"That's my future wife." He stared at her while he shoveled food into his gaping mouth.

"Be less creepy," Nadra whispered.

I'd seen the female look up and meet eyes with Rhogan several times. Apparently, she didn't mind creepy.

"What's the plan for today?" he asked, still staring at the female.

"Well, I thought we could go check out the training arena Sabra was talking about after our chore, whatever that is, and then we could see if we can find Murtad."

"Murtad will find us, trust me. I wonder if kitchen duty is a chore."

"Oh, for gods' sake," Nadra said, standing and marching across the room to the female.

Rhogan gasped and turned away, hiding his face.

"Holy shit, Rhogan. I think you're blushing."

"Did you just cuss, Temir?" he asked, flashing his infamous smile.

"I think I'm spending too much time with you. Don't look now, but here they come."

Nadra brought the female over to us and gestured to Rhogan. "Wren, this is Rhogan. Rhogan, this is Wren."

"Wait a minute," she said, finally taking her eyes off my larger-than-life friend to notice me. "I know you. You're that rebel we helped near Volos." I nearly choked. "Your horns are shorter, but it's you, isn't it?"

"Yes. It's me."

"I'm so glad you're here. You have to come see Fen and Ara. They'll be so happy you've come."

"Wait, you can get us to Ara?" Nadra asked, grabbing her arm. "We seriously need to see her. She's my friend."

"Huh, I didn't know she had friends," she answered.

"Yep, that sounds like her." Nadra giggled.

Wren laughed. "I can take you to see her."

"That would be really great. We've just got to do a chore and we could go."

"Fen was crowned king only a few days ago, so they are super busy. I'll need to set up a meeting first. But I could take you somewhere else in the meantime?"

"I'd like to see the training area." Rhogan subtly flexed his muscles like an animal trying to impress a female.

Nadra rolled her eyes. "Sorry about him. Where can we find the list of chores?"

"I'd take kitchen duty." Rhogan wiggled his eyebrows until Wren blushed.

"Deal," she chuckled and walked back to her station.

"What are the odds?" Nadra asked, shaking her head.

"About once in a lifetime," Rhogan answered, forgetting to blink.

We worked as a group, cleaning the kitchen and wiping down the tables, until Wren deemed it clean enough and we followed her through the city and to the lists. "Sometimes Ara comes down here to kick everyone's asses. If you're lucky, you might catch her here. She and Gaea put on a pretty good show."

I tried not to react to that, but the excitement from Nadra jolted me. "Thank you so much. I hope we see you soon," she told Wren.

"Some of us sooner than others," Rhogan followed up.

Wren pursed her lips. "Do you always try this hard?"

"I don't know. This is my first time."

This time she rolled her eyes and walked away. Rhogan opened his wings just for show, and she looked back over her shoulder and nearly tripped.

"If the king refuses an audience with us, I'm blaming you," I said, slugging him in the forearm.

"She totally likes me," he answered.

We stayed at the lists for quite a while. We watched a giant practice with a royal guard, and we watched the guard work with several inexperienced northerners. At least here they were getting training.

"The prince went down to the compound and recruited these guys," a voice said from behind us. "You Rhogan?"

"Who wants to know?" he answered, instantly lethal as we turned to see a whelpa standing with his bony hands crossed over his hairy chest.

"Murtad sent me for you. The wings were a dead giveaway. We got a message you were coming."

"Great, let's go," I said.

"You the healer?" he asked, squinting.

I nodded.

He jutted his chin toward Nadra. "Fine, but she can't come."

216

"She goes or none of us do." Rhogan stepped so close to the messenger his chest pushed into him.

"It's rebels only," he answered, completely unfazed.

"She's one of us." I moved to stand next to Rhogan, my blood instantly boiling. "I find it ridiculous that the first sign of prejudice we see here comes from the rebellion, even worse that you single out my mate."

The messenger finally took a step back as the predator in me came forward. "Sorry, I didn't know. We don't have a lot of high fae rebels come in from the north."

"Let me punch him," Rhogan said, his fists clenched.

"Calm down. We can't have traitors in the rebellion and he's just doing his job. Let's go." Nadra took charge and probably saved the messenger's life as she grabbed me by the cuff and yanked me onward.

He walked back down the hill and we followed right behind him.

# Ara

"Besides being a well-rounded bitch and trying to take over this court, tell me anything else we actually know about Morwena's actions. My father said this was important. He said there would be a genocide. The Hunt matters, Fen."

"Ara, I get it. I know it's a giant red flag, but it's just not safe." He sat across oversized table from me, his hands cupped as if it were a professional meeting.

I'd had to chase him down into the castle library to get him to finally sit down and talk to me. He'd been avoiding this conversation for days. Though Coro's library was grander, this room always stilled me. Stacks of books so high you needed ladders to reach the top, rows of shelves filled with leather tomes, carrying so much history. So many stories of bravery and beasts written along pages so fragile they may see their final day soon and take those precious memories with them.

My eyes snapped back to Fen. "I don't think we have a choice. We have to find out how tight Coro's reins are on the Hunt. I'm telling you it matters. It mattered when my parents were killed. It matters now."

He stood, rounding the table so he could pull me to him. Cupping my cheeks, he kissed me soundly. "If it means this much to you, and this is what you think is right, then go ahead. But I want to come with you. It's my job."

I moved away, so I wouldn't fall for the distraction of his adoring gaze. "I wasn't asking for your permission. I'm trying to be a team player here, instead of rushing into danger. I know you're the Guardian, Fen. But you've also got an entire kingdom to run, and it's just a conversation. I can navigate a conversation without having a bodyguard."

He raised a knowing eyebrow at me.

"Don't give me that look."

"I have no idea what you're talking about," he smirked.

"Fine, I'll take Gaea and Greeve and we'll be back after dinner. I just want to know."

"If I go, as a king, he's more likely to talk to me."

"That can be the backup plan, good thinking."

"That's not what I meant." His tone was flat. "And you'll have both travelers with you, so I won't even be able to get there quickly, if something happens."

"I think, between the three of us, you won't have to worry about that." I pulled the knife from the band on my thigh and set it on the table beside us.

"You're supposed to kill him," he said. "We've got enough going on trying to figure out what to do in the Sea Court right now."

"You don't trust that Kai is working on it?" I asked, slumping back in my chair.

"No, I'm confident he is. But he can't stay down there and babysit forever. I need him with Brax, training the new recruits."

"How's that going?" I asked.

"We're not changing the subject right now. I'll concede that the Hunt is important. You have my blessing to go if it's what you needed. But just keep in contact with me the whole time." He tapped his finger to his head, and I sighed.

"Yes, Your Highness."

"Are we fighting?" he asked, sitting back in his seat with a glint of humor in his eyes.

"No," I said sharply.

"Oh good, because, for a second there, I thought you might want to murder me too." He grinned.

"Not funny."

"Listen, you can do whatever you want in the whole world. I'm not in charge of you, I'm not trying to command you. I'm your equal, Ara. I just want to know what you're doing." He put the book he had been reading back onto the shelf behind him and sat back down, folding his hands.

"That's why I've been trying to talk to you instead of just disappearing, but you can't really say you've been fair to me. You scold me when I do something you don't like, and then when I try to sit down and talk about it, you avoid the conversation."

"I'll make a deal with you." His eyes turned dark and seductive.

"I love a good deal." I pressed my body into the table.

"I promise to never avoid a hard conversation with you if you let me clear out this library and lay you across this table."

"You can't brush this off with sex," I laughed.

"I'm not brushing it off. You want to go, go. I just want to seal the deal."

"Right here?" I asked, patting the surface.

"And over there." He pointed at the bookshelf.

"And there?" I asked, indicating the windowsill.

"Especially there," he growled.

I threw my head back and laughed and he was out of his chair and placing me on the table in an instant.

"I thought you were going to clear the room?" I whined, making eye contact with a female smiling at me from another table.

"Fun hater," he whispered into my ear.

"At some point, I want them to respect me, King."

"Out," Fen roared, leaving no room for argument as the library emptied in a frenzy, with me still sitting on the edge of the table. "Undress."

The command in his voice was provoked by my use of his proper title. His magic crept down my spine. I pulled my top over my head, eyes glued to him as he stroked his bottom lip with his thumb, watching me, consuming me with that salacious look.

He moved in, placing his hands on either side of me, pressed flat on the table as he kissed me so hard I couldn't help but lean backward, the cool table caressing my skin as he hovered above me. He lowered his head to my collarbone, pushing soft kisses down my body until he got to my navel. He shifted, pulling the wrap I'd worn to the side so he could move his rough hand up my thighs as his other caressed my neck, moving down to follow his trail of kisses until he took a full breast into his hand and squeezed.

He moved a finger across the sensitive bud between my legs and desire pooled within me, that ache grew as he rubbed, his eyes burning into mine as he watched me squirm. He dropped to his knees and pulled me to the edge of the table, his mouth closing over me. The scratch of his trimmed beard along my thighs caused a moan as he pushed my legs open, stroking me with his tongue. His dark hair fell forward, covering his brow and I squirmed again and he used his magic to pin me into place. My body was his to devour.

He drove a finger inside of me and released his magical hold as my back arched off the table. I thought he'd keep going, hoped for it, but just as I felt that climax building he pulled away, leaving me yearning. He lifted me from the table and purred into my ear as we crossed the room, crashing into the deep windowsill, as promised. He ripped the wrap from around my waist and slid it behind my back. I disintegrated his clothing, the only bit of magic I would allow myself. He held onto both ends of the fabric, twisting it around his wrists as he pulled, holding up my hips as he plunged, shoving me backward into a pile of discarded books that tumbled to the floor.

I wanted to laugh but couldn't as he withdrew so slowly and then slammed back into me. His muscles strained as he struggled to keep the slow and powerful pace. I dug my nails into his arms as he growled, slamming into me again as my hips hovered in the air. Over and over until we were both on the brink of destruction and then he pulled away again, breath ragged as he lowered me, then took my hand.

That ache he'd created in my body built even as we stepped through the library, his fingers brushing my back as he guided me to a ladder leaning against a shelf along the wall.

"I will never get enough of you. There are days when I wonder if this overwhelming pull to touch your skin, to taste your lips will subside, and then I think of these moments and know it never will." He kissed my shoulder as he pointed to a lower rung of the ladder. "Hands here."

A wicked smile spread across my face as I bent over, holding tightly to the step as he positioned himself behind me. Hands on my hips, I sucked in a breath as he pushed forward, every inch of him stroking me as he moved. He did not breathe as he took me, kneading with his hands as I hung my head and thanked the gods for a powerful male that would always keep me guessing.

There was no such thing as gentle anymore as his body slammed into mine. As I felt that growing sensation of the most incredible orgasm, I held my breath, knowing he would deny me once again as we lived through this scandalous fantasy. I wanted only more of him. He stepped away, as predicted though, and I stood, legs quaking.

He took my face into his hands, kissing me gently as our hearts pounded in unison. "I love you so much it hurts."

I wrapped my hands around his neck, consuming him with my tongue as I kissed him. He lifted me from the ground and pressed my back into a bookshelf, as he entered me. I knew this would be the final time. That desperate look on his beautiful face was undeniable.

The stacks rattled as he moved in and out, still watching me as he always did before I shattered. And this game he'd played would be my utter undoing as that pressure built and built, as my legs trembled while I teetered over the edge of endless pleasure. A single roar from Fen and that was it for me, for him as well as he pressed me harder into the shelf, and we both climaxed, every bit as desperate for each other as we always had been. Even from the very beginning when I'd tried to deny him.

Later, I stood with Fen, Gaea, and Greeve in the kitchens. The air was filled with the thick scent of salted gravy and honey butter. Meat stewed in a pot and I was crushed we wouldn't be here to eat it. Loti promised to save me some of the midday meal and the soft spot in my heart for her grew. She'd become a mother to our group in more ways than one and I was constantly grateful for her. And the lemon tarts she had wrapped in embroidered cloth and stuck in my empty pocket.

"So, what's the plan?" Gaea asked, dressed in black, matching Greeve, who was armed to the teeth and emanating death incarnate.

"How do we get a private audience with the king?" I asked Fen, who was snacking from a fruit bowl on the counter.

"You'll enter the castle from the front, just as we always have." He looked to Greeve. "Find Pret. Tell him I've sent a messenger for a closed meeting."

"Do we mention I'm your mate?" I asked, grabbing my own handful of red grapes.

"I wouldn't. Don't give him a reason to think he has anyone special within his grasp."

"So, you're saying I'm special?" I asked, stepping into his arms.

"Had I forgotten to remind you?" He bent down, kissing me slowly.

Gaea cleared her throat and I smiled against his mouth. "See you soon, King Fancy Pants." I looked to Gaea. "See? It just doesn't have the same ring to it."

"We can work on it," she answered, thrumming her fingers on the counter. She was just as eager to go as I was. I got the feeling Gaea

224

wasn't one to stay in one place too long if she didn't have to. I'd caught her long glances at my fearsome friend and worried for him. At the very least, Gaea would not be tamed. Maybe that was why we got along so well.

She took us both at the same time. I'd worn the suit Nadra's mother had made for me to travel in, hoping it would deter any lingering thoughts of capture. Something felt off with the magic, but I didn't give myself the time to wonder about it. I left my sword behind, but my favorite knives were well hidden, the familiar bite of metal not quite warming my heated skin.

Standing outside the Marsh Court castle again was jarring. Like taking a long step back into the past. A big part of me wanted to run down the hill behind us and visit Nadra and her mother in the seamstress's shop, but we had business to take care of and this trip wasn't for memory lane. I missed Nadra though. She was the only one I had left from my past.

"Stay close," Greeve said under his breath as Gaea and I shared a look.

We walked up to the castle gates and Greeve introduced us as royal messengers from the Flame Court. We were given easy permission to enter Coro's castle, even taken to a sitting room with vaulted ceilings and ancient paintings on the wall, after being asked to wait.

"I've been told to seek Pret specifically," I said to the guard, my chin high and face entirely unamused by him.

"While that might be true, Pret is no longer serving His Majesty King Coro. You'll need to wait for Hivan to make your requests." The guard walked away with a bounce in his step, clearly amused to have the upper hand.

"Pret's always been a sympathizer to the rebellion. I can't say I'm surprised things are changing in the north," Greeve said.

225

"This isn't the north," Gaea and I answered in unison.

"You know what I mean." He paced the floor, weapons clinking against each other as he moved.

"He's going to recognize you," I told Gaea an hour later, lounging across the floral-printed settee that matched the dusty drapes. We had agreed not to discuss anything important while waiting, but this was obvious.

"I don't care. I don't belong to anyone."

"Autus will know where you are though."

She flickered. She was there one second, gone the next, and then back again.

"Sorry. Just nerves. Autus is coming south no matter what. We all know that. Especially when he finds out about . . . you know who."

Greeve jerked at her words and she shrugged. I was beginning to think leaving us to sit and wait this long just for the liaison was a military tactic meant to rattle us out of our secrets. Either that or the creepy eyes on the paintings were watching us.

*Anything?*

*For the hundredth time, no. I promise I'll let you know soon.*

*I'm bored.*

*Why is it that when I'm there, I barely see you, and now that I'm away, you suddenly have all this time?*

*I'm listening to a lecture from Knocky on setting proper schedules.*

*We should have sent him to the ocean.*

*No, he'd come back with the hydra as a mate.*

I giggled and Gaea shook her head at me. "It's really creepy when you guys do that thing."

226

I couldn't respond. Wouldn't give away any information. So instead, I stuck my tongue out at her like the child I was.

The door finally opened and a tall, pudgy fae walked in, shoving his oversized glasses up his tiny nose. We stood as he crossed the room and took a seat on the large chair in front of us. "The meaning of your visit?" A fae we could only assume was Hivan asked, failing to look up from the leather-bound book he was writing in.

"We've come to request a private audience with the king."

"The king isn't taking private meetings." He slammed his book shut and tried to walk out.

Greeve was there, blocking his path before he could even register the movement. He crossed his tattooed arms over his muscled chest and stared at the male in the eyes. "King Fenlas has sent us to speak to King Coro. You will either make that happen," he said, pulling the curved blade from his back, "or I will."

Instantly Gaea was beside him, and I'd never been so jealous of their magic. Then I remembered mine and the fact I could take the castle down with a single thought and felt slightly better.

"He's having his meal in his study right n-now. Perhaps after."

"Now's a really great time for me." I crossed the room. "Lead the way."

He looked at the tip of Greeve's sword and nodded. They stepped aside, letting him out and he hurried down the hallway. We followed closely as he rounded a corner, scurrying behind several guards blocking us with their lances. He turned his instantly smug face in our direction, and without missing a beat, Gaea grabbed my hand and we were on the other side of the guards as well, looming over Hivan.

The guards rotated, holding their weapons out, and Hivan shook his head, his neck rippling with the effort. "You have to wait here. You can't come barging in on the king. Give me just a moment."

"Aw, but we are so very good at barging." I opened the door and walked in to find Coro sitting at a long, marbled table with two guards behind him.

He looked up, his eyes instantly on Greeve.

"Why are you always the one everyone worries about?" I asked, pulling out a chair at the opposite end of the table. The guards were moving immediately, but Greeve and Gaea were armed and ready. I slid the knife from my wrist, hiding my hands below the table.

"What's this?" Coro asked, pointing with the half-eaten food left on his gilded fork. He held his other hand up, stopping his guards from coming any closer.

"Sorry, my king." Hivan bowed to hide his tremble. "They've requested a private council quite ardently."

"I know you." His eyes narrowed on Gaea. "But what are you doing with him?" He jutted his fork toward Greeve. "And who the fuck are you?"

"Which question did you want answered first?" I asked, sitting back comfortably in the padded chair.

"Take your pick," he said, finishing his bite.

"Well, she's not important. I've come as a messenger on behalf of King Fenlas."

"Ah yes, the little princeling is now a ruler. We must have missed the invite to his coronation."

"It was a private affair," I said sharply.

"Nothing's private in Alewyn." He wiped his mouth with his napkin. "Please, come sit closer, I hate to yell across the table."
228

"I have good hearing. No need to shout." I sat the dagger on my lap and brought my hands forward, planting them firmly on the table.

"Indeed," he said, smiling. "Tell me why you have come, then."

"My king extends his apologies for not coming in person, but as I'm sure you can imagine, he has his hands full at the moment."

"Go on." He waved his hand in the air, huffing as if he were bored.

"My king wishes to know how tight your grasp is on the Wild Hunt."

He coughed. "What is it with everyone trying to take my Hunt from me? Why is your *king* so concerned?" I wasn't a fan of the tone, but Coro had been playing this game a lot longer than I had.

I held a neutral face and answered honestly. "King Fenlas is concerned because before I traveled south to work for him, my father was a part of the Hunt, and even then, Morwena was trying to get her hands on it. She'd poisoned the minds of the fae she could get to, trying to steal it. My father was steadfast in his loyalty to you. He turned her down. She was so angry, she had him killed, so I'll ask you again, do you have it secured?"

"Who was your father?" he asked, as if he hadn't heard or cared about any of the rest of it.

"It's not important."

"Ah, but it is. I wish to know who remained loyal to his king until death, only to have a daughter run traitorously to the south."

I bit the inside of my cheek so hard, the taste of blood tinged my tongue. *I hate this motherfucker.*

*Don't let him get under your skin. In and out. Don't cause waves.*

"You shouldn't meddle here. Especially when you can't hold a conversation. The prince should have sent someone more qualified."

I gripped the edge of my knife below the table. "My qualifications are quite vast, I assure you."

He took an oversized bite and through his disgusting chewing said, "Go back to your kingdom and tell your prince that when he grows up, he can come see me himself if he wishes to talk of wars and traitors."

Greeve flinched beside me and the guards did also.

My muscles tightened, ready to move. "What do you know of the ocean, Coro?"

A look of amusement crossed his features, and though I wasn't sure he'd answer, he did. "I know Morwena would eat you for a snack before her main course."

I slumped back in my chair. "Would she, now?"

A giant grin spread across his face as he seemed to imagine it.

"That's strange, because to my recollection, I'm the one who killed her."

He jerked his head back and sucked in an audible breath. Greeve cleaved to the door, pulling his sword. Coro stood and stared me down.

"Is that supposed to be a threat?"

"Oh no, only listing my qualifications," I answered, tucking the knife away as I stood to lean on my knuckles flattened against the smooth surface of the dining table. "You see, Morwena had a habit of underestimating me too, and while the news of her unfortunate death hasn't spread too far, you can bet Autus already knows about it. You seem to be out of the loop though. That's too bad."

"You're a liar," he yelled.

"Yes, I am. But not about this."

Red tinged his skin as his anger rose to the surface.

"You know the most interesting thing about her death? It wasn't the way fear glinted in her eyes, it wasn't even the shrill sound she made right before I ended her." I slid the chair behind me away with my foot. "It was the fact that she honestly didn't see it coming at all."

"What the fuck do you want to know about the Hunt?" he asked, still holding his guards at bay. "Morwena could never take it from me because the magic to cross into the human lands cannot be stolen. It has to be freely given."

"Now was that so hard?" I asked.

A cheeky grin slathered his round face. "You're going to die. When this is all over, which will be soon, you, your king, his entire kingdom will be nothing but ash." His voice rose. "You think you can come in here and force information from me like I am not sovereign? As if I'm not the king of a more powerful realm than yours. My army," he said, now screaming, "is the greatest army in this world! I'm not afraid of you or your king!"

I tapped my fingers to my lips. "Do I detect a hint of denial?"

I'd pushed too far, and I knew it, but apparently angry Coro liked to spew information.

"No, and do you know why? Because I've given Autus the Hunt in exchange for immunity from the war. I've given him free passage through my lands. And guess what, he's capturing a human army to solidify his rightful place as High King of Alewyn."

"Why the fuck would you do that?" I yelled, matching his volume. "You have the greatest army in the world and you just bend over and take it right up the ass from Autus? You're a fucking idiot."

"I've just decided to add my army to his. Thank you for helping me make that decision." He sat down slowly. "Kill them," he ordered.

The guards rushed toward me, but Greeve was there in a flash. I sunk my blade into the fae on the right as the door crashed open and more guards poured into the small room. Gaea spirited and slashed while Greeve tried to watch over both me and her. I hopped onto the table, battling my own fate. If Coro handed over his army, we wouldn't have a chance against Autus.

But there was only one way to prevent it.

I stepped closer to the king. A hint of worry shone in his eyes, but still he doubted me. They always did. I kicked the heel of my boot on the table, triggering the blade at the toe to come out. Their guards rushed me, but they weren't quick enough. I planted my foot deep into Coro's neck, and for an instant, the room went still, his gurgling filing the silence as his court members seemed to flinch. But then Greeve swung his sword, taking off another guard's head, and the chamber became a blood bath until only three remained standing.

"I'm pretty sure this was the only thing Fen told us not to do." Gaea said, heaving.

"It came down to them or us, G. We always choose us."

"How the hell are we going to explain this to Fen?" Greeve asked, wiping the blood from his blade.

Gaea pointed at me. "Look at her. She's covered in blood. The second we get home, he's only going to wish he got the final blow." Gaea reached forward, grabbed Greeve's arm, and spirited away, leaving me behind, just like we had planned.

# Temir

The rebel headquarters in the Flame Court were hidden in plain sight. The male who retrieved us from the lists, thanks to Rhogan's unmistakable wingspan, led us through the bustling city and to a large shop with a hammer chiseled into the modern sign hanging above the heavy wooden door with etched glass.

The front room of the repair shop was full of busy workers and patrons. Several worked with magnifying glasses and others beat on metal with hammers. Some of the workers tinkered and a few moved inventory around the store. High fae and lessers working side by side. We passed a pixie fixing a clock being held by a high fae with sharp cheekbones and shoulder-length silver hair discussing his lunch plans with her as if they were friends.

Nadra squeezed my hand tightly. This was exactly where we were meant to be.

I was still surprised by the rebel's initial reaction to Nadra, especially considering the atmosphere here. We followed the fae to the back of the store and through an oversized door. The first room we entered was empty aside from the rows and rows of vacant chairs that faced a raised platform in the back. We continued walking until our guide led us to a door and knocked three times.

"I'm naked," a male voice called.

"Oh. Sorry, sir," the rebel replied, his cheeks flushing.

"I'm just fucking with you, Davok. Come in."

He laughed nervously and opened the door, gesturing for us to enter. A fae male with goat horns similar to Rook's and golden-brown hair lounged in a chair, his shirt completely unbuttoned, and his feet kicked up onto the worn desk in front of him. He waited for us to be seated in the unmatched chairs before waving his hand for Davok to leave us. "I bet he gave *you* a hard time." He looked at Nadra like he wanted to devour her.

A growl echoed through the room and it took a minute to register that it was my own.

"Sorry." He put his hands in the air. "We don't get a lot of mates around here. Anyway, Davok is still getting used to the fact that high fae and lesser fae play in the same sandbox in the Flame Court. How was your journey?"

"Long," I answered sharply.

He faced Rhogan, examining his wings for several minutes. "I got a message you were coming, but damn. You should have flown."

"I was helping my friend escort a bunch of rebels south. They're all at the compound right now."

"We'll get someone down there to invite them up to the next meeting. Wren's usually too busy, but Sabra isn't."

234

"I forgot they were part of the rebellion," Nadra said. "That guy said there weren't many high fae."

"Not from the north specifically, but he isn't a reliable source of information. Plenty of southern *high fae* are also part of our rebellion. But they mostly just support the cause from a distance. Even the king wears our phoenix symbol on his skin."

"Yes, we've met," I answered. "They helped me and some others fight King Autus' soldiers near Volos in the north." I paused, examining his cluttered office. Rebellion leader apparently didn't mean organized. "We won't keep you. I've brought a serum south I believe you'll be interested in, but we also want to know what the plan is. Most of our northerners were killed or fled south."

He shrugged casually, as if we weren't discussing a war.

"Do we have a plan?" Rhogan asked, shifting forward on the squeaky chair he had turned backwards to compensate for his wings.

"Right now, we are going to sit back and see how the kingdoms move against each other before we commit anything to them."

"Are you fucking kidding me?" Nadra asked, flying up and out of her chair, letting it ricochet off the wall behind her. She pointed a shaking finger in the direction of the palace. "This king has been funding the rebellion for years. You can't just do nothing."

"That king has only been king for the blink of an eye," he answered, slumping backward.

"Fine, this *court* has been. And you don't know shit. You don't see what's happening up there. How long have you been down here in this hole collecting the king's coins and divvying them up amongst yourselves while the lesser fae in the north die in packs?"

Her hands shook as Rhogan and I stood at the same time. I reached for her, but she jerked away.

"No, this isn't right. Your claim to be a rebel is really fucking convenient when you don't have to actually fight anything. When you don't have a king breathing down your neck and mind fucking you. This isn't a rebellion, it's a gods-damn fifth court. And you think *you're* king, shelling out false hope likes it's motherfucking candy."

She turned on her heel and stormed out of that room so fast, the flash of red was the last thing Murtad would see of her. Rhogan and I followed quickly behind. Odds were, there was more to Murtad's motivations, but at that point, I didn't care at all. The self-proclaimed shallow female had just rocked the rebellion leader's world.

"So, that went well," Rhogan said as we crossed the city again, heading back to the lists, hoping to see someone who could get us into the castle.

I wasn't above begging Gaea, but I didn't think it would come to that. We joined the crowd, and I wrapped my arm around Nadra's shoulder. She was still shaking, and I could feel her frustration as if it were my own.

"I don't want to talk about it," she said, plopping onto the bench.

"I've never been prouder or more turned on in my whole life," I whispered.

"Really?" she asked, her shoulders melting.

"Really."

"He had it coming." She pursed her lips together. "We survived the king. We climbed a mountain. We came all this way." She faced forward but slid her hand on my thigh, rubbing her fingers back and forth in such a way I thought I might have to find a dark alley. The desire was so strong. We were so desperate for a moment alone together, I don't think she would have even protested.

236

The males training in the lists were the same ones that were there when we left, only now they were broken into groups and practicing swordplay as several guards and a giant directed them. I couldn't believe training was a spectator sport. This was the south though. They were bred for fighting. Or so I'd heard.

A northerner I had seen at breakfast had footwork like a dancer, but he couldn't keep his arms up. The moment someone swung at him, he dropped his shoulders, and Rhogan and I began counting how many times he'd been hit. But by the time they had switched weapons, he'd actually made pretty good strides. The southerners were skilled trainers.

"Think we'll get to watch the giant fight?" Rhogan asked.

"Who would ever fight with him?"

"I would." Rhogan shrugged, a shiver going through his wings.

"Because what you lack in brains you make up for in muscle?" Nadra asked.

"Damn, you're vicious today," he answered.

"I want to be sorry but I'm just not," she laughed.

I nudged him. "Someone has to remind him that he's mortal."

"Barely." He turned back to watch the trainees try their hand at archery.

"Hey guys!" Wren bounded up to us. She was talking to the whole group but only looking at Rhogan. "Ara's not around right now, but Fen said he could meet with you, if you still want? Otherwise you'll have to wait for her to get back."

"The king would be perfect," Nadra said, smiling sweetly. She knew exactly what she was doing to me.

"He's in a meeting with Tol . . ." She cleared her throat. "The former king's closest friend. He can see you after." Her smile became sad, and I wondered what it felt like to love a king so much you mourned him.

It was beginning to feel like we were puppets on a string being guided this way and that, but as we followed Wren to the castle, the anticipation built. I hadn't quite decided how much information I would disclose to the new king, but at the very least, he needed to know his mate was in danger. Mortal danger.

"Are you hungry?" Wren asked Rhogan, forgetting we were even near. "Loti has leftovers and Fen might be a little bit."

"I'm always hungry," Rhogan answered. His devilish grin left us wondering if he meant for food or other things.

"You guys go ahead," Nadra offered. "We can wait here until he's ready."

"You sure?"

I nodded to Rhogan. He needed no persuasion to follow Wren down the hall.

After only a few minutes, the door opened and King Fenlas and his father's friend walked out. "Temir. Come in."

He dipped his chin to Nadra, and she bowed low. I did the same.

"No need for that." He ran his hand through his dark hair, the strain on his face obvious.

"Is now a bad time? We could come back?" I asked, noting his distressed face.

"No, please, I could use the distraction."

He welcomed us into a comfortable large office with bookshelves and tapestries lining the walls. He fell onto an oversized chair and we took the couch across from him. The colors were vibrant and cheerful, a direct opposite to the atmosphere the king was creating. His distracted glances and faraway looks reminded me that we were kindred spirits: his mate was away from the castle and he was struggling with it.

"So, she really is your mate?" I asked, his eyes finally meeting mine.

"She is." He lifted a glass and emptied it in one swallow.

"This is Nadra. We are also mates."

He looked at her, then back to me, then back to her. "Nadra from the tavern?" He stood.

She pressed her hand to her chest. "I can't believe you recognize me."

"Ara's going to be so surprised."

"In a good way, I hope," she answered.

"Of course. Where are you staying?" He crossed the room and filled his glass, and then two others, bringing them and the decanter back on a tray, then handed us each a glass of wine.

The fact that we were just served by the king resonated with me. He was the king but still a male. Still good.

"We're staying at the refugee compound. Just until we can get some work lined up," Nadra answered, sipping her wine. I'd almost forgotten this was her natural element. She was not intimidated to stand before important fae and speak of casual things.

"You can stay here," he offered. "I'm sure the moment Ara knows you've come, she won't settle for anything less. And you know how she is once she's decided something."

"Oh, I know." She laughed.

"Why the meeting today?" he asked, nearly finishing another glass.

"I've got something serious to tell you." It was my turn to finish the whole glass. "As you know, I worked on the king's council as a spy for the rebellion. I wasn't always a rebel and Autus trusted me. He enchanted Nadra, telling her his plans, assuming she would never escape, but when Nadra's mother was taken as prisoner, I took Nadra to safety and came back for Megere. I was captured and exposed and spent some time in the dungeons. Autus enchanted me and, long story short, the majority of the northern rebellion that hadn't already fled was killed. There are maybe five hundred still scattered through the north."

"I'm sorry to hear that." He rubbed his temple as he hung his head. "Thank you for sharing this with me."

"That's not all." Nadra refilled all the glasses and sat back down beside me. "It's about his plans. He aims to capture Ara and bind her to him. He's found an ancient scroll that has given him the recipe to do it, if he can procure certain artifacts for the ritual."

His head snapped up from his glass and, again, he was on his feet. "What specifically do you know?"

"He's gotten four of the seven items," I answered. "We tried to block him from several, but he's been one step ahead of us. Unfortunately, Nadra's mother died trying to keep him from one of them. The only items left are Ara's blood, something in the dunes, and a certain flower we have hidden from him."

"I'm so sorry to hear about your mother. Can we destroy the flower?" he asked, his brisk pacing making me dizzy.

"No," Nadra and I said in unison.

"It's not a typical flower. He mentioned needing to sever a mating bond, but I have no idea if that is something he has to do or something he wants to do just to make you suffer. Even so, can you think of anything that's fabled to be missing and in the dunes?"

240

"I can't, but I'll get the staff to start researching immediately." His body jerked, and he audibly swallowed. Seeming a million miles away, he was wherever his mate was. Perhaps a feeling she had sent down the mating bond.

"Is everything okay?" Nadra asked, setting down her wine glass and rising to her feet. "Can I get you something?"

"No, no. It's fine. Is there anything else?" he clipped.

"Nothing that can't wait until tomorrow, King Fenlas." Nadra looked at me like I knew what to do.

"You can stay here if you wish. There's plenty of space, and I'm sure Ara would love to have you near," he said to Nadra.

The color in his tanned face began to fade as the door slammed open, the walls shook from the force, and the draconian fae that was with him in Volos stalked in dressed in black from head to toe with his hair tied back and blood dripping from his entire body.

"Where is she?" the king asked, his voice barely audible as he fell to his knees.

Nadra grabbed my hand and dragged me out of the room.

# CHAPTER
## 21

# Ara

*W* *here are you?* Fen roared.

*We're just about to head back. Things got messy and I had to kill Coro. If he unleashes his army on us, we're fucked.*

*But you're fine?*

I could practically hear the sigh that accompanied the relief in his voice.

*Yes, I'm okay. Not even a scratch.*

I still stood on the blood-covered table deep within the Marsh Court castle, Coro's dead body stiffening before me. Gaea watched the door carefully. We'd made a plan together if things went terrible here, and they did. But the plan didn't involve Greeve and his dominating bullshit. Some days he was worse than Fen. So he had to go back to the Flame Court.

*I'm not coming directly home. We've got to make a stop first.*

I bit my lip waiting for the retort, the infamous argument that always came when I had a plan that didn't involve him. It didn't come.

*How long do you need?* Though his voice was tight and his words clipped, he was trying.

*No more than ten minutes and we will be back, but we're still sitting in Coro's castle, so we've got to go.*

*Be safe.*

"I think someone switched my mate, G."

"Worry about it later. Ready?"

She was nervous, her eyes focused but her hands fidgety. She'd done this a thousand times, she claimed, but still, never with someone in tow.

"Should we practice first? What if it doesn't work?" I asked.

"Let's pop in on Fen and Greeve. If they can't see us, we know it's going to work."

I nodded and hopped down from the solid table, standing on the back of a fallen guard. Gaea grabbed my hand and we disappeared, but rather than reappearing like we usually did, we spirited fluidly through a room I recognized. It took me a few seconds to acclimate myself with the process, and I thought Fen would sense my nearness if not able to see us, but he looked completely unaware as he and Greeve stood, each with a decanter in their hands.

"Ten minutes," Fen said, his voice surrounding us as we moved, never in one spot long enough to be seen.

"And if they aren't back?"

"You're not helping." Fen placed his arms behind his back, gripping his wrist tightly as he worked his jaw.

"Why didn't you tell her no, then?" Greeve's voice was a step away from commanding.

"Because I'm not in charge of her. Because I don't want to fight with her. Because she can make her own choices and she's smart and just as lethal as you are."

My heart jumped a little at those words; though his conviction was not as strong as I would have liked, he was trying. Gaea spirited us to her new room, and we stood for a moment, orienting ourselves. Or at least I was, she was wringing her hands.

"We don't have to go. We can find another way." I rested my hand on her forearm, trying to comfort her. She was afraid of being trapped and stuck there again. I didn't blame her. "I won't let anything happen to you, G. Promise."

"You're the closest thing I've had to a real friend, Ara. You know I'm in this with you."

I bumped her shoulder. "The closest? Don't be an asshole. We *are* friends. Suck it up."

"Yeah, yeah. Tell me about the Hunt. Everything you know." She sighed, trying to build her courage.

"Most of what I know is lore. It's not specifically true. The Hunt was the one thing my father did not want to talk about." I took a deep breath and sat on a chair in the corner.

She crossed the room, uncorked a wine bottle and took a healthy swallow, then held it out to me.

But I shook my head and continued. "Coro's father was gifted the Hunt. Some say he made a deal with the devil himself, and others say it was the work of the elves. Regardless, the magic was dark and dangerous. The Wild Hunt's job is to enter the human realm and drag their souls to hell. In exchange, they said the God of Death gave him the power to take the vilest of faeries also."

"So maybe Coro's wrong and the Hunt can't be used to bring the humans here." She took another drink.

"I've seen a human recently. I know they can still come. I'm guessing Morwena enchanted a member of the Hunt and he did just that. I think he was probably the test. She wanted more power and that's why she was trying to steal it. Unaware that it couldn't be stolen. My father would never agree to meet her face to face, and I think that's why. So he could make sure the Hunt wasn't used as a weapon and so she couldn't enchant him."

"Tell me about your magic," she said carefully, picking at her fingers.

I let out a long breath. "No one has really spelled it out for me, but from what we have put together, it was gifted to me so I could destroy the world. Only I would never do that. I'm trying so fucking hard to keep it reigned in every day. I can barely control it when I let it loose. I'm working on it. But when I use a massive amount, it basically tries to suffocate me so I will lose control. And even worse, every time I use a big piece of it, it creates a tear in our soul. If I'm not really, really careful . . . my magic could end the world, or Fen and I, or literally everything."

She dropped her hands to her side and shook her head. "Then we have to go. We have to see if we can find anything to help us."

"We have to hurry too. Fen's counting the minutes, I promise."

She grabbed my hand and we were instantly traveling around a cold, stone castle, devoid of color or any sign of happiness. A thousand voices echoed through the halls as we moved, unable to lock onto one single conversation for more than a few seconds. Gaea was hunting and she knew what or who she was looking for. I just had to watch and listen, never being tangible in one space for more than a fraction of a second, as if the particles of my body were scattered and moving as fluidly as her magic directed them through the Wind Court castle.

One second we were scouring through the castle, and the next we were outside, a blizzard tearing through us as we searched the grounds for proof of a large human army. Finding nothing, she spirited us back to her rooms. "There's one more place we can try. I didn't see a single council member as we were spying. I think they're in a meeting. We won't have long though."

I nodded and she reached for me again. This was going to be the most dangerous part. The king would also be in the council meeting. Still, we whisked away and were instantly circling a large hollow room with a grand table and several large gaps between each chair. I held my breath as we moved, hoping not to make a single sound.

The king was unaware as he screamed at his council. "How many have died?"

A tall skinny old fae with beady eyes stood, shaking. "Nearly a thousand. They grow thinner by the day. We did not know they required sustenance so frequently."

"They're like animals," the king roared. "If you don't feed them, of course they fucking die."

The sniveling fae moved to hide behind his chair.

"Humans are worse than—"

"My king," another fae said, standing. "We're not alone."

In another jerk, we were standing corporeal back in the Flame Court with Greeve and Fen.

"It's true," I whispered, eyes locked on Gaea.

She looked as sick as I felt. "That was Evin. He can detect magic," she mumbled into my ear.

"Explain." Fen crossed the room in three strides to stand beside me. To put his hand on me. To know I was safe and home. He couldn't help that need and, in this moment, I needed him also.

I turned into his chest and buried my head. "Everything got messed up."

His mouth flattened into a line, clearly trying to control his words. "Greeve told me what happened with Coro. If you hadn't baited him so much, he might still be alive."

My head snapped to Greeve. Fury coursed through my veins, the mental repercussions of another murder still fresh in my mind. "If I hadn't pushed him, he would have never told us a thing. He has been on Autus' side this whole time. He claimed Autus was the rightful High King of Alewyn, Fen. And Gaea and I just confirmed that he does, in fact, have a human army. I did what I had to do, I won't apologize for that. And you and I both knew Coro was destined to die."

"But now we have two kingdoms with no leaders. Did you think about that?" Greeve asked.

Fen grabbed my arm, holding me back as I attempted to storm over to him.

"Where's the dark draconian that fears nothing and only wants what's best? You know what your problem is?" I yanked my hand from Fen's arm and got right in his face. "Your fucking mating bond is turning you into a territorial asshole. The sooner you guys figure that shit out, the better. Don't talk to me, don't look at me, don't even think my fucking name until you can get that beast inside of you in check."

He looked at Gaea, and she gasped, taking several steps backward until she stumbled into a table and knocked over a glass. It shattered on the floor as I stormed out at the same time as she spirited away. Fen followed, and about halfway to the room, I felt like an asshole. I'd known and hadn't told her. Just as Wren had done to me. And more so, I'd just outed Greeve, who was supposed to be my family. I could feel the rage swirling with the sorrow in my soul, and I knew if I didn't get out of the castle and somewhere safe soon, I was going to explode and take it down with me.

I stopped, faced Fen and told him what I needed to do. He grabbed my hand and led me to the room, where we got what we needed and left the castle together. I slipped the earring into my ear and Fenlas did the same. The pressure of my magic, my emotions, and my fear still pushing me quickly to a jagged ledge I wasn't sure I could come back from.

Murder was such a seductive, terrible thing. Justifiable to the hands that served it, no matter the consequences. The king who could kill a half pixie because she ran out of wine. The Promised One who could stand on a table and kill a king because her fate told her she could. But who was holding fate accountable? More so, would the self-loathing I felt watching the life leave their still bodies suffocate me?

We swam. Fen leading the way until we came upon the ruins of the sea castle. We found Kai and Leora and called them to a meeting in a castle room with a table anchored to the ceiling by chains and carved white chairs anchored to the floor. I couldn't sit down, couldn't keep my body still as they reported, Leora's glow and Fen's calmness the only thing grounding me.

"Can I get you something?" Leora asked, her gaze flickering between me and Fen.

"We need a full report of the sea. Who is with us, who is going to fight against us," Fen said, looking directly at Kai.

There were no jokes, no humor, pure business today. Kai could tell something was wrong, but could he tell I was about to explode? Doubtful.

"The sea is vast, Fen. The court doesn't sit in one spot, they roam. We've got a few thousand maybe a little more willing to fight with us. The others either haven't seen us or won't talk. We're still running into trouble with the fae that thinks he's owed a kingdom. Morwena kept prisoner camps. She was basically forcing anyone that wouldn't fight with her into chains." His eyes flashed to Leora.

She smiled at him. "We've set them free." She glowed bright.

"And the others?" Fen asked.

"The hydra's been hunting. She's brought back anyone that didn't piss her off enough to get eaten. We haven't kept them chained up, but they are all under guard at Morwena's largest camp, which is on an island."

"Why would she use an island?" I asked, my hands starting to shake.

"She has the water gated off and she was forcing them to share the evada pearls. Only the strong survived."

Anger rolled down the bond.

"Have we done the same?" I clutched the back of a smooth chair in my hands, knuckles white as the chair began to crumble.

"No. We've tried to treat them kindly, though they haven't done the same. Leora was attacked twice, so she had to stop going when food is delivered."

Leora's bright light instantly went out as she sank into the floor.

"Take me to them," I said, my voice a thousand miles away.

"They . . . they are dangerous," Leora warned.

"So am I."

Leora stayed behind as we followed Kai and a few others, including a female he kept particularly close to. Something about our commander in the sea still shocked me. He was like a sea god. Beautiful and commanding as he not only moved through the water but seemed to control it.

We surfaced and swam the last bit of distance to the guarded island. The hydra was waiting. Watching the prisoners with six sets of hungry eyes as she let the sun warm her massive serpentine body.

"Hello friend," she said as I approached. Her heads leaned close to me and she took a long, deep breath, scenting me like the dragon had. She shriveled away, one head looked to Fen and the others watched me. "Do you wish me to kill them all?"

I shuddered. Ordering death was no better than dealing it. I recognized the thirst in her all the same. Death was like a drug to her. She needed it to satiate herself. "Why are you serving me?"

"You knew I was there," her voices sang in eerie unison. "In the dark, when I was trapped, you did not fear me."

"I should have."

"Yes." She laughed. "But you are brave, and you are good."

I narrowed my eyes and tilted my head. "How do you know I'm good? What makes me different from them?" I asked, pointing to the barbed fence.

She curled in close to me again, while the others watched, keeping their distance.

"You freed me." Her heads breathed me in again. "You are of the world. You are water and fire and air and land. You are creation. But you are also kind. Remorseful."

250

"I am not kind."

"Wrong." She made a chortling sound I assumed to be her version of laughter. "Your heart is good. You let the tree sprite go."

"I was a child then."

"A child with more kindness than a queen."

Fen's magical fingers caressed me. *Your heart is good. Even she can see that.*

"I'm a murderer, gifted the ability to destroy," I whispered, the words like a lashing as they left my lips. That pressure built within me again.

Her great body rose above me, cascading out of the water. She moved until she was on the sandy beach of the island, where she writhed and shrieked and shriveled, the lack of water killing her.

"What are you doing? Stop. Get back into the water."

She pushed off the ground, leaped over the top of us, splashed into the water, and then swam back to me. "Do you see?" she asked. "The sun, the land, even the great sea are murderers. Is the land evil?"

*A dramatic, philosophical sea beast,* Fen said. *Of course.*

I couldn't tell if he was surprised or intrigued. Maybe both.

"No," I answered. "But the land doesn't have a choice, and that's the difference."

"You're wrong. The difference is the remorse. The land has none for those it kills, you do. Who would seem the most evil?"

"What are you doing here?" I asked, pushing her questions out of my mind.

"I'm guarding the island until you give me something else to do." She moved her tentacles back and forth in the water.

"You've been trapped in Morwena's castle for who knows how long. Now that you are free, you're blindly serving me. Wouldn't you rather be free?"

"I am free, am I not?"

"You are. But why stay here?"

"The food is plentiful." She looked at the island and showing all of her teeth. "And I owe you a life debt."

"You don't owe me anything."

"I come from an archaic time. It is not your choice, but my own."

"Suit yourself. I have to go deal with these assholes now."

"Let me eat them." She licked her lips and smiled eagerly. "I would take the kill from your own hands."

I rolled my eyes. "Not yet, but you might want to get back."

"I'd rather enjoy the show." Her face beamed with ornery excitement.

I stepped out of the water and onto the shore, pulling the earring from my ear and clinching it into my fist. My hands were steady. The emotional pressure? Not so much.

"The gate is here," Kai said.

It took all the fae accompanying us to slide the door and enter the gated island. The minute we stepped inside, the sea fae, some wearing only their evada pearl, ran for us. Their anger intensified. I held out my hand, but Fen threw up an invisible barrier with his magic because mine could only destroy and that wasn't the actual point of this visit.

"You killed our queen," one of the sea fae yelled, slamming a staff into the ground repeatedly until others joined him in unison. The sound of grinding sand was so distracting I couldn't get a word in.

Fen stepped forward, waved his hand, and every one of the sticks burst into flames.

The crowd began to scream as they tossed them down. Still their taunting and yelling continued, as if I were the true evil in this world. As if I concocted this plan to take over. To destroy everything one person at a time. The voices scrambled my mind as I tried to control my thoughts, my own vision of myself. The murderer. Louder and louder they grew until Fen's voice was lost amongst the fray. Until I realized they were screaming but it wasn't what was drowning me. It was me. The pressure in my mind was so great, I ripped a hole into the wall holding my magic back, shoved my emotions into my magic and let everything rip from me. Because this is what I needed. To release the pressure.

I knew it was a choice. It had a cost, just as Aibell had said, and each time I used that eradicating magic, I lost a part of my soul. A part of Fen's soul. That was what being the Guardian cost him. And I couldn't just take it from him. It would always be our choice. Because once I had used it, there was no repairing it. But he understood why I had to do this. Why we had to show our strength.

This time, instead of just letting it go and dealing with the aftermath later, I directed it. I moved the magic this way and that. I let go of my fear of being a murderer, of being just the mate. The pressure of being Alewyn's Promise. I let it all go. Everything that overwhelmed me and scared me and tormented my dreams. All of it.

"Ara," Fen said.

*I'm fine.*

"You may hate me," I screamed over the crowd. "You may even want to kill me, but you will *never* touch me." I turned to the giant wall of sea I'd created—the precipice of their own destruction, if I willed it. A towering ocean wave loomed over the top of the island, blocking the sun. I could already feel the magic closing in on me. I pressed onward. "I will not kill you unless you give me a reason. Because I'm not like her. Because I'm not like any of them. Because I am not like you."

No one moved as they stared at the barrier, jaws open, as silent as the deepest part of the sea.

"I can't let you free into the world. I don't want to kill you on the battlefield. I don't want to see the ocean full of fae blood. After this inevitable war, the sea will have to rebuild, just as we will on land. I'll crush you all before I let you kill innocents. None of you are better than the fae you had in chains. Remember this day. Remember the mercy you've been given. The lives I've spared. Because she may have given you favor. She may have allowed you to showcase hatred, but I will not. This world will not. I've been sent, made, to fix Alewyn, and you will not change that with your hateful words."

I turned, lifted my hands to direct the ocean, and brought it calmly back to soft waves crashing against the shoreline. I hadn't used enough magic to debilitate myself like I had with Morwena's death, but that was also a very real boundary. My magic could destroy me just as easily as it destroyed the world. Fen, my Guardian, was the only reason why I would never let that happen.

"She commands the sea," I heard someone say.

"She is a god," another gasped.

"She is nothing," another answered.

My head snapped to the voice in the crowd. A wave of my hand and he was on his knees, breath ripped from his fragile lungs. The magic again threatened me. "I am everything!"

Another fae tried to rush to him, but Fen used his wind magic to hold him in place. But I didn't kill that fae pounding his chest for air.

Instead, I showed him mercy. Because the hydra was right, and remorse was the difference between me and them.

I pulled the magic back and the fae fell face first into the ground. I turned and walked out of the camp without another damn word to any of them. I saw the hydra swimming through the water in the distance as she moved to the surface, bowed graciously low and vanished.

It was time to go back to the southern kingdom. Time to plan for war.

CHAPTER

22

# Temir

"This will be your private room while you stay with us at the castle. Breakfast will be served downstairs in the dining hall. If you have need of a staff member, please do seek anyone out. All jobs are shared."

"Thank you," Nadra said to the high fae as we stepped into the room. There were no servants here, apparently.

"Do you think Ara's okay? The king looked devastated."

"I think if she weren't, there would be a bigger response from the castle."

"I'm sure you're right." She took several steps through the large room, then slid her hands through the fabrics that hung from the ceiling encasing the bed that sat directly on the floor. She felt the smooth surface of the pillows and meandered through the room touching each of the luxurious fabrics, including the upholstered furniture and the gossamer curtains.

"I've never seen anything like it," I told her. "It's completely exposed to the elements."

She stood against the wall, pulled the fabric aside, and I joined her, staring at the evening sky. A thousand faint stars splashed across the world like the splatter of a paintbrush.

"It's peaceful here," she said. "Happy."

"Do you still miss home?" I slid my hands down her arms and around her chest.

She shook her head and leaned against me. "Not really. I don't think it would feel like home anymore, you know? Without my mother, it's only an empty shop. I just want to be where you are, Temir." She spun in my arms and ran her fingers through my hair, then locked them behind my neck and pulled my face down to hers.

I leaned, grabbed her by the bottom and lifted her up to me. She was so close I could see the depth and swirls of color within her golden eyes. The scattering of freckles across her cheeks and over her perfect little nose. Finally, we were safe and alone. I pressed my lips to hers, softly at first. She opened and I massaged her with my tongue. I took several steps backward into the room, carried her to the couch and laid her down, never parting my mouth from hers.

She made soft groaning noises as we kissed and it was nearly my undoing. The sound of pleasure coming from my mate was like those perfectly placed stars singing a chorus from the heavens.

She reached between us and began unfastening my pants. Approval jolted through me and she licked the roof of my mouth, then bit my bottom lip. She was anything but shy.

I moved my hands to her waist and began to lift her shirt.

A pounding on the door barely convinced me to stop. A deep-throated snarl was the only response I had. To which Nadra threw her head back and laughed. I stood, walked to the door and nearly yanked it open before she stopped me.

"Your button, Temir," she laughed.

I quickly fixed it, cracked the door, and glared outside. Rhogan stood waiting for me. I was so distracted by the thought of finally having Nadra to myself, I'd completely forgotten we left him with Wren.

"So, Wren said we're moving to the castle?" he asked, trying to peek into the gap of the door.

"Let him in, Tem," Nadra said from behind me.

"No, no." Rhogan winked at me and flashed his infamous giant smile. "I'll go down and get our things from the compound and plan to meet for breakfast in the morning."

I nodded and shut the door before he could say anything else.

Nadra burst into more laughter.

"That really is the most beautiful sound in the world," I told her, walking back to the couch.

"Okay, goodbye, then," Rhogan yelled from the hall.

"Bye." She giggled until I lifted her from the couch and moved her to the bed.

I slipped off my boots. She propped her lithe body up on her elbows, locked her eyes onto me, and watched as I began to remove each piece of her worn clothing, one item at a time, until she laid before me bare and beautiful. My mouth was bone dry as I memorized her perfect form. She crawled to the edge of the bed where I stood and her hands began to move over the panes of my chest as she lifted the seam of my shirt and pulled it smoothly above my head.

I was rock solid and pressing against the limitations of my pants. Her eyes dragged down my body and her lips parted as she got to my

258

waist. She reached for me again, unbuttoning once more and letting them drop to the tile floor.

I placed my hands to the sides of her face and pulled her up to me until she was on her knees and her silky lips were pressed to mine. Her breathing was as rapid as my own as we explored each other's naked bodies. I shifted, taking her full breast into my hand and massaging.

She began to make those sounds again as she leaned back to give me full access, my hand at her waist holding her upright.

"Tell me you want this, Nadra. Tell me," I growled.

"Oh gods," she said in answer as I moved my hand down her body to find the dewy folds between her legs.

I massaged gently as she reached for me, taking me into her hands. My body roared to life, pushing to claim her, to finally leave my mark on her as my mate.

She rocked against my hand, her hips moving in a way that only a female could.

I pulled her upright, dragging my teeth along her neck as she continued to move against me, until she was whimpering and her breaths were scattered. Until her body went completely rigid. I stroked and stroked her until she came.

"Temir." She said my name like it was a final prayer on her lips, and I swept her up again, carried her to the head of the bed, and laid her down, where I crawled on top of her, my length resting on her navel as she spread her legs wide and pushed up from the hips. "Please, Temir."

"Say the words, Nadra. Tell me what you want."

"I need you." Her soft, throaty voice enraptured me.

I pressed the tip against her dripping core, and again, she lifted, searching for me. A hiss left my clenched teeth as I pushed into her inch by inch until I was deep inside her. She wrapped her feet around me, and I held her thighs as I began to thrust. Slowly at first, until the urgency to claim her, to mark her, overwhelmed me.

She dug her nails into my back, her gasps and whimpers sending shivers down my body as I moved in and out of her. My labored breathing grew sparser and she began to moan so loud I thought maybe the entire kingdom could hear her.

And I loved it.

Her body went tight again, spasming around my length, my own pressure beginning to build. The desire to mark her, brand her as mine was powerful. I wanted my scent all over her. I leaned down, breathing onto her collar bone as she cried out and I bit into her salty skin. She went limp below me and for a moment I paused to let her breathe, but then she moved, pulling me out of her and rolled over. She lifted her full ass into the air. I didn't hesitate, I slammed myself deep within her again, feeling every inch of texture between us. I tangled my hands into her copper hair and pulled her back, forcing her to take all of me until we found a rhythm. Until she was screaming and I was barely holding on.

I needed it to last forever. I wanted to stay looking over that ledge, but as I plunged deep within my mate, I moved closer and closer to it until I erupted inside of her, sending pulse after heated pulse.

We collapsed onto the bed, and I pulled her naked body to my bare chest. I smothered her lips with mine and frantically claimed her mouth until again I was hard and needing more of her. She climbed on top of me and rode, swaying those hips and making those sounds until, again, we both climaxed. Eventually, sometime that night, we fell asleep as one.

We woke tangled in each other's arms.

"Are you happy?" she whispered, her voice hoarse from the night of love making.

"I didn't know this feeling existed," I answered. "I've felt happiness in my life, at least I thought I had. But being here with you is like soaring through the sky. It's like realizing life could be eternal, and for the first time, actually hoping it is. You make me laugh. At one point, I forgot how to do that. I love your fire and the way you command a room when you want. I've never had that ability. You're everything I never knew I wanted, but so much more." I pulled her closer to me, never feeling satisfied with the distance between us.

She trailed a fingertip up and down my antlers as she sighed. "I feel the same way. In the midst of chaos, I still feel so lucky."

Later, after a long bath and a visit from a few staff members, we were freshly dressed and being led through the castle to the dining hall for breakfast. Ara and the king were not in attendance, but Rhogan was already halfway through a heaping pile of eggs. The draconian who was with the king in the study the night before was there, but he didn't so much as lift his eyes to acknowledge us as we sat down. We were served generously, though we ate in near silence aside from the groaning from Rhogan as he tried different types of fruits and felt the need to express his undying gratitude as Wren laughed and added more and more to his plate.

The doors opened and Gaea walked into the room.

"Oh," she said. "I guess I was expecting everyone to be in the kitchen."

Greeve jumped out of his seat as she approached the table.

She looked up to him, reached for an apple and turned and walked back out of the room.

He sat again, barely touching the chair before he leapt back up and vanished out of the room.

"That was awkward," Nadra said.

"Don't get me started." Wren shook her head as she looked to the ceiling.

"So, what's the plan for the day?" she asked no one in particular.

Rhogan tossed a folded paper onto the table between us. "We've got another invitation from Murtad."

Nadra rolled her eyes and huffed. "Not interested."

"I've got to get the serum to the rebellion, Nadra. I have to go."

"You could come shopping with me if you want," Wren offered. "I've got some things I need to get for the compound."

"Sweet baby boggarts, I haven't shopped in so long, I think I forgot how," Nadra answered.

Rhogan rubbed his hands together. "I heard the giant is training today. We should go check that out."

"A lot of fae will be down there," Wren warned. "He always draws a crowd. Especially if Ara joins in."

Nadra's eyes lit from within. She had crossed the world to be reunited with her friend. I only hoped she wasn't disappointed. The female I met in the north was vicious, and there wasn't an ounce of kindness to her.

Later, Rhogan and I entered the repair shop just as we had before, but this time it was empty. I shifted the weight of the bag on my shoulder and pushed through the door in the back of the store. The chairs were full of fae and Murtad stood at the front of the room.

"At least he buttoned his shirt this time," Rhogan murmured.

We stood at the back of the full room. A few curious heads turned to see the massive male standing beside me, but for the most part, Murtad held the attention of the crowd like he was offering them deliverance. We waited until he was done with his sugar-coated sermon. The rebels rose from their seats and several familiar faces moved toward me.

I felt my heart leap as Iva's beaming smile approached. "You made it out," I said. "Both of you?"

"Yes. Roe's with Oravan and his family right over there." She pointed and my eyes followed until I eyed a large group of northern fae in the crowd.

"I'll catch up with you soon," I told her. "Don't let them leave, Rhogan."

He moved to block the door, expanding his enormous wings until there was no way around him.

"What's this?" Murtad asked, picking invisible lent from his unbuttoned shirt.

"It's time to weed out the traitors from the rest of the rebellion. I'm sure the Weaver told you why we've come."

"She mentioned it." He shrugged.

"About what Nadra said yesterday—"

He shook his head. "I've heard it before. Things aren't the same down here as they are in the north."

"But if you choose not to fight with King Fenlas, they will be."

"That's why I've asked you to come today. I already sent word that we would join the south, but I won't be offering frontline rebels."

"I think that's our decision to make," I balked.

"Not everyone is meant for battle, Temir," he said casually as he stepped away from me and toward Rhogan at the door.

"How the fuck did that guy become the leader of the rebellion?" I asked Roe as I made my way back to them.

He reached up to clap me on the back. "You'll get used to him."

Voices rose across the crowd and I was instantly moving toward Rhogan at the door. "You cannot keep us trapped in here like criminals," a male centaur shouted.

"Actually, he can." Murtad stepped forward, crossing his arms over his chest. "I've called you all here today because the king has asked us to join him in the war against the northern king, and we will. But first, we need to know who is loyal to this rebellion. Fenlas had a traitor in his own inner circle. There's no reason to believe we don't as well. I'd be interested to find out who let that fucking harpy in here a month ago."

I lifted the bag from my shoulder and set it on a table in the back. Iva and Roe joined me as we laid out the unbreakable vials I'd gotten from the glassmaker before leaving the Marsh Court.

"It's a quick and simple process. You there." I pointed toward a short fae in the crowd with a long neck and feathers covering half his skin. "Would you be willing to volunteer, so I can demonstrate?"

He pulled his head down to his chest and stepped bravely forward. "I will be the first."

I lifted a small vial with blue liquid and handed it to him. His hands were steady as he took the vial and drank. The crowd watched, but no one moved or said a single word.

"You've just taken a truth serum," I announced. "Do you report about the rebellion to anyone?"

"No," he answered.

264

"Have you ever been enchanted?"

"No," he said again.

"Where are you from?"

"I worked in Coro's castle," he answered, shame crossing his face as he rubbed his wrists.

I handed him the red vial and he drank it. "That's the entire process," I said over the crowd. "Rhogan and I will stay until you can get your guards through questioning, and then we'll let you run it from there," I told Murtad.

He nodded and called out several larger fae males. We watched the process until the door could be covered and then left them to it. I stopped to invite Oravan to the castle and then we headed back to the training arena to watch the giant.

I didn't think Rhogan had ever been so excited in his life.

# CHAPTER
## 23

# Ara

"Nadra? You're sure?" I asked, stepping into my training gear.

"Without a doubt. Curly red hair and all," Fen said as he watched me dress with hooded eyes.

"Where is she? Why haven't I seen her?"

"We've been busy." He leaned against the doorframe to the bathing room.

"Do you think the war council went okay last night?"

He scratched the back of his head. "As good as one can go, I suppose. I wish we had some final numbers, but I did get a message back from Murtad about the rebellion."

"Oh, yes. The mysterious rebel leader." I rolled my eyes.

"I would go with obnoxious before mysterious, but essentially, yes, him."

"And?" I asked, pulling the shirt over my head.

"The rebels are in, conditionally."

I shoved my foot into one boot and then the other. "Conditionally?"

"Trust me, it's how he works. He always has to make it seem like he's doing me a favor."

"Sounds like a winner. When can I see Nadra?"

"Now if you want."

"Of course I want to see her now. I'm surprised she isn't banging the door down and tearing through our closet."

"She was social at our meeting, but she didn't seem like the same girl I saw at the parties in Coro's castle. I think she's changed."

I snorted. "I doubt it."

We hardly used the dining hall, but the number of us was growing and the kitchens weren't, so we strode the halls, hand in hand, until we got there.

"Ara?" A beaming redhead shouted as she shot out of her chair and launched herself at me. "I thought we'd missed you." Her simple clothes were tattered, her skin tanned by the sun and her eyes were the only thing gleaming. Even her hair had lost its luster.

"What happened?" I asked, pulling her away to examine her. "You look . . . different."

"Mother . . ." Her voice broke. "It's just . . . It's a long story. It's so good to see you."

"I'm so sorry, Nadra. But you made it and you're here with Temir?"

"My mate." She smiled behind her tears.

I pulled her into a hug. She was the only reminder I had of my former life and I never thought I'd be so happy to see her. "You can shop my closet later if you want to," I whispered into her ear.

She giggled and hugged me tighter and then began sobbing and I just stood there holding her until she could compose herself. "Wren and I are going shopping for the refugee compound. Do you want to come?"

I pulled away. "Absolutely not. Still not a shopper."

She sniffled and smiled. "It's so good to see you. I've been so worried about you." Her eyes flashed to Fen and I caught the subtle shake of his head. He wasn't telling me something.

*Haven't had time, that's all. We will talk about it later.*

"You're staying here now. I'll see you for dinner, I promise."

"We better get going," Wren said from behind us. "If we're late to Deci's, he will sell our flour."

Nadra pulled me into another hug and then she and Wren were gone.

I rounded on Fen. "Keeping secrets?"

"No. It's just something we should talk about with just the four of us. I've got to stop into the study and then we can go down to the lists." I eyed him carefully, but his relaxed posture and steady eyes gave nothing away. "After you." We walked silently side by side. He held the study door open for me. I narrowed my eyes but stepped inside anyway. He didn't follow. Instead, he slammed the door shut and held it with his wind magic as I beat on it with the flat of my hand.

"What the hell, Fen?" I yelled. "I have magic too. I could shred this door right now." A throat was cleared behind me. I hadn't even looked to see if someone else was in the room. I pivoted furiously, and

268

as soon as I saw Greeve, I turned and continued to beat on the door. "I'm going to kick your ass, Fenlas. Open this gods-damn door right now."

"Family fights, but they also forgive," he said like some fucking children's book.

*You're cut off,* I fumed.

*As if you could resist me.*

I spun to Greeve. "Was this your idea? Because you've been a real asshole lately and I'm not going to apologize for what I said."

"I'm not asking for an apology." He crossed his arms over his chest. "But you could at least sit down like an adult and talk to me."

"You can't tell me what to do," I argued, jamming my hands into my pockets.

*Like adults,* Fen reiterated.

"Stop listening behind the door!" I yelled.

"Look, I just wanted to say that you were right."

I paused. "I'm listening."

"This whole time I've asked you to join our family and let us protect you and be a team player."

"You forgot to mention the part where I was right," I said, tapping my foot.

"Things have been . . . strange lately. As soon as she got here, from the moment I saw her, I think I knew. Something within me did. But every time I've tried to get close to her, she pushes me away or just vanishes. It's caused some tension."

"So, you thought you'd redirect that onto me?"

He crossed the room until he stood right in front of me. I had to strain my neck to look up at him. "You're my family now." A slight breeze surrounded him, his magic thrumming even now as he reached for me. "I'm sorry I was a jerk and I didn't talk to you before I went to Fen. In the future, you can trust me. I'm working on the temper."

Fen cleared his throat in the hallway.

"Go away, Fen," we said in unison.

"Not until you hug it out," he answered.

I raised an eyebrow to Greeve. "I'm not hugging you."

"Will you talk to her for me?" he asked, his eyes pleading.

I shook my head, throwing my hands up in mock surrender. "She's more pissed at me than anyone."

"Please. I'll get on my knees right here. She won't talk to me."

"Oh my gods, fine. But you have to do something for me."

"Anything."

I smiled wickedly. "You're going to regret that."

"Probably," he answered, pulling me into the hug I didn't want.

Fen opened the door grinning.

I rolled my eyes and stormed past him, headed to the lists.

"Fine, I'm an asshole." I leaned against the fence as Greywolf began to warm up.

Gaea kicked the sand below her feet but didn't answer. Of all people, Loti was the one who convinced her to come down and talk to me.

"I was so pissed when Wren did that to me, so I get it. I should have said something in private. I just . . ." My voice faded away as I struggled to explain the rage.

"Was that a complete thought?" she asked finally.

"I suck at this." I pulled myself up and sat on the top of the fence lining the arena. "Sometimes I feel like I'm okay and I have confidence that we can do this, and then shit hits the fan and I can't collect my thoughts long enough to consider we might actually all fucking die."

"But you knew before we went to Coro's court. You could have told me."

"I only guessed. I didn't know for sure until you grabbed him and I saw his face right before you left me behind. He knew what was happening and it wasn't me he was worried about."

She considered that for a moment, picking lint from her shirt. "Fine. I'm going to forgive you because I somewhat like your snarky attitude and all around badassery, but I'm not sure you're going to convince Greeve as easily as me."

"He's the one who asked me to talk to you. Besides, he can suck my dick."

"There's that attitude," she laughed and I winked at her.

"Seriously though, are you going to accept the bond?"

"I mean, have you seen him? Tall, dark, handsome."

"Moody as fuck," I added.

"Also that. I guess I thought when the mating bond snapped into place, it would happen to both of us at the same time."

"I think they are all always different. I'm not even sure the exact moment mine and Fen's bond really snapped. There was a moment in The Mists, but there was something more between us before that. Still,

271

you might have some competition with the hydra. Just maybe keep him away from the sea for a while."

*Is it safe yet?*

"They're getting lonely," I told her, tilting my head to the two draconian fae huddled in the arena, watching us as they got their weapons ready.

"Let's do this, then." She took us to the center of the arena with her magic.

"You're sure this is a good idea?" Brax asked from the fence line.

"I'm like eighty percent sure," I answered, grabbing several wooden knives and strapping a sword to my back.

"Okay," he announced, more for the growing crowd than for us. "The rules are simple. Male against female. If you take what would be a fatal wound with real weapons, you're out. Last fae standing wins."

"What do I get when I win?" Fen asked, jumping back and forth like he was ready to pounce.

I sent him a very suggestive mental picture and he instantly dropped the sword in his hand.

Gaea laughed and even Greeve smiled before he groaned remembering who was on his team. "We're screwed." He shook his head.

"On your marks!" Brax yelled.

We walked to the center of the arena. I moved my feet into position and bent slightly at the knee, ready to run as soon as the signal was given.

*Have I told you how sexy you are when you're about to kick someone's ass?*

I ignored him of course. My father taught me about distraction tactics when I was a child. Fen was only doing it because he knew he was about to be embarrassed in front of his people. I almost felt bad. Almost.

Brax took a deep breath in to yell, but he was stopped by a commotion in the stands. Fae were yelling for guards and Greeve grabbed Fen and cleaved him away before we could even see what was happening. Gaea reached for my arm to do the same, but I yanked free.

"Unless you're taking me over there, don't bother." I moved to the stands before she could protest, but she did follow. I jumped the fence and my arm jerked as Temir reached for me.

"Where's the king?" he asked frantically.

"He's probably back in the palace." I stepped back to take in the large, winged male beside him.

"Rhogan," the male said, dipping his chin. "And this is Murtad, if you haven't met."

"Pleasure," the satyr said, measuring me carefully.

"What's going on?" I ignored the rebel leader. I'd heard his name. I wasn't impressed.

"We've caught a traitor in the rebellion. The rebels are dragging him to the castle."

"So, the rebels want the security from the southern court but conditionally offer their own services to the crown? That's fucking convenient." I held my hand out so Gaea could take us to the study. She didn't hesitate. Fen was arguing with Greeve about going back when we arrived. "The rebels found a traitor and they're bringing him here now."

Fen was out the door in an instant.

I looked over my shoulder to Gaea as I followed. "Can you go back and get Temir? You can leave the leader to walk."

She bit back a smile. "And the other one?"

"He has wings, let's see if he can use them." We stepped into the foyer as she spirited away.

Two large males, both with hoofed feet and knobby horns, dragged a third between them. He was a fae with elongated canines, lanky limbs and jeweled bracelets up and down his arms, something about them familiar.

"He's knocked out," one of the rebels said.

Fen looked to Greeve, who nodded, grabbed the traitor, and disappeared.

"Tell me everything," Fen said to Temir as he and Gaea appeared in the doorway.

"I created a serum. I've been manufacturing it as we traveled and while we were in the northern kingdom. It's a truth serum. If taken, you can't tell a lie. We dropped it off at the rebel meeting this morning and then Rhogan and I left. Apparently, someone got nervous and tried to escape the guards."

"He stabbed a guard before those two got him," Murtad said as Rhogan dropped him at the door, his wings pounding the air.

I rested my hand on the dagger at my waist. There was familiar comfort in the carved handle. "Do you have serum left?"

"It's in the room you've let me have." Rhogan stepped around Murtad. "I brought it back with me last night."

Fen nodded. "Grab it. And meet me back here in ten minutes. Murtad, I'll send a report with what we find."

"Oh good, I was hoping I wouldn't have to sit through a boring interrogation." He moved backwards, strolling down the steps to the castle.

*I don't think I like him.*

*I don't think anyone really does.*

"I'd prefer you to come for the administration, if you don't mind," Fen asked the healer. "It might not be pretty though."

"You won't have to force information out of him. He will have to answer anything you ask."

"That doesn't mean I won't punch him in the fucking face," I said as Gaea grabbed onto me.

"Do you need to know where Greeve took him?" Fen asked, already watching the hall for Rhogan to return.

"I can sense Greeve. Don't ask," she said as we spirited away and landed in a large, empty stone room, save a single chair in the center.

The traitor was already tied down while Greeve stood before him like a statue, the wind from his power blowing through his hair as he clenched and unclenched his iron fists, waiting for an excuse to use them. He hadn't even registered our arrival.

Gaea looked to him and moved carefully across the room until she reached out and gently touched his arm. The wind beating around him vanished as he finally looked away and into his mate's face. They didn't speak a word as I stood, awkwardly watching. He blinked and his shoulders relaxed a fraction.

The door to the room slammed open, and the three other males burst in with the force of a gale, knocking the door from its hinges. We stood in a half circle around the traitor, watching his chest rise and fall until finally Temir spoke. "I can wake him if you're ready."

"Should we make a plan?" Gaea asked.

"Wake the asshole. Find out what he knows. Kill the asshole," I answered.

Greeve and Rhogan nodded.

At least someone agreed with me.

Temir reached forward, placed his hand on the traitor's forehead, and within seconds, his bloodshot eyes opened. Greeve grabbed his fuzzy head and yanked it back as Fen poured a vial full of liquid down this throat.

He spat it out, coughing.

"Don't worry," Temir said. "He's gotten enough of it down."

Suddenly the traitor was laughing, full-belly, shoulder-shaking laughter as the group of us stood around him ready to murder. The golden bracelets stacked up his arms rattled, drawing me in; something familiar about them still tapped my mind.

"You're a lesser," Gaea said. No pretense, just point blank.

"So are you, traitor," he answered. "Our king wasn't giving it to you hard enough so you had to come searching for a better tumble?"

Greeve's hand was at his throat before I blinked. He lifted the traitor off the ground as a smile crossed his face. Even I was scared of him in that moment.

"Stop." Gaea placed her hand on Greeve's arm. "He wants you to kill him. Don't you see? He's baiting you so he won't have to give up information. Put him down."

Greeve dropped him and paced behind us as the fae gasped for breath.

"What is your name?" Fen asked first.

He pinched his mouth shut, biting down on his own lips so hard he began to bleed, but still, he couldn't fight the magic. "Throng."

"Have you been enchanted?" Temir asked.

"No." He smiled. "I've faithfully supported King Autus and I have done his bidding for years."

"Why?"

"Because you were always the favored ones. Both of you." He looked between Temir and Gaea. "You lived in his castle and ate at his table and he promised me I could have the same things. That I could be like you." He spat at the floor in front of Temir.

"What have you told Autus?" Fen asked.

"Everything."

"Be more specific," Rhogan demanded from the corner.

"He knows you're mated to that," he said, as if I were not a fae at all. Just an object.

I felt the fury building. My magic called me to end him. To end it all.

"He knows Tolero is dead and the sea queen. He knows your mate killed her. He knows she has a lot of power and he's coming for her."

"What else is he planning?" Fen asked, holding my hand as if he could save me from the words.

"He has asked me to help him release them and I have." His psychotic laugh filled the room.

"Release who?"

He shook his head and suddenly blood poured from his mouth. He choked on his own blood.

Temir leaped for him, pried his mouth open and turned to Fen. "He bit his own tongue off."

"Can you heal him?"

"Yes," Temir answered. "But it's going to hurt like hell."

"Good."

He reached forward and placed his hand on his forehead. His brows furrowed and we waited until he shook his head. The traitor was turning a deep shade of blue as he continued to choke.

"Oh my gods, the bracelets." I rushed forward. "They're charmed." I began yanking them down his arms and off one by one, but I wasn't fast enough. He went limp before I could remove them all.

"Fuck," Fen yelled.

"I don't understand. How did the serum work if your magic didn't?" Gaea asked.

"The serum isn't magic. There's magic in the making, but the serum itself isn't."

"I should have seen it sooner. I knew they looked familiar."

"How so?" Temir asked.

"I lost it so I can't show you, but my mother's necklace. Originally, it was used as a promise. To my mother from another, but the stones were the same. Then Aibell did something to activate it before I left her cottage. It protected me from a different type of magic. Morwena's trackers."

"I've seen that stone before," Gaea said, picking up a bracelet. "I think I know where your necklace is." She was gone and back before I could even register it. She held my mother's necklace out to me.

I couldn't explain why, but tears filled my eyes as I reached for the last thing my mother had given me. "Where was it?"

"We found it when we were searching Lichen's rooms."

"I wish I could kill that asshole again." I clasped the charm around my neck and swayed with the memory of my mother's hands in mine. Her final moments. Her rushing me out the door and to my destiny.

To Fen. Though I hadn't known it at the time. It seemed a lifetime ago.

"I have bad news." Temir stepped forward, yanking me from my memories. "I know what he has released. He told Nadra there are dangerous creatures trapped somewhere within this world. Behind a hidden door. Autus intended to find it and release them upon Alewyn. I'd bet a coin that's what it was."

"When the fuck did Nadra have a talk with Autus?" I asked.

Rhogan and Temir shared a look.

"She was his prisoner, of sorts," Temir whispered. "He enchanted her to love him, though he wouldn't let her touch him. Essentially, he tried to drive her to madness. Haven't you told her?" he asked Fen.

"Told me what?"

"He's found a way to control your power. He just needs a few more items and you."

*Tell me this isn't what you were keeping from me, Fenlas. Tell me you didn't know this,* I begged him. A single look was answer enough. I shoved the feelings of betrayal away.

Temir cleared his throat. "That's not the biggest concern right now, though I think we need to search for the lost artifact in the dunes before he finds it."

"I'm so confused," Gaea said, shaking her head.

"Later," Aibell answered as she popped into the room. She faced me and placed her hands upon her staff. "The creatures of the book."

I blinked, trying to process what she'd said. "No," I gasped.

"They rattle," she answered.

I didn't want to consider creatures so strong they rattled Aibell's bones. She was not of this world. What did that say of them? "The banshee was released from the book, but it wasn't the only creature locked within," I told the others, then turned back to her. "I thought releasing the book into the Soul Repository destroyed it?"

"Every door has two sides. You destroyed one, child." Aibell's large eyes dropped to the ground. "He's been hunting its match."

"You seem all powerful," Temir said with more disdain than I'd ever heard from him. "Why can't you take care of them?"

"I am but one. I will hunt them, but you will have to destroy them."

"Get Kai," Fen ordered Greeve, and immediately he was gone.

"I will return. Prepare." Aibell looked gravely around the room, letting the tension in her words settle before she vanished.

Fen took over. "We won't be able to hunt in big groups. We will be slow. We need to break up. Gaea, you'll have to take one team and Greeve will have to take the other."

"What are the teams?" I asked.

"You and I stay together," he answered. "We have to."

I wanted to argue, but he was right. If I needed to use as much magic as I had with Morwena, he would have to protect me through the aftermath. While I faced the price of my magic. "We can take Kai with us as well, since he is a tracker."

"And Gaea, because she can sense where Greeve is, which means we can always get to them." Fen answered.

"Right. So, Rhogan, Temir and Greeve will fight anything close by that Greeve can get to quickly. We will take anything farther away that Gaea can spirit to." We turned to the room of eyes watching us. "Any objections?"

"Wren and Nadra?" Temir asked.

"Nadra can't fight at all, she would only be in danger," I said.

"I've been working with her, but I think you're right," Rhogan said. "She can hold her own against a simple fae, but probably not an ancient beast."

"Wren can stay with Nadra and Inok. Someone has to be here at the castle," I answered.

"Let's go. Everyone meet in my study in no more than ten minutes." Fen grabbed my hand and we were tearing through the palace, searching the halls until we found Inok. "I need you to watch the castle. There's no time to explain. Send word for everyone to go to their homes. I want no one on the streets of the city. No one outside. Wren is to join you here. Get word to Sabra to lock down the refugees."

Inok didn't say a word, simply bowed and sprung into motion. If Fen was worried, he didn't let it show at all. He was militant. Commanding. Poised.

"Don't be sexy right now, Fen. I love you, but there's no time for all the things I want to do." I yanked him to our room so I could change. I needed all my weapons.

By the time we got to the study, Temir and Rhogan were already waiting for us. Greeve and Gaea still hadn't arrived, and Aibell was standing, wringing her wrinkled hands, impatiently waiting.

"There are three to kill. Two are moving through the Marsh Court, one is nearly here."

"Do we know what they are?" I asked. "More banshees?"

She shook her head. Actual fear shone from behind her ancient eyes. Aibell was foreign, but I always believed she was from some place far worse than Alewyn. Whatever the king had released upon us, whatever had caused this reaction from her, was likely something close to death. I looked around the room. As Greeve and Gaea walked in, I realized we likely wouldn't all be standing here once this was done.

# Temir

*R*hogan was easy. We'd spent so much time together recently, we knew how to fight together. His great, long sword was his favorite weapon, and though I was skilled with my own, we both knew he was a far better fighter. My magic was what brought me here. Why I was included in the hunt for the creatures the king had released. Locked away for thousands of years, and now somehow, we were supposed to hunt and kill them. I doubted the probability considering those who fought them all those years ago, though they had more potent magic, were unable to kill them. Still, as I looked to the dark draconian fae appointed to our team, felt the breeze constantly surrounding the darkness that encompassed him, and heard the clinging of the weapons he was trained with since birth to fight with, I wondered if we might actually have a chance.

"I know where we are." Greeve looked around us studiously. "That rise over there leads to the borderlands."

"At least when the old lady dropped us, she didn't plant us in the middle of a barren desert." Rhogan wiped beads of sweat from the side of his face. Neither of us were acclimated to the dry heat. His wings shifted as he pulled a sword longer than me from his back.

The sound of metal rubbing against metal pierced my ears.

"We aren't in the middle." Greeve's voice was lethal. "But if there's something near, as far as I'm concerned, the fewer victims it has, the better."

"What's the plan?" I asked, blocking bits of sand from my eyes as the wind blew around us in waves, my teeth grinding along the grains blown into my mouth.

"We go hunting," the drac answered, completely unfazed by the nature of the desert or the breeze surrounding us. "We walk, you fly," he told Rhogan.

He shot into the sky, his wings opening so fast a feather drifted to the ground. He circled above us, the batting of his wings became the cadence to our march through the scorching desert. He carried his long sword in his hands as he flew. He was born for this. Ready.

I was not.

A scream came from somewhere behind us and then another.

"Fly toward the sounds," Greeve yelled at Rhogan as he grabbed my arm turned us to dust on the wind.

My body ripped through a rush of pressured air until we landed smoothly, Greeve already running. My feet sank into the sand, and though I pushed through my thighs, I wasn't nearly as fast as he was.

But then he slammed to a halt.

"Fuck." Rhogan dropped beside him. "Is that what I think it is?"

"Yes." Greeve pulled a curved blade from his sheath. "A gods-damn tharraing. Do not let her get her hands on you."

284

Ahead of us, a group of ranchers stood together surrounding a creature I'd never seen before. There were two shredded bodies already on the ground as the tharraing, a beautiful female being, hovered above them, enthralling the remaining group with her smooth movements and seductive eyes. The generous curves of her body, her long black hair, the way she moved, everything about her aided her attempt to lure the small group closer so they were within reach.

We continued slowly forward, my eyes darting through the gathered fae trying to swing weapons at her.

She lashed forward, a crack audible as she grabbed one of the males. Her face became sinister. Her smile wicked. She spun him around so quickly he was a blur, an insect in a spider's invisible web. She whispered into his ear as she continued, the crowd moving back as we edged forward.

A female screamed again as the tharraing's unfortunate victim was suspended midair, his head tilted to the sky and his body limp. The creature towered over him, blocking the sun as she plunged her needle-like fingers into both of his eye sockets. The sound of his skull cracking reverberated through the dry air as his body jerked from her invasion. She slowly pulled a silky, delicate substance from him.

"His soul," Rhogan breathed, though I wasn't sure he meant for it to be out loud.

"Please, no," the female in the crowd begged. She tried to run forward, pushing and pulling, but several males held her back.

Her sobs were the only sound to the tharraing's movements as she held that fae above the ground. Her nimble fingers seemed to dance in the sunlight as she gathered the tendrils of his faerie soul and wove them into string. She held the gossamer-like ends high in the air until the unforgiving sunlight shone through them. She sliced his soul with those fingers. The corpse she held in front of her shriveled into a hollowed heap as deep red blood streamed down his empty face. Done with her victim, she dropped him to the ground with a thud, the cold chill that shrouded me a direct contrast to the heat from the endless desert.

"Get back to your homes. Save yourselves!" Rhogan expanded his wings, trying to block the creature from the ranchers.

The smart ones ran. Perhaps we should have run also.

"You're beautiful." Her honeyed voice enraptured Greeve as he stepped forward. "Perhaps I'll keep you."

I felt the physical pull to her words. Rhogan dropped his hands to his sides and his sword dragged along the ground as he took several willing steps toward her. I sank my fingers into his feathered wing and yanked him backward. His heavy body was reluctant to submit. "Don't listen to her," I barked.

Greeve shook his head and disappeared, the wind carrying him like a cyclone. The creature screamed as black blood poured down her arm. I could feel the thrum of my heart, the sweat pour down my neck, the tension in my muscles as I stood useless, watching as the drac continued to slash at her until she hissed and crouched, still not standing on the ground. Lashing out with her sharpened fingers as he surrounded her, her body jerked each time he made contact.

Rhogan moved in to swing his enormous sword from behind, but he hesitated.

Greeve landed several feet away. His shoulders rising and falling as he tried to catch his breath. Blood poured from his wounds, glistening down his back and dropping to the deep red sand below his feet. He may have been hurting her, but she was definitely doing more damage. With Greeve on the ground, Rhogan stepped in, his sword giving him some distance from her vicious claws.

286

I ran to Greeve and reached to heal him, but he pulled away. "Let me help you. It's why I'm here."

He was reluctant but nodded. I placed my hand on his shredded back and tugged on my magic until it was flowing from me.

But then Rhogan yelled and Greeve whisked away, barely receiving any healing as he moved back in toward the female.

A farmer who stayed behind began shooting arrows at the tharraing. Rhogan was trying to dodge them while still swinging his sword and trying to avoid hitting Greeve, who we couldn't see at all as he struck the creature. He took an arrow to the shoulder before I could tackle the rancher to the ground. "You'll kill them both," I screamed into his ear.

"Fine, as long as she goes with them," the fae grunted as he tried to shove me off of him.

I drew my arm back and cracked him in the face, his nose shattering as blood poured from his nostrils. I grabbed his shoulders and slammed his head on the ground. I didn't want to use my power to debilitate the bastard if I didn't have to. "Do you really think you're going to kill that thing with an arrow when those two together can't take her down?"

"Get the fuck off of me." He breathed through his nose, and blood splattered across my face.

"He's right, Ullo," another rancher said as he grabbed his friend and nodded at me. "Best we leave the drac to it." I moved off of him as the one who spoke up pulled his friend to his feet. "Better get to the others and make sure they're locked in. Good luck," he said over his shoulder as the rest of the bystanders backed up. Not all of them left, but they kept their distance, observing.

I turned back to the battle, watching her body twist back and forth. She kept an eye glued to Rhogan while dodging Greeve as he struck her time and time again. Her eyes began to calculate, her smile spreading again as she struck like a snake and snatched him from the air. She slashed and slashed at him until he was bleeding from every surface of his body.

"Save him," Rhogan yelled as he pounded forward, lifting the sword high above his head to bring it down upon the tharraing.

She dropped the drac and turned just in time to dodge his blow, the weapon landing inches from Greeve's discarded body. She wanted Greeve. She moved back toward him multiple times, but as Rhogan became the more pressing threat, he drew her backward far enough that I could reach the draconian.

I sank to my knees in the sand and placed my sweaty hands on Greeve. The phantom pain reverberated through my own body, and I had to push it away. The last time I had laid my hands on someone hurt so bad his pain seeped into me was Oleonis, and he died. I closed my eyes and tried to keep my ears open as I immersed myself into the well of magic guiding it through him.

"Hold on," I ordered his unresponsive body.

I didn't take the time to numb him from the pain. As my magic moved through him, it was going to burn like hell, but I had to reserve what I could because he would need nearly all of it. Starting from the top and working my way down, I closed the severed blood vessels, nerves, and tendons.

I glanced up to check on Rhogan. One of his wings hung awkwardly behind him, and much like Greeve, he was bleeding profusely. He could barely lift his sword to block blow after blow from the creature that must have clawed her way from hell upon birth. Rhogan fell to one knee, his face utterly defeated. Each of his breaths as labored as the draconian's were faint. He collapsed to the ground, face first into the burning hot sand as the creature reached for him, lifting him until he hung suspended in the air. This battle was already almost over.

I pulled my hands from Greeve. I couldn't save him. I couldn't heal him and do what I knew I needed to do in order to save the rest of the world. I wouldn't have the magic for both.

"Hey," I yelled, trying to draw her attention before she could tear Rhogan's soul from his body. "Take me first."

Her head snapped sideways, the smile once again spreading across her striking face. "Why should I?" she asked, drawing me in with that siren's call.

"I am mated. If you sever my soul, you kill both of us."

Her eyes went wide, and she was before me in an instant. "Two souls for one?" She tilted her head as she watched me.

"And I won't even fight you," I answered, hoping she moved a few inches closer.

"No," Rhogan grumbled from the ground. "Temir."

"Too late." The tharraing grabbed my shoulder.

I didn't hesitate. I laid my hand over her arm and let the dark magic nearly drain me in an instant. The breath shot from my lungs at the immediate void. She didn't shriek, moan or even blink. One moment she was alive and the next she was dead.

I crawled to Rhogan, the sand scraping my arms, my muscles protesting each of my movements. There was only a small bit left. Just enough for his wings, I hoped. My eyelids weighed a thousand pounds. The exhaustion threatened to take me before I could get to him, but I fought as hard as he had, as hard as Greeve had, until I stretched my hand out far enough for one finger to gently graze the top of his head. He moaned as I moved that last bit of magic forward, avoiding the final drop that called to me. Spots filled my vision and I felt him shift just before the world faded away.

CHAPTER

*25*

# Ara

*O*f all the places. Of all the places in the whole fucking wide world, we had to come here.

"I don't see anything," Gaea huffed, searching the horizon.

And of course, she didn't. Because the barn that used to fill that view, the warm cottage that used to sit in the background had been burnt to the ground. The ash of the buildings, of my parent's bodies, nothing but a memory as the green grass filled the ever-evolving land. I knew we were there to hunt an ancient creature, but my heart called me in a different direction. Home.

"The forest." Kai drew his sword.

That gods-damned forest. I'd nearly died in there once, and because we had not one, but two creatures to kill, we would probably come close again. I turned my back on the memories that haunted me and followed the rest of the group into the dense forest. The sun quickly vanished as the canopy of leaves and branches grew above us. Even the air was familiar here—the smell of the woods, moss-covered ground, and rotted bark a staple from my childhood. A low, murky fog crept along the terrain like veils of haze slithering along the forest floor.

Though Gaea's eyes were that of a feline, so were her movements as she silently walked beside me.

Kai and Fen used hand signals to guide us forward. I'd seen them navigate a forest, had formed a friendship with them in one, but this was different. Dangerous.

"Stop," I whispered, my face tightening.

The air had gone still. The forest that had always felt aware somehow was now completely silent—not a whisper of wind rushing through the fallen leaves. As they all looked to me, I pointed to my ear.

*Something's here.*

The hair on my arms rose, invisible fingers trickled down my spine, and my senses screamed that someone, something was watching us. I looked over my shoulder and saw nothing. Still, I pulled two throwing knives from the band across my chest, relishing in the comfort they brought to my callused hands. I hardly dared to breathe as we stood, four hearts beating, the only sound in the reticent forest.

Movement out of the corner of my eye gripped me. As slowly as I could allow my coiled muscles, I turned my head. The three of them did the same. There was nothing there, but I knew I had seen something. I kept my hands loose and my feet shoulder-width apart as I continued to rake my eyes over the scene. It could be anything. I looked back and forth, searching frantically for anything that felt out of place, something that felt like a violation to the world.

I hadn't seen a thing, but Kai did. In a single swift movement, he yanked an arrow from his quiver, drew back his bow, and released.

"A vysa?" I asked out loud as the creature separated from the tree it was camouflaged against.

The woodland sprang to life. A flock of startled birds shot from the forest ceiling as he moved.

"A what?" Gaea asked.

"Secure your minds," I demanded.

I strained my neck to look up at the tall, lanky creature that reminded me of a stilted festival performer. His face was like an unfinished sculpture, featureless apart from two obsidian stones where his eyes should be, the lack of a mouth more unsettling to me than the long skeletal fingers. Swaths of moss draped over his bony arms and hung between his limbs like a blanket crafted by the forest itself. Between the deep canyons scored across his bark-clad shoulders, small mushrooms and seedlings sprouted from deep within. He moved leisurely, the wooden crust of his skin cracking as he stalked forward. A shield of magic surrounded him, dragging along the ground until the forest floor began to swirl below him and the weight of his magical shield ripped the roots of hundred-year-old trees from the ground, filling the forest with the sound of its own desecration.

"He's incredibly strong and exceedingly magical," I yelled.

"I didn't know the vysa was a real creature," Fen answered, pulling his own magic forward.

"Looks like you were wrong." Kai strapped his bow to his back and pulled out a sword, as if that would do any more damage to the behemoth than an arrow.

"We're fucked if we can't get past that shield." Gaea spirited behind the vysa and back again. "It surrounds him."

*Should I use my magic?*

*No. You know what happens. If the power of the destruction incapacitates you, I'm not sure what we'll do for the next fight.*

He was right, of course. It was too big of a risk. The cost was too great.

"Uh, guys?" Gaea snagged our attention.

We both looked in her direction as Kai lifted his sword and moved toward her.

"I knew it." I strapped the daggers back to my chest and pulled my own sword. "It has taken control of his mind. He's the only one without magic."

"Occupy Kai while I take on the vysa," Fen barked, moving away.

"Two for Kai, one for the creature?" I protested.

"Keep him alive." He stared up at the vysa standing eerily still, observing the chaos unfolding before him with those ebony stones for eyes.

Gaea spirited away as Kai got closer and pivoted to make me his new target. I thought his mind was blank and he wasn't really in there, but a flicker of emotion showed me he was. The vysa had convinced him we were the foes. I had trained with Kai enough to know how he moved. I knew he favored his right side because of a pain he sometimes got in his left knee. I knew he would block a second late when he should have countered. I could do this.

But could Fen defeat a vysa on his own?

"Go help Fen," I told Gaea as she landed beside me. "I can take care of Kai."

She huffed and spirited away.

I raised my sword in time to block Kai. He swung to punch my ribs, but I was faster. I moved to the side and then advanced on him, watching for Fen out of my peripheral vision. But Kai was strong, and if I let myself become too distracted, he would take the opportunity. I swung, blocked, and countered. The familiar vibrations of our swords crashing into one another jolted through my body, the sound of a deadly sword fight reminding me of my father. I felt him speaking over my shoulder, whispering to me.

"Tighten your core," he would say. "Shoulders back."

I moved. I spun. I kicked.

"Chin up, Ara." He was there. I could feel him.

I blocked.

"Balance your weight."

Jab. Slash. Pivot. Shuffle.

"Faster."

Tears stung my eyes as the phantom of my father's memory overwhelmed my senses. Why was this happening? Was it the proximity of home?

Kai swung through my blurry vision and struck my thigh. The burn of his blade pulled me from the distraction of my recollections.

Gaea spirited beside me. "My turn." She pushed me toward Fen.

I stumbled, turning to see the creature watching me instead of Fen and Kai. Had he known? Had he felt my misery? Something was off.

Fen tore through his own magic.

The vysa's shield was nearly gone, so he shifted forward. He was no longer going to sit back and watch this battle and that was when he became very, very dangerous. We moved quickly, deeper within the forest, beyond the familiar parts I knew and closer to the river I had used to outsmart a knovern.

Gaea spirited back and forth, keeping Kai occupied as we went.

*Where are we going?* I asked Fen as he struck the shield with magic.

*Only deeper into the forest. Away from the edge.*

I knew what that meant. He was worried I'd eviscerate the world. If not the world, then a good radius.

*Just in case,* he assured me. His hands were steady, but the bond never lied.

We stopped moving. The crack in the vysa's shield slid down the side like a raindrop and then the entire thing shattered into a million pieces of ancient magic.

"You're up." Gaea's shoulders drooped from the battle with Kai.

But Kai didn't come for me; he didn't focus on Gaea either. Kai and the beast were both headed toward Fen.

"We have to stop Kai, G."

"I can't fight him. He's too strong."

"Then you have to help Fen. I'll worry about Kai." I pulled a knife and threw it until it landed in Kai's calf. I had no choice. It wouldn't kill him. He would heal. But I had to pull his attention back to me.

He drew an arrow and shot.

I dodged it, but the wound in my thigh burned from the movement. I threw another knife, intentionally missing him, but it was enough that he stopped chasing my mate.

I pulled my sword once more and Kai came at me with a vengeance. The power of his sword crashed down on me so hard it took all my strength to block him. This was the warrior Fen had known him to be. Ruthless. He pulled the sword back and swung it so quickly forward, the fog on the ground moved with him.

Again, I blocked, but that familiar feeling of nostalgia threatened to overtake me.

The ground shook and Gaea screamed.

I couldn't look behind me or I would die. There was a sheen of sweat on Kai's forehead. Several times it looked as if he was trying to fight against the vysa's control, but it didn't matter. He still pressed on. He swung. I blocked. I advanced. He blocked. I could have made so many lethal blows. I could have killed him time and time again, but I was only meant to occupy him. To continue to be worn down by his strength. I heard Fen call and I couldn't help but look. I couldn't block the dread and anger. The beast had him pinned to the ground below his long, lanky fingers.

*It's time.*

I shoved Kai away from me and ran. He chased, but Gaea blocked him, spiriting in from the side and shoving him to the ground. I got close to the vysa and steadied myself. Closing my eyes, I moved that wall deep within me, letting the power of eradication rain down on the vysa, on the forest, on me. I knew, unquestionably, the vysa was dead.

The suffocation moved in.

*Fight it.*

But I couldn't. The darkness swept me up and slammed me to the ground. The guilt of such raw power drowning me. I couldn't see, but I could guess I had leveled all or most of that forest. That forest was the last place that held memories of my parents, and I had destroyed it.

"Murderer." My mother's voice caressed my mind.

Perhaps it was my magic creeping to life to remind me of the darkness within me. Tolero's face flashed before me. I watched as his final smile became serpentine and he said, "Kill them all."

I pushed on the magic but the pressure crushed me into the hallowed ground.

*FIGHT IT, ARA.*

He was there, I could feel him reaching for me, heaving the bond. But what could I be to a king, really? What could I offer him when the only thing that followed me was death? When I was the true executioner of the world? I was the one who needed to be locked behind a door. They didn't know. None of them knew how badly the magic begged me to end them all. None of them knew they still walked in this world because of my stubborn will.

"Slaughter," Morwena's voice rattled my brain.

I couldn't breathe. I couldn't move. The cost of using that archaic, undiluted magic had been a piece of our shared soul. But it was also this. And though I fought it, I succumbed to the darkness just as I heard the world-shattering wail of the final creature and realized it had been here the entire time.

A secrer. A leech. It conjured and fed off my memories. My misery had been a magnet. It was already jumbling my mind, sending me thoughts of my family even before I killed the vysa. And as my mind began to splinter, I surrendered to the pull. They were on their own.

I drifted through a vast emptiness of despair. This was comfort. This was safe and calm. This place, whatever it was, was vacant. Void of emotion. I lingered in that space. I needed to be somewhere else though. Someone needed me.

My mind was stronger than this. I couldn't be here. Someone could die. Someone I loved could die. I pushed up and up until I heard

298

the scream of a female I thought I knew. Her cry was familiar. And then I remembered. I began frantically digging within the tendrils of my subconscious for reality.

The tiny flame from within me flickered, lighting the darkness as I clawed my way out of it.

The weight on my chest lifted, the cloud through my mind still thick as I heard Fenlas shouting Kai's name. I felt his instant desperation. Again, I heard Gaea scream. Only this time, it seemed to stop the world, bringing with it absolute mental clarity. I used that as an anchor to pull myself out of my own self destruction.

Before I could open my eyes, before I could even move, a shock wave ripped through me. My ears rang, my body shook uncontrollably. My heart stopped. The breath was stolen from my lungs. The bond, that single connection to Fen, was gone.

I jerked upright and opened my eyes. Kai was on a knee gasping for breath as he looked down at the fallen body of the final creature. He had killed it. Behind me, I heard Gaea sobbing. My stomach lurched. I didn't want to look. I knew with every part of my soul what I would see. Still, I turned.

Fenlas, King of the Flame Court, my best friend, my mate, laid still upon the scorched ground. I crawled on my hands and knees to him, dragging my splintered heart with me. I wiped my soiled fingers on my clothes before I touched his beautiful face, but they wouldn't come clean. My heart beat so loud, I knew it was trying to wake him. His eyes were closed. He did not breathe. Did not pull for me. I felt only the softest, most faint whisper of his presence within me. That single flame began to flicker, and I knew he would die. I think I heard the actual sound as my heart cracked. I tried to swallow the jagged lump in my throat. I tried to force back the tears, the ringing in my ears.

"Take him," I begged Gaea. "You have to take him to Temir."

"I can't," she cried, tears leaving tracks in the dirt upon her face. "It took . . . It stole my magic." She looked toward Kai and back to Fen. "Greeve . . ." Her gentle voice broke. "I think he's gone too."

Too. The word that shattered my fragile world.

# Temir

hogan's wings beating in an uneven pattern woke me. He grunted and strained carrying me, his arms under my armpits, my feet hanging high above the ground.

"Greeve," I croaked, still nearly drained, exhaustion pulling me away, even now.

"I'll go back for him," he grunted.

"No. Rhogan, you have to take him first. Come back for me. I'm only tired, he needs a healer, or he isn't going to make it."

"We're over halfway back," he answered from above me.

"I don't care. Leave me here, just go get the drac."

My stomach plummeted as he descended. We nearly crash landed onto the ground.

"Can you fix my wing? It's better than it was, but it's still broken. I can't fly well." His eyes were bloodshot, the veins in his muscles protruding from the overexertion. His icy blond hair was a mop of sweat and dried blood. Those raven wings were so damaged he probably shouldn't have been able to fly at all.

"I'm drained, Rhog. I gave you all that I could."

He didn't answer. Only managed a half turn and jumped into the air before he crashed to the ground, sand flying around him. He stood, cursed and tried again, and this time, those broken onyx wings carried him away. It wasn't graceful, but he was gone.

My muscles screamed at me. Fatigue threatened me, but step by step, I inched my way in the same direction we were flying. I was lost. With each step, I sank deeper into the crimson sand. I pulled at my legs, begged them to keep walking. The horizon began to waver in the heat. Sweat poured down my head and stung my eyes. Still, I trudged on. Nadra appeared in the distance, her curls blowing in the wind, but when I reached for her, she vanished. It hurt to swallow. My swollen tongue became a foreign object in my sandy mouth.

I fell. Pulled myself up. Fell again. I could not go on. I would either die burned by the relentless sun, starving, thirsty and lost in the desert, or I would be found by my broken-winged friend, face down in the sand that began to bury me. As I closed my eyes, I sent wave after unyielding wave of love to Nadra. Because if I was going to die in the desert, I never wanted her to question how I felt about her.

I woke, never fully realizing I fell asleep. The beating sun had moved farther across the sky. My lips were cracked and bleeding. I blinked, and the sand covering my entire body fell from my lashes. Pushing from the ground, I willed my body to stand. To fight against the debilitating fatigue. I walked, twisted mirages appearing sporadically. Autus stood in the distance, flipping his faithful gold knife, the one charmed to never miss a target, in his hand. The sun glinted off the jewel in the center and I felt fear like I had never known tremor through me.

I braced myself for the impact of that knife, my mind convinced that he was real, that he had actually hunted me down and was ready to kill me. But he vanished. The fear did not. I saw Rhogan for the fourth time hovering above me in the sky.

"Just leave me alone," I yelled, my voice hoarse.

I beat my palms into my temples as the desert continued lashing out in my mind. I stumbled forward as the vision drew closer. The familiar sound of his wings grew, and I pulled my sword I could barely lift from the ground, but still I swung at the mirage haphazardly. "Go away," I rasped.

"Tem, put the sword away."

I blinked the gritty sand from my eyes and stumbled backward. "You're real?"

"Real," he said.

I dropped the sword and hung my head.

"It's going to be a long ride back, but Greeve still hasn't moved. We have to hurry."

I nodded. His movements were sluggish as he stepped behind me. Likely the strain on his broken wing made him more tired than I was.

"I've rested. Not a lot, but I might be able to heal it," I said.

"No, Temir. Greeve is going to need every bit you can give him."

He shoved his hands under my arms, and it took three times to leave the ground. His body trembled as we moved.

"Is Nadra at the castle?"

Exhaustion rumbled through his words. "She's with Wren. She's a wreck. Everyone is."

"Are the others back?"

"Not yet."

I grabbed his arm and shoved the bit of replenished magic into him, focusing solely on his wing. He dipped low for a moment. My feet hit the ground, dragging trails into the sand. "You needed that."

"So did Greeve."

I didn't want to tell him that Nadra could refill the void, but I didn't want anyone to know her ability. That was the only way to protect her. But as Rhogan bounded higher into the air, the wind pushing against us as we moved, I realized I was going to have to tell him. If no one else. He knew I was empty. "I need to tell you something," I started.

"No time like the present," he strained. Though his wing was repaired, he was still tired.

"Nadra is . . . special."

"She's your mate. Of course she is."

"No, I mean there's more. She's going to need extra protection."

As we flew, I went through the whole story: what she had learned from the king, the items he hunted, and what he was trying to do. I explained the flower and how it had claimed her somehow. How its power was now somewhere within her.

He was silent for a long time. He processed things differently than I did. While I was analytical, Rhogan was far more emotional. "I'll protect her always, brother," he said, low and deadly.

As the castle came into view, I pulled and tugged on the bond until she was doing the same. I needed her to meet me at the door. When we dropped outside, she was already there, running for me.

She crashed into me, nearly bowling me over. "Oh gods, Temir." She cried, hugging me, pulling away to look me over, and then hugging me again.

304

"I'm fine, love. But I need your power right now if we are going to save Greeve."

She nodded and held out her hand. The moment our bare skin touched, that foreign power began to vibrate and thrum through our fingers.

"Let's go." She yanked me into the castle. They hadn't moved him from the entryway. His body, no longer bleeding, laid still upon the marbled floor. His shirt lay discarded to the side and deep red welts covered his body.

"I couldn't move him or he would die. I've done everything I can to help him," an old fae in long robes said. "He's breathing, but only just."

Wren cowered in the far corner of the hallway, her eyes withdrawn and rimmed with tears. She held a tissue to her nose and watched, sniffling as I knelt over him.

I placed my hands upon him once more as the healer stepped away, closed my eyes, and drew the power forward. Nadra put her hands on my shoulders, and suddenly Greeve's body jerked in response. Not to me, but Nadra.

Pulling my hands away from his perfectly restored skin, I looked up to her and back to Greeve. Nadra had not just refilled my magic, she amplified my power.

Shifting, Greeve groaned and sat up, swaying.

"Gaea," he mumbled, trying to pull himself to his feet.

Wren rushed forward, shoved her head under his arm and helped him stand. His eyes were half open. Seconds ago, he was on death's doorstep and now he was standing. Assisted, but standing. I could not wrap my medical brain around that.

I spun to look at Rhogan, shocked to find the old hag standing beside him. She dipped her chin to me, and I knew she was confirming the thoughts swirling through my mind. I hadn't just imagined it. Nadra was powerful.

"Where have you been?" I snarled at her.

"Not that it's your business boy, but I was handling my own beast and restoring The Mists to keep what lurks beyond from pushing back into this world. And you will watch your tongue when you speak to me." She slammed the solid end of her staff into the hard floor, the sound ricocheting around the castle entryway. "We must go, dear," she said to Nadra, holding out her hand.

Rhogan and I stepped forward, blocking Nadra from Aibell's site.

"Good grendel, you male fae are insufferable. There's no time for this."

"Take me to her." Greeve stumbled toward Aibell, arm still around Wren for support.

"Very well." She shook her head. "Everyone who wishes to come, hands on the staff."

We stood in a circle around her. Nadra sandwiched between me and Rhogan. The floor fell out from below us, and my heart dropped into my stomach as we traveled by whatever means she decreed necessary.

We landed on charred ground, my boots crunching as ash fell from the sky like a soft winter snow. Half a forest had been blown to smithereens and we stood directly in the center of the rubble. Stepping away from Aibell, Greeve released the staff and cleaved away.

Wren cried out and bolted, falling to the ground beside Ara. Kai walked somberly toward us. Our eyes met for only a moment before he looked away, watching Greeve as Gaea buried herself into his arms. He pulled her close to Wren, and together they knelt with Ara.

I didn't even know Gaea had made friends here. Still, I watched as she cried and Greeve stroked her long chestnut hair, holding her fiercely to him.

"Go to them." Aibell pushed Nadra forward, jutting her chin to the group.

"Temir?" Wren demanded from the huddled group. "Temir, you have to save him."

Only then did I see the king laid before them. I ran, inhaling the falling ash as I knelt beside them all and placed my hands on him. I felt for his heart first. No response. His lungs were empty. His body completely still.

A hand gripped my shoulder. I looked up, expecting Nadra, but found Aibell instead. "Not even your magic can save him now, boy."

"No," Ara whispered. "He can. He has to try."

Aibell reached down to Ara, pulled the jewel on her necklace forward and carefully examined it. Ara gasped and lifted the trinket from her head. She stood, clasped it in both of her hands and bowed her head, saying a silent prayer.

She stayed like that, unmoving, until a tiny creature came out of the woods in the distance. Kai was suddenly moving. Trying to block Fen's body as the pixie flew passed Ara entirely and moved to the king.

"What are you doing?" Ara asked, stepping beside Kai to protect the fallen king.

"You've asked for her helpsies. Ofra has agreed."

"Where are we going?" Kai asked, moving to lift Fenlas from the ground.

"No one elseies. I will take hims to the glen."

"Do it," Ara said. "Move," she commanded Kai.

His face fell and he stepped away.

"Ofra makes no promises. It will takes a miracle." The little forest pixie fluttered her wings. She laid the palm of her hand upon the king's chest, and then they were gone.

Greeve and Gaea stood as Nadra approached them. "If I may, Aibell thinks I can help you," she offered.

I wanted to stop her. I wanted to keep her secret forever, but it was her secret. Not mine.

"No one can help me now," Gaea answered. "The wind has abandoned me. I am nothing without it."

I opened my mouth to disagree but Greeve turned her to face him. His dark eyes looked down upon her and she moved her hands to his bare chest. It was a private moment we probably shouldn't have witnessed. "Never nothing." He ran his fingers through her hair. "I have enough for both of us." He called the breeze forward to encompass them.

She shook her head as fresh tears began to fall.

Her magic had been her identity. It had saved her from so many things, but it had also been the cause of so many other problems. Still, Gaea had always been like the wind. The storm at sea and the blizzard. It was the only constant in her life.

"If I could just try." Nadra reached her hand halfway to Gaea.

"You have nothing to lose," I encouraged her. "Aibell brought us for a reason, and if it wasn't for Fen, then it was for you."

"Are you sure?" Rhogan gritted his teeth but didn't move.

I didn't answer. Couldn't. Gaea closed the distance, grabbed Nadra's hand, and her eyes rolled back. She began to fall, but Greeve caught her.

"What did you do?" Greeve barked.

I pulled Nadra away from him as Rhogan stepped in.

"How?" Gaea cried, her feline eyes opened and locked on Nadra.

"It's a long story." She shrugged, refusing to offer more as she took my hand and pulled me and Rhogan away. Toward Kai, who had sat on the ground with his back to everyone. He tucked his knees to his chest and tried to hide his face as Wren sat beside him.

"What happened?" she whispered.

His shoulders shook. The warrior was crying. Greeve came, offering solace to his friend. Soon, everyone but Ara, who still stood, staring into the forest, sat in a circle around him, waiting.

"Tell us." Greeve leaned a shoulder into him.

"It was a secrar," Gaea said first. "The first creature was a vysa."

Rhogan took a deep breath beside me, his wings twitching.

"The vysa turned Kai against us, and Ara and I had to keep him occupied while Fen . . ." Her voice shook. She swallowed and squeezed her eyes shut as if the memory was wrapped in physical pain. "Fen had to shatter the vysa's shield. He did, but then Ara had to use her magic to kill him. He was too big. Too powerful. Her magic hurts her." Gaea's voice faded away as she looked into the evening sky. Greeve wrapped an arm around her, and she continued, though quiet. "Her magic overwhelmed her, and she needed Fen. But he couldn't protect her when the secrar came. We think it was feeding off her emotions. That's how it found us, the leech. We didn't know she was struggling until it was too late."

"The creature stole Gaea's magic almost instantly," Kai murmured, saving her from having to speak the words. He looked to Greeve. "I tried to save her. I swear I did."

"You did save me," she whispered.

"Fen was standing in front of Ara, using the little bit of magic he had left to try to shield her on the ground. But when I blocked the secrar from killing Gaea after it stole her magic, it turned on me." He ran his hands through his hair, burying his face into his arms and began to sob again.

"Fen left Ara on the ground to take the final magical blow, saving Kai and sacrificing himself instead," she whispered, turning to look toward Ara, who still hadn't moved. "And then Kai killed it before it killed the rest of us."

"I'm not a hero. If he dies, it's my fault," Kai said quietly, tears tracking down his face.

# CHAPTER
## 27

# Ara

*I* could still hear them, the words they spoke. But I was numb. Numb to it all as I stared into the new crippled edge of the forest. Half of it was gone, blown to ash because of my terrible magic. But so was Fen, so I didn't care. A deafening silence crept over me. I could feel myself screaming and screaming in my mind, yet I didn't move, wasn't even sure if I was breathing. I reached for the familiar link that had carried me for so long, but still, only hollowness echoed back. That was all that was left of me, a vacancy of where he had been.

I had told him I loved him, but I can't remember if he said it back. I couldn't remember the last time he'd uttered those words to me. The last time I felt his lips pressed to mine. His hands in my own. He had told me he didn't want days or weeks. He wanted a lifetime. The vision that I had shown him. He wanted that too. He wanted it all and had gotten nothing.

*Please. Please come back to me.*

Silence.

The sun began to set. The voices behind me grew hushed. Someone came and wrapped an arm around me, but their body weight only added to my own until they stepped away. I heard mumbles of voices. Eventually, my legs gave out and I fell to my knees on the charred ground, still watching the forest for any type of movement. Still hoping, praying to one of the many gods I couldn't name for a miracle. A blanket fell over my shoulders. I closed my eyes, the memory of emerald filling my mind. I replayed everything.

"Hello you," he had said the first time I'd seen him. So familiar. He'd known me my whole life. He had waited for me, so I would wait for him. And if he did not come back to me, if the northern king had taken my mate, I would walk. I would crawl. I would dig my way into his gods-damned castle and I'd blow that motherfucker to pieces. Then I would destroy the world.

"You must come now," a voice said, pulling me toward the forest.

I stood. My movements were hardly a thought as my heavy feet dragged and I stumbled. I thought he would come back. I thought he would be the one to walk out of that forest. Instead, I had been called. And I knew why. I could feel it. Or the lack thereof. The tiny flame within me flickered and dimmed. The bond, nothing more than a memory.

No one followed. I wasn't sure if it was because they left, they fell asleep, or they knew after I said goodbye to my mate, I would no longer be safe to be around. Without Fen, we weren't a family anymore. The lump in my throat continued to hinder my swallowing as I moved forward, unable to take a full breath into my lungs. I passed tree after tree as Ofra's magic pulled me.

"You've come a long way since last I saw you," she said as the forest fell away and I stood in the middle of the pixie glen.

He was there, lying on the ground as I once had after my parents died. Ofra's long black hair flowed around her as she motioned to me.

"I'm sorry," I whispered. "Maybe I should have just stayed here when you had asked me to. Maybe none of this would have happened."

"Fate is not that simple, Ara. You either fulfill it or you die."

*Or both*, I told myself.

"Is he . . ." I couldn't say the words. Wouldn't.

"The glen will not bring the dead back to us. He is not dead, but he is not alive either. He teeters on the brink of somewhere in between. I cannot help him as you've asked. I've tried. He is so close, yet the magic cannot reach him."

I nodded, that numbness beginning to spread through me again. I laid on the ground beside his warm body and trailed my fingers down his face. Placing my hand upon his chest, I begged and begged him to come back to me. I wept, and the forest pixies came out from hiding to form a circle around us.

"I can't lose him. I can't."

"This is the moment you have to say goodbye to him."

But I wouldn't. Instead, I said goodbye to the moments we never had, to the future that was stolen from us. To the fae child that would have been his heir and looked like his father. I said goodbye to the memories.

"Thank you," I whispered into his ear, tears trailing down my face as I pushed his hair behind his pointed ear. "Thank you for saving me and loving me."

'Thank you is just as good as goodbye,' I had told him.

Several of the pixies floated through the air, weeping alongside me. Somewhere deep within me I felt my soul begin to tear. My spirit drowned with the realization that he was really gone. The last wisp of hope I'd held so desperately left me. Just as he would.

*Take me with you.*

I laid my head upon his chest, upon his heart. Though I knew he was gone, I still pulled him to me. Still tugged and lurched and heaved.

The ground began to rumble. The glen reacted, and Ofra moved to sit beside me.

"You're doing it." She placed her warm hand on my back. "Your soul is the anchor. He is pulling, fighting to come back."

The flame.

The flame flickered, just dim enough to warm something within me, but then it grew until I could feel him. So very faintly, but he was there. Pulling as desperately as I was.

"Oh gods," I said as his heart began to beat beneath me.

"You must move away now." Ofra stood.

"I can't leave him."

"Let the magic do what it is meant to do. Come."

As I lifted myself from him, willing to do anything to bring him back, I felt the magnetic pull—as if physically leaving his side strained everything—but I carried that tiny flame within me as I moved to the edge of the glen lit by starlight alone. I lifted my head to the sky and thanked the gods for answered prayers and hopeless dreams.

And then we waited.

*Marry me.*

I cried out and ran to him, throwing myself over him again, so fucking grateful for the arms that lifted from the ground and held me as I sobbed and sobbed into the chest that rose and fell.

"I love you," I wailed.

I pulled myself up to stare into those beautiful emerald eyes that I thought I'd never see again. I ran my fingers through his jet-black hair. I kissed his cheek and his lips and the stubble along his sharp jawline.

He sat up and pulled me into his lap and held me as desperately as I was holding him.

"You were dead," I murmured. "You left me."

"I'm so sorry. It wasn't supposed to happen that way. I was supposed to save you."

"Kai saved us all," I told him. "Because we're a team. A family. And right now, I don't think he's okay either."

We rose, moving toward our savior. "Thank you," I told Ofra as Fen and I stood on the edge of the glen. I held my mother's necklace out to her. "You've fulfilled more than your end of the bargain."

"Keep it." She smiled. The light from the moon moved through her pale figure. "Maybe I'll see you again one day."

"I hope not," I said honestly as we turned to walk out of the glen. I jerked to a stop, catching a glimpse of a massive black horse out of my peripheral. "Brimir?" Refusing to let go of Fen, I dragged him with me as I ran to my family's fae horse. He was just as beautiful as I remembered, perhaps his coat even a bit shinier.

He recognized me. The moment I stepped close enough to touch him, he shoved his long nose over my shoulder and yanked me into a hug, just as he did when I was younger. The tears I thought had run dry began to fall again as I held the last member of my family once more. "What are you doing here?" I whispered into his twitching ear.

"I hope you don't mind." Ofra reached a hand forward as if to stroke the beast but pulled back. "He was running from a knovern and Esa found him. She brought him to the glen for safety and he remained. The pixies are all quite fond of him.

"I don't mind at all," I mumbled into his neck.

"Shall we take him home?" Fen asked, patting Brimir's neck as my father always did.

I stepped away and studied his deep eyes, hooded in thick lashes. He loved me and I loved him, but I knew the answer. The one he seemed to have given with that look. "He's happy and safe here. I can't say the same for the desert. He should stay."

"Hes gets to staayyysss!" Esa, the little pixie, shouted to the others shooting out of the tall grass, only to realize what she'd done and darted back into the safety of her hiding spot. The other pixies didn't make a sound.

"Goodbye again, my friend. I'm glad you've found a home."

"You can visit him anytime," Ofra said as we made our way toward the edge of the glen once more. There was a pull there. She wanted Fen and I to stay, and now I'd felt the magic behind her words. We wouldn't stay, of course, but it would have been so much easier if we could have.

"Is she a god?" Fen asked as we wove through the trees.

"When I first met her, I thought she was. Now, I'm not sure. The gods don't seem to involve themselves."

Fen looked off into the distance, silent for a long time. "But they do," he said finally, squeezing my fingers as he quickened our pace.

I would never ask him what he had seen, where he had been as he balanced between life and death, but I knew it would probably stay with him for the rest of his life.

316

We came upon a heap of fae lying on the ground, but at this point, we were only worried about the one that stood, his back to us as he watched the moon in the sky above.

"Kai?" I whispered.

He turned. His face looked like he'd lived a thousand lives of torture. Until his eyes landed on Fen. He didn't say a word, only crumbled to his brother's feet and began to cry. "The king," he managed. "The king does not sacrifice himself for the warrior."

Fen reached for him, pulled him back to his feet, planted his hands on his shoulders, and shook him. "I am not a king, and you are not a warrior in this family."

"Fen?" Wren peeled herself from the ground. She rubbed her eyes. He held a hand out for her and she joined their group hug.

I nudged Greeve with my foot, trying to not wake Gaea, curled in his arms. He was on his feet in an instant, knife ready in his hand. I tilted my head to the group and the moment he saw Fen, he dropped the knife and joined them.

I stood back watching the reunion, my heart bursting, though mentally I was exhausted. Greeve turned toward me, grabbed my arm, and yanked me into the center until they were crushing me. My heart had never been so full, tangled in the arms of a group of southerners.

"Let's go home," Fen mumbled.

We woke the others and Gaea happily took us home. I wanted to ask her about Greeve. About what had happened. But it wasn't the right time. She followed him down the hall, and that was enough answer for me.

"Tired?" Fen asked, pulling me toward our rooms.

"Utterly exhausted."

"We'll rest tonight, but tomorrow we have to start hunting for that lost artifact in the dunes. I didn't nearly die to lose you to Autus."

"I'm not scared of him," I said. "I lived through the death of my mate and nothing could be worse than that. We know his plans. We have an army."

"It's not enough. It's never going to be enough until he is dead. He released those creatures as a distraction. He's scheming. We cannot be complacent. We don't have near the numbers we need to fight him."

"Then we find more." I opened the door to our room.

"Easier said than done," he answered, kicking off his boots. "Tell Friar she can burn these clothes tomorrow. I never want to see them again."

"What's wrong with your magic?" I asked, stepping away.

"Nothing," he pulled me back to him. "I've just got better things to do."

He grabbed the back of my neck, lifted my chin, and kissed me thoroughly. Until my knees had gone weak and my hands began to remove my clothes.

"Consider it done," I said against his mouth. "Is there anything else I can do for my king?"

"I can think of a few things." He lifted me and walked into the bathing room.

# CHAPTER

## 28

# Temir

"What do you think she wants?" Nadra asked as we stepped out into the heat of the south.

"I'm not sure. She just said to meet her in the lists."

We walked down to the training area and I think it was the first time I'd seen it nearly empty. I wasn't surprised though. Ara had a way of commanding a crowd. If she didn't want an audience, she wouldn't have one.

She threw metal daggers in perfect succession at scattered targets. Her body danced through the air and around the ground as she moved. A perfectly honed weapon. I could see why she always drew a crowd. She jumped backward, spun and slammed the final blade into the last target so hard it tipped, a cloud of dirt her standing ovation.

"I knew you were scary," Nadra said. "I had no idea how much."

Ara shrugged. "What do you know about the Winterlands?" she asked, wiping sweat from her neck with a cloth.

She'd been distant lately. She rarely came to meals unless the king was there, which was rare, and she didn't spend time with Nadra or Wren. No one had seen Greeve and Gaea in the week since we'd been back. We spent most of our time training with Rhogan and the rebels. Rhogan insisted on training Nadra himself. He'd fought with Kai the few times he tried to step in.

"I've never heard of them."

"That's what I thought. Neither have I," she huffed.

"Okay?"

"Come with me," Ara ordered, spinning on her heel and walking away.

Nadra lifted her shoulders and followed. We strode to the armory, where the weapons were stored. Stacks and stacks of swords and shields were piled along the floor and the giant was carefully examining each one as he put them away. His oversized hands were careful as he handled them. Oravan walked in right behind us with arms full of more weapons.

"Hey Tem," he said as he began to unload.

"You." Ara pointed. "Join us." He dropped the swords in his hand. "It's time to talk about the Winterlands," Ara told Greywolf.

"I can't." He took several steps backward, his kind eyes showing fear. "It isn't spoken of." After realizing what he'd said, he covered his hands with his mouth.

"Have you heard of them? You're from the north." She looked at Oravan, but he shook his head.

"When I was a child, maybe eight or nine, my mother made me memorize every village, every city, every single town. I can tell you almost exactly where they all are on a map. But I've never heard of the Winterlands." She looked again to the giant. He shook his head. "If there are fae there who can help us, Grey, we need to know. We need all the help we can get right now. We know Autus is preparing to move south. We are running out of time."

"For you, queen sir." He nodded his head.

"I'm not . . ." She stopped. "It doesn't matter. Go on."

"You know The Bog?" he asked me and Oravan.

I pulled my head back in surprise. "Of course. But no one goes there. It's dangerous."

"Yes." He smiled. "Very dangerous."

"So, The Bog is the Winterlands?" Ara asked impatiently.

"No, queen sir. Beyond The Bog. North. The Winterlands is a great city of hidden fae. And churches and trade shops and good foods."

"There's an entire city?" I asked.

Oravan shook his head. "It isn't possible. If there were a city in the Wind Court, Autus would know. He would have destroyed it long ago."

"Wards," the giant answered. "No one comes and no one leaves. The Winterlands is hidden."

"How did you leave? Why?"

"They tell stories to the children. I knew I wanted to come to the warm. So, one day, I left. I walked through The Bog and kept going."

"Why don't others leave?" I asked.

"Heva doesn't let them. Says it is to protect everyone. But I snuck out." He kicked his toe on the ground. "If they find out, they will have me killed."

"Don't worry, Grey." Ara reached to pat his arm. "They will never know it came from you. I promise." She locked eyes with me and tilted her head toward the door. We left Oravan and the giant to continue their work. She paced in front of us for several moments. "Tell me about your magic, Nadra," she said finally. "I've been waiting for you to come to me, but you haven't."

"You've been gone." The pitch of Nadra's voice rose as she became defensive. "I've barely had a chance to say hello to you. I might have changed, but you haven't."

"I'm sorry I've been a rotten friend, but it's complicated," she answered. "It's time though. I want the whole story."

So Nadra told her. Everything. More than I would have, including our time in the dungeon and the loss of her mother. The mountain top, the glass maker, all of it.

Ara reached for her hand, examining it. "Who else knows?"

"Everyone who lives in the castle. That's it."

"Tell no one else." She squeezed Nadra's hand and released it. "We're a team, a family. We will keep you safe."

"Temir and Rhogan keep me safe," Nadra answered.

"Then welcome to the family," she said to me. "I need to ask you to do something for me. I need someone from the Wind Court."

"You want me to find the Winterlands and ask them to join us."

"I do. And I want you to leave Nadra behind. It won't be safe for her there."

"Rhogan stays with her," I answered. "It's not that I don't trust the rest of you, but I know him. He will want to be here."

"If that's your wish," she replied. "I'm sending Gaea also. You can choose your team. In and out. Don't take no for an answer."

"You need to contact the Weaver. She needs to come south."

"I already have." She walked away before I could reply.

"I don't like this," Nadra said, pulling back slightly. "I want to go."

"You know she's right."

"Listen, last time I got left behind, Greeve almost died, and I didn't think you were even coming back at all." She crossed her hands over her chest.

"But I did, and we both know war is coming. We need to be prepared."

She bit her lip but conceded.

Later that night, everyone showed up for dinner in the hall. The older female from the kitchens fussed and snipped as she filled the table with food. I surveyed the fae around the room and realized Ara was right, this was a family. Maybe not my own, but they certainly were. They bickered like siblings and laughed at memories, and I wondered what that felt like. Until I saw Rhogan and Nadra teasing each other and realized I was the only one distancing myself.

War was coming. The closer we became to one another, the worse it was going to hurt everyone when someone died. I looked to Gaea filling Greeve's plate. How easily she had fit in here, with them. As if this is where she was meant to be. I just didn't think this was it for me. A step in my journey, that was all.

The king motioned to me.

I squatted down to speak to him at the head of the table.

"I'm working on figuring out what the lost artifact is. Ara told me about Nadra's magic. I give you my word, we will keep her safe. Not only because Ara's life depends on it, but because you are a member of this court. If you'll have us."

I looked away, wondering if Fenlas could also read minds.

"It's not a requirement," Ara leaned in. "You don't have to stay here. It's only an offer. Have you decided on your team?"

"I have."

"Apart from Gaea, who will you take?"

"Greeve only."

She bit her lip, her mind working. "You're sure?"

"For many reasons. He'd kill me if I didn't, but also, I'm guessing the more people we bring into their sacred city, the more unsettling it will be for them. If it is the way the giant described, then they aren't going to be welcoming to outsiders. I need a warrior. Someone their legends have spoken about. A draconian should do it."

"You're smart." She popped a grape into her mouth. "I'm glad you're here, Temir."

I looked to Nadra, and she winked at me, lifted her wine glass in the air and laughed at something Kai said. Perhaps I needed to try harder. Kai had been spending a massive amount of time in the sea court, and still he'd found time to be a part of this family. Limited as it might be. I'd healed him after an injury down there and I had a feeling he was struggling in his own way. Thought he didn't lean on anyone with his troubles. As the commander of the Flame Court army, he ran a tight ship. Yet here he was.

The next morning, we stood in King Fenlas' study as the smell of old books and the vision of the cracked spines brought nostalgic feelings and thoughts back to me. He had piles of them all over his disheveled desk. Some were spread on the floor. There were discarded papers and notes everywhere. I could tell by the king's bloodshot eyes he hadn't slept. Possibly for days.

"All set?" Gaea asked, the last to join us as she walked in with more weapons strapped to her than I'd ever seen her wear.

"It's important you explain the full situation. Whoever Heva is, he has to understand that he still has a stake in all of this," the king said.

"How much force do I use?" Greeve asked, tightening a strap on Gaea's back.

"None," Ara answered. "We aren't trying to create more enemies."

"But don't take no for an answer," I said, nodding. "No problem."

We spirited as close to The Bog as Gaea could take us, and a shock of cold air ran down my spine. I wasn't acclimated to the desert yet, but I was certainly growing used to it. I pulled the furs closer to my ears, blocking the icy breeze that chilled my neck.

The water never froze here because of the magic of the gryla population that lived below the surface of the long body of shallow water. It was as still as glass. A mirror to the painted sky above. Tall, barren trees lined the water as our feet crunched along the ice-covered ground.

Gaea slowed our pace, each of us watching for movement in the water as we walked along the edge. Greeve pulled his infamous sword as we went. She had warned him of what we would find here. Why no one came to The Bog. Why no one knew what lay beyond it.

"There." Gaea pointed at a gurgle of bubbles along the surface of the water.

"New plan," I spoke just as the gryla rose to the surface, her long, wet hair covering her face and half of her naked green body. "Greeve, take Gaea to the other side. As far as you can get from here."

He grabbed her arm.

"Wait, what about you?" she asked, staring at the hideous creature crawling out of the water.

"Come back for me," I said.

They were gone on the breeze.

I held my sword out as the gryla stood and cocked her head sideways in an unnatural way. Her eyes hidden. "I know you." Her voice was scratchy as she pointed at me. "My payment to the king."

"Stay back," I warned.

"You don't come to my land and tell me what to do." Her voice split into two tones as the demon within her rose to the surface. She moved quicker than I had expected, knocking my sword to the side and gripping my neck.

I swung the weapon up and sliced into her. Her blood sprayed across the snow, but she did not flinch. She stunk of rotted fish and seaweed. Even through my labored breathing, I could smell her decrepit body. One of her sisters hissed behind us as I pulled the blade back to swing again. Spots filled my vision.

Gaea landed beside me and brought a sword down over the gryla's arms at my throat, chopping them clean off her body. The creature screamed as we were both sprayed with rancid blood. Gaea grabbed my hand and spirited us away before I could even catch my breath.

We landed and Greeve flinched. Likely from the lingering smell. I put my hands on my knees and tried to pull the cold air into my lungs. Greeve clapped me on the back, which was no help, but eventually I was standing up right.

"Look." Gaea pointed.

I turned around and couldn't believe what I saw. Absolutely nothing. The giant led us to the northernmost tip of the world, far away from everyone for nothing. I shook my head.

"Why?" I asked. "Why would he send us here for nothing?"

"He has to be working for Autus. He had to have a reason."

But something didn't sit right with me. Something was off. "My payment to the king."

"What?" Greeve asked, still scanning the horizon with his keen eyes.

"That's what the gryla said before she attacked me. What do you know about the giant, Greeve?"

"Anyone can be enchanted. Even a gentle giant," he said, but something caught his eye. "Watch." He pointed to the sky in front of us.

"I don't see anything." Gaea shoved her sword back into place.

"There," he said.

And I saw it too. A bird. Flying high above the horizon and then dipping low, as if hunting, but it disappeared.

"What the hell?" Gaea asked, stepping forward.

"Wards," Greeve answered. "The giant mentioned them. Fae used to use them all the time to keep others away or things hidden. I recently had to take some containment wards out that Morwena was using on a hydra. I don't think the giant was lying at all. I think the city is hidden in plain sight." He tugged Gaea forward.

I followed.

"Can you feel that?" Gaea asked, rubbing her chest.

"It's the wards," Greeve answered. "Their purpose is to make you feel like you should turn back."

She huffed. "At least we know why they've never been discovered. Not only do you have to travel around The Bog, you have to push through this gods awful feeling of dread just to walk toward a city you can't even see. Fen needs to look into warding."

The flat land of freshly fallen snow was the only thing we could see until two male voices called in unison. "Stop there."

"Add guards to the list," she mumbled.

The scene before us remained untouched. No fae, no creatures, nothing to give a hint of settlement.

"Turn around. Only death awaits you here."

"We've come to talk to Heva," I said into the emptiness.

Two figures stepped in front of us as if they had just landed from the sky. They wore golden armor that glistened in the sunlight and held long javelins with pointed ends. "Who are you?" the one with brown, tufted hair asked. Something foreign crossed his face as he took me in.

"I'm Temir, and I come as a messenger on behalf of King Fenlas of the Flame Court.

"We do not recognize the southern royalty here. We govern our own."

"All the same, we'd like to talk to your leader."

"Stay here," he answered, his gaze lingering on me. They stepped backward and disappeared, the veil of the ward encompassing them. We waited for several long minutes until they returned. "You may come. They must wait." He pointed at me.

"This is my draconian guard," I said, knowing the words would strike them with at least curiosity. "I am ordered by my king to stay with him and the female at all times."

They exchanged a look and hesitantly motioned us forward. The moment we stepped beyond the veil of the ward, the entire scene changed. A thriving city appeared before us. Paved streets, tall

328

buildings, thousands of fae everywhere. I froze. Unable to move as I closed my eyes and listened to the sound of fae children running through the streets, the smell of fire from chimneys, and laughter from a world of people living as if all hell hadn't broken loose.

I couldn't imagine why anyone would leave this. Convincing the king, leader, whatever they called him, to join us when his world was completely safe and undamaged was going to be a chore. We strolled the bustling streets. Gaea took in the sights. The buildings with art hanging in the windows and the musicians singing on the street corners. Greeve hadn't taken his eyes off the guards leading us. He was dark, lethal and completely unaffected by the Winterlands. That was why I'd chosen him.

The fae began to line the streets, gathering to watch us walk by. Their eyes were wide and some pointed and whispered to each other. I couldn't help but feel that more eyes were on me than the draconian, but likely they didn't know what he was. Who knew when the last time an outsider had passed their wards?

"We worship the seven gods here. You will stop at the temple to beg passage before you can be brought before Heva."

Gaea opened her mouth to protest, but I grabbed her hand and shook my head. "Whatever is required," I said through clenched teeth.

We were taken to the tallest building in the city. We climbed a hundred gilded stairs until we reached the top and I turned to see the view below us. The fae were tiny but the city was massive. There were no decrepit buildings, nothing that indicated one portion of the city was not as rich as another. This was a city of prosperity. Even the winter weather seemed to subside here.

"Come," the guard said.

We walked into the ornate church. The sun cast colors of light onto the shining floor as rows of perfectly aligned cherrywood pews lined each side of the aisle. At the front of the church, along the dais, were seven empty gold basins.

"Choose the god you wish to ask for passage. Kneel before their offering bowl and lay something meaningful to you inside." The guard set the tip of his weapon carefully onto the floor.

The gods were represented by sculptures. The Warrior was symbolized by a fae with a knocked arrow. The Mother, a female and her child. Nature, a tree. The Scholar, a book. Time, an hourglass. Death, a hooded figure. And finally, Life, a seed. I didn't know their names. I'd had only a brief lesson on the gods from Oleonis.

Gaea moved first. She knelt before the god of nature's statue, hands shaking as she placed something small into the bowl and bowed her head, her hands flat on her thighs. Greeve chose the Warrior. He dropped a knife inside, the sound echoing through the entire church, and assumed the same respectful pose as Gaea. I stood between Life and Death. I was a product of both.

The guard cleared his throat behind me, and I stepped forward and kneeled. "The offering," he barked.

I had nothing but the barrier ring I pulled from my finger. The ring Gaea had given me. The ring that had saved me from King Autus. My heart skipped a beat as I dropped it into the golden offering bowl and bowed my head.

*Why have you chosen death?* a feminine voice asked into my mind.

*Death is only a door to eternity.*

*Indeed. But you feel connected to me, do you not?* the god asked.

*I carry a power that is yours.*

*You have made a great offering. No longer immune to the northern king's magic, what will you do when he captures you?*

330

*I may pray to the God of Life then.*

I heard the God of Death's deep, ominous laughter within my mind, and the hair on my arms rose.

*I will enjoy our eternity together. For now, you may take back your offering. You do not need to seek passage to the gods' city. You were granted that privilege at birth.*

*I don't understand.*

*You will.*

My mind went quiet as the God of Death left me. I stayed hunched over for several moments thinking about what she had said, then stood, pulled my ring out of the bowl, and placed it back on my finger. Greeve and Gaea were motionless on their knees. I could see the strain on their faces as their offerings vanished. Their eyes opened and they looked at each other.

Whatever messages they had received, they were also granted passage into the Winterlands, or apparently, the gods' city. We left the church, and the crowd at the end of the stairs had only grown. As the guards led us down, they cheered, knowing the gods had blessed our passage. They only stared at me and waved and clapped, not at my companions.

We followed the fae males, clad in armor down a city street over a bridge and toward the largest cottage I had ever seen. Heva's home. They knocked on the rounded, wooden door and a female answered, dropping a glass to the hardwood floor as her eyes landed on me.

"P-please," she stuttered. "Come in. Heva is in his study."

At this point, there was no question that something strange was happening. Gaea and Greeve both moved closer to me as we entered the house. We walked down several long, bare hallways until we came to the very end.

One of the guards knocked on the door and let himself in, shutting it behind him.

"This is strange to you as well, right?" Gaea whispered.

I could only nod as the door was opened and we stepped inside a study.

Gaea gasped and her head jerked to me as Heva turned in his chair. He brought his hand onto the desk and leaned forward, examining me.

My features . . . My horns so similar to his own.

He sat back and nodded to the guards. "Hello, son."

# CHAPTER
## 29

# Ara

*I* stood on the balcony of our room and memorized the motion of the pewter sea as it tossed and tumbled. Once again, I had been left alone as Fen continued his work. Whispers and gossip flooded the Flame Court—hardly any of it was good. Fen was not a seasoned king, and the loss of Tolero was a heavy blanket across this land as we prepared for a battle we were not ready for.

Nearly dying can change you. At least, it had Fen. Maybe it had changed me too. I wasn't sure. I saw shadows of him lying still on the ground every time I closed my eyes. I saw our soul leave his body each time I lay down to sleep. I became haunted by what could happen in the days and weeks to come.

He, on the other hand, was obsessed with the lost artifact. Convinced, if he could find it, Autus would give up hunting me. It didn't matter how many times I told him that wouldn't happen.

The soldiers were in training in the lists, and we had taken over both fighting pits for additional space. The dracs were sending warriors on their cetani to teach anyone who wanted to fight. Umari led flights to the Marsh Court villages, warning them all of Autus' plans.

I sipped the tea from my tray and closed my eyes as the breeze blew my hair to the side. I wondered how she did it. Fenlas' mother. She'd left such a mark on this kingdom, yet there was never time to love a king. Always busy, always being called in a thousand different directions. I missed him. Missed traveling to The Mists with him. Missed his singular focus. But that was a selfish battle.

"Ara?" Wren's voice cut through my thoughts like a knife.

"I'm here," I called.

"Why are you out here?" she asked, pulling up a chair.

"The view, I guess?"

"I've missed you." She poured herself a drink. "You haven't been around."

"I've been here. Waiting."

"For what?" She blocked the sun from her eyes with her hands, staring at me.

"Everything." I shrugged. "Every day I wake up with this feeling of dread, wondering if it's going to be the day I die. If he dies."

She shook her head.

"You don't understand, Wren. I felt him. I felt him slip away from me. I felt the fracture in my soul. I'd choose to die a thousand deaths before I ever want to feel that way again. I'm scared." That familiar pressure began to build in my chest again as I remembered, for the thousandth time, what it felt like to lose him.

"It's weird, isn't it?" she asked, slumping back into her chair. "We can live forever if we're careful. But we can also die young if we're careful. I think the key is to live. It isn't to hide away from the world and wait for it."

"It doesn't matter what I do." I sipped my tea and looked back to the water.

"It matters a great deal what you do. The city is full of fae starting to question everything your mate does because he isn't out there holding their hands. He isn't reminding them every day that he is confident. But you could be. In fact, you should be."

"So that's my job? Wave Fen's flag to the world and smile graciously?"

"No. Your job is to protect your people. Sometimes protection is simply reminding them that you are both more than qualified to handle this."

"I could end this. I could ask Gaea to spirit me into Autus' chambers and kill him in his sleep." I watched her reaction carefully.

"Then do it, Ara. Save us all the trouble. But don't sit in this room and forget what you mean to all of us. Fen is lost, but so are you." She stood and set her teacup on the table between us. "Don't make me kick your fucking ass."

"You could try," I answered, the shadow of a smile on my numb face.

"Come on." She held her hand out. "Let's go wave that flag."

"You can wave it. I'll stand beside you."

"That's all I ask."

I spent the afternoon walking through the city. Wren stopped to introduce me to everyone we saw. She knew all their names and I felt as incompetent as ever. But the fae were kind, if not cautious, and I realized that she was right. I needed to do more. I needed to be Fen's teammate and help him when he struggled. If he was so busy working, I could share that workload.

I made it back to the castle feeling lighter than I had in days. "Thanks for holding my hand," I told Wren as she began to walk away.

"Anytime. You're going to be a great queen, Ara. And you're not alone."

I headed back to the room to change for dinner, convinced to eat in the hall, even if Fen wasn't going to join us.

Inok passed me, jerked to a stop, and cleared his throat. "I wondered if I could have a word?"

I'd been leery of him since King Tolero's death, but I couldn't deny him. I faced him carefully. "I suppose."

"I never thanked you. In fact, I think I might have done the opposite."

"I'm sorry?"

"Tolero," he mumbled, looking down to the floor. "You . . . eased his suffering, and I was so angry about that. I wanted to be selfish and have that last bit of time with him. But you did the right thing for him."

I nodded. I really didn't want to think about those moments. The sound of Tolero's final breath. "I wouldn't have done it if he hadn't asked. If Fen hadn't given me his blessing."

"I know." His sad smile wrenched my heart. "I knew him my whole life, you know. He was already king when I was born."

"Really? I just assumed you were the same age."

"Not hardly," he chuckled. "He would have loved to hear you say that though."

"Can I ask you a question?" I leaned against the wall.

"Of course."

"What am I supposed to do? For Fen? He's drowning in work. The people are getting worried about Autus and I think he's struggling with his near-death experience."

He tapped his finger to his lips. "I have an idea." A smile grew across his face. "Something Tolero would have killed me for."

"I'm all ears."

Later, we stood together in pits on the far side of the city. Kai, Wren, Rhogan and Nadra stood with us. Inok had convinced Fen to make an appearance and check the northerners' progress as they trained with the southerners. We even had a few sea fae training as well. Inok had sent a messenger to the draconians, and the entire fleet of cetani filled the sky.

Umari sat strong upon her beast and I hoped she had really come to talk some sense into her grandson. But as she landed and kept her eyes trained on me, I understood that was not going to happen. We had invited the devil, and she was not on my team. Maybe Fen's but not mine.

"I see you've left your cave, Grandson," she said, watching only me.

"We weren't expecting you, Umari," he answered.

"I've heard word on the wind that you nearly died. I've come to see you in the flesh. And to challenge your mate."

"What?" He jerked. *Do not agree to this.*

"Having a mate got my daughter killed. I'll not watch the same thing happen to you." Her black eyes hadn't left mine, her stone face hateful.

"So, are we going to fight, then?" I asked, smoothing a wrinkle from my shirt. "I seriously wouldn't recommend that, but if you insist."

"No." Fen pulled me backward. "You cannot challenge my mate, Umari."

Finally, her eyes left me to scrutinize her grandson. "I am still your elder, boy. King or no king."

Fen's posture turned rigid as they squared off.

I wondered what any of this would actually solve, but if nothing else, it was a show for the ever-growing crowd that watched the cetani land.

I rested my hand on Fen's forearm. "I accept the challenge."

"Hm." Umari stuck her nose into the air and stepped in front of me. "I will not fight you this day, girl. Instead, I challenge you to claim a cetani. A ritual that has always been done in the dunes, but today I'll allow it to be done here, amongst your peers."

*It can be dangerous. It's not worth it.*

*It's worth it to me, Fen. Look at the people. Most of them have never seen this done.*

*And if you aren't chosen?*

*Then I guess Umari and I are just going to have to throw down right here in the arena, so they still get their show.*

He rolled his eyes and I genuinely smiled. It felt so good to do that.

"I will agree on one condition." Fen's smile matched my own.

"No," Umari answered.

"What?" I asked.

"I get to paint you." Fire lit his eyes.

I looked around to see who had heard. "Like right here, in front of everyone?"

"No. We will step away, go over the basics, and then we come back."

"If you fail, you aren't good enough for my grandson. Draconian blood is sacred. Yours is not. Failure means agreeing to denounce your mating bond. If you succeed, I will claim you for the rest of your days." Her eyes narrowed on me.

"No. Absolutely n—"

"I agree," I cut in.

"Your words are binding. It is done."

*Why would you agree to that?*

*I've already denounced it. It doesn't work. But she doesn't need to know that.*

*Clever little vixen.*

*Let's give them a show, King.*

"Make it memorable," Inok said from beside me, nodding. I hadn't given that old fae much credit. I'd grouped him in with the rest of the staff at the castle, but truly, he was probably like family to Fen. He likely watched him struggling just as I did. Perhaps he wasn't as vocal about it, but I knew he had a reason to want better for him. For us. And I was grateful. Even though now I had to claim a cetani.

There was a small enclosure in the pits where the fighters would wait their turn. Fen took my hand and a drac followed us with a wooden box. Fen waited for the draconian to leave, then turned to shut the door behind him. He lit a flame using his fire magic and suspended it in the air, giving us the only source of light as he opened the box.

"You're sure you want to do this?"

"I'm sure." I wasn't sure at all.

He yanked out a single strap of fabric. Strolling over to me, he placed his callused hands on my exposed waist and turned me. Unfastening the top of the shirt I wore, he pulled it above my head, then wrapped the piece of fabric over my eyes and tied it securely behind me.

"I don't think I remember you telling me anything about being blindfolded," I said.

"Did I forget that part?" Happiness filled his tone as he rustled in the box again. Then his hands were on me. He pushed his thumbs below my waistband and pulled until the bottoms I wore fell to my ankles.

"Step forward," he commanded. The familiar seduction in his voice soothed me.

I did as I was told until I was standing in a room, completely naked, and blindfolded doing whatever that male told me. It was the first time in a while I'd felt him absolutely present and I would do anything he asked.

He moved away, back to the box. I listened for his breath as he came close once more. I gasped as his cold, wet hands covered my chest. He massaged, stepped away, caressed, stepped away, stroked, stepped away.

"Are you enjoying yourself, my king?"

"Immensely," he answered as he ran two fingers down my throat.

"So, if the king thing doesn't work out, body painting is a firm backup option."

340

"I have many talents," he said, his voice thick.

"What will we do while we wait for it to dry?"

I felt a lick of his magic between my legs as a response. A gasp caught in my throat. "I'm not sure that's a good option just before I have to perform in front of a crowd."

"I'm pretty sure it is," he retorted.

His wind magic began to move in gentle circles, starting at my ankles and moving slowly up to my calves, my knees and then my thighs. He was drying the paint but loving every minute of it. "You never answered my question." He stood directly behind me, though I hadn't heard him move.

"What question?" It sounded breathier than I'd planned.

"Marry me, Ara. I know we're mates, and it's not required, but I want it all with you. I want every title. I want the ceremony. I want to stand before the world and make you mine."

I shuddered. My knees suddenly weak. "I'll make you a deal."

"You would bargain with me on this?" he asked, straining because I would not just agree.

"I'll marry you if you ask me in front of the entire kingdom."

He leaned forward and spoke right into my ear. "I didn't think you would want something like that."

"It's not about what I want. It's about what the people want. It's about giving them something to celebrate on the brink of war. I'll marry you, Fen. But we need them to support us. Wren says reminding them who we are will help. So, let's remind them."

"Deal." He pulled the blindfold off, the paint completely dry.

My brows furrowed. "Don't I need that?"

"No, that was just for me." He winked, his face glowing in the light of the flame.

I laced my fingers behind his neck and smiled. "I love you. I've missed you."

He pulled slightly back, looking at me strangely. "Missed me?"

I looked up into his brutal, beautiful face. "Fen, you haven't even come to bed for most of the week, haven't eaten with the others. You've been so distant."

He rested his hands on the side of my face, pulling me gently to him. "I would give anything to make sure you are safe. My own life, Ara. I'm sorry I've been so focused on that. But it's important. We can't just start walking through the desert with no idea what we are looking for. There has to be something in the history books." I didn't say anything, just stepped away from him and turned. He grabbed my wrist and spun me back around. "I'll try harder. I'm sorry."

I nodded at his attempted promise. "Are you going to tell me how to do this?" I asked, waving at the door. I'd prefer to change the subject entirely than fight with him.

"Cetani demand respect." He became a tutor in an instant, walking me through the ceremony and the steps. He made me say them back to him three times until I had it memorized. Then, he wrapped the blindfold around my chest, blocking almost nothing, removed fabric from the box, and tied it around my waist. It was a skirt, with two high slits up each side.

I cocked my head to the side. "You didn't write your name on me, did you?"

"I promise I didn't," he chuckled.

"Still a badass?" I asked.

"Yes, Ara. You're still a badass. And humble too."

342

I could feel the eye roll, but I didn't care. I had a reputation to keep. He gathered the jars of paint and placed them back in the box. He snuffed out the flame and opened the door to the pits.

I had to give it to Inok and Umari. They put on quite a show in a crunch. I couldn't be sure of course, but it seemed like everyone, even close to the city, filled the stands; there were even fae lining the fence as the draconians danced around the arena with circles of fire and batons with blades on the ends. They flipped around and yelled as they performed and the crowd loved it. Loved them. But Fen was one of them. Or at least his mother was. The moment he walked out into the arena, the crowd quieted. The hiss of whispers filled the air as they discussed their king.

"Today, Umari, leader of the draconian fae, has challenged Ara, mate of your king, to perform a sacred rite." Inok's voice was loud and clear, and I only semi cringed at my singular title. No need to mention I was Alewyn's Promise. No need to mention I was actually born here too. "She will attempt to claim a cetani."

The crowd grew loud again, shifting around each other for a better view, as I stepped out and stood in the center of the pit, nearly naked and smothered in ceremonial paint. The cetani did not need a fae to lead them as they walked forward in a line, Asha at the head.

My heart thundered in my chest as their feline claws pounded the ground in unison as they moved. After parading the fence line, they moved in until they had formed a circle around me. Asha lifted her giant head, her feathers ruffling as she roared. The rest of the cetani followed until the only thing I wanted to do was cower and cover my ears. I was not allowed to move though. Not allowed a single flinch as they each walked up to me.

"This is fine," I whispered. "We can be friends."

*Are you talking to them right now?* I could hear the laughter in his voice.

*Don't you judge me king high and mighty. I'm trying to make friends.*

A laugh vibrated down the bond and I had to shut him out as I focused. As I watched them circle me. "Which one of you wants to conquer the world with me?"

Their eyes were huge. I could see myself reflected in each one as I memorized the difference between them. They kicked up dirt as their circle wound tighter around me. The crowd disappeared as they stomped in closer. The ground rumbling as their feet marched, the sound filled my mind. The entire world was gone as they marched around me, so fast they were nearly a blur. My head spun as the cetani completely overwhelmed my senses.

*It's normal. Stay grounded.*

He could feel my confusion. The urge to move. It was difficult to make myself vulnerable to anyone. Especially a beast. But I kept my head lowered and spoke the words Fen had taught me.

"Tha mi a 'seasamh romhad mar do cho-ionnan. Do dhìon, mo dhìon. Biodh a 'ghaoth gar giùlan mar aon air iteig."

I'm fairly certain I skewed some of that, but I hoped I had gotten enough right for this to work. I'd asked Fen what it meant, but he would only tell me it was a promise to protect the cetani.

Closing my eyes, I held my hand out, willing my heartbeat to slow, just like he had told me to do. I listened to the thundering begin to subside. The world went completely silent. I waited. Nothing happened.

*What do I do now?*

*Open your eyes, my love,* his voice awed.

344

I dropped my hand and opened my eyes to find a cetani, nose to the ground, bowing before me with his wings spread wide.

"Hi there," I whispered, taking a tiny step forward.

*Totally knew this would work,* I beamed.

*Do you recognize him?*

*He looks like Asha, only smaller.*

I reached down to pet the massive, feathered wing of the Cetani. The crowd was completely motionless. As far as they knew, I wasn't from here, I was a foreigner that had come only because I was the mate. But this meant something. It meant I was more. It meant I belonged.

Fen marched forward and addressed the gathering as I continued to pet my Cetani. *My* Cetani. It didn't even feel real. "Years and years ago, a child was born right here in this city. Her fate, gifted by my mother, marked her as special."

I stood, realizing what he was telling the people. My heart responded to his words in terror and pride as he continued to tell my story.

"Not only was this child a gift from Alewyn, we learned that one day, she would save the world. Her parents took their own lives to protect her. The people who raised her, her second parents, trained her just as she would have been raised had she stayed here, in her home. She is a warrior. But she is far more. She is more than a promise from this world, she is more than my mate. As you can see, even my own cetani has claimed her."

My head snapped back to the creature rising from the ground. I hadn't realized it. He had of course.

"Many of you witnessed my father riding my mother's cetani. It would stand to reason that my queen would also ride my own."

He had never called me that before. We'd always skirted around that conversation. Chills covered my body.

"Just over a week ago, the king of the Wind Court opened a door that was closed several millennia ago. The door released fabled creatures into this world. I'm not telling you this to worry you, I'm telling you this because that female," he said, pointing at me, "saved us all." He turned toward me and held his hand out.

*A deal's a deal.*

*I didn't mean today, Fenlas.*

*I did.*

I walked forward and took his hand. Before his people, before his grandmother, before the world, he knelt before me. A hush fell over the crowd as he brought my hand to his mouth.

"Right now, I'm not a king. I'm simply a male asking the most beautiful and badass female in the entire world to marry me. I love you. I think I've loved you my entire life. I've walked the edge of death with you. I've traveled this world with you. And now I'd like to live the rest of my life with you, if you'll have me. I'm asking you now, before our kingdom as my witness, will you marry me?"

I smiled down at my faerie king and nodded. "Every lifetime."

He stood and swung me around in a circle. I looked over my shoulder to Inok, who dipped his chin in approval. And then to Umari, who stood watching us with neither happiness nor contempt. I hadn't planned for this at all, but I hoped this really would get Fen out of his head.

We ambled over to Cal, who knelt while Fen helped me onto his back. He climbed up behind me and held my waist tight as the beast leaped from the ground, threw his wings out and soared into the air, leaving nothing behind us but a cheering crowd and a cloud of dust.

# Temir

"*I*'m sorry. Did you just say son?" Gaea asked the male leaning against his desk. "I mean, there's no question you look alike, but Temir isn't from here."

"Who are you?" he demanded, already annoyed with my company.

"How?" I asked, interrupting their budding argument.

"It's a long story."

His vague answer grated my nerves. This wasn't what I was sent here for, but I needed to know. Ara chose me because I was from the north, she just had no idea how far north. Neither did I, apparently.

"I've got time." I crossed the small office, picked a stack of discarded books off of a chair, and sat.

Gaea, more direct than I had seen her in a long time, mirrored me and plopped down, crossing her arms over her chest as she waited. I was happy to see that even though things hadn't gone as she and I had once planned, she was still in my corner.

"What specifically do you want to know?" he asked, raising an eyebrow.

"I specifically want to know why you called him son," she answered for me. Her tone as sharp as her glare.

Greeve crossed the room, gripped the back of her chair, and stared Heva down. He looked up to him, back to me, and then shuffled some papers around on his disheveled desk. Completely unfazed by the draconian, likely a warrior in his own right.

"Many, many years ago, a seer prophesied a great divide in the world."

"How long?" Greeve asked.

"Before your kind fled from the north. Before the Iron Wars. Before the dynasty of the elven race fell. Our people prayed to the gods, which was more common then. They spoke to us and told us to come here, where they would keep us safe."

"Still not seeing the point," Gaea cut in, tapping her fingers along her arm.

"One year," he continued as if she hadn't interrupted. "One of our own decided he would travel south and explore the world beyond. The gods told him not to leave, but he disobeyed, and we were punished as a people for it. He tore a hole in the veil they created for us. We eventually replaced it with wards, but as you are standing before me, you can see how effective those are."

I leaned forward. "Why would the gods shield your people specifically? There are lesser and high fae in the city. I saw them both."

"We are the same," he barked. "There is no divide here."

348

It was the first time he had spoken with absolute authority.

Greeve moved forward an inch, nearly crunching the back of the chair in his hands.

"The gods chose to shield my people because we listened to the prophetess. We made sacrifices to them and begged for them to have mercy on us."

"So, you're telling me you're a gazillion years old?"

"No, girl. Our ancestors have passed on. We likely do have more children here than you see in the south because we pay homage to the Mother. We still die. We still age. We still bicker amongst ourselves."

"What does any of this have to do with me?" I asked, trying to pull everyone back to the actual point.

"I'm sure you met the creatures of The Bog as you passed through. The gryla?" He pulled a piece of paper from his desk and began to write as he continued. As if we had already bored him.

"Unfortunately," I answered.

"When the fae traveled south and left a tear in the veil, he traded our information to the gryla for safe passage. Occasionally, they are able to slip past our guards. They steal children from their beds at night and give them to Autus so he will leave them alone. A tax. We've lost several children this way." He paused. "Including my own son. Did you never wonder where you were from?" His pen wavered long enough for him to look up at me with disgust.

"I was raised in the king's stables. I had no reason to question the things that were said." My face mirrored his own.

"Fae children are so rare. They would never be discarded. Never thrown out to the stables." He looked back to his paper and shook his head as if I were the ridiculous one.

"And my mother?"

His eyes moved to a painting on the wall. I didn't bother looking. I knew what I would see there. The face of a female I never had a chance to know.

"She passed bringing you into this world." His voice turned dark, raw with emotion. "I wasn't fit to raise you, so I sent you to live with a caretaker. A friend of your mother's. She lived close to the border of our wards. When the gryla came in at night and stole you, she slit her throat." His eyes became dark. Sinister. "You've been the cause of two deaths in this city."

Gaea scrunched her nose in disgust. "He was a baby. You can't possibly blame him."

"I can fight my own battles," I said, rising. "And none of this is why I came here. None of this matters anymore. You can hate me, that's fine. But I've come on behalf of the king of the Flame Court."

He snorted, focusing solely on the paper he had been working on.

"Autus is gathering a human army. Coro and Morwena are dead. He is bored with the north and wants to take over the entire world. A world that you are part of."

"A king that wants to claim the south is no problem of mine. He doesn't even know that we exist."

I pressed my palms onto the desk and leaned over him, ire filling my blood. "Your gods gave me passage to beseech your help. Doesn't that mean anything to you?"

"They gave you passage because you were born here."

I pointed to my companions. "They weren't."

"The gods have many whims that are rarely explainable. I've learned over many, many years you can never be sure of their motive for anything."

"What do you think will happen after the king decimates the south?" Greeve asked, a brisk breeze moving through the room. "Once the king has claimed the rest of the world? If we know you are here, do you think it will take long before he learns the same?"

"What if he uses the Hunt to move into the human world or another? What if he wants to claim that for his own as well? What if worlds are destroyed because you want to sit behind this desk and claim immunity?" My hands trembled as I held back the fury.

"I am within my rights to protect the identity of my people. I will not suffer them to a war that is not their own. Get out."

"But you can't—"

"I can and I will."

Gaea jerk upward. "You're a coward."

"Perhaps, but when you're dead and I'm alive, I will know I've made the right choice."

"I'm glad you were never raised here, Temir." Gaea faced me. "I'm sorry for everything your life put you through, but it made you a hell of a better person than your father." She stormed out of the room. Greeve followed closely behind her.

I turned to walk out, and he stopped me.

"You could stay. The gods have allowed it."

I shook my head. "I'm not like you. I would never let the weak suffer while I stand by. I have a family. One that will defend me to my own father who cannot see past the end of his nose." I closed the door and followed my team out of the house and back into the city.

"What now?" Gaea asked, throwing her hands in the air.

I quickened my step. "Ara said we don't take no for an answer."

"That was a firm no," the drac added.

"Was it?" I asked, continuing down the bridge as the guards came running from Heva's home. "Time to make a scene."

Gaea grabbed my arm, understanding what I meant. "Where to?"

"Can you take us both?"

"Of course."

"The middle of that main road should do it, then."

Greeve lunged forward and we were gone. We landed as if dropped from the heavens. The crowd scanned the skies, trying to figure out where we had come from.

"A show, then?" Greeve asked, pulling out his favorite sword.

"Indeed," I answered, doing the same.

"A draconian," I heard someone shout.

"Heva?" someone else asked.

We began. Our swords clashed as Greeve took his time. He made a show of dancing around me as I blocked his moves and tried to press him back. No matter how much I'd been relentlessly training, I would never have his skill. His precision. Especially as he called his magic forward and began to cleave around the street, striking my sword, cleaving away, zooming up behind me, cleaving away. It became a show as Gaea started moving through the crowds with her own magic, whispering about the draconian fighting Heva's lost son.

The streets overflowed with fae calling out, cheering, and exchanging coins as they bet on us. On our show. I held my sword high above me and took a knee, forfeiting the match to the better opponent. Some in the crowd began to boo.

But Greeve landed beside me and held his hands up. They quieted, eager to hear what he might have to say. "Today we have come to ask your leader for help. Not only for ourselves but for the world below.

A world where draconians like myself ride wild beasts into battle." He waved his hand for me to continue.

I stepped forward. "A world where a child, stolen away in the night, can be raised in the evil king's castle and still be good."

"A world," Gaea said, landing beside me, "where a fae with magic can still find love and friendship and happiness."

"Down there," Greeve continued. "It's not everything the rumors say. There are still fae worth fighting for. This great world has made a promise to us. But we need help in order to see that promise through. We come now, asking you to beseech your leader to join the fight, before the fight comes to you."

The guards were pushing their way through the crowd and were nearly upon us. Taking a knee, I knelt before them. Greeve did the same. Gaea followed directly in the center. We bowed our heads in unison as she placed her hands on our backs, and we were gone.

"Do you think it worked?" I asked, standing as we landed at home.

"We did our best, didn't start a war with them, and put on one hell of a show. If I know Ara, she'll appreciate the dramatics." Gaea smirked. "See ya later?"

I nodded, and in a snap, they were gone.

"Just the guy I wanted to talk to." I turned to see King Fenlas walking up to me in the hall. He put his arm on my shoulder casually. "Got a minute?"

"Sure," I said, taken aback by his relaxed nature. He'd always been like this, but it seemed so bizarre coming from a king.

We walked into his study, and his pile of books had doubled. He seemed happier though. Lighter.

"I want to talk to you about morals." He shifted a pile of books from a chair so I could sit, then cleared the other chair so he could sit beside me instead of in front of me. I had déjà vu for a moment and realized Fenlas was twice the male my father was.

"Morals?" I asked.

"Where did this all start for you, Temir?" He turned his chair so he could face me. "From the beginning, what led you to us?"

"I was working in the Wind Court. I was the healer there. The king enchanted everyone so they would never know what my ability was. He never wanted anyone to know he held a key to immortality. I did basic healing without my magic as well, and I'd been creating medical journals and medicines that would help common ailments and non-magical healers. Autus announced his betrothal to Morwena, and I think we all began to feel the shift in his momentum."

He thought about that for a long time. Sitting back in his chair and rubbing his chin. "Go on."

"If I'm being honest, I hadn't planned on leaving him. I hadn't even considered that an option until one of my experiments went awry. I thought I was numbing nerve endings, and I ended up numbing a combination of brain cortexes, or so I believed once the truth serum emerged. I sat back and thought about what that power might mean in Autus' hands. I knew he would use it for something terrible."

"I see." He watched me closely. "So, where did you go from there?"

"I went to my mentor. A male I trusted with everything. I told him what had happened and he also believed it wouldn't be sensible to tell the king."

"He was wise." Fen shifted forward. "So, then what?"

"Gaea, my mentor, and I were trying to make a plan to escape without being hunted. We'd kept the serum a secret. It wasn't quite finished. I could only get it to work on sea fae at first. We planned to stay until it was perfect and then leave. But Oleonis was killed and I discovered the rebellion and Gaea left and the rest you know."

He ran his fingers through his hair a few times.

"Just ask me what it is you wish to know."

"Part of me wants to use your serum on the entire kingdom. To weed out anyone who shouldn't be here. To find the ones who won't run when we go to battle. But that also feels wrong. It feels like I would be violating my people."

I relaxed, my horns resting on the high back of the chair. "Autus is a strange king. He has the ability to enchant the mind. Sure, you can try to skirt around certain truths, but for the most part, his magic could have changed the trajectory of this war before it even started. But he is fae and prideful and thinks that people should follow him because they believe in him. So, in his own way, he does have morals. He just has a skewed perception of himself."

"Enchantment doesn't work as easily as that though. I have the ability myself. More powerful now that my father has died. But when you twist the mind, you're bending it to your will. A weaker mind would be easy, but I imagine someone such as yourself would take more skill to manipulate. I would guess the king's ability to enchant isn't as strong as you give him credit for. Our magic is diluted. Sure, with singular focus he could change a strong-willed mind for a certain length of time, but not forever."

"That's interesting. I had no idea he had that limitation. I just assumed he chose not to use it. I've seen him do it a thousand times or more. He would enchant each person I healed so they would not remember my ability. He enchanted a whole ballroom to forget my power."

"It is nothing to remove a memory, Temir. A simple pluck of a thread in the mind. Using magic to control someone or larger groups to do something for a long period of time, that's a greater feat, for sure."

I thought back to all the times I'd seen Autus struggle with his magic after I received Oravan's ring. Of course. He wanted people to believe it was a powerful threat.

"Which brings me back to your serum. What would you have me do with it, Temir? If I used it on the entire kingdom, would you feel guilty or responsible for that violation?"

"Today, I went to a secret city hidden on the very tip of the Wind Court. I stood in front of a fae, my father, and begged him for help. He refused because he is safe in his bubble. He claims to be blessed by the gods and therefore safe from everything that happens here." I reached down and picked a book from the floor just to occupy my hands. "I'd never known where I came from. I had no idea I was kidnapped and sold to Autus. I think if any other fae stood there today, in my shoes, they would have felt robbed of a life they could have had."

"But you didn't?" he asked.

"No. I felt . . . abandoned."

He leaned his head back and stared at the ceiling.

"I would give you my blessing to do whatever you wanted with that serum because I have realized something I've been missing in this whole adventure."

"What?"

"Family isn't just your blood, Fenlas. It's who you decide to stand beside and fight with no matter who is right or wrong. That male was not my family. But Gaea? She stood there and defended me. Greeve was ready to cleave across the room and take his head off. That's what a family does for each other. I didn't think I belonged here. I thought

I was supposed to move on and find something else after this was all over, but today I realized this is where I'm supposed to be. Choice after choice and fight after fight all happened so I could be in this one place. With you and with your mate. With my family. Even if we are still trying to figure out where we all fit."

"Trust me, no one knows where they fit. We just do."

"So, what will you do?" I asked him.

"I'd like you to make a store of serum. I don't think I'll be using it today, but as we go to war, we may need it."

"Consider it done." I stood and made it halfway across the room before he stopped me.

"I'm sorry to hear about your father."

"Don't be. At least now I know."

CHAPTER

*31*

# Ara

*lease, Fen? Don't make me beg you.* I wasn't above pouting.

*But you look so pretty on your knees.*

*I will cut you in your sleep, King. Or we can fist fight in the bailey. Up to you.*

*Fine. I'm almost finished and then we can go.*

*YES!*

"He said yes," I told Cal as I massaged his head, burying my fingers into the pure white mane around his face, as soft as a rabbit. He pushed into my hand and closed his amber eyes.

"You'll spoil him rotten," Loti said from behind me, carrying a bucket of meat across the rooftop.

"You've been up here as often as I have," I answered defensively.

"Well, I always liked these beasts." She plopped the bucket down.

I stepped aside so Cal could eat. "You should pet him."

"Oh no, I prefer to just look at them. Are you going out again?"

"Fen's on his way," I answered.

She wiped her hands on the pressed apron she wore daily. "I would have made you a meal to take had I known."

"We'll be back for lunch, Loti. Thank you. Just a quick ride, nothing fancy."

"That's what you said last time," she laughed.

I shrugged. I loved flying with the cetani. I wouldn't apologize for that. She tucked her hands into her apron pockets, and we stood together in a comfortable silence as we waited for Fen to join us. He stepped out onto the roof and smiled at me. I felt that gaze all the way to the pit of my soul, his bedroom eyes glued to me as he crossed the roof, tousled hair and all.

"Ready?"

"Be safe, now," Loti said as we mounted Cal. "I'll see you for lunch."

"See you later," I squealed as Fen led Cal right off the edge of the castle, and he plummeted before spreading his wings and drifting just above the ground.

"That's my favorite part." Fen tightened his hand around my waist and nipped at my ear.

I leaned back against his broad chest, feeling it rise and fall as he held me. "This is mine."

"I thought I'd take you to see the border of our lands today."

"Take me wherever you want." I closed my eyes.

The low growl sent a shiver down my spine and I laughed. Cal rose high into the sky and flapped his lengthy wings enough to gain a bit of momentum. Fen leaned forward and snuggled into me as we rode through the heat of the day. The wind just cool enough to protect us from the sun's burning rays.

The ebb and flow of the beast below us lulled me into a deep, hypnotic state of mind as I cuddled into Fen and enjoyed the precious moments we had together. I wasn't healed from the trauma of almost losing him. The nightmares were proof. But today, things were fine. He was here with me, and it was easier when he was. We rode for a long time in silence, enjoying the feel of our bodies pressed together until, finally, he spoke.

"See there?" He pointed to a spot where the sands began to fade to patchy grass. "That's the border to our lands."

"Is it now though? Who does the Marsh Court belong to? Coro didn't have an heir."

"I suppose that will all be decided later. Autus likely thinks it's already his."

"Do you think he's—What the fuck is that?" I jerked up, squinting my eyes to the horizon.

Fen leaned forward, yanking Cal to the side and pressed his heels into him.

"Autus' soldiers," he said. "A small brigade. We've got to get our army to the border."

"Why would he do that? I thought he wasn't moving yet."

"They're small enough that they might not be detected. He's testing us."

I felt the rigidity of his posture and that call to battle began to creep over me. I wanted down. I wanted to stand before them and destroy them. But something better came to mind. "I have an idea."

"I don't like the sound of that."

His heart raced against my back. The adrenaline and push to save his people drove him. We made it back to the castle bailey in half the time it had taken us to fly out to the border. Fen launched himself off Cal and was running before we could even lock down a plan. He knew what he was doing though.

Greeve and Gaea appeared as soon as the alarm sounded.

"What's wrong?" Greeve asked, shoving the tail of his shirt into his trousers. His lips swollen.

"Send an urgent message to Kai in the sea and then find Fen, Autus has a group of soldiers headed for the border."

He was gone on the wind.

I raised an eyebrow at Gaea.

"What?"

"Straighten your shirt, G. We've got to go."

She didn't bother, just clutched my hand. "Where to?"

"Umari."

The world disintegrated into a thousand pieces. The ground fading away as we spirited. Within seconds we were standing near the oasis. We ran, sounding the alarm until the sky was filled with dark draconian fae, riding their beasts, screaming into the air and flying toward the border.

"To the battle, then?"

"No, they can handle the battle, we've got somewhere else to go. But we need to change into something warmer."

She shook her head and crossed her arms. "I don't like the sound of that."

I rolled my eyes at Fen's echoed words. "Did I miss a secret family meeting? My ideas are always genius. Just trust me."

She grabbed me and we spirited to her room, which was actually Greeve's room, apparently. There were weapons strewn about, his leathers tossed over a chair, and only a small pile of clothes that belonged to Gaea. "Here," she said, shoving layers of long furs into my hands. "Put these on."

"Where to?" she asked after we were both dressed and nearly sweating in the clothes.

"How close can you get me to the Western Gap?"

"Volos?"

"That will do."

The shock of cold ripped through me as we landed. A blizzard blew so relentlessly I could hardly move. Gaea gripped my hand again, and the winds became tolerable, but the visibility was still a joke.

"We have to get to the Gap," I yelled over the roaring winds surrounding us. "Quickly."

We trudged through the snow, moving as fast as we could. We were close to the mountain range, close to the area Lichen had called the banshee, but I couldn't see a single landform to pinpoint exactly where we were.

"What's in the Gap?" she yelled back to me as we sank into the thigh deep snow.

"Dragons," I called, still moving.

She stopped. "You're fucking kidding me."

"Nope."

362

"This is why I never trust your ideas."

"Have I led you astray yet?"

"Oh, no. Swimming with the hydra last week was a real riot."

"If that was sarcasm, I'm telling her you said that," I yelled, pulling her into motion.

"I hate you," she answered but kept the pace anyway.

"Love you too, G."

We walked forever, moving at a snail's pace in the storm. I could have tried magic, but it wasn't worth the cost, unless we got lost. And I couldn't stop the storm anyway. I played out the battle happening at the border over and over in my mind. Fen was smart, he was a warrior. He had Kai and Greeve there as well as the dracs on the way and the rest of the soldiers. Still, I couldn't get the picture of him lying on the ground out of my mind. I couldn't stop myself from worrying over him, though I tried not to distract him with the bond. I willed my mental shields to protect those emotions as best they could.

Eventually the storm settled, and though we were still stomping through deep, deep snow, sometimes waist high, we did eventually make it to the base of the Dregan Mountains.

"This is a terrible idea."

"For the thousandth time, you don't have to come with me. Just go home, I'll meet you there."

"Fuck that. I'm not leaving you here with these beasts." She paused. "Oh gods, is that … ?"

"The Mists." I turned to face them. "The old hag actually did put them back."

"I get it now." She hugged her chest. "I never did before. But Greeve, life without him …"

"I know."

We continued on in silence, both rolling through a thousand scenarios of our mates' deaths. Autus was moving his army. Even if it was only a small piece right now, we needed to get a plan in place. We couldn't let him come to our lands.

"Hello, little liar," Pathog said, standing at the opening of the gap. "Have you brought me someone to play with?" The tremendous lemon-colored beast moved in closer, his wings tucked to his side as he breathed in Gaea. "Her kind are rare. I would keep her."

I kept my tone flat. "She's not available."

"Are you sure?" he asked, tilting his head so he could see her through one massive eye.

"She's sure," Gaea snapped.

"I've come to strike a bargain with you." I crossed my arms over my chest and dug a boot into the ground while I waited for his response.

The scales along his back rippled as he shuddered at the word. "Why would you make a bargain when you are at liberty to demand?"

"Because I would never wish to be enslaved to anyone and I imagine you don't either."

"The bargain, then?" His yellow tail dragged along the muddy ground, rocks and pebbles scattered, and sludge flew through the air.

I looked to Gaea, hoping I was right in trusting her with their secret. "I will open my mind and allow you to take back the name I hold over you in exchange for your entire hoard agreeing to patrol the border of the Flame Court until Autus or I am dead. I will not ask you to join our war against him, but I would ask you to protect our lands."

"You are strange, little liar." He sniffed me, his snout inches from my body.

364

Gaea reached slowly forward and pulled me back a few inches.

"Yes, yes. I know. Do we have a deal?"

His great claws curled, digging valleys into the tampered ground below him. His muscles coiled and he leapt into the air, roaring over his hoard until every dragon took to the air, circling and bellowing into the winter sky.

*We have a deal,* he hissed into my mind. The static of our magical bond rippled across my skin, and a light flashed as the deal was struck. Making a deal with a dragon was always binding. I opened my mind and felt the pluck from my memories as his name escaped me. "You will ride with me to your lands. I will grant passage for the air walker."

"Ever wondered what it was like to ride a dragon?" I asked Gaea, who marveled at the beasts in flight above us.

She shook her head slowly. "Absolutely not."

"You can ride back or spirit back."

"You just want to make an entrance," she smirked.

"I want the southerners to know their new king is not without his allies."

"Let's go." She sighed as the dragon landed before us, his wing stretched low across the ground.

We soared through the sky at breakneck speed atop the back of the dragon that led the rest. Both avoiding the hard conversation. Refusing to acknowledge that our mates were likely battling Autus' soldiers. Hoping that, for once, he hadn't gotten the upper hand and no one would be dead as we landed.

"Can you see anything?" Gaea shifted her weight, trying to look around the serpentine head as we descended.

"Your mate is well," the dragon said, circling and tilting so that we could see the battlegrounds below. At least three hundred bodies were spread across the blood-covered ground. But as we moved lower and the line of southerners began to cheer, I finally relaxed my shoulders.

"We won."

I turned to Gaea, but she was already gone. Already steps from Greeve, who stood beside Fen, stoic as ever, as the great beast I rode landed then lifted his head and roared, the heat from his flames causing the crowd to move back as the other dragons joined.

Fen walked slowly to the beast, held his hand out and helped me dismount.

"They will guard the border until the end," I whispered. "And then I will have no claim over the dragons."

He briefly dipped his chin and raised my hand into the air. "Your future queen has secured our borders with a full hoard of dragons."

The southerners erupted into cheers again, but as I turned my head and saw the bodies lying across the ground, suddenly it was him lying there. Me standing over his body. Broken, gone. I couldn't celebrate. Could only manage the shadow of a smile as we walked through the crowd of our soldiers. The gaping wound from Fen's near-death experience still raw. I turned once more, bowed to the dragon who carried me home, and walked away.

He narrowed his eyes at me only briefly and then lifted back into the sky. *Until next time, little liar.*

*They didn't even have a chance. We caught them by surprise.*

I nodded, watching my feet take step after step, forcing myself to breathe as we walked. He didn't die. He was safe. It was easy, he had said. Still, my mind was clouding over.

"Do you mind if I have Gaea take me home? I'm not feeling well."

"You don't want to ride Cal with me?"

"Another time." I stopped.

The remnants of the battle were still fresh on his skin. Blood. Not his blood, I had to remind myself.

His concern wrapped around me as firmly as his arms. I could have crumbled right here, and he would have carried me. Would have protected me from appearing weak to the others. He leaned away enough to look into my eyes, brushing my cheek with his thumb. "Are you okay?"

"I will be. It's just been a long day."

He pulled me back in and kissed my brow. "I'll see you at home?"

I nodded and spun to Gaea behind us. "Take me home, G." I held my hand out, waiting for her to say goodbye to Greeve.

She reached for me and we were in my room the next instant. "What's wrong?"

"This!" I threw my hands in the air. "All of it. One minute I'm fine and the next minute I remember he almost died, and I'm consumed by it. I have to end this. I can't just keep waiting around for a war."

"What's the plan?" she asked, ready for whatever I was going to throw at her. Even though I know it would probably scare her.

"Something I was talking to Wren about. What if we spirited to the Wind Court and killed Autus in his sleep? What if we could end this before it goes any further?"

"Tonight?"

"So, talking to a dragon is a terrible idea, but sneaking off to the Wind Court isn't?"

She pressed her lips together and shook her head. "No, they're both terrible ideas. But the dragon thing worked out, I guess."

"I think we should take Wren. Can you carry both of us?"

"Yeah, sure."

I nodded and sat on the edge of the bed. "Tonight, then. I'll tell Wren at dinner. You can't tell Greeve, Gaea. I mean it. He will rat us out in an instant."

"I won't," she promised. "Meet in the sitting room next to the study?"

"Come armed."

Dinner was a basin full of emotions as I tried to justify one final murder. I attempted to hide them from Fen, but he kept looking my way, full of worry. I'd smile and try to reassure him that I was just tired, but I think he knew, on some level, something more was going on. Still, he ate dinner in silence while we listened to the rest of the group discuss the battle and watched Kai's reenactment of several of his kills. He used a sausage for a sword, and it was certainly the best part. Especially when he shoved the whole thing in his mouth at the end and began to choke on his pretend weapon.

I'd slipped Wren the note I had prepared as we entered the room and I knew the moment she had read it. Her face became pale, but she locked eyes with me and nodded. She would come, of course. No matter the danger, she would be there. The males in the room may have been born and bred for battle, but the females were too.

I waited and waited for Fen to fall asleep that night. I listened to his breathing for a long time before I slipped out of bed, grabbed my leathers, and crept out of our bedroom. Padding down the hallways, avoiding the staff, I eventually made it into the sitting room. Wren was already there.

"Are you sure this is a good idea?" she asked, pulling her hair back and tying it.

"If it works, think of all the lives we will save."

"And if it doesn't."

"Then at least we can say we tried." I slipped my shirt off and hurried into the other clothing.

"Sorry I'm late." Gaea handed my weapons to me as soon as she popped in. "The battle put Greeve in a *mood*."

Wren shoved her fingers into her ears. "La la la. I don't want to hear it. La la la."

"Super glad you brought the child," Gaea said, her voice flat.

"Hey." Wren dropped her hands.

"Only kidding." She nudged her.

I strapped the sword onto my back and stepped forward. "In and out. We spirit into his rooms, as close as you can get us to his bed. Wren keeps us hidden. I make my move and we go. No one hesitates. No one let's go. Got it?"

"He's a king. He'll still see us," Wren said.

"Yes, but if he's smart, he sleeps with a guard. He won't see us and Autus will be dead before he gets a chance."

I stuck my hand out, Wren put hers on mine, Gaea grabbed them both. "Ready?"

"Ready."

The king's chambers were cold, grey, and unwelcoming. But they were also empty. We poked around the room for several minutes, finding nothing but dust and soiled bed sheets.

"Where else might he be?" I whispered.

"No idea. We could search around, but we will have to be careful about Evin. The moment he detects us, he'll sound an alarm and we will have to go."

"Do it," I ordered.

We spirited throughout the castle seamlessly. It was empty. Not a single guard, not even a servant was left behind. It meant only one of two things: Autus was in hiding, or he was already on the move.

"Take us home," I said finally after searching for anything that would help us. "There's nothing here."

We spirited back to the sitting room. "At least we tried." Wren reached her hands above her head and yawned.

"Tried what exactly?" a deep and deadly voice asked from behind us.

Together, we turned to find Fenlas and Greeve standing shoulder to shoulder in the doorway. Red faced and chests heaving. His anger rippled through me.

"We tried synchronized skinny dipping." Wren shrugged. "Turns out the sea was far too cold."

"With all your weapons?" Fen lifted a brow, not buying it for a second.

"Gaea's a scaredy-cat," she said, shoving past the seething males.

I would have laughed if not for their faces. If I didn't know that, like it or not, I was going to have to tell him.

"Come find us when you get that ragey male shit under control." Gaea wound her arm around mine and spirited us away.

"That's not going to help anything," I said as we stood in a barn filled with hundreds of glass sculptures.

"I've spent most of my life cowering within the shadow of an entitled male. I'll be damned if I'm going to do it for the rest of it. We can make our own decisions."

"If he left in the middle of the night to do something suicidal, I'd be pissed too."

370

She shrugged and walked out. I followed her. There was a small cottage across the yard. She quietly opened the door and snuck inside, her slow steps becoming quick. Her tiptoeing turned frantic, running as she realized the house was empty. "They're gone." She sat on the edge of the couch, wringing her hands.

"Who is?"

"I'll tell you tomorrow. Let's try to get some sleep. The back room is a guest room if you want it."

"No, you're not getting off the hook that easy. I need some more information here, G. I want the story. Your story."

"There isn't one." She didn't miss a beat as she turned away from me.

"A female who runs always has a story."

She let out a long breath, plucking a small glass figurine off the end table. "There was a boy. And before the boy, there was a male, and before him, there was another that was like a father to me. And he died, and the world changed. And I tried, Ara. I fucking tried to get over it, but my heart wouldn't let me. I couldn't wake up and walk past his bedroom door. I couldn't eat a meal in silence. I couldn't breathe. Losing Oleonis broke a part of me. And the male. He was right there. Fighting for me. Waiting for me. But my heart wasn't ready, and neither was his. I thought if we'd given it time, it would have gotten better. But then his mate showed up. And again, everything changed in heartbeat."

"I also lost a male that was like a father to me. It never gets easier, but somehow you just learn to deal with it. Every day, every minute. I'm always here if you want to talk, or cry, or be pissed at the world. And as far as the other male—Temir, I'm guessing—it's okay to let go."

"You're far too observant." She sat back on the couch and wiped a fallen tear. "The thing is, I think I'm happy. I am meant to be with Greeve. The way he makes me feel, his strength, his darkness . . ." She paused, letting her mind wander. "I love him. And I'm terrified. I loved Temir. Even when I didn't want to, I still did. Because he is such a good soul. But he was also reckless. And I was terrified I was going to lose him. I thought I'd come here, move on, and be safer. And now I've found my mate and I'm the reckless one."

"Okay, stop. First of all, you don't get to take credit for my brilliant ideas. I own those. All of them. They are mine. You're the unfortunate best friend. And as far as your past, we all have one and you can't blame yourself for trying to find happiness. For trying to escape the life of a prisoner, G."

"You don't know what it's like to be the bad guy. To be the one who has to walk away."

"Oh, so I should have brought snacks for the pity party?"

She threw a pillow at me and smiled. "It's not funny."

"I don't know what you're talking about. I'm hilarious and you've got to let it go. Live a little. Let yourself be happy. I don't think Temir blames you. In fact, I think he's just happy that you're here and safe and with us. And because I'm selfish, I'm glad you did whatever you did to get here."

"I've never had a real friend before. Except Temir. I'm glad I have one here."

"I mean, I won't tell Kai you said that. He'd be pissed."

She flashed me a smile. "Fine, I guess I'll claim him too. But dealing with Greeve when he tries to control me is hard. I won't let myself be controlled ever again. I lived that life long enough to know it's not what I want."

"Trust me, it's not what he wants either. He just has to figure that out. Give him time."

She scooted closer to me and laid her head on my shoulder. "The boy that lives here means the world to me. His name is River and he hates being called Rock." She laughed and shook her head. "I should get some sleep. I'll see you in the morning."

I stood and stretched. "I hope the bed isn't made of glass." I walked through the strange home, sat on the edge of the bed and couldn't help but reach for Fen.

*I love you. Even if you can't understand why I did what I did tonight, I still love you.*

Nothing.

*Good night.*

Silence.

CHAPTER

32

# Temir

*A* firm knock on my door woke me. I untangled myself from Nadra and jumped from the bed, expecting an emergency, but when I swung the door open and found the king standing with a bottle of amber liquid, half smiling, I realized this was only a social call.

"We're going to the tavern. Get dressed."

I rubbed my eyes and yawned. "Do I have a choice?"

"No." He spun on his heel, walked down the hall to Rhogan's room, and began pounding again.

I dressed quickly and met him at the front of the castle with Greeve, Rhogan, and Kai in tow. He and Greeve had clearly already been drinking.

Fenlas swung his arm around my shoulder and leaned his body weight into me. "You know what I like about you, Temir?" he asked, breathing into my ear. "You're just a roll with the punches kind of guy. You know who's not that kind of guy? Me. I am not."

He shoved the bottle he brought into my hand, and though I wasn't much of a drinker, there was no way I was getting away from it this night. Err, morning?

Rhogan looked over his shoulder and wiggled his eyebrows at me. A night of drinking was right up his alley.

Fen beat his fist on the locked door of the tavern he had chosen. A short burly fae with hairy arms and a beard that touched the floor swung the door open, looking ready to murder. Until his eyes landed on the king. He stepped to the side and addressed Kai. "Lock up when you're done."

"Thanks, Gillie." Kai moved behind the bar as the owner waddled back up the stairs. Chairs were piled on top of tables and the floor was still wet from being mopped. The room smelled of citrus and stale bread, but the windows were clear and the corners were clean.

Rhogan and Greeve cleared a table for us, setting the chairs on the floor. Fen grabbed several mugs while Kai filled pitchers from barrels that lined the side of the countertop. I wasn't sure how to help, so I just sat in a chair and waited for them to be seated. Greeve sat beside me, leaning his arms on the table. Rhogan swung the chair around, as he usually did to sit on it backwards, accommodating his wings.

"What are we celebrating, boys?" Rhogan asked, grabbing a mug and sucking half of it down before wiping his mouth with the back of his hand and slamming the cup back on the table.

"Misery," Fenlas answered, drinking the full mug and refilling.

"Your mating bond grating on your nerves?" Kai asked, a sparkle in his eye.

Greeve grumbled, lifted the pitcher, and drank straight from it. I took a long drink from my own glass as Kai pulled a deck of cards from his pocket and dealt each of us a card.

"Be careful," Greeve slurred. "Kai's drinking games never end well."

"Highest card drinks and keeps his card. Whoever has the most cards at the end gives Loti a big ole smooch tomorrow."

"One day, she's going to poison you," Fen said, still brooding.

"Nah. She'd miss me too much." He grinned, but his smile didn't quite reach his eyes and I wondered if there was more going on with Kai than what he showed on the surface.

Round and round we went, drinking and talking about war and females and life and how they were all so similar. My eyelids grew heavy and my smile wide as we continued the card game. Kai kept pulling more cards from his pockets until the table was stacked with them, we smelled like a brewery, and none of us could sit up straight.

"Last round," Kai mumbled, his eyes unable to focus.

We all turned our final card over. Rhogan lost that round, grabbed the pitcher and chugged what was left. He belched and slammed it back on the table. "Enjoy your smooches," he said to Kai, who clearly had the tallest stack of cards. "I've got a female to find." He stood, swayed, and laughed, his wings helping him balance as he crashed into a side table.

"We could just sleep here." My tongue was so swollen I didn't think anyone could understand me. I laid my head on the cool table and closed my eyes.

Fen grabbed the back of my shirt and pulled me to my feet. "Isnot too far."

As one, we stumbled out of the building, leaning too far to the right and then left, our feet dragging and bodies heavy. Kai sang a bawdy tune about a big-chested mermaid as we walked back to the castle. We got close enough to the door that I could see a beautiful red-haired female standing against the frame, her arms crossed over her chest and her eyes level with me. Nadra.

"Ohhhh," Kai drawled. "Tem's in trouble."

We all burst into laughter until I realized Temir was me and I was the one in trouble. The smile fell from my face. At least I thought it did, until she shook her head and smiled, and I realized it never had.

I'd needed that night with them. To let go, to vent about the world. And she knew it. I left the group behind and walked quickly to her. In my mind it was quick, but I imagine it was quite lopsided and a little laggy. She slid her hands up my chest and looked up at me in the doorway. I leaned down, kissed her hard and pulled her inside, ignoring the catcalls from Kai and Rhogan as we left.

"Did you have fun?" she asked later, still trying to catch her breath, lying naked and glorious beside me.

"Tired," I answered, unable to open my eyes.

She ran her hands through my hair, avoiding the horns as I feel asleep to her sweet laughter. Moments later, she was shaking me awake. She had bathed and dressed, and the blinding sun coming through the window told me it was nearly noon. "We've been called to lunch, Temir. Are you going to bathe and dress or go down naked?"

I felt like holy hell. My stomach turned and the smell of my own breath made me almost vomit. I slumped into the bathing room, keeping my eyes closed tight so the sun wouldn't burn my retinas. I shut the door and took several deep, grounding breaths. I called my magic forward and cured the hangover that would have consumed my full day. My shoulders relaxed and I was in and out of the bath in no time. I brushed my teeth and hummed that tune Kai had sang on the way home.

"It's not fair, you know." Nadra gleamed as I pulled her into my arms. "Normal people get hangovers and have to suffer for drinking enough to poison a kingdom."

"Luckily for me, I'm not normal." I flashed her a smile and pulled her out the door. I hadn't felt this happy, this carefree, in so long. Not because I was in denial about the coming war, but because I was actually happy. I'd accepted complacent for so long, this just felt so foreign.

We proceeded into the dining hall, and all four of my drinking buddies looked as if they'd regretted every decision they'd made last night. Fen held his head in his hands and moaned as Loti piled his plate. Rhogan was just laying his head on the table across from Kai who groaned and slid his plate away from him.

Gaea and Ara sat with Wren at the end of the table, smirking as they relished in the suffering of the males. Nadra sat down with them, and I crossed the room. I placed my hand on Fen's back and pushed my magic through to him.

He sighed and sat up straighter. "You are a godsend, Temir."

"Me next," Kai groaned.

I healed the rest of them and filled a plate, sitting next to the king. Greeve began to shovel food into his mouth. I'd never seen the draconian so out of character. He looked down the table to Gaea. She looked his way, and his head snapped forward. I'd heard what happened in the tavern last night, but we still didn't know where they had actually gone.

"Loti, you are looking lovely today," Rhogan said, smiling wide at her.

He wiggled his eyebrows at Kai as Greeve and Fen snorted. I tried to keep my face neutral as Kai stood from the table, a tart in his hand, and moved in her direction. Rhogan buried his face so he wouldn't laugh. Within seconds, Loti was screaming and running around the table while Kai chased her, lips puckered.

He caught her around the waist, and she squeezed, squirmed and swatted him while he pressed his lips onto her cheek and held them there. He swung her around for show, and by the time he released her and she took off running, the atmosphere of the entire room had changed with Loti's infectious laughter. The divide wasn't quite as wide.

Fen stood and cleared his throat. "We've had some new arrivals come in today. Someone I think you'd like to meet, Kaitalen. I am calling a meeting in the open council room before dinner, though the doors will remain shut. Everyone in this room is to attend. Wren, if you could invite your sister, and Greeve, if you could call in Brax? I'll have Inok join us as well as Umari, who should already be on her way."

He locked eyes with Ara down the table and then quickly looked anywhere else. Nadra turned to whisper something into her ear, but her face didn't give an inch as she watched Fen carefully avoid her. He walked out of the room and she stood, following him out of the door.

"That was awkward." Kai scooped a pile of eggs into his mouth.

Greeve reached over, snagged a piece of meat from his plate, and then stood. He watched Gaea, but she didn't so much as look at him as he walked out. She didn't stand to follow him either.

"No," Greeve told me later in the training yard. "If you put too much weight on your left leg, you won't be able to turn to the right quickly enough. You have to disperse your weight evenly. Again."

He had agreed last night to help me train with swords. Rhogan had taken that as an invitation also, and now both barked orders at me while Kai attacked. I was getting better. I was a far cry from the warrior I'd been when we left the Wind Court. Still, I'd been almost useless against the tharraing. I couldn't let that happen again.

"Good. Again," the drac barked.

"Give it a rest, Greeve. Just because your mate's giving you hell doesn't mean you have to take it out on him."

I stumbled. "Mate?" I knew they had grown close. I knew he was sulking over her. Had I avoided the signs? Refused to see them? She hadn't told me.

"Yeah, didn't you know?" Kai asked.

"No." I raised my sword back up. "But I suppose it makes the most sense. You're similar."

"I don't run away. I don't fear the way she does," Greeve said, his eyes going dark.

"I've known Gaea for a long time."

"I know." He gripped his wooden sword tighter and gave me a look.

I wondered how much she had told him. Probably everything. I took a step back. "I'm only saying when she needs space, the only thing you can do is give it to her. At least she's here. When we . . . I mean . . . the old Gaea would have just disappeared."

He nodded, and the conversation was over. He walked away before I could say anything else.

Kai held his fingers close together. "Little tip. Maybe don't remind him you banged his mate."

My eyes doubled.

"Yeah. We all know." Rhogan kicked the sand and turned to hide his obnoxious grin.

"It's not like I think of her that way anymore. I'm happily mated."

Kai picked at a piece of lint on his sleeve as he casually asked, "How would you like it if I gave you advice on that sweet little fox you're keeping locked up in your room?"

I balled my hands into fists, and Rhogan slid between us.

"Exactly," Kai smirked. He'd used those words just to provoke me. To prove a point.

It worked.

"We've got a meeting to get to." Rhogan pushed me toward the door. When we were far enough away, he let go. "He didn't mean that, you know."

"I know," I snapped and stormed into the castle.

I found Nadra in the hall and pulled her into the room, smashed her against the wall and kissed her until my nerves calmed and I realized my response was completely irrational. I brushed the hair from her face and then kissed her gently. She reached up and ran her nails down my back in response, and I grabbed her around the waist and threw her onto the bed.

# Ara

"You could just talk," I barked at Fen as I chased him down the hallway. "Instead of glaring at me and making it awkward in front of everyone, just ask me."

He opened the door to his study, and I followed him in, slamming it behind me. I crossed my arms as I took in the state of the room. The books that had filled the floors were still there, but the desk had been completely cleared off, everything thrown to the floor.

"Fen," I said softly.

"You want to talk?" he answered, his voice the only thing I'd longed for since the second Gaea spirited us away last night. "You should have done that before you went on whatever your secret mission was. Whatever you thought was so important it was worth sneaking out of bed for."

"You wouldn't have let me go."

"Then you shouldn't have gone. And I won't apologize for saying that. I may not tell you what you want to hear, but I'll always tell you what you need to hear, Ara." No anger, no emotion at all. The defeat on his face was worse than anything else.

"I had to. And maybe you won't understand it, but fuck, Fen. Every single time I let my mind rest, the only thing I see is you lying dead on the ground. Every time you hide in this room reading this book or that book, I'm alone, and it plays over and over."

"I thought it was better. After the cetani." His eyes finally lifted to mine, and I shook my head.

"But that's the thing. As soon as it felt manageable, Autus attacked and just brought everything right back. I don't know if it will ever get better. You died." My voice broke. "You fucking died, and I had to listen to it. I cried into your chest and your heart didn't beat."

"I never left you. I never would."

"Don't you see? As long as that threat is out there, as long I know that bastard is plotting, I can't let the fear go."

"Ara, why do you think I sit in this room and hunt through these books. I feel exactly the same way. Exactly."

"Then why aren't we working together? Why don't you ask for help?"

"Why didn't you?" He walked over to me and grabbed my hands. "Tell me where you went."

"I . . ." I searched the depth of those beautiful eyes, knowing what my words would do to him. "We went to the Wind Court." His grip tightened on my hands. "We spirited, Wren kept us hidden. It was supposed to be a quick in and out job. He was supposed to be there, Fen. He was supposed to be asleep in his bed, I was going to kill him, and we were coming home before anyone knew we were gone."

"But you didn't," he said. Not a question.

"No." I dropped my head, but he lifted my chin with his finger.

"What happened?"

"He was gone," I whispered. "His entire castle, every single fae, gone."

"Shit." He jerked, stepping away from me. "Shit," he said again. "I thought we had time. I thought we had so much more time. Kings never rush anything."

"So, you think he's already on the move?" I sank into a chair.

"Well, he isn't hiding. Temir can tell you that much. It's not in his nature."

"How long until he gets here?"

He took a lengthy breath and sat across from me. "I don't know when he left. It takes time to move an entire army down the continent. A month, at least. Maybe more if he has a human army. But no one has reported spotting them yet."

"Maybe he's just left."

He shook his head. "But why would he take his entire castle? I don't get it. They would slow him down."

I shrugged.

"We can't keep fighting. I never want to spend another night away from you. I don't think my liver can handle it." A great pause lingered between us as his emotions swayed. "I would have let you go, Ara. I might have asked to come, but I wouldn't have stopped you."

"None of it matters anyway," I said. "It didn't work. And I'm sorry you got a stubborn, reckless asshole for a mate. I'm sorry this isn't all happy and perfect."

"I don't want perfect, Ara. I just want you. I love the fire. I love how passionate you are. I love that I never have to be anything but myself with you. I will fight these small battles with you now so we can learn how to be perfect together." He stood and stared me down until my eyes met his, lit with fire and passion and our soul. "There's not a damn thing in this world or the next I wouldn't go through to be with you." He pulled me to him. Hugging me tight, he lay his head on mine and we stayed there, holding each other, until Inok walked in.

"Sorry. They're ready." He bowed, keeping the formal demeanor he wore like armor.

"I wish you wouldn't do that." Though Fen's face was neutral, a tinge of pride pricked me.

"Like it or not, you are king and no one else will treat you as such if those around you are given exception."

"I don't care if everyone bows to me," he said and we walked out of the room.

As we entered the meeting room, shock hit me as I saw the Weaver sitting coiled beside a row of chairs, her snakeskin glossier than last I'd seen her. I was not as surprised as Kai though, who stood at the door watching her with his mouth gaping. Rhogan had to shove him out of the way just so he could squeeze his wings through the doorframe.

"Welcome home," Fen said as we passed by.

She dipped her head and winked at me. "I hear you are the dragon rider."

"Was," I answered, following Fen.

Almost everyone had come. Only Umari was missing. Fen and I sat behind the table on the raised platform while everyone else sat in the audience seats, waiting for him to begin. "There's been news," he began. "Temir, Gaea please stand."

Temir looked around and then stood as everyone shifted in their chairs to look at him.

"Ara, Gaea and Wren left for a mission last night," Fen said, addressing the crowd. "They discovered King Autus' castle was completely empty. You know him better than the rest of us. Has he gone into hiding, as kings have been known to do in the past, or is he on the move?"

"He wouldn't go into hiding when he believes himself to be the rightful High King of Alewyn," Temir said. "He has mobilized."

"But why does he think he is justified?" Wren asked.

"Because," the Weaver answered, "his father was from the Wind Court. His mother was a cousin to Coro. Now that Coro has died with no heir, he could claim that territory. He was betrothed to Morwena, who was killed." She arched an eyebrow at me. "With no heir, he could have a claim if she has no relatives. And as far as the Flame Court . . ." She turned to look at Fen. "Autus has no claim. But he could refuse to acknowledge yours."

A great wind gust whipped through the room as Greeve disagreed. "Ara killed Morwena. She has more right to claim the sea than he does. As well as the Marsh Court. And he made that claim before Coro was dead."

"I've not come to argue politics. I'm only explaining why he *thinks* his war is justified." The naga swayed back and forth, her serpentine nature showing through.

"All of that aside," Fen interrupted, raising his hands and gesturing for them to all be seated. "Why is the castle completely empty? Where have the servants gone?"

The door slammed open and Umari walked in dragging two limp bodies behind her. "Because he's killed them all." She heaved her prisoners toward the aisle.

"What?" Nadra jumped from her seat. "All of them?"

"That's what this one said before I knocked him out." She plopped down into a chair. "I found them trudging across the desert. Thought someone ought to know why."

I'd seen that same lethal look on my mate's face enough times to know she had enjoyed the hunt.

"Temir." Fen gestured to the northerner Umari had indicated.

"Wait," I jumped to my feet.

*How many in this room do you think have good mental shields? You don't know their abilities. What if one can communicate with the king somehow? We need to contain this.*

"Right." He scratched his head. "We trust everyone in this room obviously, but we don't know these fae or their powers. Do you recognize them?" he asked Temir, Nadra, and Gaea.

They shook their heads.

"Best take them down, Greeve. We'll be there in a bit."

Greeve stood, grabbed one of the fae, and was gone. We waited until he came back for the other. Once they were out of the room, we spoke freely again.

"If we take all of our numbers, the sea fae, the draconians, the rebels, the southerners all of them, how many do we have willing and able to fight?"

"I have two thousand draconians prepared for battle." Umari stood taller, her chin raised.

"The sea fae total over five thousand," Kai rose. "But they have said more than three times that many went north."

The Weaver grew on her stacked coils. "I tried recruiting Coro's army before we moved south. Rebels have been infiltrating them for months. We were able to bring two thousand soldiers and about the same number of rebels. The rest are held up in the castle right now."

"Between the rebels that were already here and the refugees, there are at least five thousand," Sabra tapped a finger to her lip, the wheels spinning in her mind reflected in worry on her pensive face.

"Our own numbers?" he asked, turning to Inok.

"Ten thousand," he answered.

"Twenty-six thousand total," I mumbled.

"I want every single soldier, every sea fae, every drac in motion as soon as possible. I don't want that bastard on my land. Brax, see it done. Kai, you're with him. Get them to the border lords' properties. The dragons will keep everyone safe. I guarantee those two got through while we were fighting the first wave of Autus' attack. The battle was a distraction so his hunters could come."

I took a long, deep breath and felt the makings of war settling over me. This was it.

"King Fenlas?" Nadra stood beside Temir, her arm linked through his. "I think I can help with the Marsh Court. I'm from there and was an apt courtier. I know a lot of them. If I could just try to talk to them—"

My fists tightened at my side. "No, absolutely not. It's dangerous and you are not trained. It's not going to be like having lunch with the court ladies."

"I'll go with her," Rhogan answered, standing and letting his wings spread. "I'll make sure she is safe."

I looked to Gaea and raised a brow.

"I'll take them. We have to try," she said.

She'd used my own words against me. She knew how valuable Nadra was, but we'd need those additional numbers. The last correspondence we received told us Autus had just over forty thousand soldiers. And now he was mobile.

I nodded subtly and looked to Fen.

"Greeve goes too," he said. Discussion over.

The room emptied, Temir stayed back, as did the Weaver, Kai and Gaea.

"I've sent Nadra for the serum, but there's something I've just thought about. Have you talked to Oravan?"

"The blacksmith?" Fen asked. "Not that I can recall, other than pleasantries in passing, why?"

"He made the sword for Autus' recipe to trap Ara, so maybe the king said something to him that could help give clues to the lost artifact you're trying to find."

The Weaver slithered closer. "Lost artifact?"

"It's a long story, but basically, Autus thinks he can bind my power to him if he finds certain items. But he won't find them all," I said nonchalantly, though I knew it drove Fen mad.

"What's the artifact?" she asked, lowering her voice.

"We don't know. That part was vague. Just something from the southern kingdom, that's all we know."

"Where have you searched?" She looked only to Fen now.

"I've been searching books for anything touched by a god or forged in powerful magic, since that seems to be the connecting factor."

"The naga ruins. They are full of ancient artifacts, I'm sure most of them are gone by now, but certainly if something is hidden, that's where it will be."

"What makes you so sure?" I asked.

"Because I'm the one who brought the temple down," she said, as if she were speaking of the weather.

I realized the only thing I really knew about her was what Kai had mentioned about her in the forest. *She's a legend in the south. She's the one who killed an entire horde of her own kind to try to help her lover escape.*

"It's worth looking into," Fen decided. "For now, I've got to go deal with Umari's prisoners. Temir, you better come also."

Leaving the others behind, the three of us hustled through the familiar levels of the castle and back to that hideous room from before. I'd watched a traitor bite off his own tongue in this desolate room. I'd hate to think of the other memories these barren walls carried. Greeve had both fae tied to the wall this time. He wasn't taking any chances. We checked them for jewelry of any kind, and Fen was quick to remind everyone to shield their minds. He nodded to Temir, and the healer walked forward, placed his hand on one of them, and then stepped away as the high fae with pale skin slowly opened his bloodshot eyes. The lump on his head from where Umari had struck him remained.

"Who are you?" Fen asked, casually leaning against the wall, arms crossing his broad chest in a terrifyingly calm tone.

He smiled but didn't answer.

"I won't bother wasting my time." Fen nodded to Temir.

Greeve cleaved forward, grabbed the fae by the hair, and held his head back as Temir administered his serum. The fae's face turned red, rage moving through him as he realized Temir was in the room. They loved to hate him in the north.

"Who are you?" Fen asked again.

"Desim," he spat.

"Why are you in the Flame Court?"

"The one true king has sent us to find something for him."

"Find what?" Fen examined his hands, refusing eye contact with the male.

He tried to press his lips together, but Greeve punched him in the stomach and he squawked. "The chalice."

"What chalice?" Fen's tone was smooth, neutral. He'd get his answers one way or another and his relaxed demeanor was a show. A deadly façade.

"I don't know. We were told to walk through the dunes until we found old buildings or caves. Supposedly, there would be a chalice the king requires."

"Do you know how many caves there are in the dunes?" The corners of his mouth twisted up.

"No idea."

"Did your king tell you how to find the chalice?"

"No."

"What does the chalice look like?" I asked, stepping forward.

His eyes narrowed on me. "I don't know," he gritted out.

I double checked my shields, but they were fully intact. I hadn't felt any intrusion or prodding from the fae. "What happened to the servants in the king's castle? Why is it empty?"

"We had a very large bonfire." He grinned. "It was cold, we needed to warm our army."

I stumbled backward. The dark smile grew across his face as he witnessed how his words affected me. Gutted me. "How many?" I whispered.

"Thousands. Lessers burn up pretty quickly. We had to keep piling them on."

I stumbled backward as if I had been shoved. Temir cracked him across the face before I could respond. My mind reeled. Thousands. *I have to go. The pressure is building.*

I couldn't think, couldn't breathe, as I shuffled out of the room and down the castle hallways. Thousands he had said. Gone. Their lives, meaningless. My magic pressed in. I slid my back down the cool wall just outside the room and pressed my palms into the side of my head. A tapestry hung across from me depicted a hunting party; though hung with innocent intentions, my stomach turned. Oh gods. I forced the air into my lungs. I needed Gaea. I needed to get out. I needed to get away from people.

I stood, stumbling. My chest swelled as the magic, locked behind the dam, shoved against me. Begging me to end it all. To end the entire world. All the problems, all the hatred, all of it. Let the world become reborn. Let the fae rise from the ashes of hatred and damnation.

*Ara, breathe.* Fen placed his hands on my arms. *Look at me. You are in control. Look at me.*

I shook my head. I couldn't. I couldn't pull a full breath. I started to panic. The deadly magic right there. So beguiling, yet so much tension.

"Use the bond as an anchor, Ara. Just like I did. It's there. Grab it, pull yourself back to me. Don't lose yourself. You're in control."

I tried so fucking hard to hear the words he said, but I couldn't. The ringing in my ears overwhelmed me.

*Thousands.* It was the only word that came to my lips. The world was going dark. I was dangerous. I was lethal. Suddenly, I was gone, standing in the middle of Autus' empty castle. I saw them. The thousands who worked here, the lesser fae who might have cooked meals and cleaned rooms. They were here, and then they weren't.

"Blow this bitch sky high," Gaea muttered, refusing to judge or look away from me. "You need to take something out on the world? Do it here, where it hurts him."

"Go," I rasped as the magic began to crest.

But she didn't. She didn't let go as the pressure finally burst and the magic ripped from me. She squeezed my hand as all the nerves and worry that had been building for days roared through me. As the castle walls came down and the world faded away. As my magic threatened to destroy me, just as thoroughly has it had a good portion of the Wind Court. She never let go.

I felt arms below me, the summer sun and then nothing at all. And then I knew, without a shadow of a doubt, that this was how it would end. I would shatter the world into a million pieces and take every person I loved with me. I'd kill myself in the process. That's what I was created for. Not to save the world, but to destroy it.

*You're wrong,* a voice said into my mind.

*I'm not.*

# CHAPTER
## 34

# Temir

"Go," Greeve said, his voice cold.

He pulled that long, curved blade out, and though I'd shut the door behind me, my hearing was still keen enough to hear the final gasp of the second fae before he was killed. I walked to my room carefully. As much as I didn't want to picture the faces of the servants who had likely died, I couldn't help it. The cook that always gave me extra food for a starving stable boy. The laundress that never questioned why my bedding would go missing from time to time. They were gone. All of them.

I opened the door to find Nadra changing into something Wren had likely brought her. The female fashion in the Marsh Court was quite different than what they wore here and even in the Wind Court. The Flame Court replaced layers of fabric with something light and sheer to combat the hot weather, or they wore something they could fight in. Leathers, they had called them.

"Are you sure this is wise?" I asked as she sat to brush out her hair.

"Everyone knows Coro has the greatest army. Had," she corrected herself. "If we can sway them to come south, it could make the difference between winning and losing. I'd say that's a wise decision."

"But your power . . ."

"No one will know. I'll have plenty of guards. They aren't going to listen to anyone else like they would listen to me. I'll go straight to Xanth, plead our case, and come right home."

I crossed the room to stand behind her. "No one knows the current state of Hrundel."

"Exactly. We need to know, and hopefully Rhogan will have some time to check the skies for Autus' army."

"If you think he is going to leave your side, you're wrong."

She shrugged and twisted her hair into a knot on the top of her head. I handed her the pins she liked to use, and before I knew it, she was kissing me goodbye.

"Be careful."

She moved her hands along my antlers and leaned in close. "I promise," she whispered, and then walked out the door.

I thought I would try for a nap since I'd barely slept off our drunken night, but my mind wouldn't stop. I pictured everything that could happen to her and knew I'd be up the rest of the night. I would probably be a wreck by tomorrow. So instead, I found myself wandering down to the city to find Oravan. King Fenlas needed to find that artifact, and if I could help at all, that was what I desired to do.

He was working in his own small corner of the blacksmith's shop, pounding a red-hot piece of metal against an anchor. Sweat beaded on my forehead the moment I stepped inside. Though a soft breeze carried the smell of burning metal through the open window, it did nothing for the heat. Oravan wasn't fazed at all, his shirt still clean as he worked. He was focused. Banging and rotating the iron. I had to walk in front of him to get his attention, avoiding sparks that flew through the air.

"'Bout time you came by." He shoved the metal into a pot of water, the sizzle concluding his work as plumes of smoke filled the air around him.

"I've got a question for you." I stepped back as he grabbed another rod.

"No serum this time?" he asked.

"No. No serum. We're on the same side now."

"We've always been on the same side, Temir."

"Can you tell me about the day the king asked for the sword. The one forged in death?"

He dropped the rod he was holding, and it clanged to the floor. He looked around the room cautiously and then pulled me closer to him. "What about it?"

"The last time we talked about it, you were working on it. You said it would be the most powerful sword ever made. I know you finished it before you could escape, and I know he has it. But he isn't planning to use it the way you might think. I need to know what he said to you when he ordered it made."

"But he didn't order it," he said. "He sent Eadas to order it. He asked if I'd heard of the legendary sword, and of course I had. He asked me if I could duplicate it and said it needed the same amount of power as the original, if not more."

"How did you forge it in death?"

His eyes dropped to the floor as he sat silent with his haunted memories. "I was brought ashes, and I combined them into the metal as I was forming the sword. I'll never do it again, if that's what you're getting at, Temir. Not for all the freedom in the world. There is a darkness in that kind of magic. It felt . . . wrong."

"I'm not asking you to do it again. But you said it has a brother. Do you know where?"

"Some say it's hidden in someone's home, right in plain sight, and others swear it was melted down and forged into something new. I've no idea the truth of it. I've never seen it myself."

"No matter. You're sure that's all you know of it?"

"I'm sure."

I left him to continue his work and made my way back to the castle. Fen was easy to find. He barely left his study anymore. I knocked quietly on the door and let myself in. "Thought you might like a hand."

"It's boring work," he said, circles under his eyes from his own lack of sleep.

"I've got nothing better to do."

"The far wall hasn't been touched. I've been going through the oldest books looking for anything that talks about an artifact with immense power. Now we know it's a chalice, that should help. If we can figure out what it is, then maybe we can check the archives and see where it was last."

"And if it isn't in the books, Fen? What then?"

"It's not logical to start digging through the desert. Autus' males would have never found it that way. There has to be more to it. Something we hadn't specifically asked or that fae was not told."

"I'll get started, then." I walked to the back of the room and ran my finger down the textured spines of several books until I found one I thought looked promising. I sat on the floor, pressed my back against the bookshelf, and skimmed the pages for anything that might be helpful. There was nothing, of course. I sat the book onto the floor beside me, stood, and repeated the same process. Several times I looked up to see the king wringing his hands, rubbing his eyes, and flipping frantically through worn pages.

There was a library here, but he'd had the staff swapping out books as he completed them, preferring the privacy and comfort of his own study. But the space was filling fast, the staff unable to keep up.

Loti brought us dinner and didn't say a word as we nodded our thanks and continued searching. My pile of books began to grow. Fen had nearly buried himself in his.

"Have you checked for books on the naga?" I asked, stretching. "If the Weaver is to be believed, perhaps they had an archive list we could look through."

"Try that bottom shelf there." He pointed, but his voice sounded like boots on gravel. "There are several books on the fae of the southern kingdom in the corner."

I stood, shuffled my pile to the side, and sat back down in the corner. The words ran together on the pages, but still, we searched. Fen nodded off and several times I cleared my throat just to wake him. I was used to research. I'd done it most of my life. I'd written hundreds of medical journals, but even I would be strained after searching for as long as he had.

"Shall we come back to it tomorrow?" I asked.

He looked out of the small window and smiled sadly. "I think it already is tomorrow. Let's call it a night, Temir. We're worthless running on the amount of sleep we've gotten."

"Tomorrow's a big day." I stretched my hands above my head. "All of your forces will be gathered at the border."

"Indeed it is," he agreed.

I walked the quiet halls back to my room, sent Nadra my love down the bond, fell face first into the bed, and slept like a rock until morning. My eyes were still tired when I woke, but I quickly dressed and made my way down to breakfast.

It was only Fen, Inok, and me today. We ate quickly and went back to the study immediately afterward. Inok didn't join us. He'd left for the stables to meet with the soldiers gathering at the borders. Fen would only be researching until his cetani arrived.

"Are you certain you don't want to come to see the numbers?" he asked again as I sat on the chair across from him and dropped a stack of books on the floor.

"I'm not sure how much help I'd be there, but if I'm here, at least we're still searching."

"You're a good male," he said. "Ara's not even concerned with the threat. She's confident he will never find all the pieces. I just can't have that same outlook. I have to protect her."

I thought of Nadra and the imprint on her hand. "I understand that more than you know."

It wasn't long before one of the castle staff came to announce that the king's cetani had arrived. He thanked me again for working and then was gone. Pulled in a thousand directions. We hadn't even discussed Ara's absence. I'd seen her face when that fae told us what Autus had done. She was absolutely destroyed by it. More than I was.

399

But I wasn't born to protect those fae. I hadn't failed them all. She thought she had. I could see it in her eyes before she stumbled out of that torture room.

I continued searching books for several more hours, finding nothing helpful. There were a lot of new things I'd learned, but nothing about ancient magic, chalices or binding magic.

"Temir?" Nadra called, yanking me from the book in my lap.

I scrambled out of the door and met her in the hallway. "You're fine?"

"A promise is a promise," she said, smiling. "No one was hurt."

"How did it go?"

"The fae of the city have walled themselves in. The only reason we got past it was because of Gaea's magic. We stayed in my mother's old shop." Her voice wavered for just a moment, but she shook it off. "We talked to as many people as we could and told them to travel south. Then we spirited into the castle."

"What happened?"

"I searched for Xanth. His cousin and I used to attend court lunches together. He said the soldiers weren't leaving the court defenseless and they planned to protect the city. But they did hear Greeve and Rhogan speak. After that, they seemed divided. Some left to come south in the night, some stayed."

"Did anyone leave to check for Autus' army?"

"Rhogan and Greeve took turns guarding the door to the shop and searching for the king's soldiers. Gaea even left a few times to check for them. Eventually, Rhogan found them about a day's march north of the city."

I could see the worry on her face. I pulled her into my arms again. "You gave them a warning, Nadra. You did what you could. If they chose to stay, it's their own fault."

"I know." She sniffled. "But some of them were my friends. And they wouldn't listen. They laid their eyes on Rhogan and Gaea and instantly shut their minds. They were so cruel. If they stay and they die, they deserve it."

"I'm glad you're back," I told her as Rhogan came around the corner, his wings tucked in close and still touching the walls.

"Did you tell him your idea?" he asked, practically bouncing.

She gasped. "I forgot." She pulled away and held my arms. "I could feel the oak tree, Temir."

"Okay?" I searched her eyes for an explanation.

"It's the power from the adda. It felt the same as it does when you pull that power from me. We didn't know it then, but it was the flower."

"Holy shit." I looked down at her hand. "Holy shit."

"There's our favorite scholar." Rhogan clapped me on the back, knocking the wind out of me.

"We have to get to Fen," I said. "We have to get to the borderlands right now."

"I'll go grab Gaea." Nadra darted down the hall.

"Oh good, I won't have to carry you." Rhogan smirked.

"How many Marsh Court soldiers do you think you realistically recruited?"

"Rough estimate, maybe a couple thousand."

"Coro had over twenty thousand soldiers. His army used to be the biggest."

Rhogan shrugged. "I can tell you there weren't twenty thousand holed up in that castle. I'm guessing some of them have already left. They might have gone north, they might be coming south, I don't know. Nadra was worried about the people in the city. None of them would listen to her. Not one of them."

"Prejudices can run deep," I said as Gaea came marching down the hall.

"Sorry." I could tell she was tired.

Still, she tied her hair back and held her hand out to me. "I'll live."

We made it to the borderlands before the king. I couldn't believe the sight. A giant yellow dragon paced back and forth like a caged animal in the distance, swinging his barbed tail around and blowing fire into the air. Thousands and thousands of soldiers gathered to watch him, and clearly, he was enjoying the audience.

I'd never seen so many people in my life. I'd seen the soldiers in the north in scattered training exercises. I'd seen Coro's guards on parade. Still, the sea of soldiers, the dragons, the sky full of cetani and draconian fae, they gave me the hope I'd been lacking. There were fae for as far as I could see. Satyrs passed out weapons, pots of stew were cooking, commanders were shouting clipped orders.

"It's incredible, isn't it?" Gaea asked. "To see all of these fae fighting for the same thing we have been?

"If only Oleo were here with us now," I said, hardly blinking.

She slipped her hand into mine and squeezed. "He's here, Temir. He is still with us."

A scream in the sky silenced the entire crowd as King Fenlas landed his cetani in the distance. A wave passed through them like a ripple as they all took a knee before their king. Our king. Gaea and I were no exception. When we stood, she reached for me again and spirited us to the front of the crowd.

Fen saw us right away. His eyes became frantic as he rushed toward us. I imagine he lived on the edge of that fear. Something was always happening. "What is it?"

"Autus' army are still a day north of Hrundel," Gaea said. "We recruited a couple thousand soldiers but that's all. Hopefully they can stay ahead of Autus."

He nodded and turned to me. "Did you find something?" I could see the hope on his tired face.

I looked around cautiously. "I didn't, but Nadra did. She can detect the artifact."

He squinted his eyes and tilted his head, concern transforming into fear of hoping. "You're sure?"

"She could feel the power in the tree we desecrated. I hadn't thought about it, but she's sure she can help find the artifact. We need to get her out into the dunes and start searching."

"Let me finish up here. I'll meet you back at the castle and we can make a plan. We'll start tomorrow." He smiled and walked toward Kai in the distance, his steps a bit lighter as he marched.

"I'm glad he said tomorrow." Gaea yawned, pressing the back of her hand to her mouth.

We were back at the castle and parting ways moments later.

Nadra was already asleep in bed when I walked in, so I took my boots off and slid in beside her. She opened her eyes long enough to wrap her arm over me, and then she was gently snoring again. The sound was so peaceful I fell asleep not long after.

"So, Fae horses, then?" Fen asked the next morning at breakfast. I wasn't sure he'd slept at all.

"We could try wind cleaving with Greeve," Nadra said, "but I think he will move too fast for me to pick up anything."

"No, horses are a better option. Temir, you've hunted down two of these already. You better come along."

I nodded and looked at Ara for the third time that morning. Her eyes were heavy. Sad. She was so affected by the loss of the lesser fae in the Wind Court, I'd begun to feel guilty for not being more upset about it. But a lot of them hated me just as much as the high fae. I was the same as them in all ways but rank. As if status ever mattered to me.

She caught me staring and then caught Kai staring, and before long, she pushed her plate away and walked out of the room. Though everyone remained quiet, Fen's face said it all. She was trying but failing. Her guilt was eating her alive.

"So just the three of us going, then?" Nadra asked, bringing the attention off of her friend and back to the room.

"I need the others working with the soldiers. We had a large group of Marsh fae come in last night after you left. Somehow, the dragons knew to let them through."

"Dragons are actually very intelligent," I offered. "I've read quite a bit about them from your books."

"Let me know if you can figure out how to make them join a war." He stood to follow Ara. "Otherwise, I'll meet you in the stables."

I had no idea how to speak to dragons, of course.

"How's it looking today?" Wren asked Greeve, sitting at the end of the table.

"Same as yesterday, I suppose. We have a lot of mouths to feed at the border, but at least the city is safe. If they get past the dragons, they'll have an army waiting for them."

"That's not the plan though, right?" Nadra asked. "We aren't going to let them get that far south?"

"We wouldn't want them to suffer the desert sun." Kai winked. "We're working on a plan right now."

"I could help out with a plan, if you want?" Rhogan said with a mouth full of food.

"You have battle experience?" Greeve asked.

Rhogan nodded. "Iron Wars."

"Great, you can meet us at the borderlands after breakfast." Kai clapped him on the back. "Have a nice flight. Don't get those wings too close to the sun, pretty boy."

Nadra and I finished and walked together to the stables. Fen was already there with three large fae horses. I helped Nadra onto the smallest of the great animals and then jumped onto my own.

Fen pulled back on the reins, his horse antsy to run. "The Weaver says we should check the temple ruins of the naga and Autus sent those fae to the dunes. There are dunes close to the draconians or there are some closer to the old naga colony. I say we head in that direction and see if they were both right. Objections?"

I rubbed my hands together. "Sounds like a solid plan. Let's go."

We ambled through the red desert for hours. I'd eaten more sand than I cared to admit before I followed Fen's lead and covered my face with a long scarf. His habit of flicking glances to Nadra as she shook her head at him set the tone for the arduous journey across the scorching hot court.

The desert appeared endless upon my beast, so dark he seemed a shadow, apart from the heat his black hair drew from the sun. We crossed hills and great caverns within the ground, flatlands and an endless supply of that crimson sand I was sure would haunt my nightmares. There was never enough water.

"Anything?" Fen called.

"Still nothing," Nadra answered, defeat lingering on the edge of her words.

I felt a flush of panic from her and caught her eye. "The desert is huge. Don't get discouraged."

She nodded, but I knew she was losing confidence.

Fen pointed to the west. "The naga ruins are over there. If you draw a line straight east, you can see the dunes."

Far in the distance, along the horizon, I could barely make out a landform. The desert sun was hard to trust. Mirages in the distance showed many buildings, when really it could have been only one or two, or possibly none at all. Still, Fen knew exactly where we were, and when he kicked the flank of the horse and he took off flying through the desert, we followed, throwing sand behind us in ripples. I knew it was difficult for him to be out here and not home, with his soldiers or his mate.

The naga's temple ruins grew larger and larger until they were great, shattered serpentine pillars laying half buried in the ground or still partially erect. Fen kept a wide berth as he began to move south, now more slowly. "The naga who once lived here were very traditional. Those who survived claim this land is sacred. It's important we do not disturb anything unless we absolutely have to."

I thought for sure as Nadra continued to shake her head that we were going to have to go digging through an ancient graveyard, and knowing our luck, we would probably resurrect a deadly monster. But Nadra gasped and Fen stopped short.

"There." She held her hand to her chest. "It's close. Maybe just over this hill."

We'd nearly crested the top when my heart raced. If we found the chalice and had Oravan melt it down or found another way to destroy it, the king's plans would be thwarted and we would just have a battle. Fen and I had equal stakes in finding the chalice, as both of our mates depended on it.

"Fuck," Fen yelled calling his magic forward.

We topped the hill to find Autus' damn harpy twins. The moment the sun glinted off the metal in one of their hands, Fen sent waves of fire in their direction.

I moved my beast into a full run, holding my breath as I willed the horse to go as fast as he could down the sandy hillside. But we were too late. They had already bounded into the air and were successfully dodging Fen's magic. He called forward a breeze so hard it nearly pinned one of the bastards to the ground.

The other swooped low, grabbed his hand, and they flew off. We had lost them. Had lost the chalice.

I followed Nadra's gaze to Fen, who had come off his horse and fallen to his knees, watching those fae disappear into the distance. Everything he'd worked for was for nothing. And now we knew the king was still trying to bind Ara to him. The only thing he needed was Nadra and Ara. Fortunately, he had no idea Nadra was so special.

# Ara

"What are you doing up there, little liar?" that yellow dragon asked me from the ground. I lay down, digging my hands into Cal's soft, furry mane, and wondered what it would be like to have a simple purpose in life. Like a dragon. What could their purpose be, really?

"I'll try not to take offense to that," he answered.

*Get out of my head.*

"I am outside of your mind, just on the doorstep."

Cal soared through the sky like a boat on a still lake, smooth and steady, providing the escape I'd sought. His great feathered wings made no noise as he slowly lifted one side, turning to make another rotation down the border.

The sky was full of patrolling cetani. Umari called out orders and they dove and roared and climbed back into the sky like dancers.

Meanwhile, Cal carried me through as if they weren't there at all. As if he felt my sorrow as his own. As if he helped me carry my burden of fate.

"What is your burden?"

*I don't want to talk about it.*

Again, we turned.

"Do you fear the king of the Wind Court?"

I considered that question, though I didn't want to at all.

*I fear what he will do to the world. Or what I will.*

The dragon was silent for a long time. I sat up, holding tight to Cal, and looked down. Twelve. We had twelve dragons patrolling our border, and still, his males had gotten through. Fen was right the whole time, and I'd been so very wrong. And the only thing I'd felt aside from complete sorrow was absolute rage. There was no in between unless I became numb.

"The world will be what it will be. Even one such as I cannot change that."

*We are not the same. You don't know what I am.*

"Tell me, little liar. What are you?"

*Death.*

"We are all death, if motivated."

*What motivates a dragon?* I asked, pushing Cal to the side so I could look into the slits of his clever eyes as he soared beside us.

"Many things. Anger, curiosity, loyalty, revenge."

*Why would a dragon ever need revenge?*

"You've held my name in your mind. I cannot think of another time a faerie has released the name of a dragon. Bloodshed is usually how those situations end."

The dragon flew around us in circles. No matter the great size of the cetani, the dragons made them look trivial in comparison, though Cal never cowered.

"I've grown quite fond of you, little liar."

*I have that effect on people.*

"Again, you lie."

*I'll try not to take offense to that.*

I watched as he jerked to the side, observing the line of dragons, even the ones I couldn't see in the far distance. He closed his eyes and his golden yellow scales rippled like a drop of water in the sea.

"I have a gift for you, little liar. Call your mate."

Fen met us on the ground. "What is it?" he asked, barreling through his soldiers.

We watched as another from the dragon's hoard flew in. The blood red color of his massive body filled the sky. The soldiers moved away as the crimson dragon landed beside his leader, opened his two front paws, and deposited his gift to the ground. The yellow beast made a guttural noise, and the crimson dragon snorted and took to the sky once more.

"I believe this is a human," the dragon said out loud. "He was traveling with two others that didn't make it."

410

"Can you read his mind? Where was he going?"

"His mind is quite weak. Your enemy has sent him ahead to deliver a message."

The human stood tall and puffed his chest out. As if he was the higher species here in this world.

"What is your message?" Fen asked, his voice dangerous.

He raised his chin to the faerie king. Such bravery in humans. "I can only speak to the Promised One."

Fen's eyes were cold and unwavering. "I am the Promised One."

"The woman."

"My *female* is here. Speak."

I heard a rustling in the crowd behind me, but I didn't bother turning. I couldn't take my eyes off the human. His glossed-over eyes. The way his hands were held limp at his sides. "He's enchanted," I mumbled, though no one seemed to hear me.

"I've been sent to inform you that the High King of Alewyn is coming for you. He wishes to give you an opportunity to save the city of Hrundel. Surrender yourself to him and they live. Do nothing, and they all die."

*Don't even think about it.* Fen took a step toward the human, his hand on the carved handle of his blade.

"Stop!" Kai yelled from behind us. Apparently, he'd been the one causing the raucous in the crowd.

"Don't kill him," Rhogan begged, running at his side.

"We need him." Kai pushed his way through the last of the crowd and grabbed the human. Rhogan followed, protecting the man with his wings.

"Yes. Now you see." The yellow dragon turned his great body, nearly knocked down a tent with his massive tail, and vaulted back into the sky.

"Temir!" Fen shouted. "Someone find Temir."

"He's here," a voice called as Greeve landed, a hand clasped tightly on Tem's shoulder.

"Back to work," Kai barked over the crowd and suddenly everyone sprang into motion.

Tents had been lined up along the borderlands. A great city of soldiers, Wren had said. And it was. Thousands of all types of fae had traveled south or were already living here. The irony was the southern army, those who would fight with us, was made of more than half lesser fae. Those who had been sacrificed and enslaved had something to fight for. Something to protect. Autus had started a genocide. These fae could either fight with us, or they would die. A life or death decision was no decision at all.

Hrundel though. The city outside of Coro's castle. The merchants, the soldiers, the court I'd once called home. They would all die. Autus had given me the ultimatum, but we had given them their chance to flee. We'd offered them an open border to escape and only a few thousand had taken that option. Still, could I fault them? Could I condemn them to death?

I stared off into the distance, watching the tiny grains of sand blow in the wind like an hourglass. Time. We'd nearly run out of time. We were so confident Autus would move slowly. There was never a rush in the land of fae. He was tactical though. Had used our confidence against us.

I felt my body crushing beneath the weight of this decision. The world grew louder as it passed me by. I'd spiraled into my own mind. Not for the decision I'd have to make, but for the world that would suffer no matter what. For the madness on the other end of that offer.

"Hello?" Gaea waved her hand in front of my face. Startled, I reached for a blade. "Woah. Calm down. It's just me." She took several steps backward.

"Sorry." I sighed, looking away from her. Beyond.

"You need to get your shit together," she said, as blunt as ever. "Come on." She wrapped her arm around mine and began walking. I followed, my feet moving before my mind could register where we were going. The tent where they had taken the proud human.

"We know where they are right now," Kai was saying, "it has to be done. She needs to go."

A sharp breeze whipped through the tent. Greeve was furious. "We can wait until they get closer," he argued.

"Where am I going now?" Gaea asked. Her eyes locked on her mate.

"Hrundel." He jerked around and stormed out of the tent.

"We need to know the size of his army. Our last three scouts haven't returned," Fen said quietly.

I laid my hand on her arm. "It's your choice. Greeve can go with you."

"It makes more sense to take Rhogan. I can spirit us in, he can soar above, get the numbers and I can get us back. Hrundel is flat terrain. Unless I can guess a safe place up in the castle, I think a higher vantage point is the best option."

"He's going to be so pissed," I heard Kai say as I stepped out of the tent and went to stand next to a brooding Greeve.

I put my hand into his. We stood there, silent. Fighting our own internal battles for a long time. He'd heard the plan. He'd be staying behind while his mate went to a city taken over by the enemy. Everything felt dark and heavy. There were no simple answers and no reliable outcomes.

"This is it," I said finally, maybe just to break the silence. Maybe to welcome him to my level of anguish. "I thought it was supposed to be easy."

He nudged me. "Nothing worth doing is ever easy."

We watched the sun drop. The crowds of people around us created an ambiance of voices like water rushing over the rocks in a brook. Peaceful, blended.

*Tell me you aren't considering his offer.*

The constant concern thrumming through the link between Fen and I hadn't wavered in days. Of course, he would be worried. I hadn't always made the best choices when it came to my own safety, but I'd settled into the numbness in my own mind.

Perhaps I would have considered it days ago. Perhaps I would wake up in the middle of the night and change my mind. For now, I considered nothing. Not what I would wear tomorrow, not what I would eat, not where I would sleep. Not even how I looked to the others.

*I'm not.*

"Time to go in, Princess." Greeve pulled me back into the tent.

I hadn't noticed the cool air settle over us as the sun had dipped behind the horizon.

The human sat in a chair surrounded by Wren, Kai, Fen and Temir. Arms crossed and staring down at him like he was a puzzle. Rhogan and Gaea must have left already.

"Any other ideas?" Fen asked, though he turned to us when we walked back in.

Temir shook his head.

"It took me months to convert the serum from sea fae to land dwellers. Humans are entirely different. I wouldn't even know where to start."

Greeve raised an eyebrow.

"He won't speak other than to repeat the message for Ara," Temir informed him. "We are trying to work around the magic, but the truth serum doesn't work on him and neither does Oravan's barrier ring."

Fen crossed the room to where I stood. He put his hands on my arms and looked down into my eyes, searching for me somewhere within. *Are you okay?*

I nodded, but I felt the lump grow in my throat as the truth threatened to escape. I was not okay. I was nowhere near okay. He pulled me close and rubbed his hands down my back as I laid my ear against his chest and listened to the rapid beat of his frantic heart. No matter what Fen showed the rest of the world, the pressure had been building on him as well. And these last few days, I hadn't made that any better. In fact, I was probably making it worse.

*I'm sorry, Fenlas. I'm sorry for all of it.*

*Never apologize to me for something you have no control over. Autus was coming with or without your power drawing him. Don't get it twisted in that beautiful mind of yours.*

I nodded my head. He was right, of course. "Have you tried healing him?" I asked.

Everyone looked at me like I'd grown three heads. When was the last time I'd contributed to a conversation?

"Healing what?" Temir asked.

I took a deep breath, steeling myself. I needed to push away the cloud that hung over me. I needed to be the weapon I was raised to be.

"The dragon said his mind was weak. Maybe the enchantment damaged his mind. There is no magic in the human world. Perhaps that's why. Fen thinks Autus isn't using his magic on fae because his power is diluted and most of our minds are too strong for him to hold it for long periods of time. But what if the humans aren't?"

"If I was stolen from my world and dropped into another and told to fight, I'd plop down on my ass and refuse," Kai said. "The king has to be enchanting all of them at the same time. I'd say their minds have to be weak against it."

I saw a hint of something flash over the human's face.

416

"I'm not saying humans aren't strong willed or smart," I said to him, though I wasn't sure why. "I only mean you are weaker against magic because you have no reason to resist it in your world."

Fen nodded, the shadow of a smile crossing his face simply because I was engaging with the others. "Try it."

Temir placed his hand on the human's head, and he went from a mindless puppet to extreme emotion. "Who are you?" he asked, trying to slide backward on his chair. "Who the fuck are you?"

"Relax," Temir said in a calm voice. "We aren't here to hurt you. We'd like to help you."

The human shook his head. "The last one of you that said that to me . . ." He couldn't finish his sentence. "My wife, you took my wife. Where is she?" He jumped from his chair.

Kai grabbed him midair and slammed him back down. "You can either sit there and listen while we try to help you, or I can end this right now." His face was serious, his voice a weapon.

The human turned red. His hands shook, but he remained quiet.

Wren stepped forward. She got down on her knees before the human. "We will not hurt you. We really are trying to help. What is your name?"

"Dustin." He balled his fists at his side.

*Weird name.*

"My name is Wren." She kept her voice light and her smile sweet. "Do you remember anything that happened after you were captured?"

"They took us to a place that was so cold, many of us died that first night. They hadn't thought to keep us warm. They didn't feed us. Nothing. They had two big fuckers with wings guarding the gates they kept us behind. Then they took us to the castle and lined us up outside."

He looked to the ground for several minutes.

"I was holding my wife close to me. Then, the leader came out and began to talk to us, and I don't remember anything after that. I don't know where my wife is." His voice broke.

"I'm very sorry," Wren said. "I don't know where she is either. Are you hungry? Can I find you something to eat?"

He shook his head.


Fen stepped forward. "The king who stole you from your world is our enemy. He is amassing an army of your kind to fight against us. Most of them will die unless we find a way to save you all before the battle begins."

Gaea and Rhogan appeared in the room, and the moment we turned to see their stricken faces, we knew.

"How many?" Fen asked, his voice low.

"Sixty to seventy thousand," Rhogan answered, the words trapped in his throat.

No one moved. No one breathed. The ringing of silence flooded the tent. I pushed and pushed and willed the magic that threatened to pour forward behind that wall. Of all the times, now was not it. I couldn't fight myself and Autus. I just couldn't.

418

"Aibell," I whispered.

She did not answer. So, I tilted my head back and screamed her name. It ripped from me. From the deepest crevice of my soul. There was a thunderclap outside, the tent flap blew open, and she stormed in like a god.

"Not alone," she said, an odd smile on her face. "You must call on her too."

"Who?" Fen asked, stepping between us.

She raised her staff and pushed him aside.

"Nealla," I breathed.

"Absolutely fucking not. Whatever you're thinking, unthink it," he demanded.

"We have to do it, Fen," I said, trying to convince myself as well.

"Do what?"

"We have to destroy the magic that allows The Hunt to collect humans." I pointed to the foreigner. "There will be two times as many of them if we don't. Autus could set up court in Coro's castle and just build and build his army. That's his plan, don't you see? He knows the humans will be wiped out like bugs against our fae army. But at what point are there so many we don't stand a chance?"

"We're there." Greeve moved to step beside me. "She's right and you know it."

Rhogan stepped forward, his wings scraping the top of the canvas tent. "He's got the giants, he's got more trolls than I've ever seen, he's called in the centaurs, he has three grendels, and he has a manticore.

He has an army of over forty thousand humans. He has the high fae from the Wind Court. He's got more sea fae than we thought. There were lutins and brownies ravaging the city when I flew over. It's a mess."

"So, he hasn't killed all of the lesser fae, then," I spat. "Only the ones he couldn't control with bribery or enchantment."

"Basically," Gaea answered.

"Do it," Fen said. Though I could feel the regret wash over him the moment the words left his mouth. "Not here though. Keep her away from the soldiers. I need them to sleep tonight."

Aibell stepped forward as Gaea moved toward me.

"I know I haven't shown it lately, but I can still kick your ass, G. I'll be fine. Don't worry."

Her smile was fake but still appreciated. I grabbed the end of Aibell's staff, and we were gone. We landed in her old cottage though, not on Nealla's island. It was exactly as I remembered it. Not a speck of dust out of place.

"Why are we here?"

"To sort the things that need sorting."

"Oh, fucking fantastic. The riddles have returned."

She whacked me in the head with her staff. "This is not a game, child. This will come at a cost. If Nealla agrees to help, she will want assurance it's for a purpose."

"What cost?"

"That is for her to say," she said.

She brought her pole forward again, but I blocked it. Her magic froze me in place, and she repeated, whacking me. I couldn't move. Couldn't fight back. The cottage I'd once known faded away around us, and the training arena I had built with my father appeared.

"Fight it," she commanded. "You have magic, use it."

"You don't want me to do that," I gritted out, suppressing the growing anger.

"I do." She spun in a circle and slammed the edge of her staff into my stomach. "Fight back."

The magic began to grow. To crest that wall once again.

"No, Aibell. Don't make me do this."

"Control it," she snapped.

The shadows I had once fought in this barn walked toward me. As one, they pulled the arrows from their backs and nocked them. Inches from my face, they threatened me.

"I'll take this place to the ground." Like a storm brewing, the magic pressed on. Until I couldn't hold it back, until I knew I'd be taken with it. The emotions, the despair, the anger, the fear all pushed forward.

"Control it," she said again. "You are not weak. You are strong. You are in control. Siphon it. Aim it. Shield your mind from your own magic and release it," she screamed so that I could hear her over the wailing in my head.

Having no choice, I squeezed my eyes shut, and she smacked me with her staff again.

"You cannot aim with your eyes closed, foolish girl."

And that was it. I managed a small partition in my mind from my own magic as it exploded out of me. The familiar smothering feeling crept over me as a small piece of my soul ripped away.

"Again," Aibell called, her voice echoing from a distance. "Open your eyes, you coward."

My eyelids weighed a thousand pounds. Still, I did as she ordered, difficult as it was. I needed help. Desperately. And if this was the key, if she could help me, I'd do anything. Fight any battle.

"Good. There's that fire."

The building was completely gone, of course.

"The only thing threatening to drown you is your own fear of your magic. Do not fear your power, command it. Fenlas is your Guardian, but you cannot expect him to protect you from your own mind. He will need to help you with the aftermath. It is the price you pay, child. But do not let it destroy you. You do not succumb to it. You do not forget who raised you. You do not back down. Control it."

She released her hold over my body, and I stood. Wobbly, but I stood.

"Nealla will need you to control that magic if you expect to destroy the Wild Hunt. It will take the power of all three of us. If one fails," she said, stepping closer, her eyes pinning me, "there will be a steep price. This time, aim."

Again, the shadows pressed in on me as the building reappeared. My magic didn't build, though. The pressure wasn't there. Until Aibell grabbed my mind and forced me to watch as Autus lit a pile of lesser fae bodies on fire. As he threw a living, screaming fae on top of that fire. As their wails for help fell on deaf ears through a cruel world. I saw the laughter in his eyes, I saw the glee. What a sick motherfucker he was.

And then she showed me Nadra standing before him. He enchanted her to need him, to want him so badly it caused her physical pain. But when she reached for him, he slapped her face, and the rage that thundered through me was unbridled. The magic followed.

"Eyes open, focus."

A shadow changed forms. Autus now stood before me.

"Touch nothing with your magic but your enemy," she ordered. "You've done this before, do it again."

I moved into a fighting stance and narrowed my eyes. I wanted nothing more than to destroy that sick bastard. I released the magic as if it were a weapon, an extension of me. I forced it into my own control, lashing out until it struck the king and obliterated him . . . and half the building.

"Better," Aibell said.

I felt the rage, the magic pushing me down as I dropped to a knee.

She stood before me and stared me down. Half my size, frail and furious. "That is always a price you will pay for such magic. You will never use it without losing a part of your soul. You either learn to control it, or it will shred you to pieces and control you instead. Understand?"

I bared my teeth. "Yes."

"Let's go, then." She shoved her staff into the floor and tilted it toward me.

I grabbed the top of it and the world fell away. We landed outside of Nealla's cabin, me still on a knee.

"Get up, child. There's no time for weakness."

"What are you?" I asked, shaking my head.

"What indeed." She climbed the hill to the cottage. "I am ready."

She rapped her staff against Nealla's door until I was sure it would shatter. When she didn't answer, Aibell pressed her hand against the wood and blew it to pieces.

"Why must you always do that?" Nealla asked, swiping her hand through the air to remove the fallen debris with her magic.

"I knocked this time," Aibell answered, letting herself in.

Nealla sat, her face hidden behind a beautiful cloth wrapped around her mouth and a hood over her head. Only her eyes, barely visible in the shadow, showed through. "Who will care for the humans left in Alewyn when the Hunt is destroyed?"

"My king and me. I vow it."

"Such honor," she balked. "Where's the mouthy little fae girl who stormed into my cottage before?

"She's still in there," Aibell assured her.

"Seventy thousand soldiers march south for war. Will you help us?" I wasn't proud. I knew we needed all the help we could get.

"We cannot," Nealla said. "We've moved all the pieces into motion to help as much as we are able."

"How can you play with us like puppets for my entire lifetime and then step away now? Why would you lead us to failure? The king has three times the army we do."

Her words were daggers propelled by anger. "The gods will not allow us onto the battlefield."

I threw my hands into the air and huffed. "What fucking gods? I haven't seen a god or heard from one. No one worships the gods anymore."

"You are wrong, girl. You know nothing." She leaned forward and narrowed her deadly eyes at me.

"I know all of this will be for nothing if you refuse to help."

"That power living in your veins? That's your help," Nealla said, her voice short.

"We have to stop the Hunt. If you will help with nothing else, please help with that." I sat down across from her and Aibell took the final seat.

Nealla pulled her hand from her long robes. A black stone sat flat in her palm.

I looked to her hidden face, the question obvious.

"The sword?" She held her hand out, her long fingers extending past the ends of her dark robes.

Aibell snapped her fingers with a flash of light and a sword appeared in her hand. Not just any sword. One I had seen a thousand times. Nealla reached for the blade and ran her finger down the sharpened end until I was sure blood would drip down the metal. It didn't.

"I don't understand." I couldn't look away from my father's sword.

"This stone," Nealla said, placing it on the table, "works as an anchor. When I gifted the Wild Hunt to Coro's ancestors long, long ago, I wrapped it in a specific magic."

Aibell rolled her eyes. I'd never seen her stoop to such a low. "Here we go."

"Don't be bitter, old female," Nealla bit out.

"How can you call me old? What does that make you?"

I stood, leaning forward to break the old lady fight up. "Why is everyone else's magic so specific and yet the two of you seem to defy those laws?"

"The laws do not apply to us. Don't ask questions." Aibell slammed her staff into the floor.

"She's always liked the dramatics." Nealla shook her head. "And she's just mad because I could never open the door to her world so she could go home."

"So, it's true, then." I looked at Aibell. Her slightly oversized eyes, her deep embedded wrinkles.

"Mind your business," she barked. "Back to the stone. Sit down, child."

426

"There are three of these. One in the human world, one attached to the beast that leads the Hunt, and this one. Each an anchor. Each stone allows the Hunt to travel between the worlds. This stone calls the beast home, the one in the human world draws it there. The Hunt is to travel to the human world and do the bidding of the God of Death. It captures those that are to travel to the underworld and delivers them."

"What does that have to do with my father's sword?" I felt the pull to reach for the blade I'd oiled so many times. The handle my father had lovingly polished. I could still hear the sound of him slicing the air as he used it to show me proper techniques.

"This sword has a brother now. Touch the blade, girl, and feel the power it wields." She placed it on the table between us.

"I've touched it before. Carried it." I crossed my arms over my chest. "It has no power. You are mistaken."

"When your mind was closed off from magic, it might have felt like an ordinary sword, but this sword has been forged in death." She spoke the word death like it was an orgasm. Like the very thought seduced her.

"But my father—"

"Your father meant to destroy the stone in the human world, girl. That is why he carried this sword for so long. It was his mission before he was given a fae child to look after." Nealla looked pointedly at me, and I recoiled on pure instinct.

"Who gave him that mission?" My mind reeled.

"I did. And after you were given to him, he said he would only continue with the plan to destroy the stone if I agreed to bind your magic and the knowledge of you." She lifted the blade from the table.

"Why? If you gifted the Hunt to King Coro's ancestors, why not just take it away if you didn't want him to have it anymore?"

She clicked her tongue. "So many questions."

Aibell sighed dramatically and rested her chin on her hand, elbow propped on the table.

Nealla cleared her throat, pulling the attention back. "The power nestled between the worlds is vast. It isn't something anyone, even one such as myself, should tinker with. At the time, I didn't care. But Coro abused the power I gifted his ancestors. Thassen was a great warrior. I believed him strong enough to destroy the stone. That is why he never left Coro's hunt, though many times I think he would have liked to."

She swung the great blade through the air, and for a brief second, a memory of my father doing the same flashed before me. Nealla's laugh at my response was like a spider walking down my rigid spine.

Fen tugged on our bond.

*I'm okay. I'll be back soon.*

"Why didn't he ever destroy the stone? Why not just destroy that one, or the one on the beast?"

"Without magic of his own, he had to rely on only the power within the blade. The stone in the human world is the only one weak enough for him to destroy, and he didn't find it in time."

"And that one?" I asked, pointing to her hand.

428

"This one will take all three of us." She handed the sword to me.

The moment the cold metal touched my skin, I came alive. The power pulsed like the beat of a hollowed drum.

"Finally." Aibell stood.

"You will call your magic forward and strike the stone at the same time. We will try to contain what comes from within."

Aibell shared a withered look with me, something like regret filling her eyes. "Tell her the cost if she is not able to control her magic."

Nealla leaned in, that dangerous glare stealing my breath. "This will take a great mass of power. You must strike the stone, and then each of us has to feed our magic to destroy it. If there is not enough power, if the power is erratic or unstable, one of you will die and the other may be stuck between the worlds forever."

"Not you?"

She chuckled. "I cannot die."

I'd never seen such a level of excitement on Aibell's ancient face as she rubbed her hands together. Nealla placed the black stone down on the table once more. I considered telling Fen that I might die in the next moment. But I couldn't. Wouldn't. Aibell's words rang through my mind.

*Do not let it destroy you. You do not succumb to it. You do not forget who raised you. You do not back down.*

I held the heavy sword above my head, and in one swoop, I released my magic and brought it down with a crack. The table split in two.

"Now," Nealla screamed as the cottage faded away and we were falling through a dark expanse of nothing. As if the stone had broken open and we were soaring through the tear between worlds.

A wicked smile crossed Aibell's face. My racing heart thundered in my chest as I finally put the puzzle together, seconds too late. She had done it. Had finally left our world behind. Wherever we would land, it would not be Alewyn. Nealla cursed in the distance as she too realized that Aibell would not use her magic to destroy the stone. She would choose death or desertion before returning to Alewyn.

Everything Aibell had done was to get us to this single point. She had moved all the pieces together so carefully, helping only when she needed to. Had held my father's sword for this moment. Had been denied the ability to leave our world for so long, and now it was here. I wanted to hate her. I wanted to destroy her. But I couldn't. I couldn't even blame her. There was still kindness in that old hag. I still didn't think she wanted me to die. Why else would she have forced me to control my magic?

A great mass of emptiness surrounded me and Aibell, like falling through the heavens, I imagined. Occasionally it felt as if something solid would approach and then we would jerk sideways, continuing to fall through the veil of worlds. And I had no idea if this was going to be my eternity or if I'd die soon. Nealla was gone. She'd not taken the journey with us, but Aibell's face held peace as her eyes shut and she held her arms out beside her as if she were a child seconds from landing in a softened pile of autumn leaves.

But that wouldn't work for me. I couldn't accept this. I had been ripped from my home with no idea what world or what state of in-between I was suspended in. But like Aibell, I would do anything to go home.

Anything.

I shattered that iron wall in my mind. I let the magic rip through me with a singular purpose. Destroy the obsidian stone. That was the ultimate goal.

*Yes,* Nealla said into my mind. *More, child. Find my magic.*

As I fell through the obsidian, night rushing past me as if it were tangible, I pushed magic forward until I found the black poisonous magic that was Nealla's. The moment I touched it, I felt the wrongness. The instinct to turn and run nearly overpowered me. Nealla's magic was far vaster than my own. Still, I pushed and pushed forward with precision. Aibell had abandoned us, but I felt the world coming back to me, and then I felt the rip in my soul. That familiar tear that threatened to overtake me as Alewyn slipped away again.

I pushed back, shielding myself from the magic. I tossed and tumbled through nothingness. Nealla and Aibell were gone completely. Panic began to set in. Was this the plan? Had I somehow missed a clue.

"Did you want me to destroy the world? Was this what you wanted?" I screamed.

*Open your mind, girl. Come back.*

I fell blindly into endless depths of nothingness. And then I remembered my own anchor. Fen. I scrambled for him. I dug my claws in and scraped my way back to him and that flame. Until the world began to reappear and the blackness faded. Until I was once again in Nealla's cottage and Aibell's still body lay spread on the floor.

I could hardly string two thoughts together to realize what had happened. I stared at her for a long time, my father's sword still in my hand, the power still thrumming through me.

"You refused her, didn't you? She wanted to die and you wouldn't let her. Wouldn't or couldn't send her away and yet selfishly forced her to live. You took away her choice."

Nealla didn't respond. Didn't acknowledge I had spoken. The hood she wore, the Soul Repository, the gift of the Wild Hunt, The Mists, the bone graveyard. I stumbled backwards. I was such an idiot. So caught up in everything else, I couldn't see what was right in front of me.

"Take me home," I said blankly, my eyes still upon the crumpled old body on the floor. "Take me home."

Nealla's head jerked up finally. She moved an inch toward me, snapped her fingers, and I was standing once more in the tent beside Fen.

Wren stepped forward and squeezed my arm. "You look like you've seen a ghost."

"Not a ghost." I shook my head. "The God of Death."

# Temir

*W*e sat together in the war tent after Sabra came to take the human someplace safe. Trays of food were brought in, and we helped ourselves as Ara spoke.

"I don't know what happened. I wish she would have told me her plan."

"Would you have gone along with it?" Fen asked.

She lifted her shoulders and shook her head.

"Well," Kai said, talking with a mouth full of food. "Let's say I locked you in my closet. And then you were like 'let me out,' and I was all 'no, never muahaha,' and then you had to sit in there while the dust bunnies started a war, and as menial as it seemed to you, what else did you have to do with your time but meddle? So, you did. I mean, in the end, you'd probably off yourself too." He swallowed and took a gulp of wine.

"What the fuck is wrong with you?" Greeve asked, shoving him off his chair.

"This is how my brain works, you know this," Kai said.

"And you're sure Nealla is the God of Death?" I asked, leaning my antlers against the taut canvas tent behind me.

"Completely."

I thought about mentioning my own conversation with that particular god, but I didn't see how it would be helpful. Nadra leaned over and rested her head on my shoulder. It had been a long day, a long week. We had all moved out to the borderlands and set up tents to join the rest of the soldiers, then practiced fighting most of the day, took shifts helping Oravan and a few other blacksmiths mass produce weapons, and tried to eat meals together when we could. Life in a tent in the desert was a far cry from life in a castle. We made it work though. If nothing else, we were all together.

"My tent's got extra room for a pretty faerie." Rhogan wiggled his eyebrows at Wren as he stood.

She snorted and turned to Gaea, blowing him off as Nadra and I exchanged a look. We'd seen her sneak into his tent several nights and caught him walking out of hers just this morning. He didn't seem to mind her reaction. Instead, he turned and strode out of the tent as if it hadn't happened at all. By this point everyone knew, and if they didn't, Wren's flushed cheeks as she ducked down were an absolute giveaway.

We followed shortly after, and as we entered our own small tent, I found myself remembering that old crazy lady. The way she popped up all over the place. When she found Gaea and I on the beach and told me to let her go. She'd known Greeve was her mate. Was waiting for her. I pulled open the squares of fabric meant to be windows, allowing the stuffy air to blow through.

"What are you thinking about?" Nadra asked, standing on her tiptoes to kiss my cheek.

"Aibell," I answered.

"I thought you hated her."

"I didn't hate her. I just didn't understand her. Completely illogical most of the time."

"That's the scholar in you."

We lay down to sleep, and though Nadra fell asleep within minutes, I found myself tossing and turning and going over the battle plan in my mind. Thirty thousand against seventy thousand. No matter what we planned, the truth was: run in, kill everyone who tries to kill you, and don't die.

Eventually, I snuck out of bed and the sweltering tent. I found myself ambling toward the border. I played the battle over and over in my mind but could not find a way for the south to defeat an army twice its size. Most were humans, based on Rhogan's report. My feet sank into the deep sands, pulling at the muscles in my legs. Humans were no match for a fae warrior. But did they deserve to die? How easy would it really be for me to swing that blade?

*What a rare power you have,* a strange voice said into my busy mind.

I jerked, searching the dark night for someone to come into view but I saw no one. "Who are you?"

435

"Don't worry, little healer. I'm not allowed to eat you."

What creatures lurked at night in the Flame Court? I wasn't keen to uncover that secret as I turned to leave.

"It has happened before. A battle won with all the odds stacked against the victorious."

I halted, the sand pulling me down as if it were forcing me to talk to the mysterious stranger. "When?"

"Long before your time, during the prime of my own kind."

"If you show yourself, I'll hear your story."

"It makes no difference to me whether you hear my story or not, little healer. But if you prefer it, I will step out of the shadows."

"I prefer to know whom I'm speaking to." I focused my eyes, straining to see through the darkness of night. If he hadn't spoken, I would have never known he was there, and that was . . . mildly concerning.

The ground rumbled as two giant, clawed feet landed in front of me. My heart stopped as I looked up to see a massive yellow dragon staring down. It was certainly not a sight for the faint of heart. He leaned all the way down until his long snout lay on the ground before me, his elongated teeth each the size of one of my arms.

I stumbled back.

*Hello, little healer,* the beast said. There were words somewhere in my mind, but I stumbled to find them. The hiss of a dragon filled my mind. "So, you aren't all as brave as the little liar."

I shook my head. I knew he meant Ara. And no, I was not as brave as she was. I didn't think anyone was. I think she could scare Fen if she wanted to.

"Certainly, she could." The dragon chuckled.

"Having your mind read is quite unnerving. The story?" I managed.

"Ah yes. Once upon a time, I don't know why but that felt important to say, Alewyn was a world of elven faeries and creatures that lurked and lived in shadow. The elven faeries had one king only. His name was Luchar. The elven territory grew too small for the growing population, but the creatures that lived in this world would give the king no more than the land he already had. At first, he thought he was unable to fight them, to push back his borders so they could all live."

The dragon paused for several moments, blowing divots into the sand as he remembered his story.

I locked my hands behind my back, waiting patiently for the point.

"Luchar had no way to force the creatures back because there were twenty of them to every fae. He prepared for a great battle with the creatures. He had no choice, as they were running out of room in the city. The creatures lined up outside of the king's territory ready to kill the moment anyone left. But the king was smart. He sent half his kingdom to the battle lines to set up tents. To show that he was ready for war, but the other half, the males, hollowed out the ground below the creatures, carefully digging so they would not know what was happening."

"And then?" I asked, though I guessed the outcome.

"The day of the great battle that would have wiped out Luchar's army, he pulled all of his soldiers back toward his castle. He launched boulders at the creatures until the ground below them crumbled. And then his people rained arrows down on the creatures stuck in the holes until they died. It was a bloody mess, but it worked. And those that survived never attacked the king again."

"So, the moral of the story is, we may not beat them one on one, we will need to be tactical if we aim to win."

"But you knew that already." The dragon slid his claws across the ground.

"I did. But we cannot build a great trench below Autus' army."

"No. But you have other weapons. Use them." With those final words, he backed away and into the shadows. *Goodbye, little healer.*

I continued to walk for hours, thinking about what the dragon had said. What I had already known. We needed a greater plan than just letting all hell break loose and hoping we landed on top. An open sky full of stars and an untouched moon were my only companions as the world around me slumbered. I found myself standing outside of Fen and Ara's tent just as the sun was rising.

"You look like hell." Ara pulled the tent flap open and stepped outside. "Glad I'm not the only one." She handed me a cup of tea and went back in to pour herself another.

I sipped the warm tea and watched the camp come alive one warrior at a time.

"What's on your mind?" Ara asked, stepping back out of the tent, with Fen in tow.

"I've got an idea. It's a terrible, dangerous idea, but it's all I've got."

"Oh, my favorite." Ara blew into her hot cup. "Shall we gather the team?"

"We'd better." I locked eyes with Fen. He nodded, and we spilt in three different directions. I covered my eyes when I opened Rhogan's tent and found Wren naked inside.

"Oh relax, Temir." She laughed. "I'm sure you've seen breasts before."

Still, I backed out and apologized, then wove through tent after scattered tent settled into the desert floor like a temporary village of desperate souls and eager soldiers. I stopped to get Nadra, warned her of my plan, and then we met everyone in the tent we used for meetings. Kai was still bleary-eyed, and if not from the forlorn look on his face, I wouldn't have been surprised if Fen had found a female in his tent too.

"We're all here, Tem," the king said. "Let's hear it." He sat down in his usual spot, able to see the door at all times.

"Right." I pressed my palms into the round table and stood. "I've been thinking. Autus' army is a lot bigger than ours."

"You called us in here for that?" Kai asked, rubbing his eyes and yawning.

Greeve punched his arm. Kai socked him back. Wren giggled and Gaea snorted. Rhogan flashed his giant smile, and I had to rub my temples to collect my thoughts.

"No. I mean yes. Kind of. Hear me out. Fen, if you could step forward for me."

"Oh, a show." Wren clapped her hands.

"Hold your palm out flat and make a small flame. Something about the size of a marble should do."

He did as I asked, and I nodded to Nadra. She stepped forward and placed her hand on Fen's forearm. The moment she touched him, the flame tripled in size. She pulled her hand away and again it was small.

"Not everyone here is aware, but Nadra has two magical abilities. Perhaps they are the same, but in a nutshell, she can refill magic by touch, but she can also amplify its power. Imagine if the king has all the humans crammed into a few tents, or even just corralled outside in a group. What if Gaea could take us in the cover of night, assuming most would be asleep then. Wren could keep us invisible, and Nadra and I could do mass healings over the humans? Enough so they could escape, or at the very least, refuse to fight."

"No." Greeve stepped forward. "Gaea's taken enough risks."

My eyes landed on Gaea. She opened her mouth and shut it again. I could see the war within her.

"Temir," Ara said. "You realize you'd have to take Nadra close to the king to do this. It's risky."

"I told you it was a dangerous plan. But what else do we have? We've been going over terrain in the Marsh court, we've talked about weather, we've talked about funneling the army. No matter where we land, we still come back to the size of his army, and we can't get past it. And maybe I can't cure thirty thousand minds, but what if I can cure fifteen thousand? That's fifteen thousand less innocent lives we have to take."

The room was absolutely silent. Each crucial member of this makeshift family weighed the pros and cons on their faces as I turned to the king.

"I wasn't gifted this ability for nothing. I know it's not ideal. And I know it's risky. But you have to see it's the only way we get an advantage. With Wren and Gaea there, we won't be seen, and we can leave in an instant. The king won't be mingling with the humans. He won't be anywhere near them."

"It's true," Gaea said. "Autus has always thought humans were disgusting, lowly creatures. He would sit at a table full of lesser fae and toast to their good health before he got within twenty feet of a human."

"I'll open the table right now for anyone else to present a better plan." Fen gestured to the space in the middle of the room. "Any plan other than that one."

"Realistically, how many humans do you think you can heal in a single night?" Rhogan asked, his battle face on and wings twitching.

"The human that was here took a single touch and he was healed. The enchantment from the king was gone entirely. It would depend on how the king has the humans camping, but if we walked through their camp invisible, I imagine it would be plenty. Thousands."

Ara turned to Fen. "Do we have a choice?"

"My king?" Inok's frantic voice called from outside of the tent.

"Come in, Inok," he answered.

He walked into the tent, looked around, and bowed his head to Fen. He was the only one who did that. When he lifted his face, sorrow filled his eyes as they flicked to Ara and then to Nadra. "There's news. Autus massacred the city last night. The aerial scouts claim there were no survivors. Autus is on the move."

Fen watched his mate, but she was unfazed. A far cry from the reaction she had to the last mass murder. But this time the city had refused to save themselves. Or maybe she was just steeling her heart. Perhaps we all were.

"Everyone but Greeve out," Fen ordered. "You stay too, Temir."

Kai stood and cleared his throat. I'd learned in small moments, he was the most tactical, the most observant. His humor was a shield, a façade to the clever fae he was. "The hills are still our best terrain. He is only two days out from that spot now that he has left the city. If this is going to happen, it has to be tonight. If Autus decides to march his army through the next few nights, until he's on our doorstep, we won't have time for Temir's plan at all. We still have to move our army as well."

With that, he and the others exited the tent, except for Ara. "What?" she asked when Fen looked at her. "You didn't possibly think I was leaving."

"Speak your mind," he told Greeve, jutting his chin to him.

"I don't like it. You wouldn't send your mate into the king's camp, I can't agree to send my own."

"To be fair, I sent myself to the king's castle," Ara responded. "We lived."

"And if I ordered it?" Fen asked.

442

Greeve looked absolutely stricken. I hated that for him. Hated all of this.

"Then it would be done," he said, void of emotion.

"I won't go if she doesn't want to go, Greeve," I answered. "I respect her too much for that."

"And I will not order it if you don't want it to happen," Fen added. "But I think we have to consider it. Take the day, think about it. We'll discuss again at dinner."

"I would talk to Gaea," Ara added. "She won't like this decision being made for her."

We split ways, and I found myself shirtless, running drills with Rhogan in the dry desert heat to pass the time. I should have rested. I should have let my mind shut off after the very long night, but I couldn't. Instead, I got lost in the swordplay and moved by memory alone as we shuffled through everything we were working on.

I'd beat Rhogan several times these past few days. The practice and the coaching from Kai had helped me so much I'd found confidence with a sword in my hand, had earned each of the blisters on my palms.

By dinner, the tension in the tent was high. Kai, of course, made it his personal mission to distract us. "Ten coins says I can catch fourteen grapes in a row," he said, nudging Wren.

"Five coins says you choke on the first one." She smirked.

"Deal." He tossed his little coin bag on the table and buried his hands into the bowl of fruit, plucking them from the vine until he had a pile in front of him. "One." He showed her the grape like it was a magic trick, then launched it into the air, tilted his head back, adjusted to the left, back to the right, and just as that grape landed into his mouth, it caught in the back of his throat and he lurched forward.

Wren slammed her hand into his back and the grape shot across the tent. "Thank you." She slid the coins across the table.

"Best of three?" Kai offered, slamming his fist into his own chest as he coughed.

"Nope. Next time I'll just let you choke."

"Oh, let's do that." Ara set a bag of coins in front of her.

"Let's not." Fen grabbed the bag and tossed it back to her. "We have enough to worry about without choking out the commander of our army."

"Fun hater," Ara grumbled.

"So, where did we land on the plan to go to the enemy camp?" Wren asked, stealing one of Kai's grapes.

"What do you want to do?" Rhogan asked from beside her. "You get a say as well."

"As long as Gaea's got my back, I'm okay with going. I think Temir's right. We need to save as many humans as we can, and we need to reduce the size of Autus' army."

"I've always got your back, girl." Gaea leaned her head onto Greeve's shoulder. "I'm in too. If we are careful and do everything by the book, we will be fine. And if anything seems fishy, we leave."

Fen looked to Nadra. "You've been silent through this whole thing and you're a part of it also. What say you?"

444

"I never wanted this power," she said honestly. "But I have it now, and if something good can come of it, even if we only save one single life, I think we have to do it."

"Greeve?" Fen asked.

"Gaea can make her own choices," he said as if he'd been practicing the bland line all day.

She patted his hand and smiled.

Kai snorted, but the smile vanished with one sharp look from Greeve.

"Then you should leave as soon as dinner is over," Fen said. "They may be distracted with a meal and that will give you a bit of extra time."

I ignored my racing heart. This was what needed to happen. This could change everything. Voices from thousands of soldiers filled the silence. Nadra grabbed my hand under the table and I felt her reassurance vibrate through me. Because if everything went awry, it was all my fault.

"Have you slept at all?" Nadra asked me later as I strapped my sword to my back, just in case.

"Not a wink. I don't think I could if I wanted to."

"This will work, Temir. It's a solid plan and the only one we've got."

I hugged her for several minutes within the confines of our tent. She understood more than anyone my reservations, but still, we had no choice. Not really. Burying my hands into her wild, curly hair, I tilted her head back and kissed her until we both needed a breath.

"You're sure you don't want to take a guard?" Fen asked.

I shook my head. "Gaea can travel with all of us because of Nadra's magic, but even that has its limits, I'm sure. The same goes for Wren. If this goes to plan, we won't need anyone else."

"And if it doesn't?" Greeve's wind magic matched his tone beating on the side of our war tent so erratically, Gaea had to step closer just to keep the sand below the layers of rugs from flying through the tense room.

I didn't answer. I didn't have the one he wanted anyway. I wouldn't change my mind and I couldn't make promises.

Ara flipped a dagger in her hand and pressed it into Wren's palm.

"Your bow won't do you a lot of good in close quarters. Keep this in your hand. Be careful." She turned to Gaea. "You'd better fucking come back."

"Aw. I'll miss you too," Gaea said.

She moved to stand before my mate. Nadra pulled away from my hands and wrapped her arms around Ara. Ara whispered something into her ear, and Nadra laughed and shook her head. She held out a knife for her, but Nadra refused to take it.

"We will be fine. I'd just stab myself with that thing. I've got the sword I've been practicing with. That's enough."

"It's never enough." Ara stepped away.

"Let's get this thing over with." Gaea held her hand out. Nadra took it first, and Gaea's eyes doubled at the onslaught of magic. "Holy shit. That's intense."

I was next and then Wren. In that moment, we all vanished, though we were still standing there.

"Did they leave?" I heard Kai ask as Gaea whisked us away.

In an instant, we stood in the Marsh Court. There was nothing but land all around us. Wren pulled her hand back and everyone reappeared.

"We're going to have to do a little bit of hopping around until we find them," Gaea said. "There's no way to know for sure where they are from the ground. Everyone keep your eyes open."

"Here." Wren pulled a rope from the bag she had on her back. "If we all hold onto this, I can keep us hidden without having to hold hands."

"You'll still have to be touching me to spirit though. My magic doesn't transfer through objects. But just in case we land right in the middle of the camp, better hold onto both of us. No one lets go."

It took us over an hour, but we finally found the massive army. They hadn't gotten as far as we thought they had, but the sheer size of them was nothing less than terrifying. Seventy thousand was just a number until you were standing there looking at them. From a distance, we could see all the giants, the beasts that moved with Autus, the humans, the high fae, the winged creatures that flew above. All of them. An ocean of enemies preparing for war.

Gaea held us in that place for several moments so we could watch as they assembled tents. Fires began to spark within the crowd as they settled in for the night. "Anyone who wants to back out, now's the time to say it." She looked over each of us carefully.

"Now, we definitely can't," Wren whispered. "Look at all of them."

"Let's go," Nadra said. "The sooner we start, the greater number we can save."

"On both sides." I added. "It looks like the humans are clustered together on the west." I pointed, though they couldn't see me. "They're smaller than the others."

"I see them," Gaea said.

I dropped the rope. "Hang on. Let's get ourselves situated. I'm going to need a free hand to use my magic, and Nadra's going to have to be able to refill Wren and I as needed. We only have so many hands."

"Right, so how do we do this?" Gaea asked.

"I'll take the lead and wrap the rope around my wrist with the hand I hold onto Nadra with. She'll be sandwiched between you and me, Wren. Then Gaea takes the back."

"We need to leave slack between everyone so we can move through easier," Wren added.

"No, we have to stay as close together as possible. We won't be able to move into tight spaces or we run the risk of tripping someone," I warned.

"So, if I'm in the back, how do you two grab me fast enough to spirit away in a hurry?" Gaea asked.

"If someone yanks the rope, we huddle and throw our hands in the middle."

"Got it." Wren nodded.

Gaea spirited us close but not into the army. We were still limited to where she had actually stepped foot, and though she'd spent many nights stretching her boundaries, she hadn't walked the entire kingdom. Standing on solid ground, fresh dirt and green grass below my feet was shockingly comforting. We held tight to the rope and began our descent down the hill and into the masses.

"We won't be able to talk once we get much farther. If anyone needs anything, remember to jerk on the rope and I'll take us out," Gaea said.

We moved as one through the grassy terrain, and I was sure we all held our breath as we stepped into Autus' camp. The humans were scattered toward the outskirts, but the closer we got to the center, the more tightly packed they were. Large tents were erected among them. Apparently, Autus had learned how fragile human life was. I led the team forward, called on my magic, and reached my hand out to the first human.

He was alone and kneeling before a fire he was trying to build. They all had the same glassy look. That mindless expression. The moment my hand made contact, it melted away. He started to panic. Looking around himself wide eyed and backing up. I felt a small pull on the rope and heard the whisper of Wren's voice until the frightened human was quiet. Listening.

This was the beginning of our plan. We needed one human to spread the escape plan to all the others. We couldn't do that and move quickly through the crowd. We had to rely on them to help save themselves without drawing too much attention. It was the only flaw in the plan. The only wild card.

The human stiffened and then imitated the mindless expression he had before. I had no idea what Wren had said to him, but it worked. We moved. I reached for another. A small jerk as the magic touched him, then our messenger, the first human, was speaking in hushed tones beside him. Again, the second human imitated the blank face. I heard Nadra exhale and felt the tension release from her. This was going to work.

And so, we moved effortlessly through the human crowd, eventually going so quickly we didn't pause to make sure it was working. There was an endless flow of magic coming from me as we drifted from one to the next and so on. But it quickly became clear that no matter how fast we moved, no matter how much ground we covered in one night, there wasn't enough time. We couldn't free them all.

A quick jerk on the rope halted us and within seconds we were miles away from the camp.

"Sorry," Nadra said. "I just need a minute to breathe."

I hadn't realized this was taxing for her. Hadn't felt a hint of it. She rubbed her head and Wren wrapped her arm around her.

I brushed my fingers along her temple, pulling the headache away. "We need to talk about the plan anyway. What have you told the humans to do, Wren?"

"They are going to march south with the army. They'll never be able to make a clean break with Autus' sentries watching."

"I've been trying to avoid them as we move," I said. "The guards posted sporadically throughout the camp are easy enough to work

450

around, but we are relying heavily on the human's ability to act at this point."

"How many do you think we've got so far?" Nadra asked.

Wren wrung her hands, looking up as if she were pulling the number from the sky. "Four thousand two hundred and twenty-three. I've been counting."

"Nowhere near enough." Gaea released a long sigh.

"Should we move north through the crowd, all the way to the rear, and then come back south or move sideways and wind ourselves through?" Wren asked.

"If we go back and forth, we have to weave in and out of the centaurs mingled in at the edge of humans. They will smell us for sure," Gaea said.

"But if we moved all the way to the northern edge, there just aren't as many. They are packed in tighter when we are closer to the rest of the army. We could free more in less time if we move sideways," I countered.

"Your call," Gaea said. "It's working so far. If we are careful, we're fine, but we need to get back in there. Are you okay, Nadra?"

"I'm fine." She sounded so tired.

"Are you sure?" I asked, pulling her close. "We can stop. We can try again tomorrow night."

"No. We have to do this now. The longer we draw it out, the riskier it is."

"Okay, but if you need another break, just say so. I couldn't tell you were tired."

"I'm fine," she said again.

Gaea stretched her arms above her head, twisted back and forth, then held her hand out, and we all reached in. Again, we were standing in the middle of Autus' war camp. It smelled of stewed meats and the sharp bite of oil as their weapons were cared for by several smiths in a nearby makeshift hut. I decided we would move side to side instead of walking all the way to the back of the crowd. It was more dangerous, but we were careful, avoiding the beasts the best we could. The humans played their parts; though as the night wore on, more of them began to move into the tents to sleep. Tents guarded by sentries posted inside and outside of them. Tents we couldn't open. We had to stand outside and wait for someone else to do it.

We moved seamlessly into one that had the doors tied back. It was packed full of humans. So many, there wasn't floor space for them to all lay. Most stood. A single guard at the front watched outside of the open door as we crept along the side of the tent until we were at the very back. And then we began. One by one, a wave of mental clarity fell over the occupants. Wren directed a few, informing them of the plan. One of the females fell to her knees and cried.

That was the first time I thought we might be discovered. But the others blocked her from view and were cautious. Humans were brave and smart. But if they weren't, they would die, and I think everyone was beginning to realize that. I'd seen several of the larger males walking mindlessly into the tent, past the guard, and slink to the back of the room whispering a bit too frantically. Any wrong move and they would be discovered. We would be safe, but they wouldn't be.

The faint light pouring in from the final rays of the day was abruptly shadowed by a beastly guard with horns of a demon. Shoving a human to the side, he scanned the packed crowd. Searching. Our group froze, holding our breath. Eventually, he mumbled to the other guard and stepped out. We edged forward. I placed my hand on a human's head and felt his fever. I cured his dehydration, along with the damage to his mind from Autus. There were so many of them becoming sick becuase Alewyn had not been kind to them. And they were stuck here now. The Hunt was gone forever, and with it, the ability to leave the world. Another guard stormed into the tent, and we had to give up our mission and spirit out before we were discovered.

Still within the confinements of the war camp, we decided to concentrate on the outside humans for a while, but eventually, as they went in for shelter, we had to move back into the tents. Which again meant we had to stand outside and wait until the door was opened so we could slip in. We successfully finished two tents and waited outside a third, slightly closer to the centaurs.

The door opened, a guard stepped out, and I pulled the team inside. Shock alone caused me to falter.

"Hello, my love," Autus said and lurched forward, grabbing Nadra by her hair. He yanked her away from our grasp, and she dropped the rope.

I pulled the sword from my back, and two guards swung wildly through the air, unable to see us as the king had. I felt a hand grab me, and I knew it was Gaea, so I lurched forward, ripping myself free. As she screamed for me, I dropped the rope, and the circle of guards in the room ran for me, creating a wall between me and Nadra as the king pulled her backward.

"No!" I yelled.

Her panic down the bond took me to my knees. She swatted at him, but he grabbed her arm to stop her. And then he froze. He'd seen it. The raised skin. The adda. But he'd felt her power the moment he grabbed her. I watched the wheels begin to turn in his mind as the guards closed in and raised their swords, and I turned just in time to see Gaea leap toward me. I tried to escape her, to stay with Nadra, but I wasn't quick enough. The moment she made contact, I heard the sword coming down on me, missing by just a hair as we spirited away.

"Take me back!" I screamed from my knees in the middle of another gods forsaken tent. "Take me back."

I jumped to my feet, bursting out and running toward her. I heard someone chasing me, but I didn't care. I felt Nadra's fear and pain. The king was hurting her. "I'm coming," I huffed, running as fast as I could through deep sand. Until I felt a jerk of my arm, a fist slam into my head, and the world falling away.

Greeve.

# Ara

"Someone start talking," Fen said as Greeve cleaved away to catch Temir.

"It happened so fast," Wren said. "He was waiting. We walked into the tent and he reached forward. I'm not sure if he was actually aiming for Nadra or Gaea, but the moment he grabbed a hold of her hair, he snatched her away."

"I tried to spirit away, I tried. But he grabbed her too quickly and then she let go and Temir let go." Gaea shook her head wildly, trying to make sense of what had happened.

"Gods-damnit," I yelled, yanking a knife out and throwing it as hard as I could into the side of the table covered in maps, spilling ink all over the top layer.

Greeve cleaved back in, a limp Temir in his arms. He laid him gently onto the floor and didn't say a word as he took two massive steps through the room and crushed Gaea into his chest.

Rhogan paced, taking up so much room in the tent I wanted to kick him out just for moving.

"What are we going to do?" Kai asked, stepping forward. "Full plan, right now."

"We have to go get her," I answered.

"We?"

"Yes, Fenlas. We. You and me. We. She's our family. We can't let him have her."

"It's too dangerous."

I roared. Actually fucking roared. I'd been storing weeks of pent-up aggression, erratic emotions, and barrels of rage. I forgot who I was, lost in the idea of what the world thought I should be. I'd had enough. "Everything is dangerous. Don't you get it? Look around you! Find one gods-damned thing that hasn't been dangerous. It doesn't matter. Look at him." I pointed to Temir lying shriveled on the ground. "Look him in the face and tell him his mate isn't worth what yours is. I'm going to get her. Either you assholes come with me, or I'm going alone. And you know I can't use my power to wipe all those fuckers out. You know what will happen if I do."

Gaea pulled away from Greeve and took my hand. "You don't have to destroy the world, Ara. Don't sacrifice your entire soul. I'm going."

"Stop," Fen said, every bit the faerie king that he was. Commanding and eerily calm. "We'll go. Together. But not without a plan."

"He won't kill her," Wren said softly. "I don't know if he will hurt her, but I saw the look on his face when he found the mark. When he felt her power."

"He knows, then?" Rhogan whispered with lethal intensity as his wings grew wide.

I could feel the world spiraling out of control. I couldn't determine if those were Fen's feelings or my own. Somewhere the boundary between our own thoughts and feelings had begun to gray.

Kai paced, holding his fists to his side. "We move the army now. We march through the night and take a stand outside of his camp."

"That won't be a threat to him," Rhogan interjected. "Even though we can move faster than his army, we wouldn't make it in time. And he'd probably love to have us delivered on a platter."

"We still have to start moving," Fen said. "We can't let him get past the hills. We don't want him much closer to our border."

"That doesn't solve this problem. That doesn't help us get Nadra back. Move the army, prepare for battle, do what needs to be done, but how do we get her?" I asked.

"I can fly overhead, see where he's keeping her, and drop Greeve into place, then he can cleave in, grab her, and shoot out of there before the king even knows what happened."

"Except no one is flying over undetected," Gaea said. "The sky is full of faeries and armed sentries and Autus had Evin in the tent with him. He'll know you're there before you're within five feet of that tent. He detects magic. I'm sure that's how he knew we were getting closer. Nadra was probably a beacon of power to him."

We stayed up the entire night trying to figure out how to extract Nadra. Temir eventually woke, but he was no help at all. We knew she was still alive based on their connection, but aside from that, he paced around the tent demanding he be included in each and every plan.

The problem with taking Temir was that he would be a wild card. His instincts would force him to do whatever was necessary to save his mate, and that could be dangerous for anyone else. He would have to stay behind, even if it meant we had to knock him out again or lie to him. My stomach rolled at the thought, but I hoped he would forgive us if it meant we could save Nadra.

The sun began to rise, and the deep, ground-shaking roar of a dragon pulled us all from the tent. The great yellow beast waited for us just outside. Plumes of smoke rose from his nostrils as he stretched low and slow, curling into a ball. "There is a messenger. Shall I eat him?" he asked eagerly.

"Well, yes, but give us the message first," I answered.

He huffed and opened his giant claws. A faerie with massive wings, damaged by the dragon, rolled to the ground. He reminded me of Rhogan by size alone. It took a great effort for the male to pull himself into a standing position, but it took an even greater effort for me to keep from hitting the asshole as he spat at the feet of my king.

"King Autus, High King of Alewyn"—he paused to sway, catching his balance—"has sent me to inform the promised one that he will trade her for the healer's mate."

Fen growled and stepped forward. "Enjoy your breakfast, dragon," he said, eyes locked onto the fae.

The dragon grabbed the faerie, tossed him into the air, burnt him to a crisp, and swallowed him in one single motion. "Thank you, King Fancy Pants," he said and lifted back into the air.

I smiled, and Fen jerked his head toward me. "I mean, it's kind of catchy." I raised a shoulder and turned to hide my smile.

"No. It isn't. Especially from a beast that size. Kai, get this army ready to mobilize. If we aren't moving by sundown, you and I are fist fighting."

"I'd be happy to throw some punches right now, if you need, King Fancy Pants." Kai bounced back and forth on his feet with his hands up.

"Not in the mood." Fen stormed back to the tent.

I released a heavy breath. "At least you tried. G, I need a favor." We stepped away from the group and I whispered to her. "I need you to take my father's sword back to the castle. If something happens to me, I want Fen to have it."

"No. Nothing is going to happen to you, don't be ridiculous."

"Just please do it. If nothing happens, then we won't even mention it. But, if it does, make sure he gets it. No one else can. It's powerful."

"Then give it to him before the battle." She looked back to the war tent over her shoulder and sank a little.

I shook my head. "He's already taking Tolero's twin blades."

"Fine. I'll take it back before we start marching." Her eyes went to the ground.

"What?" I asked.

"A favor for a favor?"

"Anything."

"This is real, Ara. Any of us could die. If I do and Greeve doesn't, will you . . ." She paused. "Will you tell him that I love him? I haven't told him yet."

"You should. Of course I will, but it should come from you."

"I know, I just don't want him to think I'm saying goodbye."

"A pact, then." I grabbed her hand. "We don't fucking die in this war. We have weddings, we marry our mates, and we have babies running around the castle together. Mine will be slightly more beautiful than yours, but that's just genetics. And when we are two thousand years old and we get tired of our males' overbearing fae shit, we'll move to an island together and make them hunt us."

She laughed, and the sun caught the tear in her eye.

"Hey, seriously though. We don't die. We fight until our last breath. Deal?"

"Deal." She jerked me into a hug and I let her. I even hugged her back.

"Females are weird." Kai shook his head, swinging a sword through the air as he worked out his own aggression.

"Don't you have an army to move?" I gave him the finger.

He winked at me and kept going.

"He seem a bit moodier to you lately?" I asked under my breath.

She nodded. "He's the commander about to go to war. I'd say if he wasn't moody that would be something to worry about."

Gaea and I shuffled into the group tent where Fen and Greeve stood hunched over the map spread across the table my knife was embedded in.

"Where are they?" Fen asked.

Gaea leaned forward and pointed to a spot on the map straight south of the castle.

"Four days march if we rest." He sank back into a chair, studying the parchment as if it might transform into better circumstances.

"While it's just the four of us here, I have a plan to get Nadra back," I said. "Gaea takes me in." I held up my hand to interrupt whatever objection Fen was about to throw at me. "She comes back, grabs the two of you and drops you outside the tent. Greeve cleaves you around the outside of the tent so you aren't seen. Gaea does that weird, intangible misty thing she does and comes back in. It looks like I'm the only one there. I'll stay back near the door and demand Nadra be let outside of the tent before I come any closer. The moment she is close enough, Gaea grabs us both and we leave. If all hell breaks loose, you two are there as backup."

Fen ran his fingers through his hair. "She has to take us first. You aren't getting left there alone for a single second."

"Fine, whatever."

"Now?" Gaea asked.

"I need to leave orders for Inok and Kai. As soon as I get back, we should go. There's no telling what he is doing to her, and I can't let her or Temir suffer any longer than necessary." He kissed me and hustled out.

I turned to Greeve. Brooding, dark Greeve. With his long hair and tattooed skin. His weapons were nowhere near as intimidating as the look on his face.

"We've always had a bond, you and I," I said, grabbing his hand.

He shook his head. "No. We don't say goodbye before a fight. Ever."

"I'm not saying goodbye, Greeve." Still, his face hardened. "I need a favor." He shook his head. "You know what you have to do. If it comes down to me and him, he is your king." He crossed his muscular arms over his chest. "He gets out before I do, do you hear me? He doesn't have an heir. He gets out."

"Don't make me choose." I heard the falter in his hardened voice, the love for me within his words.

"There isn't a choice and you know it."

He clenched his jaw, keeping still for a long time, stone cold and silent. Eventually, he dipped his chin just enough to agree and then grabbed my hand and yanked me to him. "It won't come to that," he whispered. "But if it does, I promise."

"You too." I caught Gaea's eye. "You don't save me if you can't save him. If you have to choose, you choose him."

"I hate you for forcing this," she whispered and looked away, nodding.

"Love you too, G." I stepped out of the tent, hoping she would take the hint and tell him how she really felt before we left.

I found Fen and dragged him back to our tent. The moment the door was tied shut, I was in his arms kissing him. He gave me no objections and no words as he ripped the shirt off me, kissing down my neck as I jumped into his arms. He grabbed me below my thighs, holding me up as he carried me to the piled blankets on the floor, laid me down, and used his magic to rip off my bottoms. He was frantic. I was too. Lost in a moment where we just needed to find a release in each other. I reached down and pulled the belt from his waist. He unbuttoned and ripped his own pants off, then he pinned my arms down.

Aside from his hands in mine, he didn't touch me. Didn't stroke between my legs. Didn't massage me at all. He leaned down and kissed me again. His tongue teased my lips the same moment he jerked forward and slammed himself to the hilt into me. I cried out in a mix of pain and pleasure. He rocked back and forth, quick and hard. Greedy.

My breaths fell short. The ache for release grew as he moved. I tilted my head back and squeezed my eyes shut, holding back the scream. It was there. Right there. One more thrust and I was done. Exploding alongside my mate as he pulsed.

He collapsed on top of me, and I glided my hands down his muscled back as he caught his breath and then moved to his side so we could face each other, nose to nose. I wasn't entirely sure why we needed this moment, but we did. All the pressure. All the unknown. All the danger. He was my release. My simple escape. My home.

A wisp of concern wrapped around me. Laying my palm against his racing heart, I whispered, "Draconians don't fear."

He watched me for several moments, moving his fingertips down the side of my naked body as he searched for words. "I'm not afraid of him. Or a lost battle. Even the fall of my kingdom, should it come to that." Setting his hand on my own, upon his heart, he closed his eyes and released a long breath. "Only a fool would not fear the loss of you, my love."

His vulnerability gutted me. "You are strong, Fenlas. We will get through this together. I'm scared too. But not for us. I'm scared to let the world continue to be what it is. I want it all someday, you know? A family. And I'll fight for that alone. To have that with you."

His beautiful emerald eyes spoke the difficult words he could not.

*I won't say goodbye to you, Ara. But if it all goes to hell and you have to go on without me, I'll wait for you. You'll find me on the doorstep to the Ether, waiting. No matter how long it takes.*

A could hardly drag a breath into my lungs beneath that gaze. I swallowed the lump in my throat. *This feels an awful lot like a goodbye.*

He brushed his lips over mine as he pulled me closer. *Only making a plan, my darling. So you never have to wonder where I am.*

I pulled away to look back into that handsome face that had always halted me. *A deal, then?*

A tendril of magic blew through my hair as he laughed. *A bargain? Even about this? Of course you would. I agree. Whatever it is, I agree.*

*Blindly? We've talked about this.* I smiled as I remembered the last time we'd had this conversation.

*There's not a piece of me that you don't already own. Whatever it is you wish, I'll see it done.*

*My wish, my king, is that neither of us die. Neither of us reach a place where we falter. We don't give in, we don't give up. We live. Beyond today, tomorrow, an eternity. We live.*

*I accept your bargain,* he rumbled into my ear. *I love you.*

"Tell me that later when we make it home," I answered.

"I'll tell you then also."

He peeled himself off me, and we were dressed and ready to go within moments. We made it as far as the door before he grabbed me. "I need you to say it. I need the words."

"I love you, Fenlas," I said and shoved him out the door.

Gaea and Greeve looked about as tousled as we did. And equally unashamed. I watched as the three of them vanished and held my breath until she reappeared.

"I took the sword to the castle." She held her hand out to me. "Now don't shatter the world and don't die. Don't be a hero, Ara."

I smiled and grabbed her hand, the weapons hidden within my outfit comforting as we vanished. I would make no promises this day. The ground rushed to me, and within seconds, Gaea released my hand and vanished. A slight breeze caressed my skin. It was either Greeve or Fen. As far as the guards staring at me with their jaws on the ground were concerned, I had just appeared out of thin air, armed and

464

furious. I lifted my chin and pushed my chest forward. "Where the fuck is your pansy ass king?"

A beady eyed male stepped out from the tent. "Well aren't you a pretty little thing." He moved touch my hair.

I swatted his hand away and jammed a hidden knife into his throat. "Anyone touches me, you die."

"Sir," a guard said, rushing to the bastard on the ground. "Aidas?"

The rest of them still watched me.

I widened my stance and pulled another knife out, the grip as familiar as the Marsh Court surrounding me.

"This is probably the worst greeting I've ever had. Your king called for me, and here I am, yet his lackeys don't even speak. Are we sharing brain cells today, fellas?"

"In there," one of them whispered and pointed to the tent the one gurgling on the ground had come from.

I took a step forward and two of the guards inched closer together, blocking the door. "Seriously?" I rolled my eyes.

One of them put a hand on his sword and I could feel the tendrils of rage from Fenlas as they both fell to the ground, though I hadn't moved.

"Anyone else?"

The rest moved back. Even the ones behind me.

I pushed open the doors to the tent and stepped inside, shutting away the plethora of emotions coming from Fenlas. The interior of the tent was almost entirely dark apart from a few candles scattered along the empty floor. It smelled of melted iron and rotted flowers. The king kept his back to me, adjusting the items carefully laid out on the table on the opposite side: the sword that looked identical to my father's, the ashes scattered along the hilt, a piece of fabric cresting the top of

465

a rubied chalice, and a flattened scroll. With Nadra and I both here . . .

Nadra's eyes bulged, and she shook her head wildly. Fabric had been tied around her mouth and her hands were bound with rope.

My stomach lurched as Autus turned toward me, his face wild. Possessed.

"I knew you would come. You feel the pull to me even without our bond, do you not?"

"By pull, do you mean that burning vomit feeling in the back of my throat, because I feel that for sure."

Red melted down his face and he opened his mouth to chastise me, but I stopped him.

"Let's not do that thing where we banter back and forth. You're a sick fucker, I'm just a poor innocent female destined to be by your side while we rule the world together etcetera . . . etcetera," I said, flourishing my hand.

"Great." He strode forward. "To the point, then."

I hoped Gaea was in the tent and ready. I couldn't see her at all, but I could feel the magic within me stirring to life.

"Let Nadra go first or no deal."

"Ah yes. A fool's bargain." He snatched Nadra. She tried to pull away from him, pushing against him as she shook her head, trying to tell me something. But I couldn't make it out with her mouth covered. Then she was screaming. I promised I wouldn't step in. I promised to stay by the door, but he was hurting her and she was frantic, and without realizing it, I stumbled forward. I felt the gush of the door opening and turned to see Fen and Greeve behind me.

The king didn't miss a beat. He grabbed the golden knife from his belt and threw it at Fenlas. It landed square in his chest.

466

His pain was my pain as I screamed. I moved the wall holding my magic back just as Autus looked at me and his melodic voice told me to stop, ordered the room to stop. I froze in place, unable to fight him.

His hand wrapped around Nadra made his magic so strong, I was no longer immune. I couldn't fight him as he stepped toward me. Fen vanished, and I knew Gaea had kept her end of the promise. Oravan's trinket had kept her protected against the king's magic, though my power hadn't given me the same luxury.

Greeve was also frozen in place. He grunted behind me but couldn't move.

The northern king pulled the sword from his table, stepped forward, grabbed my wrist and sliced, gathering my blood into the chalice, mixing it with another's. Nadra's. The room was deadly still. A bated breath the only accompaniment to his psychotic nature. He looked at her but spoke to me. "As I'd hoped, I don't need to sever the bond you have with your mate. He will die anyway. A deal's a deal though. I will miss you, my sweet." He shoved Nadra toward the door.

Bound and crying, she moved to stand behind Greeve as Autus grabbed me, poured his blood into the cup, and my whole fucking world shattered as the awareness of Fenlas left me. As the bond to him vanished, save that one lone flame.

Autus drank deeply from the chalice of the three mixed bloods. It poured down his face, down his robes, and onto the floor as he swallowed. He turned to bring his sword down on Greeve, but he was already gone. Already saved by Gaea. Thank the gods.

"Sit," he commanded. My legs became so weak I sat readily on the floor. "Stand." I was back on my feet before I could register the movement. This wasn't supposed to happen. Enchantment didn't work on me. But then that was the point of the blood oath he'd made. My world came crashing down. "Good. Now forget them all. Forget everything but that you are simply mine."

And like an ax to a limb, my entire life was severed from me.

# Temir

"Temir!" Gaea screamed across the chasm of my mind. "Come quickly."

I pulled my thoughts from the clouded sorrow of losing my mate long enough to register she needed something. I turned my head toward the door. I needed something too, and they had locked me into my tent, our tent, like a child, with a sentry posted outside.

The unsecured flaps flew open and Gaea stormed in, her arms covered in blood.

I wanted to care, but I could only think of Nadra. I could only focus on her.

"I can save Nadra. But you have to save Fen. That's the deal. Do you hear me?" She shook me by the shoulders. "You save the king or I don't save your mate."

My mind became clear as glass. I leapt to my feet and ran for the door, pushing through the crowds of people with Gaea right on my heels, screaming for everyone to get back. Kai and Rhogan came running and forced everyone away.

"I have to go back now," Gaea said. "You save him, Temir. Do you hear me?"

I nodded and laid my hands on his chest as she vanished. The wound was fresh, his heart was still beating, though the knife ripped through the chamber walls and fluid was filling around his lungs. I pulled the weapon out carefully and let it drop to the sand. With each beat of his heart, more blood seeped from his injury. I removed the fluid and healed the tear from within, and magic coursed through me as I tried to pull him back again. He was so familiar with death. Had been here once before, so it was hard to coax him back to this side.

I healed the outside gash and sat there for a long time with my hands on his chest, pouring more and more life into him. Until I couldn't any longer. I lifted my hands and the world came back to me. I turned and Nadra was standing there, the skin around her mouth raw. She watched me with sorrowful eyes as I crawled across the ground and hugged her legs. She crumpled over me and sobbed as I held and rocked her, telling myself over and over again that she was safe and she was home.

"Thank you," I said, hoping Gaea could hear me.

"Ara's gone," Nadra whispered into my ear. "The king has control over her."

I'd been so lost in my own despair I hadn't stopped to realize anything that was happening. Why Fenlas had a knife in his heart, why Gaea had left, how Nadra had come home. Nothing. I turned to see Gaea weeping into the Greeve's chest. His eyes lingering on Fen's body.

470

"He'll live." I pulled Nadra to her feet. "He just has to want to."

Kai and Rhogan lifted him from the ground and carried him into his tent. They stepped outside and stood guard while the others told me what had happened. The atmosphere had changed. Though the soldiers hadn't heard of the damage done to their king yet, the volume of the camp turned to hushed tones as restless soldiers moved around irritably. Even the dragons became twitchy, roaring and bellowing from the border for no apparent reason.

Inok joined us after visiting Fen's tent. "We will still press forward," he said, looking between us.

Kai moved beside him with the face of a warrior. A commander. "We move the army, we move the king, we go where we were told. Everyone has a stake in this. When Autus is defeated, he has to die. He can't be sent packing back to his lands like he was in the Iron Wars. The boundaries of the four kingdoms are no more. One king will walk away from this. Our king. There are no other options."

We packed our entire camp at the borderlands swiftly, leaving the dragons behind to guard the innocent in the Flame Court, and began our slow trek across the southernmost portion of what was once the Marsh Court. The green grass and cooler temperature were a welcomed break from the desert climate. Traveling with a plethora of fae, perhaps marching to their own deaths, was a long and tedious journey as the cetani flew ahead, and though Kai protested, we had to stop for sustenance, quick as it may be, and some form of rest.

As we moved, I considered the motives of each side. It was so hard to justify a battle, but each person had their own reason for being here. The humans may not have had a choice, but if they didn't turn and fight with us, they would die anyway. Survival was primal and necessary.

The beasts that marched with Autus, the powerful and most malignant section of his army, were there because he had promised them something they couldn't live without. Whatever that was, land, food, clemency it would be worth it to them. The high fae that fought with Autus were there because they believed in the genocide. They believed in a king who would purify the world. But Autus, he fought because he believed himself the one true king. Because something in his mind had been planted long, long ago, and he'd never been able to let that go.

The southern kingdom and all of our allies fought with us because we believed in something more. We sought the kindness and respect that grew and flourished in the Flame Court. We believed in all fae. Everyone's basic right to live and breathe in this world. We marched to save our future queen, the one a king long ago sacrificed our faerie immortality for. I fought for my mate. The red-haired, freckled faced beauty. The high fae mated and bound to a lesser fae.

We marched for days. The first night, Fen opened his eyes, remembered his own sorrow and pushed us hard and fast all the way through. He allowed us to rest the second night, though I wasn't not sure he did. He didn't eat. Wouldn't speak to anyone. The only time we saw him was when he was leading the army farther north.

On the final day, the day our scouts told us Autus' armies rested behind a row of hills, we stopped. We set up our tents, built our fires, and gathered with our friends. For the first time since we left, I sought out the rebels and the Weaver. I wished them luck. I found Roe and Iva among their group and did the same. I found the glassmaker and thanked him for leaving River at the compound. The boy I hadn't bothered to say goodbye to. Maybe I couldn't bring myself to do it again.

And then we sat, our group, in a tent around a wooden table with a knife imprint along the side and tried to find comfort in each other. Tried not to think about the fact that this could be the last time we were all together, minus one. Because when the sun rose, the fae would also rise, and so would the weapons, the bloodshed, and the death count.

I lay in bed that night curled around Nadra and stared into the woven pattern of fabric on the tent. I watched as shadows danced along the side. Listened as murmurs from across our camp filled the air, a reminder the others were also unable to sleep. But I didn't rise from the bed. I lay there and memorized each breath Nadra took beside me. I didn't want her to fight. I wanted her to stay behind, but she insisted and she could use a sword. We needed everyone. Rhogan had promised to help protect her, and that was the only assurance I had.

The noise outside grew long before the sun rose. Our allies were restless, antsy. Nadra stretched her body over mine and opened her tired eyes. Every morning I looked forward to that smile, but today, there was none.

"What happens if Ara uses her magic?" she asked quietly instead.

"If she concentrates it on just the king's enemies, we all die, including her. If she doesn't, the whole world dies, including her."

She jerked upright and pulled the sheets to cover her chest. "So, she dies no matter what?"

"Before we left the castle, Fen, Kai and I discussed war strategies. Her magic comes with a steep cost. That much, that fast, will shred their soul. And because no matter what Autus has control over, now matter how bound she is to him, she will also always be bound to King Fenlas. I'm guessing Autus thinks he already killed the king and severed her bond to him. Maybe Fen dies as well, I don't know."

"So, we just march in there and hope she doesn't use it?" she asked, taking careful, deep breaths.

"She's strong and stubborn. But no matter what, we have to do what we can, until we can't anymore. Maybe Autus wins this battle, but it certainly won't be without a fight."

I sat up beside her and rubbed her back in the dark. After reminding her how much I loved her, we dressed into our strongest fighting gear, strapped on every weapon, and exited the tent. We wouldn't bother taking them down this morning. All energy would be saved for the battle.

As we moved to the main tent, the sounds of voices were drowned out by the sounds of metal brushing against metal. Armor, swords, shields, all of it would be worn today. I saw Brax and Greywolf pass us by, marching across the camp. I'd forgotten how large the giant was. And though we only had one, Rhogan claimed Autus had over a hundred. I pushed that from my mind as I looked to see the draconians strapping protective gear onto the cetani.

The truth was, the south was lethal. Everyone knew that. Even the children here could fight, though there were few and they were precious, so they were left behind. If the humans weren't part of the equations, if it were just fae against fae, we would have a real chance at fighting Autus' army and surviving. We hadn't removed the humans from the equation entirely, but we had put a dent into his plan, and hopefully, he didn't know it yet.

Wren walked into the war tent at the same time we did, her bow in her hand and two quivers full of arrows strapped to her back. She would lead the archers with the first wave as Autus' army descended the hill in front of us.

Gaea and Greeve were already in the tent with Fen. I wasn't sure they'd left him alone last night.

474

"Everyone know the plan?" Kai asked, walking in like the commander he was and not like the jokester we had known him to be.

"The plan to stay alive?" Rhogan asked quietly.

"Yeah, basically that," he said, sitting down in a chair. "Rhogan and I will leave shortly to get everyone into position. Wren, you're on archers then sorting out the humans with Sabra. Tem, you and Nadra come in on the backside, heal anyone you can quickly and keep going. Greeve and Gaea, you'll do your thing but stay together as much as you can. You're on beasts with the other wielders so be careful. I heard there's a manticore down there. Rhogan leads aerial with Umari and Fen while Brax and I will lead the ground soldiers. Keep your eyes up. Questions?"

Fen stood. "I'm going to get Ara, stay the fuck out of my way."

And with that, he walked out. We gathered our things and followed. There was no sense in sitting around. This day had been coming for a long, long time. We stood in a row at the top of the hill, our army packed in instead of stretching out. We'd go in like a hammer, strong and impactful.

While we waited, shoulder to shoulder, we watched as a small platform was placed atop the hill across from us. Autus took his seat and Fen snarled as Ara took hers beside him. Their army then crested the hill. Just as large and intimidating as I remembered them.

Umari lifted her beast from the ground and flew toward us. The sound of her cetani's wings beating against the air, as well as the sun's gleam on the pieces of metal she had strapped on to protect her throat and heart, demanded our attention.

She hovered in front of Fen, shaking her head. "You must say something to all of these warriors prepared to die for you today, Fenlas. You want the ability to cross that battlefield and make it to your mate? Inspire this army to do that for you."

475

His eyes went dark as he glared at her, but she lifted her bo, screamed a warrior's cry into the air, and flew back to her draconian troops.

Fen hadn't brought his cetani to the battle. Instead, he stepped forward and turned. He called a great wind over the crowd until everyone was silent. Until even the birds stopped singing and the cetani stilled. "The word faerie means something different today," he yelled, deep-rooted passion in his timbered voice. "I am fae. You are fae. Those," he pointed, "those are cowards." The crowd cheered and he waited. "I see you all gathered here by strength and honor. Not by fear. Not by force. Someone I love once told me, you may look to the past, but you must never stay there. Today, we look to the past. We remember those who were massacred by that coward's whims. By the fallen queen of the sea. You fight today for those they call lesser, but you must also fight for your right to live your life how you chose to live it. You look to the future and make your dreams come true. It starts today. Here and now. You hold this line, you listen, and you never stop fighting. Not with your last breath."

The crowd exploded into battle cries, the cetani bounded into the air and from the far west side of our ranks. We stood on the peak of that hill and watched as Autus' army crested the one opposite of us, pouring over it like ants from a colony. Their soldiers were never ending.

"Hold!" Kai yelled.

The human signal was given. The great banner waved across the sky, and we watched as the entire western flank of their army broke off and turned to run. There were thousands and thousands of them. More than I had hoped we'd saved, but still not enough. Just never enough.

"Arrows, nock," Wren cried as the front of our opponents reached the basin of the hill.

The sound of tightened strings filled the air in unison as they were aimed to the sky. Anticipation became its own beast on the battlefield, in our hearts, growing as we were seconds from the battle beginning.

"Release!" she screamed.

Arrows filled the sky, casting a shadow over grass that had rarely been walked upon but would now forever be a field of death.

"Now," Kai ordered.

Nadra, Gaea, Greeve and I stood still as we watched our army explode, charging forward, like a battering ram. The strongest in the front and to the sides, the weaker in the middle intending to break their army in half, separating the humans from the rest. The cetani carried boulders and dropped them onto the giants scattered throughout the army. They dove, clawed their enemies and rose back into the sky. But the giants began to lift the boulders and throw them back. One hit, and the draconians were falling to the ground.

I searched for Kai and Fen leading our army front and center. Blades drawn and slicing through, but not as fast as we needed them to. Autus' army began to surround ours. We'd expected that. The archers from the middle shot arrows and held shields for the fighters around them.

"Call it, Temir." Gaea was already moving toward me as we surveyed the battle.

"There's no choice." Greeve kept his eyes on the sky. "Go now."

She was antsy to join the fray, and so was Greeve, whose hardened face hadn't moved from the skies.

"I'll try my best." I was not confident at all in our backup plan.

Gaea lifted her hand to mine, the hand that wasn't holding Nadra's, and the three of us vanished. The moment we hit the ground, she pulled a sword and was gone. Back to Greeve, spiriting to the beasts and starting their own wild battle.

"You." I pointed at the yellow dragon slumbering lazily in the desert sun.

"Not now, little healer. I am tired," he said with a terrifying yawn.

"You told me a story. You told me of an old king who used tactics to defeat the beasts. Tactics are weapons and so are you. We need you."

"Where is the little liar?" he asked, stretching.

"Autus has her." Nadra crossed her arms and lowered her chin. "If she's your friend at all, we need your help to save her."

"I'll admit she does intrigue me, but I don't believe we are friends."

"If you and your hoard would join our fight, this battle would be over quickly and many, many lives would be spared."

"Many of your own lives, but not the others. You forget that I, too, am a beast."

"I have horns. I am not a high fae. There is a beast somewhere within me." I gestured to the top of my head.

"Indeed," he answered, breathing me in like the first breath after emerging from water before he turned to Nadra "And you have odd power. Familiar and not."

"We could stay and debate this all day long, but there's no time. Either you take us back and help us fight, or we start walking. We made a great sacrifice by coming here. If you say no, Temir can't save anyone. We will make it back only to find our friends dead on a battlefield."

478

"You should never rely on a dragon without a deal."

I looked to Nadra, and she took a deep breath, nodding. We knew it might come to this. She stepped forward.

"I will offer you my power when this is over. You may take it from me in three days' time."

The dragon laughed. A great, deep laugh. "You cannot harness magic in that way."

"What, then?" she argued. "What can we bargain with?"

"I cannot force my brethren to fight in a faerie battle. It is not done. But I will agree to join you. I will take you back and fight your enemies for one simple thing. Your future child."

She scoffed. "You might as well kill me."

"It's not a deal," I said firmly and grabbed Nadra's hand, pulling her away. "It was a risk, we both knew that."

A beat of wings behind us and then a crash as he landed in front of us. "I will not take your child." He breathed me in again. "Your daughter. I ask only that when she comes of age, you allow me to court her, if she would agree."

"How can a fae court a dragon?" Nadra asked.

"Our ways are our own. Do we have a deal or not?"

"No deal." I shook my head. "If someday we are blessed with a child, she will have the right to choose, just as we have."

"Temir," Nadra said quietly beside me. "He said she would have to agree. We would only have to provide a blessing. A parent's blessing to try to change the tide of the battle."

"You would agree?" I asked, nearly tripping over my words.

"We're running out of time, Temir. If Autus wins, none of this matters anyway."

"One dragon isn't going to make a huge difference. A dent maybe."

"A dent that could save lives. We need to agree to this."

I let out a deep breath. "You have our consent to court our future daughter if she agrees and if we both live through this."

A ripple of power coursed through me and over the dragon's scales as the deal was struck. I'd snuck in our own safety as a contingency plan. If we didn't both live, there would never be a future child.

He dipped low to the ground and we quickly scaled his back. He leapt into the air and we held on for dear life as we soared across the Marsh Court kingdom at record speed, our hands held tight onto the yellow scales of the beast as we huddled together and prayed for more time. The wait to get there was agonizing. I had no idea what we would see when we arrived, but the vision was devastating. Our block of soldiers was completely dispersed. Cetani still flew through the air, but with only half the number we had started with. Which meant we had lost the draconians with them. I couldn't spot Kai or Fen in the mayhem, but I saw the beasts being assaulted by invisible weapons and knew Gaea and Greeve were brutally fighting.

The dragon soared around and behind Autus and Ara on the stage and roared louder than any sound the bloodied battle would make. He moved low to fly just above the ground, scorching flames pouring from him. One pass and I knew we had made the right decision. Until the giants began to lift the boulders the cetani had dropped and threw them at us. The first hit the dragon just before his tail. He roared and whipped around so fast we nearly slid off his back.

He reached forward and grabbed the giant from the ground, filling his entire claw, and squeezed. The giant exploded into pieces, and the dragon threw him to the ground. Again, he was struck by a boulder.

All of the magic wielders for both sides attacked each other with a vengeance. The ground rattled, fire burned the field along with several fallen fae. Wind whipped around as if it were a tangible weapon from both sides, and great creatures made from unsourced water pummeled the battlegrounds. Chaos took shape as the battle continued in every direction.

Again, the dragon charged. Back and forth. Until his wing became so damaged, he could barely keep us upright. Until blood poured from him to the ground like a waterfall. Until I was sure he would die too.

Thousands. He'd killed thousands with his fire, but as he crashed, just outside the battle, I knew he was done. He'd fought as much as he could, and if he dared push any further, he'd die. I could feel the pain, the wounds in his great body. I grabbed Nadra's hand and began to heal him, but he stopped me.

"Go. Tell the little liar I tried."

His body was so massive I knew he was right. No matter how much Nadra could increase my power, I would be here until tomorrow healing him. We slid down and Nadra reached for the beast one final time. She placed the palm of her hand onto his great snout and thanked him. And then we were running.

Slamming into the battle, my sword crashed into a high fae with milky skin and hard eyes. The shriek of metal came from behind me as Nadra faced her own opponent. I could barely think of myself with her right next to me. The sword fight with the high fae was a power struggle. We were equally matched, but I had southern training. I knew moves he didn't. I struck, he blocked. I turned, he swung. I dipped low and brought my sword up to impale him under his armor. He gasped, and I kicked him away, turning to help Nadra, but she had already taken down her opponent.

We made it only two more steps before, again, we were assaulted.

Rhogan came soaring through the air and landed on Nadra's attacker. He was bloodied to hell, and I only recognized him because of his wings and size. The beasts were not far from us. We worked as a team fighting, helping Nadra, moving as much as we could to the back line where I could start healing anyone who could possibly help us. I reached out to several along the way and did my best. I took several hits to the arms and one deep gash to my thigh I had to heal and I healed Rhogan twice as we moved. Feeling a rush of air beside me, I knew we were close to Greeve and Gaea. They'd left a pile of beasts in their wake, but the sky was bleeding. Greeve was bleeding as he moved on the wind.

A minotaur charged me, his head lowered, his sharpened horns a weapon. I couldn't hold him back with my sword, though I tried. Rhogan was busy helping Nadra with a slithering narb, his rows of teeth gnashing to protect his wormlike body.

Great arms came from behind and wrapped around my throat. I tried to swing back with the hilt of my blade. But I couldn't. The minotaur slammed into me at full force. His horn impaling my stomach as he continued to charge with me, limp, bleeding and still attached to him.

With the pain, so incredibly strong, my vision blurred. He'd severed an intestine for sure. I felt, rather than saw, the beast jerk to the side. He tilted his head down and I slid off his bloodied horn. He swung wildly into the air. I called my magic forward to heal the wound in my stomach before I lost consciousness. Without Nadra, and with the other healing I'd been doing, I could feel the draining. The emptiness.

I heard a gasp caught in a throat, a small whimper, and I watched as the angered beast plucked Gaea out of the air. She had been the one to protect me. She had stopped the minotaur from killing me. But now he held her in his muscled hands and roared.

A storm-like wind whipped through the air as the minotaur was slashed down his back, blood spraying the ground behind him in an arc. But he did not hesitate. Did not release his hold on Gaea as he held her in the air by her throat.

I pulled myself to my feet.

Greeve slashed the beast again.

I stumbled. Stood. Rushed forward with my sword in front of me. And then watched the greatest horror of my life as he tilted his head down, shoved Gaea onto his horns, and rammed her into the ground, severing her in two, before falling dead atop her.

The deep, primal, guttural roar—the severance of Greeve's soul— was a sound that would haunt me the rest of my life. I fell to the ground and crawled to her fallen body. If there was anything I could do, I would do it. Memories filled with those beautiful eyes and that enchanting smile filled my mind, but I shoved them away.

My vision clouded as giant tears burned down my cheeks. I swallowed the growing lump in my throat and shoved and pushed until the minotaur's body rolled off her. I reached for my dearest friend. The one I'd never given a fair chance. The one who had always been there for me, but on a breeze, she vanished, and so did that draconian fae.

"Temir!" Nadra shouted, pulling me back to the real world.

I looked up just in time to see Rhogan block an axe coming down on top of me. And that was when I knew it was over. We would all die on this battlefield no matter what any of us did. It didn't matter how well trained you were, when you were just completely outnumbered and out muscled. There was nothing to be done. I dropped my shoulders. Defeat slamming into me.

"I know it hurts, Tem, but don't lose focus." Rhogan yanked me to him by my collar. "You get up and you fight for her, do you hear me?"

I nodded, and my eye caught a glimmer in the far distance. In the north. A trumpet sounded, and then two. Rhogan released me. He turned—most on the battlefield turned—as ten thousand armored fae descended a hill in the distance. The leader was a broad-shouldered fae with horns that matched mine. My father had come.

I stood. Red filling my vision. Rage ripped through the sorrow in my mind. I had more fight in me. I was still breathing, and as long as I was, I was not yet done.

# CHAPTER
## 39

# Ara

re you watching, Princess?" Autus asked.

Princess . . . Something familiar flitted before my mind, but it faded before I could grasp it.

"Our enemies will fall today, and we will rule this world together soon."

*So confident.*

My stomach turned, though I was unsure why. We sat on a platform at the top of a hill, watching a grand performance, or so I thought it was, until the familiar scent of death, of blood, struck me. But how did I know that smell? I sat back into my chair and stared blankly forward. Watching as a great dragon flew across the battlefield below. I saw the muscle in my king's jaw twitch. The dragon lit our soldiers on fire. Ashes on the wind.

Wind.

"The boulders you stupid fucking giants," he bellowed and then turned to me more softly and said, "We will let them have their battle, but in the end, you will rain death upon them all. I do enjoy the show, though. Don't you, darling?"

I turned blankly back to the battle. Why should I use my power? I didn't care about any of them. The king believed we were bound. I believed otherwise. The only thing that pulled at me was a lone flicker in my mind. A single lingering flame that felt important. Though I wasn't sure why.

The dragon lasted longer than I anticipated, but eventually we watched him fade over a hill behind us. My king relished in his triumph. I turned to watch the soldier's brutal, lethal attacks. Our opponents fought like dancers. Again, that wave of familiarity passed me by. A great masculine cry of pain cleaved the battleground like a warrior's song of anguish. I turned just in time to see a minotaur fall. A gleam in my king's eye as he chuckled. My heart still jumped at that scream as sorrow filled me.

The inky black feeling of wrongness began to pour over me, so powerful I could hardly sit still in my seat. As if my body were paralyzed and my muscles ached for movement. To push past that frozen feeling. To jerk myself to life. I watched two fae warriors that led their army down the hill with an obsession I couldn't fathom. Though I tried to pull myself away, to see the rest of the battle, I always came back to them. To him. The warrior who inched himself closer and closer to us as he fought. His muscled body. His vengeful eyes. I thought maybe he would be the one to kill me. The bloodlust was strong enough.

They fought many high fae as they pressed forward. They fought like they'd fought together their entire lives. They moved as a team, watching each other's backs as they pressed forward, leaving a line of fallen fae in their wake. One dark haired, one messy blond.

They were slower now than they had been when they started down that hill. The momentum fading as their bodies tired. I held my breath as one of our own, my king's cousin as I had been informed over our evening meal, approached them. At the same time, a group of four harpies shot down from the sky, screeching and reaching their taloned feet forward like they would pluck them from the ground.

They sliced their swords through the air but facing five directions at once was impossible. A harpy lunged, grabbed the lighter-haired one by the arm, and lifted, trying to pull that massive male from the ground. His arm became shredded meat as her talons ripped into him.

The darker fae looked over his shoulder to check on his male just as another harpy barreled through the air, tumbled into him, and started clawing him as she held him pinned to the field. I watched as the male from our army turned on my king's harpies and began swinging his sword at the one pinning the darker fae to the ground. Their wings blocked a bit of the scene as the other two dipped and clawed and pulled back, but the darker male was back on his feet within moments, breathing heavily as he turned to save the other.

In the distance, a female's scream rang over the warring crowd. "Kai. Kai," she shouted. She ran as if the wind pushed her. As if every frantic step was rung in desperation. She fell and got back up, covered in blood that wasn't her own. Still, she ran. But it was too late for him. He'd fallen below the winged harpies, and though both of the others attacked with a vengeance, the third male, the blond one that had fought side by side with the southern leader, did not get up. Instead, he was enveloped within the screeches of victory from the harpies who tore him to shreds.

I watched the dark male turn my way. I felt his eyes burn into my own and then look back to his fallen brother. And then back to me as he began running, and something in his decision to come for me brought that flame to life within me. It forced the ice to begin to melt. Something about that male mattered to me. And then I worried; something about the fallen one mattered to me also.

Fear struck me as clarity was just within my grasp. As my breaths began to quicken and my heart began to pound. As I learned the male beside me was not my king, but my enemy, and the male running to me, for me, was my everything. And then my head snapped to where the minotaur had fallen and the scream that had pierced my heart.

Back to the king. Fenlas. My mate. That flame became a roaring fire as it seared me from within. As everything crashed back to me. A bond that could never be severed. That was what we had. Ameriala. Autus may have bound me to him as well, but it was artificial. What Fen and I had was real, raw, and chosen. It was stronger than anything Autus could do. I felt the tether to Autus thin as Fen got closer and closer to me. And then I felt him. His agony and his heartache.

Gods. Kai. Gaea. And the battle continued. My heart twisted at the force of reality.

*He is mine,* I snarled into my mind.

The king running for me froze in his tracks, stopped halfway, and fell to his knees. Because even though he was promised, too, even though he was my Guardian, I had remembered where I came from. I remembered. And I did not need a savior. Not this day.

*Make sure it fucking hurts.*

Autus had his back to me. He said something inaudible as he watched a new army come from the north in shining armor rain down upon what was left of his army after my southerners had ripped them to shreds.

488

"It's time." He turned to face me. "You will call your magic forward. Now. You will end this."

There was a pull deep within me. He had bound me to him, and I felt a jerk of my own desire to follow his commands. But never in my life had I let anyone tell me what to do. Bound or not, my will was still my own. Without Nadra here to amplify his magic, had he used it, his words were merely suggestions.

"Yes, my king," I said in a sickly-sweet voice. I reached my hand for him, though my skin crawled when he took it. I closed my eyes and saw Kaitalen. His infectious laugh. His strength. His loyalty. I saw a beautiful female with striking feline eyes. The vision of the future that we'd promised each other but now would never have. He'd taken them both from me.

"Leave my army intact," he commanded.

One single thought and the king was on his knees before me. My mind my own, my magic completely controlled. Focused, thanks to a little old hag who made sure I could protect myself one final time before she finally found her own way to escape this world. A bulging vein popped out of the king's forehead, a matching one pulsed in his neck.

The world stopped. I looked into that bastard's hateful eyes. He fought back, mentally pushing me as realization fell upon him.

"What are you doing, you wretched female?" he rasped.

I felt a wall go up behind me as Fen held back anyone who would interfere. He was nearly drained, the exhaustion jolted through me. I gritted my teeth, torn between obliterating everything, ending it all so that this entire world could start anew and pinpointing that magic. I wouldn't be enough to simply kill Autus. It would never be enough.

That faltering, the single hesitation grew as King Autus struggled back to his feet. Coated in a false sense of empowerment, that fucker had the nerve to place his hands upon my throat and squeeze. For a moment, I let him.

*Kill them all and free the rest.*

Free the rest. That was my prophecy. I was never meant to annihilate the world. Only this last fae, with his hands clung tightly around my airway.

*Ara!* The terror in Fen's voice rattled our soul.

And then I knew. I struck the king. He barely flinched. I kicked him in the groin and didn't give him a second to recoil as I followed with a knee to the kidney. He fell back. I could have used my power again, but the physical release was so necessary. He struck me across the face and stars filled my vision. I leapt, swiping the golden blade from his belt and planting it in his gut. It was just enough to take him down. Using my power to hold him there, I smiled.

"Once upon a time, there was a young female who had never seen a human before. She was innocent and naïve in so many ways. The first day she saw one, she watched in horror as you murdered a pixie because she'd run out of drink for you, Autus. Do you remember?"

"No," he grunted, barely able to hold himself upright as the pain seeped through him.

"You wouldn't. Because life is nothing to you, and now, your life is nothing to me."

"But I am the high king," he protested, his face turning purple.

I tapped my finger to my lips. "No. You're not. You are—"

"High King," he snapped.

"It's rude to interrupt someone when they are trying to kill you," I barked.

490

I let loose more power, funneling it into him until he was on his hands and knees, muscles seizing as he bellowed. I wanted Temir to be here for this moment. It was his moment more than my own, but I couldn't wait for him. Fate had given me this one task, and though I wanted to draw it out until he was laying on the wooden platform, weeping like a baby, my heart was hurting, my friends were hurting, and I was just done. Absolutely done.

I released the rush of magic, shielded myself, and destroyed him. I fell to a knee as that magic caused another rip into our soul. I only hoped it was the final one.

The entire battlefield paused as the Wind Court fae felt the death of their wretched king.

The swords did not rise again, as those who fought with Autus realized this battle was won and the war was over. That their king would not come to their aid and they no longer had a leader. The Winterlands army that had bought us just enough time to kill Autus had saved us all. Though many died. My heart wrenched at that thought. Of the losses we had learned about. The ones we already knew. Had they known that morning, by stepping on this battlefield, they were choosing to die? Willing it, should it come to that?

And then a realization melted over me so strong, it took me to the ground. A choice.

The only thing I'd ever wanted was that singular thing. Though gifted with magic to desecrate the world, in the end I still had a choice. I didn't have to use that magic. A magic no fae should ever be given. I'd beaten the gods that day. Because, though they carefully lined all the pieces for this battle, I was in control. Aibell's final gift had been a giant middle finger to the gods who had denied her.

The wall of flames came down between Fen and me and he charged, looking me over for only a moment, before crushing me in his arms and weeping silently.

"I'm sorry," I choked out. "I'm so sorry."

And I was, for not being there when he'd needed me the most, for being taken by Autus, but mostly, for his fallen brother. For Kai. We had no idea where the others were. We didn't know who else had made it.

We stepped down from the platform together. I stared down into the battlefield and my heart broke for all the fallen faeries laying in a sea of blood and bodies, of broken weapons and wounded souls. Not just from our side or his, but for all the lost lives today. All because a king couldn't see the value in life. Because a king from long ago sacrificed the immortality of all faeries so that I could save the world. But as I watched our soldiers helping each other, I realized I hadn't saved them at all. They had saved themselves.

Except Gaea. My heart filled with horror, the memory slamming into my chest as I replayed her final moments. As I heard her laugh on the wind and felt her arms around me that final time. As we made promises we couldn't keep. This war had ripped that future from me, and as I crumbled, Fen caught me, sending waves of comfort as the world around me caved in. As the loss of the best friend I'd ever had shattered me entirely. She was gone. Just like Kai. There was no justice in war, only a teetering of heartache and suffering. I remembered that female screaming as she ran to our fallen commander. A lover we'd never even known about, now just as broken as the rest of us, if not dead as well.

Wren appeared beside us. Smothered in blood and holding her arm to her chest.

"Hello, baby bird," Fen said, his voice cracking.

492

A small whimper left her, and she flew into his arms, her body shaking with tears. "I can't find Greeve," she cried. "I found Kai and . . ." She broke off again, sobbing.

"I know." He hugged her fiercely. "I know."

We discovered Rhogan, crying out in pain, but alive on the field. One wing completely torn from his back. Wren only left Fen's arms to move into his and began sobbing all over again. We knew this would happen. We knew the odds of us all walking off of the battle unscathed were nil. It didn't make the losses any less painful. In fact, it only made them greater. Because why were we spared, and they were not?

Umari found us next. She leaned on her bo like it was a staff to hold her upright. She bowed low to Fenlas, lower than she ever had, though she was injured. "You are a great king now, Fenlas. You led our people to battle and came out victorious. You've made us all proud. Now, we must reset the pieces on the board."

He shook his head. "Not today, Grandmother. Today, we simply stand ourselves up."

She dipped her chin. "We will round up the northerners while you decide what do to with their survivors."

Fen pulled me along toward the army that had come from nowhere and changed everything in the battle at the end. He approached the male who stood to the side of his gilded army with Temir. They were identical. Clearly father and son.

Nadra left Temir and yanked me into a hug. I closed my eyes and tried not to think of Gaea. I loved Nadra. She was my oldest friend. She had traveled the world to get to me, to warn me. But Gaea and I understood each other on a different level. She was my person.

"My father, Heva." Temir swept his arm to the man standing with him.

Fen bowed his head. "I'm afraid we might have lost this battle had it not been for your assistance. I thank you." He brought his fist to his chest.

"The gods shone upon you this day," Heva answered.

"I'm sure they did," Temir said in a flat tone. "Or your people forced you to get off your ass and do something for the world."

"Temir," Nadra gasped.

"I owe him nothing," he answered and walked away.

"You are still welcome to join us," Heva called out to his son.

Temir didn't turn around, but instead gave a vulgar gesture and kept walking.

I'd never seen that side of him, but I liked it.

"I wasn't sure I'd see him at all." Heva reached into his pockets. "I would ask a favor, in return for my arms this day." He pulled out a folded paper, the edges so worn it looked as if he'd opened it and closed it a hundred times. "If you would please give this to my son."

Fen took the letter. "You no longer have to hide in the Winterlands. Autus is dead. His castle is in ruins. The Wind Court is no more."

"I prefer my walls," he said simply and turned on his heel and walked away. We watched as his army moved into formation and began their march back to the hidden world they came from.

Hours later, with less than half of the army we'd come with, an injured dragon, thousands of humans and still no sign of Greeve, we did the same.

I knew I shouldn't do it, but I couldn't help myself. When the final rays of that wretched sun moved across the battlefield, I turned and looked behind me. I gasped, and Fen turned too, just in time to watch Nealla, the God of Death, raise the souls of the fallen and disappear with the last light of day.

Days later, Greeve finally came home. The look on his face reopened the wound of losing Gaea. I tried to speak to him, to tell him that she loved him. I tried to console him. But he was entirely lost. A shell of the fae I'd known. We hadn't just lost Kai and Gaea on that battlefield. We'd lost him too. And for the brief moment, he managed eye contact as we passed in the kitchens. I knew I was right. A warm tear slipped down my cheek as I understood what he meant to do.

"Please," I begged him. "Don't."

He walked away.

Fen was hardly better. I'd found him in Kai's room twice. Both times his eyes were ringed red and he couldn't say a word as he sought comfort by touching his brother's things.

"He was the best of us," Fen said, his voice catching. "He never took life too seriously. He loved so deeply. Even as a child." He audibly swallowed. "When we were just boys, he invented a game. We would pretend we were anywhere else in the world, trudging through swamps or climbing mountains, and we would have to guess where the other one was. He was shit at his own game though." He laughed, fighting back the tears. "I never knew where he was, what he was doing with his wild hand gestures." He paused and dragged in a shuddering breath. "It feels like that now," he whispered. "Like I just can't figure out where he is."

He sat on the edge of Kai's bed and buried his face in his hands. I sat beside him, my own tears falling as freely as his. My chest became so heavy, sitting in that room, looking at all the silly things he had collected. A single boot without a sole sat along on his dresser, missing the lace. He'd used it to tie back the curtains to one side. He had weapons strewn about, all worn so far down, they would never be used again. A lone seashell sat beside his bed, a token from his time in the sea court. Everything in that room had a small piece of him within it. Even our heavy hearts.

"He would have never let me die, Ara. Even when we were children. When my mother died, he saved me. He saved me even then," he sobbed. "But I couldn't do the same."

Greeve appeared in the doorway. He looked carefully around the space, seeking the same comfort Fen had been. "Do you remember?" Greeve whispered, crossing the room to fill glasses with an amber liquid and passing them out. "That time after I'd just come to the castle and you both convinced me your father was running a black market from the dungeons?"

Fen smiled sadly. "You lost that bet, and he convinced you to go down there and steal a grendle's liver."

Tears pooled in Greeve's eyes. "He found me scared out of my wits in the hallway and let me hide in his room while he convinced you all I had gone. Then we stole a pig's liver from the butcher and Sabra threw up on the floor."

"He always took better care of us than we ever did of him, didn't he?" Fen asked.

Greeve nodded.

I stood and slipped out of the room. This was a moment they both needed. They needed to mourn their brother and Greeve needed to find a reason to live. I wandered aimlessly through the halls. Finding myself standing outside of Wren's room, I raised my hand to knock on her door, but I couldn't. It wasn't fair for me to hope she would fill the void of Gaea's place in my life. I loved Wren. But she wasn't her.

Instead, I placed my back against the wall, slid down, and hugged my knees to my chest. I covered my face with my arms and began to weep. To mourn alone. We'd had a plan. We were going to grow old and bitter together. And now she was just gone. I'd watched her die from a distance without a twinge of emotion and I think I hated Autus all over again in that moment.

Wren's door opened and she came around the corner. She found me huddled on the floor, and rather than asking questions or even trying to convince me to get up, she just plopped down beside me, wrapped her arm around me, and laid her head on my shoulder as I cried.

"I'm so sorry," she said. "I wish I could bring her back. I wish I could bring them all back."

"I'm glad you're still here with me." I laid my head on hers.

A few days later, most of the surviving population, save the criminals still to be dealt with, stood alongside us in the vast open desert, watching a great, symbolic funeral pyre for all of our fallen brethren.

Fenlas spoke. His words quick, simple, and powerful. "Right now, it's hard to remember that we haven't lost everything. It's hard to smile and it's hard to heal. It's hard to find a normal in this new life. We will never be the same. And while I'm sorry for that, I'm also happy for it. There are no more divides in this world. Each of you are equal. Each of you has a place in this world. It won't be easy; in fact, picking up the pieces and rebuilding is going to be harder than any of us are prepared for. But nothing worth doing is ever easy. I'm proud to stand before you as your king and beside you as a male who has seen his own losses. I hope you'll remember from this day until your last day that life is fleeting. It is precious. Even if you live two thousand years, as my father did, the small moments still matter."

I reached for Greeve's hand, and he didn't pull away. If absolutely nothing else, he'd gotten out of bed this day. He was trying. And each day, that was all I would ask of him, though I knew some days that was more than he could give.

Fen came to stand beside me again as he led us in a final prayer.

*"Into lightness and darkness, into shadows and mist, may you rest for eternity. Over the mountains and beneath the sea, let your souls find peace. May nature keep your soul, the wind hold your memories, the river bless your spirit and the fire carry you away."*

CHAPTER

*40*

# Temir

The morning after the funeral pyre I stood on the edge of our balcony and looked over the wounded world with fresh eyes. It was done. Over. All the pain and suffering from years upon years of torment had ended. The sun was brighter, the sky clearer, but still, the cloud over our hearts remained.

*"The sun will set on this day, whether you will it or not. It will rise tomorrow on a new day, and you will once again start anew. The decisions you made in the past, will not stop the sun, or the moon, or the stars from their dance across the sky. You must always move on, son. Hard as it may be."*

Oleonis' final words to me sat heavy upon my heart. Had he known then how impactful those words would be?

"Do you want me to read it?" Nadra asked, pointing to the worn paper in my hand. I'd left it on the counter in the bathing room for days. I'd stuck it in my pocket after that. I pulled it out, ran my fingers over the parchment and placed it back inside time and time again.

"It doesn't matter what it says. It changes nothing."

"Then shred it up and toss it away," she said, challenging me.

"Fine." I pinched the paper between the fingers on each of my hands but couldn't do it. Instead, I handed it to her, tucked my head, and leaned against the ivory balcony pillar. "Just read it to yourself."

I heard the rustling of paper as she unfolded the note my father had given King Fenlas and listened to the static in the air as her eyes swept the withered page. As she sniffled. As she gently folded the paper back up and held it out to me. "Read it," she whispered.

And so, I opened the paper and willed myself to look down. Half the page was in worn text, the bottom half, a handwritten note.

*To my Aeson,*

*It's been twenty days since you were taken. Twenty days since I've slept. Twenty days of searching and scouring and threatening the gryla of The Bog for information. You're gone. The priest insisted we hold a service for you today. During that service, he spoke of forgiveness, intending to encourage me not to hold hate for your kidnapper. For your murderer. Instead, I wondered if I needed that sermon to find a way to forgive myself. From the day you were born, I was not the father you deserved. I looked at you and remembered your mother, the only love of my life. I blamed you, an innocent child, for the loss of her. I made excuses for sending you away. And now you're really gone forever.*

*They say you will realize what you had once it has left you. I had so much in you, my son. I was the fool who could not see beyond my own sorrow to the gift your mother had left me with. Now I pray that the gods have delivered you to her arms and she is smiling as brightly as the day we learned you were coming. There would never be a prouder mother. I was never the father you deserved, but she was always the mother you did. Someday, I will see you in the Ether, my son. And I will beg your forgiveness.*

*Temir,*

*This was the letter I wrote to you the day we said goodbye. We never knew the king kept our children alive. Your mother named you. She must have dreamed you would be a healer. I never thought you would ever stand before me, but I should have fallen to my knees and begged your forgiveness. I will never get it right, I'm afraid. I pray to the gods you never lose your mate, that you never have to suffer life without her. It seems I'll never be a father to you. That was never my journey. But I pray one day your heart heals and seeks me out. I'm sorry for the life you lived, suffocating under the fist of a king who would never love you. I'm sorry that I failed you, failed your mother. Broken hearts never fully heal. At least mine never has.*

*I wish you well in your life, son. The door is always open.*

*Heva*

I crumpled the paper in my fist and let it drop to the floor. I would always be grateful that he came in the moment we needed him most. But that was as far as it would ever go for me. He could hide behind his walls and send his apologies. I wasn't sure I would ever forgive him.

Nadra reached for my hand and pulled it to her chest. She searched my eyes for emotion. "He apologized. And he's the only family we have in the world. I'd give anything to have my mother back."

"Your mother loved you. Protected you. Even in her final moments, she fought."

"Heva loves you too, Tem. Maybe he is rotten at showing it, but he does."

I twisted the new band on my finger that replaced Oravan's ring. "Is this what you want? Do you want to go north?"

She kissed the hand she held. "I want you to be happy. I want you to find peace. To heal your own heart. I'm not sure where I want to be, but I know it's with you."

"Nadra, the moment I married you, I was healed."

I thought back to the small ceremony on the beach just days after we'd arrived home. The smile on her freckled face as she looked at only me when Rhogan walked her down the aisle. She fumbled her vows, and her giggle was the first anyone had heard since the world turned upside down. And I was so grateful for the birth of something new.

Later, we walked the streets of the city with Rhogan. His single wing a constant reminder that he would never fly again, and I couldn't heal that truth, nor could I grow a wing with magic. Still, he was chipper and took it in stride as we entered the rebellion's tinkering shop. I found Roe, still mourning the loss of Iva, and insisted he sit with us. We pushed ourselves to the back and sat in the seats as Murtad stood and surveyed the crowd. His eyes lingering on me before he turned to the Weaver and nodded. She joined him on the stage moments later.

"The king has asked us for our opinion. What shall be done with the rest of the fae who fought beside Autus and lived? They cannot remain locked up forever. What say you?"

502

The voices in the crowd were low murmurs to start, but they grew quickly as the words hanged, burned, and kill filled the room.

The Weaver raised her hands to silence the crowd. "Before we subject them to a fate we were all condemned to at one time, let us remember that many, many lives have already been lost. Let us remember that we also could have been prisoners of war. The fae population has been impacted so heavily. And now we have humans who live in this world, who will continue to live here. They reproduce at a much quicker rate than we do. Our world will become filled with another species most of us know nothing about. I am of the mind that we do not kill these enemies. That we educate them, we give them honest jobs, and we learn to grow together. Charging our king to govern them all carefully. Our world will forever be changed, and these moments right now will decide how. Starting with disbanding the rebellion."

"Disbanding?" someone shouted from the crowd.

"To truly erase the divide in our world, we must stand as one. We can demand a voice, but we have to trust the king. And he is worthy." She took her leave from the stage.

Murtad stood, shoved his hands in his pocket, and smiled. "This will be our final meeting. I'll see you all at the tavern." With that, he stepped down from the stage. We watched as he limped into his office, grabbed his bottle of ale and walked out.

That was it. The rebels had won. We had won.

Fenlas heard the desires of the Weaver during the council meeting. He'd already considered the growth of the humans and their sensitivity to strong climates. He'd assigned a group of southern fae to travel with them to the lands that were once the Marsh Court. They could build their lives there, and he would keep them safe because that's what Ara had promised the God of Death.

The captives were sent back to the north. Ragal, who had saved the king's life during the battle, was charged with governing them. Brax was to join him and would stay to report to the king and help Ragal rebuild. I think he also did it to remember Greywolf. To honor him by going north, just as Greywolf had come south.

"Temir," River shouted as he jumped into my waiting arms from the hall after the meeting. "Is this where you live?" His jaw was near the floor as he looked around the castle.

"It is," I answered, ruffling his hair.

"Can you show me?"

"Thank you for coming," Fenlas said to Alavon as he strode up behind me. "I'll show you where the work is to be done."

The glassmaker bowed low, and River struggled from my hands until I put him down. He turned his face to something like an imitation of Alavon and also bowed low to the king. I smiled down at him and felt a pang of sorrow that Gaea couldn't be here to witness it.

"Where's Greeve?" River asked. His face became sad as his thoughts surely aligned with my own. But of course, she would have introduced the two of them.

"He's in his room," I said.

"He's sad, isn't he?"

I looked to Fen and nodded.

"Will you take me to him?"

Fen squeezed his shoulder. "I don't think now's a good time, buddy."

"Oh," he answered, eyes falling to the floor.

Greeve appeared in front of River in a rush of wind. River's eyes lit up as he reached for him. The draconian bent down, grabbed the boy, and off they went. Alavon didn't react at all. I'd been so caught up with the rest of the world, I hadn't made time to see him, but of course Gaea had. Of course, she'd insured a bond between her mate and the boy. Her favorite boy.

I felt Nadra tug on our bond and tilt her head toward our room. We left Fen to speak with Alavon and stepped away. She closed the door gently, stepping to her tiptoes and kissed me.

"I'm so happy to be here with you, Temir. I know we have to help the dust settle, but this is it for me. This is home now."

"So we stay?" I asked, quirking an eyebrow.

"We stay," she confirmed. "With the only family we'll ever need."

# Epilogue

## Ara

My heart raced as soon as I was finally permitted to look into the mirror. I'd opted for a beautifully printed fabric I'd found one day while going through Efi's things with Fen. His breath had caught at the memory of her and I'd snuck it away for safekeeping. The cut of the gown was complimentary to the print. With a deep open back and a modest front, I'd never felt sexier. My hair was left to fall round my shoulders but pulled back at the sides. The dark coloring they'd put on my eyes made them striking.

"Wait, I forgot my mother's necklace," I told Wren, who stood behind me holding Nadra as they smiled into the reflection.

I stepped into the closet and dug through to find the box I'd given Fen to hide away. I shuffled through our wardrobe until something slid down the wall and clunked to the floor. Something long and wrapped quickly. I reached for it and knew instantly what it was. My father's sword. And then I thought of the last hands to touch that blade and suddenly the void of her came crashing back to me again. As if I'd just lost her. I couldn't help the tears that stung my eyes as someone banged on the bedroom door.

"Who is it?" Wren called.

"I need to talk to her," Inok said. The door opened and his voice became clearer. Demanding. "Alone."

I tried to push down the feelings of missing Gaea on this important day. She should have been here. Should have been the one to stand beside me. The others left the room and I stepped out to find Inok staring at me, awestruck.

"You look …"

"Divine?" I asked.

"Is that—?"

"Efi's fabric. Do you think he will mind?"

"He'd be a fool," he answered.

"Is something wrong?" I took several steps forward and laid my father's sword onto the bed. I would give it to Fen later.

Inok wrung his hands and looked away. "Greeve is gone. No one has seen him since yesterday morning."

"Does Fen know?" I asked, rushing for the door.

He ran behind me. "He's searching the city."

"Why didn't you tell me sooner. I know where he is."

"But you can't—"

"Trust me, I can, and I will," I yelled over my shoulder as I sprinted down the hallway in the nicest gown I'd ever wear.

"Where are you going?" Wren asked as I passed them.

"I'll be back, I promise."

*I know where he is. I might be late. Wait for me.*

*Do you want me to come?* Fen asked desperately.

*No, I hear its bad luck if you see me.*

*Don't take no for an answer.*

I ran to the rooftop, and Cal was already there waiting. I didn't even have to tell him. I hiked my dress up and jumped onto his back, urging him off the roof. He dipped low to the ground, as he loved to do, and then soared into the sky. We flew and flew for hours at breakneck speed. The sand turned to grass and then dense trees. Though we'd left early morning, it was already night by the time we'd made it. Cal didn't pause as we flew straight through the dragon territory within the Western Gap. He landed softly in the snow and waited as I jumped down and ran to the male standing with his back to me staring into The Mists.

"Greeve?"

He didn't move. I had no idea how long he'd been standing there ready to take his own life.

"You can't leave me," I whispered. "Not you too."

He turned, and I could tell he'd been crying. Just like his soul had been for all of these months since we'd lost his mate on the battlefield. "I couldn't save her. By the time I got to her, it was already too late." His voice was raw. As if he'd been screaming into the fog before him, begging for her to come back.

"Tell me how to help you. Tell me what to do."

"She's all I've ever wanted." He looked back to The Mists. "I could be with her again. Right now. I need only step forward."

"Greeve, please. Don't do this."

"I don't know how he did it. Tolero. How did he go on?"

I grabbed his hand, if for no other reason than to be an anchor in case he tried to move. I could use my magic, but if I obliterated The Mists, I'd free whatever monsters Aibell had hidden behind them when she recreated them.

"I can't promise you it's ever going to be better. I still cried today from missing her. But I promise to always be here for you, Greeve. I promise to never forget her. And if you have a bad day and need space, that's fine. If you want to stay up all night and talk about her, that's fine too. But you can't leave me. Fen needs you, but I need you too.

"Come home. Talk to Loti. She lost her mate a long time ago and she still manages a smile every day. But if you won't come home for me, and you won't come home for Fen, do it for Kai. Because if he was still alive, he'd be the one standing here, begging you not to do this."

He squeezed my fingers and turned back to me. "I'm sorry. You left on your wedding day to chase me down. I just can't . . ." He moved his fingers through his hair and looked back toward the mountains. "We had plans. Dreams. We were supposed to marry and have a child. We were going to move back to the dunes and raise our baby among the draconians. And now? Now I have nothing. No one. Forever."

"You'll always have me. I know I'm not a replacement for her. I know it's not the same. But you still have a family that loves you. If you want to go back to the dracs, then do it. But live, Greeve. Choose life. Find a way. I'll beg, if you need me to."

He stood staring at me for an eternity. I watched the clouds of frozen breath move through the air as his mind battled his heart. "I'll try to find a way." A single tear fell down his sun-kissed skin.

"Thank you," I whispered and hugged him. "And if you don't want to walk me down, you don't have to. I know it's going to be hard for you."

"I still want to. I was the one who gave you to the parents who raised you. I should be the one to give you to Fen." He rested his head on top of mine, and I listened to his broken heart beat for several moments.

*We're going to be late, but we're coming home.*

*Thank you. Oh gods, thank you, Ara.* I felt Fen's wash of relief. *We will be here waiting when you get back.*

"Care to visit an old friend?" I asked, pulling him to the dragons.

I whistled at Cal just in case that yellow fucker wouldn't give us a ride, but I was supposed to get married today, and the dragon was the fastest way home.

"Hello, little liar," he said as we approached.

"Hey beast. I need a ride home."

He chuckled. "You're lucky I like you."

"You're lucky I like you back."

We landed in the middle of the night. It was pitch black outside apart from a trail of Fen's floating flames.

"I'm probably a mess." I lifted my fingers to run them through my wind-blown hair.

"You've never looked more beautiful."

"That's the nicest thing you've ever said to me."

"Don't get too used to it."

I smiled and hugged him once more. He took my arm, straightened his back, and we followed the trail of flames Fenlas had left for us. They wound around the castle and down to the beach, creating a comforting warm glow against the red sands of home. We stepped into the rocking boat and rode it across the still water of the bay and out to

Efi's Aisle. My eyes landed on Fen waiting for me at the front of the aisle.

*I'm so sorry you had to wait so long.*

He pinned me with those dark eyes and my heart stopped as they crept down my body. He was beautiful and he was mine. I couldn't drag a full breath into my lungs as he took me in. *I've waited my entire life for this moment. A few hours made no difference to me.*

Thousands of tiny flames, different than Fen's, circled the aisle, darting in and out on agile wings of blue flame. A lump grew in my throat as I realized what they were. What they meant.

*Are those—?*

*Icaris. They've come to pay their respects to their new queen.*

Greeve and I walked the sandy beach, down the aisle dusted in lilies, and he placed my hand into my mate's. Fen held me with one hand and hugged Greeve with the other, mumbling something into his ear before Greeve turned to sit beside Loti in the small group of attendees.

Umari held a ceremonial knife above her head as she chanted a song with deep tones and long notes. She sang with such emotion my skin came alive, my heart raced, and the importance of this moment settled around us as if the aria had carried us off to a different land. She held out the carved bone handle, and Fen took it first.

I faced him and placed my hand into his. He sliced the blade across my palm until deep red blood seeped out. I took the blade and repeated the motion. Handing the knife back to Umari, we joined our hands as one to begin our blood oath.

As Umari laced our interlocked hands with a vine of intricately woven flowers, I looked far into those emerald eyes and watched as the light from the flames danced within them.

I felt the deep vat of emotions pour over me as he began. "Blood of my blood, I take thee. Bound by the soul and chosen by heart. I keep you from this day on."

I repeated the blood oath back to him while Umari used a candle and lit the vine wrapped around our wrists. Fen held my hand tight as the leaves burned into our skin. As quickly as the pain came, it subsided, and we were left marked for eternity. Fen's grandmother held out the rings we'd chosen for each other, my birth parents' rings we'd found while going through Efi's things. He slid the ring onto my finger and spoke through our bond.

*In all my days, Ara, I could never have dreamed of a better soulmate for myself. One who would stand on her own but still love me fiercely. I am in awe of you every day. From this day until my last day, I will love you unconditionally. I will give you the best of myself each and every day from now until eternity. I can't promise it will be perfect, my darling. But I can promise I will always be here. I will always walk beside you and encourage you. I will protect you when you need me to and let you fight your own battles when you don't. I will love you beyond the restrictions of time.*

I took a deep, trembling breath.

*I choose you, Fenlas. Until the last star falls from the sky. Until the final grain of sand is blown from the very last beach. Until my heart stops forever and then some. I don't stand here today imagining all of the good times, but rather, I think of all the bad times ahead of us. Life is hard. Loss is hard. But there's no one else in the entire world I would choose to go through the hard moments with. You will always be the blade in the dark. The one who protects me when I don't know I need protecting. My shield. I wish more than anything our parents could be here for this moment, but we have each other, and in that, we have them too. I promise to love you beyond measure from this day, until my last day. Together.*

We leaned into each other for a kiss, and then I knelt before him as he placed a small silver circlet atop my head. "My queen," he whispered.

I stood from the sandy beach, shook my dress, and leapt into his arms, kissing him passionately. The gathered fae erupted and he spun me around as he kissed me back. I turned to Greeve, afraid the joy would be so painful to him, but he flashed me a soft smile as I let Fen carry me away.

I'd never aspired to be a queen. I'd never aspired to be much, really. But this was the land of the fae, after all, and anything was possible, at least according to an old king.

# THE END

# Acknowledgements

You lived in my world, in my books for a long time and I don't think I'll be able to ever tell you what that means to me. I want to start with that. Thank you.

I know Kai and Gaea are not ideal deaths. I know Tolero isn't an ideal death. But they were necessary. I knew they were happening from the beginning. I never wanted to write an unrealistic epic battle where all the heroes lived to tell the tale. I wanted the emotions, the sorrow, and the sense of harrowing healing at the end of the book. I always knew I wanted to write a book that would grab the reader and make them laugh, and cry, and become so emotionally invested that when they closed the book—after they retrieved it from wherever they'd thrown it across the room— they took a solitary breath and let the story wash over them.

I've always said the character's reactions to death are so much more difficult to bear than the fictional death itself. Until I wrote Tolero. Until I had to let him go after getting into his mind and telling his story. I cried too. I'm not sorry for how it ended. It was their story, I was only the vessel. Someday, perhaps this story will go on. But for now, we move on. Together.

To Cheryl, who left this world far too early. We were not ready. Our hearts will forever be missing a piece because you took those with you when you left. Thank you for always having an ear for me. For daytime texts. For such fulfilling company at the campground. I hope one day my mark on this world will be as significant as yours was. We miss you. Every day.

To Dustin, Haley, Emma, and Kylie, my whole world, thank you for giving me the time to write this story. Thank you for encouraging me, giving me sparks of inspiration, and helping me celebrate each milestone. I love you. I love you. I love you. I'm the luckiest person in the world because of you.

To Tristopher, I will never not thank you for the push... shove? I wasn't going to do this. I was going to stay safe in my little bubble knowing that the haters couldn't find me in there. You refused to let me settle and I love you for that. I hope you never settle either, my friend. I hope you keep writing until you find Richard and even then, I hope you still have words.

To Jess, the one that read every single word... we did it! We cried together. I remember when you finished reading this in its roughest form and you still sat on your kitchen floor and cried with me. Maybe Ryan didn't really get our tears, but I'm pretty sure I still owe him a light saber.

To Michael, thank you for reading all the books and loving them and believing in them just as much as I do. I'm so proud to be your sister and see you do big things in this world. Thank you for your continued work on our website and taking the time to like every single post. We've come to the end of this story, but as you know, there is still more to tell.

To Darby and Claire, my ride or dies, who took this series and helped transform it into something spectacular. You are the greatest editors I could have ever asked for and I'm so happy to have worked with you on this series and anything to come in the future. More than that though, you are my dear friends and I'm so thankful for the friendship we've forged together. SPE will always hold a special place in my heart. Even if Darby can't remember what that stands for. Cheers ladies.

To Beck Michaels, my sweet friend. I couldn't have dreamed when I deigned to break a rule and message you, we would have become fast friends. You've guided me and pushed me and let me push you and I'll always be thankful for that. You don't let me falter. You let me come to you when I am weak and you curse in my ear until I feel better and I'm pretty sure that's the mark of a bestie. Because fuck them.

To Miss Karley, my sweet friend. Thank you for your empathetic heart and soul. I can hear you in my head right now yelling to bring her back. I'm not going to do it, but I love you for loving her so hard.

To Nichole, my smut queen, who sends me voice messages of random car singing performances worthy of a Grammy or messages I can't listen to around other humans, who matches my work ethic and maybe pushes me to go harder, you're a peach and I love you. Thank you.

To the BRA ladies, the reading group I never knew I needed until I realized we've never even all read a book together. Thank you. For all the love and encouragement and all around badassery you all bring to the table.

And finally, to my street team, there are not words. You are all the real MVPs here. Never once did you balk at my crazy ideas. You offered up husbands (Amber) for jobs and you always cheered me on behind doors as well as in public. When I finally decided I was going to publish this book, I dreamed of a team like you. One where we could laugh together and create a bond that was beyond a professional agreement and I'm so happy to have found that in each of you. Amber,

Ashley, Dany, Kristyne, Niki, Whitney, Sara and Kristin, thank you. So, so much. For rising to every occasion. You're stuck with me. We all know what the next project is.

# About the Author

Fae Rising is the debut series for Miranda Lyn. She grew up smack dab in the middle of the United States with nothing to do but dream up stories of fantastical creatures and powerful heroines. Now married with three children of her own, an idea sparked a buried passion within her to follow a dream and teach her children that anything is possible if you're willing to work hard for it. Be sure to follow me!

Instagram: https://www.instagram.com/authormirandalyn/

Facebook: https://www.facebook.com/authormirandalyn/

Twitter: https://twitter.com/AuthorMirandaL

Check out our website for extras, character art and exclusive content. www.faerising.com

Also, click here to sign up for the mailing list and get access to more exclusive content and giveaways!

https://www.faerising.com/subscribe

CPSIA information can be obtained
at www.ICGtesting.com
Printed in the USA
LVHW091941230421
685305LV00054B/88/J

9 781736 833902